THE ANALYST WHO LAUGHED
TO DEATH

Dec 15/16

To Michael

my dear colleague

with deep affection

Ron

THE ANALYST WHO
LAUGHED TO DEATH

Ronald Ruskin

KARNAC

First published in 2016 by
Karnac Books Ltd
118 Finchley Road
London NW3 5HT

British Library Cataloguing in Publication Data

A C.I.P. for this book is available from the British Library

ISBN-13: 978-1-78220-496-1

Typeset by Medlar Publishing Solutions Pvt Ltd, India

Printed in Great Britain by TJ International Ltd, Padstow, Cornwall

www.karnacbooks.com

To my wife Marilyn, an analyst, who steadfastly supported me, my three daughters, Danielle, Natalie, Joelle, and their wonderful families

CONTENTS

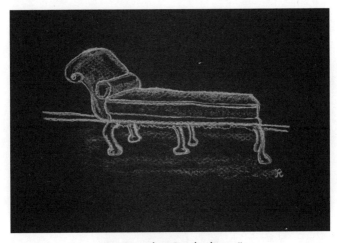

"Man tracht; Got lacht …"
Man plans; God laughs.
—Yiddish proverb

CHAPTER ONE

The analysis of M

It may seem strange that my analysis of M reads more like a detective novel than a case history. If so, it is through no intention of my own, but is related to the nature of M's clinical material. Tirelessly devoted to treating and analysing the most challenging cases, M was on a sacred quest to help patients grasp the meaning of their emotional pain. In a world sodden with outright lies and deception, M strove to bring a measure of profound truth to his patients' suffering. M saw himself as a knight errant battling against the forces of darkness which lay not only in the external landscape of society but within the deep internal regions of the soul. My patient, a sensitive and gifted physician, polite and generous to all who knew him, laughed at himself and life's folly, descending into self-mocking, scurrilous, and scatological phrases* in my office. His critical comments could be hilarious.

---

*Several of M's words and expressions in analysis were spoken in Yiddish, undoubtedly an ambivalent homage to this ancient tongue and his Bubba (grandmother). I have attempted to reproduce his comments precisely as they appeared in our sessions. Despite his courtly professional demeanour, M often swore like a stevedore.

The names of his patients have been altered to disguise their identity. —*O. Pinsky MD*

Contrary to my usual professional reserve, I occasionally burst into bouts of laughter.

The analysis carried on for two years during which time a remarkable change came over M as he unearthed long-forgotten aspects of his own childhood.

M forwarded me his diaries, his sketches, and his Bubba's recipes.

I have added, dated, and footnoted, where necessary, comments from his medical colleagues and information from the Metropolitan Toronto Police and other sources.

After M's catastrophic accident in 2009 I thought it prudent to keep private the unusual events of his illness narrative. Hovering near death, between delirium and consciousness in his ICU bed at Mount Zion Hospital, M asked that I publish his analysis.

I remained uncertain, awaiting his death or recovery and elected to keep his notes and my clinical observations confidential.

Two years passed. Owing to requests from his wife Frieda, and family, I agreed to publish a clinical monograph on M—*The Analyst Who Laughed to Death*. I have incorporated aspects of our sessions, my reflections, and M's discussion of his wayward borderline patients and anxiety-ridden psychopaths. I ask the reader to bear the shifts of focus, person, and time past-present, the basic narrative of free association. Our unconscious mind not only lives in the present but resides in past and unseen moments ushering us to our final destiny.

I console myself that faithfully narrating the course leading up to M's tragic accident will not lead to undue criticism of psychoanalysis or my therapeutic endeavour.

Could M have averted his disaster? Could I have foreseen this outcome?

I present my clinical evidence. The verdict is left for the jury of readers to decide.

2

PART ONE

THE INFANTILE NEUROSIS
JUNE 2007–MARCH 2007*

A lane behind Euclid Avenue where I ran.—R. Moses

---

*M first presented to me in June 2007, with symptoms of anxiety and insomnia, related to his wife, Frieda, informing him that she wanted a separation. While M laughingly stated this in the first session, he was unable to accept his wife's ultimatum for several months. The separation triggered a partial regression and a host of early childhood memories which M unearthed during the first phase of the analysis. The sketches in this monograph were all drawn by M. —O. Pinsky

CHAPTER TWO

Escape from childhood: June 2007

*L*ook *Pinsky*, this is where I tried to run away. I am not making up this neurotic crap, it's absolutely true—that's why I am here. Frieda, my ex-wife, doesn't think it was that bad [she had it far worse]; my late father had his headaches with Bubba and my ninety-two-year-old mother—bless her heart—she hardly talked about the past. This didn't come up in my analysis with Dr. L*—that doesn't mean I am lying, does it? Does it?

Look me in the eye. I am asking you a question.

All right, you are not going to talk. *Big deal*—go sit there like a goddamn constipated totem pole. *Fine*—don't answer. You know, when I tell you this, a part of me doesn't believe it myself. I am a psychiatrist—a psychoanalyst—I run a hospital clinic for borderlines. I treat criminal psychopaths.

I've written books. I teach residents.

Who, tell me—*who would know about me?*

Am I a criminal, a pervert, a fucking fugitive? It's a sick joke, it is totally nuts. And just because I say what I say, and I laugh at this, and I have trouble believing myself, don't give me *that* dumb look. I don't have to lie on this couch if you are not going to listen.

---

*Dr. L, a prominent Toronto training analyst. I subsequently have referred to him by his full name, Dr. Sidney K. Lippman. —*O. Pinsky*

5

Listen to me. That's an order. Is that clear?

I never listened to myself—that is no excuse for you to fall asleep.

Someone has to listen. Do you have any idea what it was like to be a kid in my family growing up on Euclid Avenue in Toronto after the war?

It was a *regular fucking nightmare.*

CHAPTER THREE

The nightmare

*W*hy was it a nightmare, you ask? Why? Because my family appeared absolutely *normal*, that's why. *Normal*—from the outside—*they were normal in a deadly psychotic way*. This is the goddamn paradox of my life. They were a decent, hard-working, religious, law-abiding Jewish family. They were nice to their neighbours, the Guttniks who ran a small grocery and the Fausts who managed a hardware store. They were decent to the third floor tenants, the Karpinskis, and Mr. Moretti who rented the basement room. They were close to my Uncle Max and Aunt Sadie, Uncle Eli and Aunt Leah. They kept kosher; they went to shul; they lived in fear of God; they followed all the rules; they never stole a cent from anyone; they gave to charity; they helped handicapped people cross the street.

They obeyed the Ten Commandments.

They lived in *Toronto the Good*. You couldn't find a nicer family.

Pinsky, are you listening? I was losing my touch. I was breaking up, disintegrating. I made mistakes—I wasn't seeing what I should see in my patients.

My first analyst missed it—I can't blame my analyst, Lippman, can I, Pinsky?

Listen, if there was *no diagnosis*, if I didn't see it and talk about it and dream about it, if it was repressed and dissociated, if I

7

was so used to it that it was part of my personality, how would others know? I discovered the syndrome, the *Bubba Complex*— but for years people denied its existence. Do you have any idea how many men walk around with this neurosis?

They haven't the slightest fucking clue why they are anxious. They tell themselves they are fine. *Yes*, they work hard, yes, they go to school, *yes*, they get married, they have children, and *yes*, they act like they know what's going on—it doesn't hit until their sixties—until they are grandparents, they are *totally fucked up*.

OK, look Pinsky; I am not saying that *you* have this neurosis.

Just agree it is a syndrome—I am not the sole victim.

I have done studies on this.

This condition exists. Are you listening, Pinsky?

My problems worsened with Paula Rose Blum—Paula Blum, her name rhymes with pabulum. I ate that shit when I was a kid—terrible stuff.

Blum was turning me into pabulum mush.

My first couch—R. Moses

CHAPTER FOUR

Paula Rose Blum

Blum was in her sixties, a mega-millionaire with a cardiac neurosis, constipation, and two bouts of cancer. To hear her talk she had every disease known to mankind. She was on the board of several Toronto charities, donated generously to universities, and was ex-president of the Mount Zion Hospital Sisterhood. Did she come to her sessions on time? *No.* She was late. You could set a stopwatch on her precise lateness—ten minutes late each session. Did she admit this fact? *No*—there was always an excuse—a traffic delay, a critical phone call, a business deal, a legal issue, an ache, a pain—did it matter? Did she tell me the truth about her medical condition? *No.* Did she accept that she was in her sixties? *No*—she had a body to kill for, Pinsky, she looked over twenty years younger—like a Jewish Jane Fonda; she told no one her real age. Did she call me to cancel? *No.* Did she follow advice? *No.* She knew best. Did she take her Celexa? *No*—she was angry and depressed. Did she get better? *No.* Did she say I was a good doctor?—*yes*, in the beginning. What made me uneasy was that I reminded her of her son—in her mind he never did anything right. *You have the same nose as Ivan Blum, my son, with the useless Harvard MBA. With that nose you stick out in a crowd.*

Blum started from nothing living with her Polish mother in a dingy Montreal apartment. She built a fortune on Italian marble

9

washrooms, Ottoman bath suites, European spa toilets—she set up a monthly magazine, *Bath and Blum* with stores across North America, the Martha Stewart of toilets. Her company outfitted the best hotels and homes. Blum was savvy. She franchised a series of companies, *Bloom-bath* she called them—in under a week, a bathroom or powder room would be totally renovated—new toilet, sink, bath and shower, tiles, fixtures, the works, all for a fraction of what independents were charging. Pinsky, what adds value to your home or condo—apart from a new kitchen? I will tell you—a new bathroom or two or three, a glass and marble shower stall, a large tiled Roman bath—that's class. The bathroom, I argue, is more important in social status than any other room. It is not where you eat, sleep, but it is how you feel when you are alone shitting.

We had one lousy fucking toilet for my parents, my Bubba, Aunt Leah and Uncle Eli, and the Karp family—all four of them who lived in the attic, plus Mr. Moretti, our tenant who lived in the basement.

This was where my infantile neurosis began.

My potty, I was attached to it—R. Moses

CHAPTER FIVE

How it all started

The laneway behind our house—R. Moses

I ran away as fast as possible. Why, I didn't know—it seemed natural, the right thing to do. I was on fire. I couldn't sit. Bubba said I was a restless soul. *"Stop running, Reuben. You will fly into the spirit world."* Bubba tied me in a leather harness—*a fucking leather harness*, can you believe, Pinsky? On streets I rushed ahead, searching for my neighbours, the Fausts and the Guttniks. Bubba held the reins. Inside the house I was on the move, jumping into closets, playing with shoes, checking under beds, climbing to the attic, going downstairs to the living room, or farther, into the dark basement inspecting the furnace and the shiny pieces of coal.

Pinsky, I wanted to find a way to get the hell out of that prison.

"Stop Reuben, you will get killed," Bubba said.

See what I am getting at? Do you see why I still have to run?

* * *

We lived on Euclid Avenue, south of College Street, in downtown Toronto in Bubba Bella's semi-detached red brick house with her sister, Auntie Leah, Uncle Eli the tailor, and my father and mother. I shared a tiny bedroom with Bubba overlooking our tiny back garden and laneway; my parents had the middle room. Auntie Leah and Uncle Eli took the bedroom facing the street. A Jewish family rented the attic for thirty-five dollars a month, the Karpinskis—a quiet mother, her two noisy boys, and their dad, a swarthy card-shark *ganif* accountant, a thief who anglicized their name to Karp. And then there was Aldo Moretti, the little shoemaker, who lived in the basement and played his accordion. Imagine eleven people and one goddamn bathroom that got temperamental and did not flush. This was the Forties; Pinsky, are you listening? Immigrant Jews and Italians lived cheek by jowl— aunts, uncles, Bubbas and Zaides, cousins, tenants, ten, twelve people to a house—who had money? Bubba had scraped together cash as a clothes peddler to buy the entire house. At dawn she left our bedroom to *shlepp* bags stuffed with clothes to peddle across Toronto. In our kitchen was a back door that led to our garden where Bubba grew vegetables. *So what did I do, Pinsky?* I slipped out the back door, criminal that I was. I ran to the garden, past Bubba's tomatoes, lettuce, onions, cucumbers, peas, and carrots. I lifted the latch that

12

led to a laneway. Behind the houses were laneways; people had wagons and horses. I ran as fast as the wind. *"Stop, stop, you will kill yourself!"*

When I was two, the Saturday July morning we were to go to Crystal Beach for a summer weekend, I was busy running from my bedroom on the second floor, chasing my nutty neighbour with braces, freckles, and frizzy fire-red hair, Ruthie-Annie. She hung out at our place, biting, pushing, and pinching me. Moretti was just getting out of the second-floor bath, a towel around his genitals, his bathrobe open. He and Karp saw us fighting. *Stop already*, the two of them said. Bubba yelled from the first floor. Reuben, don't you *dare* run downstairs! What happened? I pushed Ruthie-Annie and she pushed me. I flew head first down the stairs to land on my face in a lifeless heap. My nose gushed blood. Bubba yelled curses. I lay still as a corpse. Moretti said I was paralyzed. He wanted to call an ambulance. Bubba shoved smelling salts under my nose.

Manny Karp bent over me. *"Look*, now the kid is moving his legs."

"He hit me." Ruthie-Annie howled *she* was the injured one. She clutched her freckled nose.

"Why did you *of all people*, hit Ruthie-Annie?" Bubba said. She washed the blood off my face. Seeing that I had regained the power of my arms and legs she put me on a couch. She called Uncle Max, the doctor. He arrived with his black bag. He looked up and down at Ruthie-Annie and me. I had no words for what happened.

"Why did you hit and push Ruthie-Annie?" Uncle Max repeated. "Why?"

"Ruthie pushed him first," Karp corrected. "She is no angel."

"Stay out of this Manny Karp," Bubba warned. "This is not your business."

"I swear on the *Jewish Torah*, so help me God," Karp said. "She pushed him first."

13

No one paid attention to Karp. Everyone knew he was on the wrong side of the law; he was a liar, a gambler, a shyster. All we needed Karp and Moretti for was to pay rent.

Dr. Pinsky, I was two years old then. What the fuck did I know?

Uncle Max drove me to old Mount Zion Hospital. The doctors took X-rays. Nothing was broken. Uncle Max wanted a full inspection. "Take him home. Look him over," he said. "Watch him all night."

My parents took me home. They checked and double-checked my nose. After blaming me for pushing Ruthie-Annie, which wasn't exactly true, Bubba sat on my bed that night to watch for the Angel of Death.

This is my total recollection of that time.

This is no lie, Pinsky—I had this pain right in the middle of my fucking testicles.

The Euclid Avenue house, I fell down the stairs—R. Moses

CHAPTER SIX

First clinical impressions: June 2007

In June 2007 M was in his early sixties, a courtly round-shouldered man in a dark rumpled suit, starched white shirt and tie, with fretful coal eyes that flew about my office. His hands were never still, his legs crossed and uncrossed on the couch, he shrugged, he twitched, he smiled tensely, his fingers snapped; he twisted his head to look back—to say he was in motion was an understatement. In brief moments he became silent, frozen, and strangely distant—perhaps dissociated. Then, after a few seconds he snapped back to his hyperactive self. He told me my face reminded him of some child in his past but he was unsure. When he first arrived he sported a black eye and bruise over his face—a jogging accident he explained. Underneath his polite hypo-manic exterior M was an anxious soul who with his curly dark head of hair and rapid movements, reminded me more of a teenager than a sexagenarian. Before entering my office he limped into the washroom to check himself. *Inspection*, he told me. Sometimes he brought his golden retriever, Jaffe-Jaffe, to the office. Jaffe-Jaffe was a high-strung neurotic female dog who was to play a significant role in the untimely end of M's analysis. Yet as the analysis progressed I had no inkling of this. M's constant movement irritated me—undoubtedly his restlessness exerted an excitatory effect on Jaffe-Jaffe. I tried to keep our analytic space quiet and reflective. Jaffe-Jaffe whined when M became distressed. I suggested to M to leave Jaffe-Jaffe at home. M replied Jaffe-Jaffe did not care to be alone. Hire a dog-walker, I said. On the rare occasions when Jaffe-Jaffe was away, M's words did not slow, indeed, they could not flow fast enough—here was a man with feelings bottled up for years and always this nervous grin. I was sceptical. He insisted as a kid he knew me from somewhere. I hadn't the foggiest idea. Was M distorting his "lonely depressive" childhood or his fall down the stairs? Was this a traumatic memory or a distorted fantastical elaboration? I chafed as he ridiculed the failures of his previous analyst. He looked youthful yet hobbled into my office stooped, *kvetching* as if he carried the weight of the universe on his back. M's nose was distinctive but not the enormous caricature he portrayed. He worried that he blocked on people's names. True, more than once he mixed up his grandchildren's names. I tested his memory. It appeared intact—his problem was anxious perfectionism. Underneath his well-mannered exterior M was a savage critic and viciously

Jaffe-Jaffe, R. Moses's dog

mocking. He was irrepressibly funny—irritatingly so, indeed, I looked forward to his banter rather than analyze what it concealed—his inner emptiness. He gave me sketches, notes, news clippings from childhood. I put them aside. I wrote down M's diagnosis: Axis I: Depression. Dysthymia 300.00. I asked for a clear history, not this ping-pong digression, this present to past tense, this word-picture salad of his life. He grew furious. He roared. *Pinsky, listen to me.*

I need you to not always be my fucking analyst. I need you to bear witness.

CHAPTER SEVEN

Blum in distress

"I have to lie down on your couch, if you don't mind, doctor. Oh, it's rather hard, your couch, isn't it? *Hmm*. That way, your face and nose do not distract me—do not take this as an insult. It is easier for me to talk when I see the ceiling. I used to lie on my bed and stare at the ceiling when I was a child. It soothed me. When I saw my first therapist—Dr. Lippman—I told him that. That was the one thing he understood perfectly. Faces disturb me when I am trying to concentrate—that's a good sign—you understand. You know that I was referred to you by Dr. Bernard Bayer—*a lovely man*—your chief. We sit on three hospital committees. He recommended you most highly—I tried therapy before; I tried meditation and personal coaching, I spent time in yoga retreats—*nothing* goes deep enough. Bernard is *such a gentleman*, he refused to pry into my personal life—I have known him for years—he told me he had someone on staff, an excellent analyst, the best in Toronto—*you*."

"*Me? The best?* Dr. Bayer said that? Really, he said that?"

"He said I should go into analysis with you five times a week. Analysis would go deeper than my previous treatments—Dr. Bayer insisted. For years I had been in analysis with Lippman. He did what he could—I don't want to speak badly of Lippman. But you, Dr. Moses, are *special*."

Pinsky, I should tell you that when I hear the name Sidney Lippman, I get a sour taste in my mouth. I want to puke. A bad smell enters my nostrils. My stomach churns and cramps. I feel my rectum getting ready for an incredibly huge shit. When I first started analytic training—I looked up to him; I was searching for an ideal father in my first analyst. Lippman was six foot two, Pinsky, not short like you and me. He had a full head of raven hair—a Semitic John Wayne—eagle-nosed, hirsute, impressive, to me in those early days he appeared a thinker; he loved to flip conventional ideas on their head. Broad-shouldered, bull-necked, Lippman was a former pro hockey player with two zigzag scars from his widow's peak to his butt chin. His head looked like a Picasso, I swear. The first session I didn't take my eyes off his split face—I was fascinated by the goddamn scars. A Jewish hockey player who is an analyst? *Impossible*. It doesn't add up. Lippman sees me stare at one side, then the other side; he shifts in his analyst's chair; he leans his torso to one side, then to the other side like he is stick-handling.

Moses, what are you staring at—Moses? Is it my scar-face? Is it where I got hit by a slap shot? What's the deal? Life is a scar, Moses. When you play pro hockey you get hit in the face. Do you know how many dentists I have seen? You get whacked in the head. So you hit back. If they figure you are a Jew-boy you get hit twice as hard. You punch them in the mouth because they have to know we Jews can fight. Right?

His huge paws pointed at me with gratuitous admonitions— I didn't ask for a life history, his hockey fights, or his dental work, and you know, for a Freudian analyst he talked too much—but I ate it up. He yelled like a coach to the bench. What was my problem? Why was I so scared? Come on—open up and tell me. This was over thirty years ago when I couldn't decide about Frieda.

Get out there. Do something, Moses—why wait—don't tell me you are fucking afraid? Move forward. Take a position, Moses. You are living with this woman. What if your parents don't adore her? What if she is not your tribe? It's your life, isn't it, Moses? What is your ultimate goal?

Pinsky, this was not analysis; this was a goddamn hockey practice.

What appealed to me about Lippman? It was his veneer of intellect and swagger, he had balls—I wanted that confidence. I can't think of a decent thing to say about Lippman except that I had two analyses with him and that he was a hockey player—that was the key—do you see?

* * *

"Bayer said you do good work with mature patients. I cleared my schedule, Dr. Moses. At this time in my life, I am ready for analysis—not two times a week, not three times, but five times, to get to the heart of my problem. Are you *really* the best analyst like Bayer says?"

"Bayer is the expert. Please, Mrs. Blum, now what is your problem?"

"I can't begin to tell you."

"You can *begin* to tell me."

"I am not sure I can trust you, after what happened with Dr. Lippman."

"Mrs. Blum, tell me—what happened with Dr. Lippman?"

There was a long silence. "I keep everything locked inside."

"You are in the perfect place to unlock—let's go—I am ready whenever you are."

"You may be ready," Blum said. "I need more time."

"I am here, Mrs. Blum. I am ready and listening. Go ahead. What happened with Lippman?"

I watched this jade-eyed beauty lying on my couch. Her skin was lineless. Her body had no sags. Her luxuriant hair fell over the cushion.

Blum said nothing. She was my analytic sphinx.

* * *

Ruthie-Annie and I got into arguments. Bubba said to be nice and not push. Believe me, Pinsky, I was *always* nice—but I was no charmer like Guttnik. Karl Guttnik was four years older than me with dimples, thick wavy blond hair, brown eyes, and long dark eyelashes. Even Ruthie-Annie, who hated most of us guys, I believe, had a crush on this Adonis. Women adored him. Guttnik had *mazel*, he was brilliant, good-looking, a smoothie to boot; he became an analyst too.

I was totally envious of him—later I will tell you more about Guttnik.

On Sunday afternoons after Mass, Mr. Moretti, the shoemaker, played his accordion on our porch.

Everyone on the street listened, the Karp's, the Guttnik's. even Ruthie-Annie.

It was the most peaceful time of the week.

CHAPTER EIGHT

Mendel—the boy who went totally blind

Anyway, Pinsky, I didn't die at two. My nose was bent, deviated to the left, not broken—this was the start of the reign of terror. Yet this was not the real injury. After I fell down the stairs I had pain in my testicles—no lie. A day later, I told Bubba it hurt to piss. Bubba pulled my pants down.

Bubba's Stromberg Carlson Radio with a green electric eye.
—R. Moses

She took a good look—360 degrees, all around, up, down, sideways. *Look. Look what he did to himself.* Uncle Max made a house call and checked my genitals. "This Reuben has a sub-acute scrotal hematoma." We went to the hospital. I had to pee and be examined. The specialist said my balls were fine—a minor bruise—nothing broken or twisted or infected, except my psyche.

Each week a constant din rang out on Euclid Avenue: hollering, clattering pots, and banging doors. Our street gang, "pretty boy" Guttnik, Josh Karp, and little Herbie Faust, ran along the sidewalk. Our radio shouted music with other radios on the block.

We heard big band music, Artie Shaw, Benny Goodman, Glenn Miller, Woody Herman, Duke Ellington—no silence anywhere. Sunday afternoon we turned the radio off and Mr. Moretti played the accordion. Otherwise nobody was calm or quiet. Mostly it was complaining—*kvetching*. Yiddish was spoken when my family did not want me to understand what they were saying. Everybody spoke Yiddish—particularly when they worried. On Euclid Avenue families worried about many things—illness, death, poverty, war, the Toronto Maple Leafs, eating, sleeping, going to the toilet, not going to the toilet [of which I will have more to say later] being Jewish, not being Jewish enough, being swindled, or being alive. On Euclid Avenue, worry was how we lived life. Bubba said: "Did you hear about poor Mendel's son, playing hockey in the street?" No. "Last week someone shot a puck and of all places it hit him in the head." No—that can't have happened. "Yes, it happened, and the puck took out not one, but two eyes at the same time." Oh, my god. What then? "Then, he ended up, *nebach*, blind—*totally blind*. Imagine. You can lose an ear but both eyes? What future will Mendel have? Not to mention his family will never be the same. Reuben, *never play hockey*. If you are a good boy, you will go to Crystal Beach, *my angel*."

23

Sitting in the cockpit over water

Pinsky, an early memory—between nine months and one year—look, can you believe this? I am sitting on the potty, strapped into the cockpit hovering like a helicopter pilot over the open ocean ready to drop my bombs. "*Make ka-ka*. Be a good boy. *Show Bubba a nice ka-ka.*"

When I was about to try something exciting, Bubba warned I would end up like poor Mendel's son. "*Nebach*, that blind *boychik*, what kind of life is that?" My family sat around the kitchen, my father in his T-shirt. Uncle Eli wore a sleeveless undershirt, the women in hair-curlers served food in flowered housecoats. Bubba picked fresh vegetables in the garden. Half the evening they argued if it was safe enough to make egg sandwiches for the "Ex" during the summer. Suppose the egg got warm, turned bad, and poisoned us. After that someone went to the hospital. Hospitals were not safe—not even Mount Zion—it was only a matter of hours before death occurred. Bubba said it was unsafe to dine out: food was poorly prepared and not kosher. Bubba washed all our vegetables and fruit with soap and water, even her own tomatoes. Toronto Jews did not set foot in a restaurant, apart from United Bakery, Switzer's, Zuchter's, or Shopsy's.

"For Reuben," Bubba said, "the safest place is in bed—*asleep*."

My mother's daily weather report: June 2007

Reuben, the heat wave is worse. People die of sunstroke. Please, drink water and don't jog.

* * *

Pinsky, as soon as I understood Yiddish or English I heard my parents, Bubba Bella, Auntie Leah, and Uncle Eli sitting around the wooden kitchen table arguing about *polio*. Bubba explained that polio spread in summer—it was better for Jews to remain indoors and avoid sunstroke. Bubba and my mother were superstitious: if they dropped a knife, I was delegated to pick it up, if I stepped over little Herbie Faust, my next door red-headed neighbour with a lazy eye, *God forbid*, I had to step back the other way—or else Herbie would stop growing and live life as a Jewish dwarf. If I made a face, it would stay twisted for eternity. If I crossed my eyes, Bubba said when I woke up from sleep my eyes would tie forever into knots. "Reuben, you want to be cross-eyed like Herbie Faust?" After a bath, Bubba dried me off. She circled me with her hands and repeated in Yiddish *poo-poo-poo*. "Reuben, it is to guard your soul." Bubba kissed me. She spit out air with her puckered lips as if it was raw sewage. Mother and Auntie Leah did the same thing. *Poo-poo-poo*.

It protected me against the evil eye, devils, and death. Bubba was always protecting me.

The experts tell us trauma is caused by events that over-whelm our ego, right? Seeing death, observing catastrophes, being raped or maimed, losing parents—surviving wars and famines—you don't have to be a fucking genius to figure out why we Jews are overwhelmed. This planet is filled with trauma, agree? My cross-eyed neighbour Herbie's family fled Europe with his lunatic sister with steel braces; they spoke Polish and Yiddish to their parents. Ruthie-Annie stood armed guard over little Herbie. For Ruthie-Annie the World War was still on.

Lippman, I am thinking, what did that scar-face secretly *do* to poor Blum? I suspected he could not resist her—a wild man. He had been hit in the side of the head so many times that he was a lateral thinker. God knows how Lippman became a train-ing analyst. The analytic society tolerated him—he argued, he swore. At our analytic meetings, over theory, he threatened a fist fight with Gerber, the self-righteous self-psychologist. Lippman promised to knock Gerber unconscious—unconscious in the medical sense. There was an ugly debate when I presented my work. Analysts rarely agree. Gerber was dead against my work. Guttnik on the other side supported me. Lippman vowed to flatten Gerber. That was Lippman, he fought for his beliefs. Lippman was a real battler.

Everything these days is trauma. What is not trauma? Therapists look for trauma and God protect us if we ignore our patients' claims that they were beaten or bullied or abused—if we are not sure, we search for trauma. Where am I going with all of this? I can tell you one thing—no matter how hard I looked, I, myself, was never abused. Being abused would have been *simple*, a piece of cake—at least it would be *there in the open broad daylight*. Pinsky, I could have dealt with it in consciousness. For me the danger was buried in darkness, invisible, unpredictable, and lethal like the terrifying weather reports my mother warned me about.

It was lurking outside the house, ready to pounce on me in the dark like a *dybbuk*.

By the way did I tell you, Pinsky, someone slashed both front tires of my Volvo?

* * *

The carp from Zapinsky's fish store. Bubba put it in the bathtub and used it for gefilte fish—R. Moses

26

In the Forties ration cards, military posters, Victory Bonds, grim soldiers in uniform were everywhere. "The devil possessed Hitler," Bubba whispered: "Now the evil is over. *Poo. Poo. Poo.*" She kissed me. On Sundays Zaide Yasha visited us. He lurched, zombie-style and mumbled Polish. He patted my head. Bubba showed me a living room photo. Yasha sat with Bubba at a wedding. I saw sepia photos of our families in dark suits and dresses standing at attention.

"Who is Yasha?" I asked. "Why doesn't Yasha live here?"

Friday mornings while the Fausts and my parents worked I shopped with Bubba at Leo Rosen's kosher butcher, Guttnik's grocery, Lustig's bakery, Greenbaum's dairy, and Zapinsky's fish store in Kensington Market. Ruthie-Annie and Herbie tagged along. Ruthie-Annie was two years older than me; her glasses magnified two mirthless dark cherry eyes. She watched over little Herbie. I tried to be nice but we ended up in fights. Something was busted inside her. I didn't have words for it. She liked Rosen's butcher shop though. The floor was sawdust-covered. The air smelled of blood. Bubba saved her best maxims when Leo killed chickens. Ruthie-Annie had a fascination to see headless chickens jump. I giggled, nervous.

"What's so funny about a chicken getting ready for soup?" Bubba said.

"Bubba, can a chicken live after its head is chopped off? I asked.

"Reuben, did Mendel's son see after he lost both eyes?"

When I went to pee a huge fish swam in the tub. "Don't take a bath unless you want to be a carp." Bubba said. I dreamt I was a fish and could never be a boy again.

Bubba took Herbie, Ruthie-Annie, and me to Lustig's bakery for a bagel and we visited Greenbaum's dairy where we were given a tiny slice of cheese. In Gershon Zapinsky's fish store, fish swam in iron tanks. Guttnik left his parents' grocery to watch the chickens squawking in their cages at Kensington Market. "How are a chicken and a fish different?" Bubba asked.

"The fish swim," I said. "The chickens flap their wings."

"The chicken knows it's going to die," Guttnik said.

"*Correct*," Bubba said. "That Guttnik *boychik* is already a genius." I felt more envious.

* * *

The first years of life seal character—don't we all return to *pisherhood?* That's why I am so fond of my grandsons. Jason, Jeremy—I can't remember the third. Is my memory going, Pinsky? Is this the first sign of dementia? Tell me the truth, am I losing my mind?

I see them for Sunday bagels and lox. In those early days food was meant to fill what was missing in your body, to soothe your psyche, to halt infections, to keep bowels moving forward—to shut you up. We ate Bubba's vegetables from our tiny garden. We gulped barley soup, chicken soup, *borscht* [cabbage soup], *gefilte fish*, *potato latkes*, and our main course was the inevitable chicken with roasted potatoes. Bubba slit the lifeless fowl with a kosher stiletto, and in one bloody yank of her hand she eviscerated heart, livers, kidneys, and gizzard. *See, Reuben*, she said, like Hannibal Lecter—*see* how I cut up the chicken? When Bubba felt faint fasting during *Yom Kippur* [The Day of Atonement], she uncorked smelling salts and snorted them like snuff. On *Yom Kippur* the shul atmosphere was one of terror. *God is watching. Don't run away.* I leaned over the balcony searching for my father. All our neighbours, the Karps, the Guttniks, and the Fausts went to the same shul. I ran in the halls with Guttnik—Bubba and mother *kvelled* over Karl's beautiful eyes, dark eyelashes, and dimples. Karl's mother took him to modelling classes and acting lessons.

"Did you ever see such a little charmer?" my mother said.

I had to admit Guttnik was special. I wanted to be his friend and find out his secret charms.

After the rabbi's Yiddish sermon I joined father and red-faced Sammy Faust with ginger hair, who ran a hardware store with his wife Faggie. Sammy, Faggie, and Bubba gabbed about Bendin, their hometown. Faggie and Sammy worked dawn to dusk. I longed to be close to Father. I felt his *tallis* [prayer shawl] brush my cheeks. He clasped the prayer knots. The words were strange; the tunes cast an old sadness. Men beat their chests with closed fists and wept.

The shul where I went with Father.

CHAPTER NINE

Analytic neutrality: An overview—
O. Pinsky, July 2007

It was difficult, if not impossible, to sit with M and analyze his associations and dreams. He often brought Jaffe-Jaffe to sessions who moaned when M grew upset. Were M's childhood memories true? Who among us can remember with accuracy the earliest years of life? While I pondered this and tried to put aside his dog's vocalizing, M demanded that I take an active role. If I tried to listen and reflect on his material, M would leap from the couch and say with a sarcastic smile that I wasn't paying attention. He hurled criticisms at me. *You're not speaking, Pinsky. Where the hell are you? Are you having a silent seizure? Did you have a stroke?* He smiled but his eyes flashed with anger. *Don't I know you from somewhere?* He ached for Frieda. His happiest time was with Jaffe-Jaffe or his grandkids—particularly the eldest, Jeremy, with whom he had a deep relationship. Frieda's departure shattered his defensive shell. The separation exposed a troubled childhood that M was no longer as able to easily dissociate, joke, or deny. He increased his delinquent street jogging. M came in bruised, bandaged, and limping, yet always wore his dark but rumpled suit and tie. I sensed something struck a deep unconscious dread in his heart which he constantly denied.

"What if," I ventured tentatively, "you tried to run on a track or field? Why hurt yourself?"

"Are you my babysitter? It's those *schmuck* Toronto drivers aiming for me. Look at my notes, my drawings, my diary—I don't need you to help me cross the street."

My concerns had no effect at the time.* M was compelled to repeat his counter-phobic acts.

I collected his memorabilia in a special locked file and commented in the moment on each presentation. Through my errors and ill-attuned responses I repeated the difficulty M felt as a child—his sense of being over-controlled and misunderstood. He rebuked me for my blindness. At times he looked familiar, as if I had known him in the past—*but where?* I questioned my memory. M referred to the distant past, to childhood. Where had we met? Many times, just when I had something crucial to say, M cut me off. His actions infuriated me or made me laugh. *M was not listening.* He was enraged. I wasn't with him. He wasn't with me. He was showing me how he had felt as a child, exporting the feelings to me, which he had split-off before he could know them. A compulsive runner, he ran at dawn or night, burning off his fury on the streets challenging cars. He complained Toronto drivers were terrible—they ran him off the road. I told him I jogged. Yes, I agreed, Toronto drivers were awful. Why not run on sidewalks or a park like me? M was doggedly determined. More bruises. He limped some days. And why did he dwell in the past?

---

*In M's analysis it was far from clear which elements exerted influence on his neurosis. Dr. Sandor Gabor pointed out an unseen reality factor which was not exposed until M's final days. Jaffe-Jaffe sensed mortal danger well before anyone. I was unaware of Jaffe-Jaffe's concern about his master until well into M's analysis. The unsettling fact is that we rarely know the truth until we have failed many times to find the right answer. —O. Pinsky

CHAPTER TEN

Blum's conflict: July 2007

"Dr. Moses, why can't men stay with me? I am a woman with a sense of purpose wanting a strong loving man to share her life. You are a strong man." She lay on my couch and shifted in such a lush, wanton, seductive manner that I was sure she wanted me to possess her. At this point, Pinsky, I should have seen storm-flashes on the horizon. I should have checked with Bayer, my psychiatrist-in-chief [a well-meaning academic *putz* who does not search the dark sides of character]. Bayer has written three texts on therapy. Bayer is the short-term therapy maven—the kid, at forty-nine, is wet behind the ears. Want the truth, Pinsky? His *Bayer Method* lasts twenty sessions—after that the patient is kicked out on their ass. What does the patient learn?—idiotic fucking mantras—*make friends with feelings, walk with your wisdom*—can you swallow that superficial horseshit? Years later I see casualties. What is the *Bayer Method*? It is mood-regulation in a crap soft-cover forty dollar therapy manual for dummies. The guy is on talk shows. He is in newspapers. He has thousands of followers and writes a goddamn blog. Twenty weeks later patients say they are better—wait three years, they are back where they started from, and worse. Patients complain about his approach. What does Bayer do? He sends his problems to Guttnik—my Euclid Avenue neighbour, a turncoat analyst who gives drugs. Why shoot patients full of drugs? Does analysis do better? We treat character, not symptoms, we return to childhood—there's no shortcut. Everything you learn, to walk, to shit, to talk, to see, to feel, to love, to hate, those first steps start in childhood. If there is a problem go to where it first began.

* * *

"With my first beau, Hermann von Blumenthal, I was head over heels in love. He was tall, charming, and athletic—he reminded me of my crush on that Crystal Beach fellow.* We were *innocent kids*. My friends thought him handsome, tall with that blond Aryan look that drove my family crazy. 'What shame do you bring on us?' my mother said. 'We fled Europe. Now you invite our persecutors into the bedroom?' She threatened to boycott our wedding. Hermann was from Nuremberg. What if he was German? *Go ahead, Lippman said. Decide.* Everyone loved Hermann, except my parents. He converted and changed his name to Harry Blum. He wanted kids. I was worn down by my family. Six years later, I left him."

Pinsky, whatever form, intellectual, religious, political, I hate prejudice. Affliction surrounded the air I breathed. I grew up with victim narratives. Blum needed help. There was a coincidence—she had seen Lippman, I had seen Lippman. She had spent time at Crystal Beach. Blum talked of her failed marriage to Hermann von Blumenthal—I recalled my failures with Frieda.

---

*Crystal Beach—Blum and M cited Crystal Beach as a favourite holiday place in their childhoods. Crystal Beach was located on Lake Erie just outside of Buffalo. From the Forties to the Sixties it was a bustling small town with an amusement park and one of the largest roller-coasters in the world. In 1989 the amusement park closed, businesses left the town, and Crystal Beach faded into obscure memory. —*O. Pinsky*

"Kill the centipede, for goodness sakes, Reuben," Frieda says. "Do me a favour. It's in the sink. Hit it with your shoe—it's a lousy insect. It doesn't deserve to live."

"Frieda, you know I don't kill insects, especially centipedes."

"I can't stand all its legs waving around. Wash it down the drain."

How could I kill that poor defenceless centipede?*

It had no idea where it was.

Listen, I have nothing against centipedes; sure, they are not the prettiest insect, but why kill a centipede just because simply *to you* it appears ugly. It wanted to be with other centipedes and live a normal life. Suppose this was a test from a higher power? Suppose in the universe there is a master race of centipedes and one day they land in the vacant lot behind our house in Toronto? So I got a Kleenex.

I lifted the disoriented creature gently by its twenty front legs–the poor thing could be Kafka's cousin for all I knew. I took it outside. I put it gently on the lawn. You see, Pinsky, I was wondering if this stemmed from the trauma I underwent as a child, the trauma that was so overwhelming that I never thought of it—it was a trauma that was not a trauma that was a trauma.

On Sundays I speak with my grandkids, Jason, Jonah—*see I remembered his name*, Jeremy—explaining the world. I tell them what it was like when I was their age. I tell them about Bubba's chicken soup, her *gefilte fish*, and her *blintzes*—the food was nectar and ambrosia. I adored my Bubba's cooking. The two youngest don't understand what I am talking about and Jonah, bless him, is afraid of me. Am I too empathic? I need to take

---

*During the centipede incident [July 11, 2007] I received a call from the Toronto Police Department. "Dr. Pinsky, we are following leads on a criminal harassment case. Would you kindly call Police Headquarters? Your name was given to us by Dr. Bayer."

care of the lost, the forgotten, the misfits, the woebegone, and the downtrodden in life. I could be that persecuted centipede.

Do you see? *Pinsky, does this make sense to you? Say something.*

The centipede

CHAPTER ELEVEN

The Blitzkrieg

Uncle Eli had a big steamer trunk. He stuffed it with clothes. It was winter. For six months, from November to April, Toronto turned to ice and blowing snow. Bubba said in winter it was unsafe to play in extreme cold, children froze to death in minutes. In summer children died of sunstroke. Four days a year, *maybe*, it was safe to play in the open air.

Where was Uncle Eli going? He was taking a boat across the frigid ocean to visit his family in Manchester. *The war was over.* It was safe to travel. After Uncle Eli returned, he showed me old black-and-white photos of his family. "Reuben, the Germans bombed London—the *Blitz* killed twenty thousand people. They killed my cousin." His eyes rained tears. He showed me photos of his cousin in London. My parents had relatives in England, Poland, Russia, and Latvia. There was no news from Bendin.

"Will the Germans come here?"

"The Germans lost the Second World War, Reuben, *thank God.*"

My mother and family never spoke of the past. I lived in a tiny universe of the moment—my family, the house, the laneway, the ghetto of Jews in the middle of Toronto.

* * *

Torture #1

Bubba makes her own nightly *Blitzkrieg*; she shoves a stick of dynamite in my bum, a glycerine torpedo. "Make a nice *ka-ka*." Bubba declares all-out war on my obstinate *toochas*.

* * *

When I turned four Father opened a paper roll and spread it on the kitchen table. See the blue puddle? That is Lake Ontario. See the blue worm? That is the Don River. See the other blue worm? That's the Humber River. Toronto was between the blue worms and the big blue puddle.

"Where is Crystal Beach?" I asked.

"Crystal Beach is where everything is peaceful."

Father promised to take me to Crystal Beach but not go into the water.

"Why don't you go into the water?" I asked.

Father whispered: "No one taught me to swim."

He unfurled more paper and pointed with a pencil to the centre. Lines went this way and that. My family bent over the table discussing the rolls of paper. Their faces joined, cheek to cheek, squinting at the lines. To me, their faces looked like fruit, nuts and sweets pressed together. Uncle Eli had an orange moustache; Auntie Leah's face was a tiny lemon with raisin eyes, Bubba had soft coffee skin; Father had wavy liquorice hair and moustache. Mother's face was round, sweet as a ginger cookie. Around they walked, pointing, debating, and watching me watch them.

It was not until I saw suitcases months later that I sensed a difference.

* * *

A black-and-white squad car screeched to a halt before our house. Two cops jumped out. "Does Manny J. Karp live at this address?" They stormed up to the third floor. They dragged

The police car

Karp out of the third floor in handcuffs. That summer the entire Karp family left the attic. The rooms grew larger, the rugs were rolled up, and wall pictures disappeared. Mr. Moretti and my toys vanished. Our Euclid gang of street urchins—Karl Guttnik, Josh Karp, and little Herbie Faust disbanded. I said goodbye to Rosen's butcher shop, Lustig's bakery, Greenbaum's dairy, and Zapinsky's fish store. I hugged my teddy. A red truck stopped outside our door. Herbie Faust waved goodbye. We left the world I knew—the shops, laneways, sidewalks, parks, and people on Euclid Avenue whose faces I had come to love. I tried to run away. I became an exile in an empty countryside.

* * *

Another red truck was parked outside Euclid Avenue and behind that truck Uncle Max drove his black Chevrolet with suitcases and boxes lashed to his roof and clothes in the back seat. Like gypsies, we formed a motley refugee caravan. Along with my parents came Uncle Eli, Auntie Leah, and Bubba. Instead of living together in one house, we divided into two halves: my parents and I lived in the apartment over my father's drugstore at 739 The Queensway, and Auntie Leah, Uncle Eli, and Bubba Bella lived at the rear of Family Outfitters, a clothing store at 749 The Queensway, five doors away. Farms and empty fields surrounded the stores. I lost all my buddies. What did I do? I created a friend. His name was Captain Peacock, except he was not a captain and he was not a peacock. He was a shaggy brown dog who lived in the ceiling.

Captain Peacock told stories and kept me company. He was my best friend.

Moses' Drugs was at the corner of Royal York Road and The Queensway. "Truck drivers don't look out for little boys crossing the street. *You'll get killed.* Do you want that to happen? The trucks go faster than you. You must never walk close to the road." Bubba warned me about little children who disappeared or had been run over or lost their arms and legs. "Stay put in front of the store." She told me about a boy who ran after a ball when it went into the middle of the road. "Did he see the truck? No. Did he get run over by the truck, Reuben? Are you listening? Answer me!" He didn't see the truck I said, knowing the story. "That's right. He did not see the truck coming. And then what happened?" He got run over by the truck, I said. "That's right. He got run over by the front and back wheels of the truck and was *completely dead.* Are you listening? Do you understand?" Bubba, I understand. He was *completely dead.* There were subtle shades in Bubba's stories. People could be almost dead, partly dead, half-dead, and completely dead. Or worse, they could die once, get revived, and die again forever. I asked Leo, the butcher, if he had seen a headless chicken stay alive. Friday night I sucked the *gorgel,* the tastiest morsel, a chicken's neck.

"Reuben, watch for *gorgel* bones," Bubba said. "*You* can choke to death."

* * *

39

Zlotnik, the barber from Bendin

Every six weeks Bubba *schlepped* me back to Kensington Market to see Zlotnik the barber and my old friends. Zlotnik cut Guttnik's golden curls, Herbie's locks, and Ruthie-Annie's tresses. Zlotnik turned to Karp's son, Josh, and then it was my turn. Zlotnik had a number tattooed on his left arm. He draped me in white like a corpse. Zlotnik, from Poland, bald and half-blind with a tremor, took a straight razor to my head. I waited to be cut in two. *"You're done,"* Zlotnik said. *"Next."* I flew from the chair and put my hand to my neck—*blood*. Zlotnik had nicked me with his razor.

* * *

Blum had a "heart seizure" in my hospital office. I sat her up. I gave her a glass of water. I took her pulse. Pinsky, it didn't seem to be an arrhythmia—I believed it was palpitations. Blum talked about the tiny apartment over the depanneur [convenience store] where she lived with her mother when they first came to Montreal. The place was damp and cold in the winter. There were cockroaches. Blum left early for the local school and came home alone in the dark winter to an empty apartment. Those early years her mother worked long hours in a tailor shop.

The session after Blum's hysterical arrhythmia, she came to complain. Her Italian marble suppliers were crooks, local shippers were thieves, U.S. buyers were schemers, and the customs people were imbeciles. Her son was *gornisht mit gornisht*. She had parked beside my car and complained some idiot let the air out of her tires. Her medical specialists were nitwits, quacks, screwballs—and guess what? Men were either after her body or her money. She had a basic trust problem. Perhaps you are different, but how can I be sure? I never trusted Dr. Lippman.

"What did Lippman do?"

Blum became vague, spoke about Lippman raising his voice to her, answering his phone in sessions, and then rattled on about her bathroom woes—how the hell was she to turn a profit?

She went back to her flat tires. I read in *Forbes* she was one of North America's wealthiest women—from toilets, no less. She told me she lived with her married son. In her spare time she renovated her Forest Hill mansion, consulted with European spas, travelled to Miami, Puerto Vallarta or her Provence villa, sat on hospital committees, and ran several charities.

Blum turned to give me an ambiguous glance.

"Do you understand what it is like to be alone?"

Dr. Sandor Gabor with sparkling eyes, the finest analytic mind in Budapest

Sandor Gabor is in his mid-nineties, originally a Hungarian psycho-neurologist from Vienna by way of Budapest who speaks five languages, a kindly white-haired Jewish elf, with sparkling watery eyes that he wipes with a Kleenex—an eye condition, he explains: too many tears; at least, he does not suffer from dry eyes. Gabor met Freud before the *Anschluss*. After losing his family, after cancer, after returning to postwar Budapest, struggling against the communists, fleeing Budapest for Vienna, after two heart attacks, after a triple bypass, after bilateral hip replacements, Gabor limps with a cane. His mind is sharp as a tack. He knew the early analysts. Gabor has an incredible memory. My office is on the ground floor of a Toronto brownstone and Gabor has an office across the hall—Guttnik my arch-rival is on the second floor. We share the same garden and parking lot. Every two weeks I consult with Gabor. After listening to me about Blum, what does Gabor say? He says my big problem is my fucking countertransference.

Frieda Heintzmann from Dresden

Frieda was a knockout, blonde, blue-eyed, a real piece of German ass—as soon as I saw her I wanted to *shtupp* her. We met as interns. Whenever we weren't on call we were together

Dr. Sandor Gabor

in bed, *shtupping*. We married in residency. You can imagine my family was not entirely happy with Frieda. Lippman turned everything on its head. Who is ordering you what to do?

Frieda came to Canada as a two year old in 1950. Her aunt, uncle, and big sister were killed in the 1945 Dresden firebombing. Her *omi* put wet sheets over Frieda's mother. Everything else burned to a crisp.

Pinsky, if I wanted, I could walk five stores down to Family Outfitters where Bubba, Auntie Leah, and Uncle Eli lived. Or I could walk the other way to my father's store—as long as I did not drift near the road. Sunday I was treated to breakfast with Uncle Eli and Auntie Leah, so my parents could sleep. One Sunday Uncle Eli told me the reason. "Guess why you

42

come here? You want to know the truth?" Uncle Eli asked. "Your parents *shtupp to make babies*. Understand? Your dad is *shtupping* your mother." Like a ton of bricks, this hit me. *Shtupping*. Uncle Eli was telling me this as if I had the slightest idea. I had big worries about my testicles.

My left testicle was sagging lower.

* * *

I receive another call from the Toronto Police Department. An officer requests that I phone headquarters about a harassment case—a few questions he would like to ask. I write down the harassment unit number. I call the officer and leave my name. The next day I receive a call back. Have I recently received any threats from patients? Nothing, I say. But it gets me thinking about M. Since I have been seeing him strange things have happened. I can't point my finger to a single event—it is a feeling, an impression that lies beneath the surface of things. M tells me what is most precious in his life—his beloved family, his ex-wife Frieda, his ninety-two-year-old mother who lives two blocks away on Bathurst Street. He tells about his unsettled dog Jaffe-Jaffe, his rose garden outside his St. Clair office, and his old Volvo C-70 convertible.

M tells me of his Bubba theory. Analysts in his society are peeved, some like Guttnik, his confrere from Euclid Avenue days, are no longer enthusiastic. Others are frankly hostile.

"Tell me about your Bubba theory. Why don't analysts like your ideas?"

"Lippman supports me but most analysts think I am a nut, a radical," M replies.

"Radical? What do you mean radical?"

"They say I am too extreme. It's not just the analysts who dislike me."

"Who else dislikes you?"

43

M pauses. "The synagogue sisterhood are not pleased."

"Can you explain a bit more?"

"Listen, Pinsky, I don't want to talk about this right now."

There is a long silence.

"What are you feeling?"

Another long silence.

"I am not sure about Guttnik," M says. "He was always a pretty boy."

"Can you tell me more?"

M has mixed feelings about Guttnik, his childhood friend, school chum, jogging partner, analytic colleague, and rival. I ask him again about Guttnik but he remains quiet.

"What are you thinking about?" I ask.

I wait minutes.

"I am thinking about Fidel."

"Who is Fidel, a patient?"

"No, Fidel was my dog, a male golden retriever. Fidel was well behaved, loyal; he lived with Frieda and I before we separated. A few months later I moved to an apartment two blocks away from my mother on Bathurst Street and Fidel disappeared.

"What happened to Fidel? Did he run away? You found him eventually?"

More silence.

M shifts on the couch once. He is now absolutely still. He wears his dark suit, a starched white shirt, a dark tie. His black shoes are shiny and his dark hair gleams. He is a man of contrasts, outwardly neat, thoughtful, and polished; inwardly he is unsettled, at times volcanic, but always self-mocking.

M is devoted to his patients, working tirelessly at Mount Zion in the chronic care and borderline clinics following intractable patients, seeing them occasionally in police stations or jail. He sees long-term analytic cases in his private practice in the brownstone he shares with Gabor and his off-and-on colleague Guttnik, whom one moment he admires and the next moment he derides. M spends his free moments at his private office tending his rose garden; his rose garden offers him simple relief from the stress of his work, that and his compulsive jogging.

For a man in his sixties he looks extraordinarily young without lines or grey hair, yet as I now bend over more closely I see grey hairs sprouting on his crown and sideburns.

When he first started analysis with me there was not one grey hair.

CHAPTER TWELVE

Fidel: August 2, 2007

Fidel was before Jaffe-Jaffe. I had no idea of what happened to Fidel. Judging from M's unusual silence around the matter, I assumed that the event had affected him deeply.

It took several sessions to unravel what had led to Fidel's disappearance.

Although M was not a lefty or social activist in the true sense of the word, he recalled Fidel Castro as a teenager, the Cuban revolutionary who overthrew Fulgencio Batista, the former Cuban dictator.

How did M come to think of Castro?

It had to do with his manhood.

"You see," M explained, "I lost my virginity to a Cuban woman, Estella. She was my dance teacher. I was thirteen; Estella was the mother of my best friend, Ari Mazer."

Puzzled, I asked about Estella. M fell quiet again. "But Fidel, what happened with Fidel?"

* * *

Analysis does not proceed in a straight line. It is neither brief nor straightforward like filling a painful dental cavity. In many cases the aching root of illness reaches back to earliest childhood and extends forward throughout the entire life of the psyche. So who was Fidel?

Fidel was the dog that had grown up with M's family, his wife Frieda, and their three daughters. Fidel had joined the family as a young pup and lived with the family for seventeen years before his death.

Fidel was a consummate companion to M's wife and daughters—always friendly, never hostile, placid even when his tail and ears were pulled, Fidel became an issue when Frieda decided to separate from M. Who would care for the dog?

M assured the family that he would manage Fidel. For months Fidel accompanied M to his office and sat beside him during his analytic sessions. His patients did not mind. Fidel would come to them and offer his paw. I never met Fidel. I heard of the dog in sessions when M spoke about his unquenched desire for Estella, wanting to *shtupp* her. I did not understand more.

* * *

Shtupping—I had this sexual itch since childhood. It started after toilet training. By grade three, I had crushes on my female teachers. By grade eight I read Krafft-Ebing, Menninger, and Freud. Before my bar mitzvah I took dance lessons with my best friend's Cuban stepmom, Estella—it was not only mambo she taught me—I will tell you later. In high school I shtupped Roxanne in her parents' basement—the hottest lips in Toronto yet I can't recall Roxanne's last name. *Wait*—it's coming, it's coming—*Greenbaum, Roxanne Greenbaum*—her parents ran the local dairy.

Shtupping *and toilet training: age one*

Bubba and mother toilet trained me at one—can you believe that premature sphincter control? Was the sexual itch my revenge? I was strapped into a plastic potty. I had to sit in solitary confinement until I pushed out two full stools. One stool was never enough. And if, *God forbid*, I was constipated or fell asleep on the job, the two of them had secret weapons—not only suppositories but Torture #2—warm soap enemas. Should I complain? Am I making too much out of my anal tragedies? What they did was against the Geneva Convention. Yes, it was for my own good. What choice did I have, Pinsky? If I didn't produce my two golden eggs Bubba said there was a *bogeyman* that lived in the toilet that would come up the sewer and bite my *toochas*. Who could I talk to? The only soul who listened to me was Captain Peacock.

On Sundays while my parents were *shtupping* I went to Family Outfitters for breakfast. Bubba and Auntie Leah and Uncle Eli lived at the back of the store. I saw their living room with the furniture from Euclid Avenue—the dining room table, the side table, their big Stromberg-Carlson shortwave floor radio, just like ours, with a green electric eye that winked when you turned it on. I heard Nat King Cole sing *Mona Lisa* and Sammy Kaye's band play *Harbor Lights*. Bubba's favourite song was *That Lucky Old Sun* by Frankie Laine. Against a far wall was a fold-out davenport where Bubba slept. I wandered downstairs beside the furnace and a coal-bin, a bathroom, and rows of shelves where they kept old photos—black-and-white photos in Latvia and Poland—I recognized no one. In the basement was a Victrola with a dog listening to music. *If I only had a dog!* I learned to put 78 rpm records on the turntable, crank the handle, lower the stylus, and listen.

Summer I had nothing to do.* I felt the weight of formless hours contenting myself with Captain Peacock playing imaginary games. Bubba, who I adored, said it was unsafe to walk

---

Jaffe-Jaffe, M's beloved retriever, provided him with relief from isolation. M complained that he had nothing to do—to me it expressed a defensive need against pity. I failed to understand his profound and infinite emptiness or "nothingness" until much later. —O. Pinsky

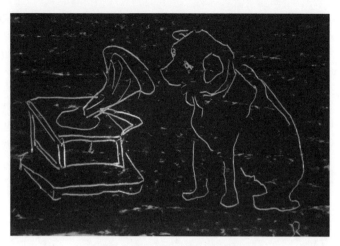

The little gramophone dog

on the road or play in public places; she warned me about polio epidemics. Auntie Leah showed me photos—roller coasters, Ferris wheels, and a sandy white beach. Uncle Eli, the world traveller, told me an astonishing fact. "Crystal Beach has the biggest roller coaster in the world." He sat me on his foot, lifted me high up, holding my hands tight, and dropped his leg. My stomach lurched. "Look what you did," Bubba said. "Now he can't stand straight."

"He will be fine," Uncle Eli said. "He is excited."

"This roller coaster is not for Reuben," Bubba said. "First, it is too big; second, it is too fast."

My mother's daily weather report: August 2, 2007

I can't walk to the corner store in this heat. I need a bottle of mineral oil, dried apricots, and prune juice. Do you see Ari Mazer? Ari was such an angel. How about your old school friends, Josh Karp and Karl Guttnik? How is little Herbie Faust?

Pinsky, why does my mother ask about little Herbie Faust?

I haven't seen him or his sister Ruthie-Annie for eons. And Ari Mazer?

Ari moved to Miami fifty years ago—is her mind locked in the past like mine?

Ari acted like a Boy Scout. The truth was that he was a total shit-disturber and psychopath. At fifteen he stole his father's Continental and drove to the local A&W with Roxanne Greenbaum, Sabrina Lustig, Guttnik, and me.

His stepmom Estella knew but she never told a soul.

Estella had her own secrets.

She taught me how to dance—I never forgot my first steps.

My father's drugstore, we lived on the second floor

August 9–10, 2007

M tells me about his precious rose garden planted on the sunny side of his office brownstone. His beautiful roses bloom throughout the summer and fall. M adores their fragrant bouquet and is careful to tend and water the roses in the hot summer. The rose garden appears to offer M a sense of caring involvement with nature much like his grandchildren and his dog, Jaffe-Jaffe. His painful loneliness is diminished with these nurturing attachments.

On Thursday August 9 or possibly Friday August 10, 2007, some delinquent has deliberately pulled out three of his beautiful dark red roses—M is not sure who has committed this destructive act.

For several minutes he lies still on my couch and says nothing.

CHAPTER THIRTEEN

Toilet phobia

Pinsky, I had a morbid fear of toilet seats. I was fine with bathrooms and urinals; I felt uneasy with crowds of men standing beside me and peeing into the communal *pissoir*, but I managed; I was not the least afraid of going to the gym and taking a shower with twenty naked men, but near a strange toilet seat I was a goner—I never told Lippman.

It's the thought of sitting on that existential black hole with my *bare naked bum and my family jewels hanging down exposed* into the dark uncertain void that drove me nuts. It led to holding in, to not letting go—it was a serious condition—in the UK alone over 4 million people have toilet phobia.

But why me, a grown man, why should I have such fears?

Latrine duty: age one to two

Bubba tied me like an inmate into my potty. She regaled me with horror stories—*Bubba mysehs*—about toilet bogeymen: I believed every word. She closed the bathroom door—that was solitary confinement. As much as I hated my blue potty, I grew attached to Bubba and my potty like a *Stockholm syndrome*. I wouldn't shit unless I sat on my goddamn stinky blue pilot seat. My parents took it everywhere, to Uncle Max's house, to my cousins and friends. I had to have my blue throne—but then, sadly, I grew out of it. No matter how hard I tried, it didn't fit. My *toochas* was too big. This led to complications. Bubba instructed me to never sit on a toilet seat with my bare *toochas*. God forbid what *terrible disease* people carried on *toochas?* Bubba gave public health talks in unrolling toilet paper and covering the toilet seat in not one but three layers, to prevent the spread of pestilence and disease. Pinsky, at my age I struggle with putting on three layers of toilet paper on the toilet. It is ridiculous but I still do it. And you know the crazy thing?

I miss my old blue potty.

* * *

August 16, 2007. Pinsky, I receive a second call from my office security manager. Someone in a trench coat and hat is snooping at night. They appear to be taking pictures of my office with an iPhone. The intruder looks at my door, the windows, the rose garden, and the mail box.

"Whoever it is seems to be checking where the cameras are," the security manager says.

CHAPTER FOURTEEN

The Bubba complex

L ittle Red Riding Hood walked across the forest to visit her Bubba. The big bad wolf ate Bubba, dressed up in her clothes and waited under the bedcovers for Riding Hood. Bubba read me that story each night. When little Herbie and Ruthie-Annie had dinner at our house Bubba read them the story. The wolf gobbled up the unsuspecting child. I knew every line, every picture in the book. I had Bubba repeat the story word for word each night. When I slept beside Bubba she became a she-wolf. Her magic stories swallowed me. Or was it night that gobbled me up? Or was it Bubba's food and Bubba herself that I devoured? I was filled with curiosity but soon fell into the dark stomach of sleep.

Psychoanalyst argues for grandparents. Toronto Star, August 20, 2007

Does the Bubba have a central place in childhood development: Yes or No?

Tuesday night Dr. Reuben Moses, before a packed audience at Beth Jerusalem Temple, Toronto, spoke on grandparents in child development. Dr. Moses, a prominent psychiatrist-analyst at Mount Zion Hospital represented the "Yes" side debating the centrality of the *Bubba* or Jewish grandmother as a key figure in addressing the anxieties of the male child. Dr. Karl Guttnik, a psychiatric colleague and congregation member debated the "No" side and failed to agree on the centrality of the Bubba Complex.

"Not everyone has a Bubba, not everyone has a Bubba Complex, not everyone has these anxieties and not everyone is Jewish," Guttnik stated.

"The grandmother keeps the family together," Moses argued.

Most of the audience expressed disapproval of Dr. Moses' description of the Bubba. Dr. Moses argued that he described the "normal ambivalence" present in all human relationships. At the meeting's end an unidentified group of individuals booed Dr. Moses. The sisterhood president stated that Dr. Moses' second planned talk entitled "Love and Hate in the Bubba Complex" planned for the following month would be postponed.

I read through the article and realize that M had a tendency to incite anger. Has he picked this tendency up from his former analyst, Lippman? Dressed in his dark suit, starched white shirt, sombre tie, fountain pen in his left breast pocket, M marches into my office bent forward, possessed, like a charging crusader on horseback in a relentless quest. It is not only the Bubba complex that he zealously defends but lost souls in his practice. He appreciates Guttnik's criticism but feels his colleague's position as betrayal. What is it about the Bubba complex that so enrages and divides his audiences? My office phone rings twice during my session with M. An urgent call, Dr. Bayer, leaves a terse message. Bayer has had a problem with M. "Has the hospital lawyer made contact with me?" When I reach Bayer he informs me that a former patient's wife has been harassing his office and the office of Dr. Karl Guttnik.

"This person dislikes doctors," Bayer said. "She detests all psychiatrists."

Had I received threatening calls? No, I say again. *Nothing*.

I feel a gnawing doubt, a concern that M is not telling me the whole story.

A few days later M's dog walker, Crystal, calls me.

CHAPTER FIFTEEN

Crystal—the dog walker: August 23, 2007

Crystal, the dog walker, is in tears. "M told me to call him here if there was a problem—can I speak to him?" M is not at my office. I explain to her that I do not accept calls during patient sessions unless there is an emergency. More tears, then a stream of insults. "Don't you dumb analysts care about human beings? You sit on your fat asses in your fancy offices, right? You don't know *fuck-all* about why I am calling, do you? You want to push me aside like everyone else, right? What does that tell me? Pinsky, *you can drop dead, fuck you*, you dumb fuck."

I plan to hang up the receiver yet sense the dog walker is not angry with me. "*Wait.*" I pull the mouthpiece closer. "M left a few moments ago. You can call him on his cell."

"He doesn't keep his cell on after his sessions with you. I already tried. *Understand?*"

I check my watch. I have a quarter hour until my next analytic patient. "Tell me what you are concerned about, Crystal."

"Are you going to listen this time?"

"All right," I say, "but I must tell you I only have a few minutes."

"*Five fucking minutes*—do you have that time?"

More tears and sighs. Crystal repeats that she was given my telephone number by M to call him if she was worried.

For several minutes I try to calm her down on the phone. She is hyperventilating so I tell her to breathe slowly. Crystal is desperate. She goes on to say that Jaffe-Jaffe is an unusual dog, sensitive, high-strung, difficult to settle—but intelligent. She wants to do a good job as a dog walker.

Crystal fears that Jaffe-Jaffe will die and it will be her fault.

"Can you explain to me why you believe Jaffe-Jaffe will die?"

"Didn't M tell you?"

"Tell me what?"

"Fidel was killed. You know who I am referring to?"

"How was Fidel killed?"

"He was run over." Crystal sobs. "I was the goddamn dog walker," she wails. "I had him off leash on the sidewalk. *Fuck.* The car didn't even see him. It happened in a flash."

"You were walking Fidel?"

"M said it would be good for me to walk a dog. He said it would help my nervousness. I have a long-standing problem with bad nerves. I don't feel secure. *Understand?*"

"Are you a patient of M?"

No answer. Crystal wails and blows her nose. She takes a deep breath.

"Crystal, are you a patient of M?"

"Jaffe-Jaffe is not like Fidel. I can't let her off leash. She almost got run over today. *Understand?* Now do you get why I worry like crazy?"

* * *

Our next session I bring up Crystal but M is off to the races rushing back to the past. I tell him that his dog walker called my office hyperventilating with high anxiety. Is Crystal his patient? He says nothing but looks sheepish. "She told me Fidel was run over by a car. Is that right?"

"Yes, that is right."

"She worries the same tragedy will happen to Jaffe-Jaffe. Why give Crystal that job?"

"Crystal has never held a job in her life."

"If Crystal is your patient, you are complicating therapy. Do you have to save the world?"

"She had a terrible childhood."

"Is she in your borderline clinic?"

"Somebody has to give her a break."

"Answer me; is Crystal in your borderline clinic?"

"Crystal was a neglected child."

"Have you considered that Crystal's anxiety is making Jaffe-Jaffe more anxious?"

M defends his reasons for having Crystal in therapy and hiring her as his dog walker.

"What about Fidel? It happened about the same time you and Frieda separated. Yes?"

I focus on Fidel, his grief over his cherished dog and ask why M has not told me about the dog's death. Has it been forgotten? "Have you pushed this back to the past?"

"Pinsky, everything is the past. Living in the present is bullshit. It is all past. There is no present moment—when we reflect we are already in the past. We are locked in a prison of time."

* * *

"When I was four I had trouble breathing and became delirious. Mother complained of spiking fever, weakness, and breathing problems. Father fretted that we had TB. Mother and I grew sicker. My lips turned slate. *See—his lips are blue—do something*, Bubba yelled at Father. Your wife can hardly breathe. Uncle Max examined us and diagnosed pneumonia. In the years before 1948, many people died of polio, TB, and pneumonia.

59

There was no treatment for polio but there was a new drug used during the war to fight bacterial infections—penicillin. "This is serious," Uncle Max said. "It is double pneumonia." It was a disease that killed thousands. I almost died.

My father, working in his drugstore, was unable to watch mother and me. Aunt Sadie and Uncle Max moved us to their house on Park Hill Avenue where we received penicillin, bed rest, and home care. After I recovered, whenever I had a sniffle Bubba warned us TB or pneumonia was around the corner. Bubba had a thing about germs—the more soap the better—she used *Lifebuoy Carbolic Soap*, she swabbed me all over with this infernal red bubbly soap—she covered me head to toe. God forbid, if you ever got it on your eyes or mouth or tongue or inside your *schmuck*, it burned like wildfire—torture #3. *"Lifebuoy burns the skin—but it kills bad germs—Don't cry, Reuben."* Lifebuoy annihilated what was on the skin, but it killed skin too. Millions of children were lathered, buffed, and sponged with Lifebuoy until skin was maraschino cherry-red.

The soap should be named *Death-Boy*.

* * *

Uncle Max wore a dark three-piece suit and carried a black bag where he kept his syringes and drugs. After I recovered from pneumonia he took me on house calls. "Sit tight. Don't you dare run away!" Uncle Max talked about patients. Some got better, some stayed the same; some died.

Uncle Max never gave up on patients. He was my hero.

Two doors from our pharmacy a new store opened—Faust's Super Hardware—little cross-eyed Herbie, my Euclid Avenue buddy and his metal-mouth sister lived over their hardware. Sam and Faggie, Polish immigrants, worked day to night. I hardly saw Herbie all week. He and Ruthie-Annie were driven to Jewish school in downtown Toronto to learn Yiddish and Hebrew. In the evenings Ruthie-Annie practiced violin. When I heard her squeaky scales at bedtime I got chills.

Herbie told me he hardly talked to his parents—they spoke almost no English and didn't have friends except for *Bendiners*. They joined the *Zaglember Society*—work, work, work was all they did. Ruthie-Annie never let her brother out of sight. Herbie was small, cross-eyed, and didn't play with boys. Ruthie-Annie demolished any guy that made fun of Herbie. The two of them were sad sacks. I was lonely. What a combination! We were all miserable. Bubba, despite her work, came home to make dinner. Many nights Herbie and Ruthie-Annie joined us.

Years later, Uncle Max gave me a children's library for my birthday—books that he had sent to his sons while stationed in Europe. Uncle Max had signed up for the Canadian Army Medical Corps. I was envious of my cousins who had a doctor-soldier father.

What was the Second World War? Why did so many of our Jewish families leave Europe?

Uncle Max said nothing.

August 23, 2007

I ask about Crystal but M has fallen quiet. After he has left Bayer's secretary calls—a woman has phoned Mount Zion, threatening Bayer, M, and Guttnik. M mentions nothing—as if these events do not exist. M has become increasingly sour to Guttnik who is not only an analyst but a drug expert for anxious, manic, and suicidal patients. M says Guttnik has turned his back on analysis. Guttnik puts his patients on drugs. M has known Guttnik since childhood. His old friend is described as a *hacham*, a wiseguy, a lady's man, suave, good-looking, an entitled prick, a rat.

* * *

61

Crystal, M's dog walker: August 24, 2007

After M leaves my couch my phone rings—a second message from M's dog walker. Crystal's voice is calmer. "Dr. Pinsky. Jaffe-Jaffe was better until last week. I am not making this up."

CHAPTER SIXTEEN

M's childhood diary
(written retrospectively in late childhood)

L ittle Herbie is thin as a skeleton with red hair. Bubba says
I should be his friend.
He speaks Yiddish, Polish, and English.

I see bones under his white skin.

His clothes hang on him. On weekends he draws pictures of flowers and trees.

He loves flowers and knows all their names.

He collects stones and painted them. He loves his sister more than anyone.

Little Herbie tells me he wants to be an artist, a painter, or a dancer.

* * *

Little Herbie is nice to me. He always says hello.

What can I say about little Herbie?

Little Herbie is quiet. He looks up to his big sister.

He is a sad little mouse. He has no Bubba.

* * *

Ruthie-Annie—she is pretty but she lights firecrackers. She throws them at boys. Bubba tells me I should be her friend. Ruthie-Annie protects Herbie. When Bubba speaks to

Ruthie-Annie I see her tears. If boys tease Herbie, Ruthie-Annie beats them up. She hit a big kid. He called her brother a sissy. She punched him. She kicked him. She bit his fingers with her braces.

One day I figure she is going to eat someone.

Little Herbie tells me she has a secret diary. During the day she carries it everywhere with her. At night Herbie says that she hides it under her pillow.

Ruthie-Annie has bruises on her arms and legs.

* * *

Bubba has a soft spot for Ruthie-Annie. She hugs her and tells her not to worry. Ruthie-Annie collects bugs. She takes care of them. She says her job is to protect the insects from evil human beings like me.

Ruthie-Annie says evil humans killed all her family in Poland.

I never hurt anyone. I never hurt a fly. One day I am going to sneak a peek at all her pet insects. One day I will read her diary and find out all her secrets.

One of Ruthie-Annie's ladybugs

CHAPTER SEVENTEEN

Sitting still: September 2007

I walk a half-mile from Mount Zion Hospital to Pinsky's office on foot, rain or shine. I jog five times a week. My mother yells at me about my running. Why do you need to run so much, Reuben? Why can't you sit still like a normal person? *Say something, Pinsky.*

"You were strapped to a potty, you wore a harness as a child," Pinsky says. "You were restricted to a block of sidewalk in front of the drugstore—look what career you chose, Moses, to sit in one place and listen to depressed patients and their *outpourings* and your mother's anxieties. You are still strapped into a professional potty. So you jogged five times a week. When your wife left and Fidel died, you didn't know what to do, so you jogged six days a week. When you see Blum you feel angry and helpless, so you jog seven days a week. You want a deep interpretation, Moses? Each day you run away from yourself."

* * *

Blum grunts in my office and craps all over me. She has been embroiled in a home renovation, she is furious with the painter—he can't get the colour right, the dry wall is not straight, and the floors are from hell. Naturally she shares her exasperation with me. Most of her hate is directed to her gay Palestinian interior designer. Blum claims she is not a racist or a homophobe; she just wants the job done right. Has she been the patient harassing Bayer at the hospital? I wonder.

Toronto has the worst traffic in North America. Blum reminds me with precise lateness, you never get anywhere on time. I take Jaffe-Jaffe out for a pee and go for a dawn jog; I drive my Volvo to my private office and see my early morning analysands. By noon I walk to the hospital where I follow clinic patients and then I march back to my private office where I see more analytic cases in the evening. I can't be still with patients—it's not toilet training, Pinsky. *I am impatient with life's constipation*. I am a good listener—but it takes all my goddamn concentration to sit still. Between patients in the late morning I take the rear stairs from my hospital office on the ninth floor to the ground floor and back—twice. In my private office I get up, walk outside; I check the garden in front of my office and return. I have this beautiful little rose garden. I tend my roses.

Oskar Pinsky, my analyst

Pinsky is seventy-one, bald, seven years older than me, a training analyst–a strict Freudian. He runs the outpatient psychiatry clinic at St. Luke's Hospital, the downtown Catholic hospital in Toronto. Pinsky is an old-timer and hard core; he says analysts should work in hospitals and reach out to the community. I like that. There is this old joke about Pinsky and Bayer. Bayer sees Pinsky walking down the street with a couch on his back.

Bayer: Hey, Pinsky, where are you going with the couch on your back?

Pinsky: Can't you see? I am making a house call.

Pinsky looks like someone I once knew. I tell him that. He nods but is upset that my dog walker, Crystal, called. I tell him about my emergency the night before.

66

On call at 2 am: August 30, 2007

Crystal sits in an Emergency Department cubicle at 2 am. She asks to see me. She coughs. She has trouble swallowing. When she was six her parents separated and she was put in a foster home, from seven to twelve she was sexually abused, at thirteen Crystal was depressed, suicidal, pregnant, and had a baby. At fifteen she was dating a drug dealer, Zeno, the leader of a motorcycle gang. Zeno himself was abused as a kid but became the most powerful guy in her hood. Zeno protected her until he went into the slammer. From jail Zeno warned me not to make Crystal more nervous or he would put a contract on me. I followed Crystal since childhood. At sixteen she dropped out of my clinic and disappeared. Two years later she returned with a new symptom—she had become a swallower. In the ED Crystal and I talk a half hour. Crystal is not exactly suicidal but admits feeling more anxious since she has been walking Jaffe-Jaffe. She admits swallowing two batteries and a ballpoint pen. Zeno will be out on parole in late 2008—I don't look forward to Zeno's release. I call the GI people about her swallowing—the third time this month for Crystal.

You shrinks should do something about her swallowing instead of talking, the GI guy says.

* * *

Father sat with me sweating on the front stoop of the drugstore on a hot summer night. The Rexall neon sign was switched off. The store was dark. Father struck a match on the stoop and lit a Sweet Caporal. We were in the country with nothing but farmers' fields, a moonless sky, and thousands of icy stars. We heard cricket music and Ruthie-Annie's shrill violin scales. Mother was in the apartment running a bath. She was seeing a doctor, Father said. When he grew emotional he sometimes stuttered.

67

"Is Mom going to be better?" I asked. "Does she have pneumonia again?"

Father smiled and shook his head. He inhaled his cigarette and leaned against the drugstore window. A Noxzema cream display sat in the window with a picture of a sunburnt little girl.

"Did you always want to be a druggist?"

"It would be b-better to be a doctor like Max or a businessman like Sam Faust."

When we climbed upstairs Mother explained that it was the baby inside that made her tired.

Mr. Rossi opened a bike store three doors away; beside him was Moretti's shoe and skate repair. Moretti, our basement tenant, married Rossi's sister that year and told Rossi about the new stores going up on The Queensway. I had three new stores to look at when I went along the sidewalk, Faust's hardware—where Sammy and Faggie worked day and night, Moretti's shoe and skate repair, and Rossi's bikes. I gaped at racing bikes with special gears in Rossi's store. They were painted bright colours from Italy. I wanted to ride a bike.

"Don't get excited," Bubba said. "What if you fall and crack your head open?"

Sunday afternoons when Mr. Moretti played his accordion Herbie took me into his parents' hardware store. We looked at the tools, nails, and paints. I stuck two big nails in my mouth and made like a werewolf—that scared Herbie. Herbie took me upstairs to his parents' apartment over the hardware store. The place smelled of mothballs and cabbage soup. Ruthie-Annie played her rusty violin scales. Herbie showed me photos of his Polish family and said they all died in the war. The mothballs and Ruthie-Annie's violin and the black-and-white photos gave me the creeps.

Herbie pointed to Ruthie-Annie's tiny bottles for homeless insects.

When Ruthie-Annie wasn't looking I found her secret diary. It was in Yiddish. I couldn't read a single word. Walking back to the drugstore and climbing up my stairs my body felt heavy and sluggish. The last thing I remembered was going to bed. I heard buzzing and my dark bedroom turning pink. Father had flicked on the neon Rexall sign.

The sign was a second moon. It shone happiness. It sprinkled warm watermelon light across Faust's Super Hardware and Rossi's Bike Shop, across farms and fields to the wooden houses far away. It shone its buzzing beacon to the heavens.

Moses' Rexall Drug Store, the most powerful drugstore in the universe.

That's what Captain Peacock whispered from the ceiling.

The Rexall sign. In the night it sent its pink colour
through the universe

* * *

Why do you want to learn Yiddish? Bubba asked. I told her that I wanted to know what my family talked about. Bubba said if I learned too much my brain would expand too fast and there would be bigger troubles.

But evenings when my parents worked Bubba taught me Yiddish.

Bubba explained Yiddish was an ancient language written in Roman or Hebrew letters that Jews used for many centuries in Europe.

Everyone in my family spoke Yiddish. They said it was their *mame loshon* or mother tongue.

To me Yiddish was a language of mystery and sadness.

It was what my parents spoke when they kept secrets from me.

I couldn't read English or Yiddish words.

Herbie told me that Ruthie-Annie wrote in Yiddish each day in her diary.

I wanted to understand why she had the strange bruises on her arms and legs.

CHAPTER EIGHTEEN

Vandalism: September 2007

Blum was externalizing—everything outside of her was troublesome. Her first husband, Hermann, her second husband, her third husband, her family, her previous analyst Lippman, her interior decorator, her specialists, even Ivan her son and Frieda who was seeing him, no one was free from blame—Blum was irreproachable. She spoke with utter certainty—this is, I suppose, the one thing she learned from the great Lippman—to boss others.

And this is when we began to drift to her problems. Her problems became my problem. The office was too cold, then it was too warm, or the couch was too hard, or the cushion too soft, or the light was too low. She didn't like the colour of my walls. She didn't care for my dark suit. I was either too silent or too verbose. I was no longer the esteemed analyst. Someone let the air out of her tires in *my parking lot*—a second time.

"Is that so?" I asked. "Why would they let the air out of *your* tires?"

"I drive a Mercedes-Benz. Some people are envious—was it you, Dr. Moses?"

"Why would I let the air out of your tires?" I asked.

"You want to deflate me," she said.

"I want to deflate your neurosis," I said calmly. During that session she asked to check her car in the underground parking lot. I dutifully accompanied her. Not only were her tires flat but someone had keyed her doors and broken a headlight.

"I should call the police about what you did to me." I walked to my old C-70 Volvo parked two spots away. It was also keyed. My tires were flat. "Look what you have done behind my back. It happened in your office parking lot," Blum said. "Why have you done this to me?"

* * *

M sent me a copy of Bayer's bestseller, *Feeling Fine: The Bayer Method of Psychotherapy*. Years later many of Bayer's original patients admitted that their treatment failed. Dissatisfied with the *Bayer Method*, patients argued that the treatment did not offer long-term relief. Some threatened legal action. Bayer countered that his method was a short-term therapy. M quipped that the method was a pile of crap, a cheap throwaway band aid. One of Bayer's difficult patients, a dentist (who lost a leg in a motorcycle accident and grew addicted to painkillers and gambling) became psychotic and threatened Bayer. Guttnik, the double agent, tried to stabilize the man on drugs. The distressed patient broke into the hospital to steal narcotics and his chart. This harassment occurred over twenty years earlier. Since childhood his wife mistrusted doctors. She joined her husband in his threats. Bayer had received phone threats from an anonymous woman. Suspicions fell on his former patient's wife. M initially had consulted on this case by phone. He advised Bayer to terminate treatment. One week later, the depressed dentist, Bayer's patient, committed suicide.

The patient's wife refused to meet hospital staff. She held Bayer and his consultant, Guttnik and M responsible. Mysteriously she vanished. I assumed the calls from the police and hospital dealt with this former patient's wife and not M's patient, Blum. I urged M to be careful.

CHAPTER NINETEEN

M's notes and sketches—O. Pinsky, October 2007

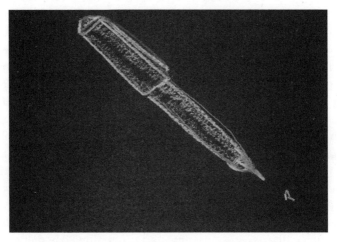

Bubba gave me a Parker 21 pen. I sketch with it.

M continued to bring sketches, news clippings, recipes, diaries, and notes to the sessions. His jumble of sketches were hastily drawn, pen or pencil drawings of his family home on Euclid Avenue, his father's drugstore, his blue potty, the Rexall sign, and his mother's daily weather reports. He sketched his patients—when they weren't looking. M's notes were dashed on crumpled hospital paper, fragments of the past. He brought his Bubba's recipe for *gefilte fish* and raved about her *blintzes*. He brought me *gefilte fish* which he made himself. I ate it for lunch, at first a little suspicious, but his *gefilte fish*, or should I say, his Bubba's *gefilte fish*, was memorable, succulent and tasty. M drew cartoons of his family and me. I kept his productions in a large manila folder on my desk during the session. Afterwards I methodically locked his work in my office filing cabinet. M brought me photos and sketches of his three grandsons, Jason, Jonah, and Jeremy, his daughters' families, Frieda, and his beloved golden retriever, Jaffe-Jaffe. He brought me sketches of hockey skates. He told me a sketch was more authentic than a photo— there was a personal bond between the sketcher and the sketched. He gave me Bayer's book on short-term psychotherapy which he despised. He mixed up his grandsons' names, calling Jason, Jeremy, or Jonah, Jason. He forgot an appointment, apologized profusely and paid me on the spot. To me his memory appeared largely intact, but he struggled with names—I believed that he had a conflict over remembering. That was why he kept his own diary and why I judiciously maintained my notes together with his notes and memorabilia. I recorded which in session and date he introduced a new personal event or story. I shared his dog walker's message about Jaffe-Jaffe acting strangely. M replied Jaffe-Jaffe was skittish at the best of times. He found an anonymous note shoved under his office door. "Moses you messed up my life." He denied it was a threat. He said he often received upsetting notes from patients. More recently he had received a couple of angry calls from his synagogue sisterhood. I discussed the call from Bayer and the police. M told me he had settled the matter and not to worry about Bayer or Guttnik. He reassured me that he was not concerned. He insisted that it was not necessary for me to respond to the police call. So I did not call Bayer or the police. I attributed M's memory block to anxiety and conflict about recalling distressing events. I knew to accept his offerings immediately. I saw relief on his face when I looked at his notes and figures—a burden removed from his psyche—an elimination of the dark menagerie locked in childhood. I was a sole witness to his early years. He had no one to show his feelings to. The muddle of words, pictures, and recipes were glyphic proof, relics of an indecipherable past. M's father had died years before his brothers left town; his mother's second husband died. M's wife had left him. He was alone except for Jaffe-Jaffe and his ninety-two-year-old mother. M recounted vivid tales of his sessions—Crystal the swallower, Zeno, her psychopathic protector, Blum, the help-rejecting complainer, and Lippman, the bully analyst. M took on the most difficult patients. Not only did he see difficult psychotic and border-line patients but he had a yen for dangerous criminal types, psychopaths who suffered anxiety. I tried to decode his uncon-scious need to cure the incurable. A few times in his career he had been pushed, punched, attacked by patients. He joked that he had seen traumatized ex-special forces ops and mem-bers of the Jewish gangs and the Italian Mafia. In this area he was intrepid—clowning about his psychic superpowers. His humour remained an immense powerful shield—he used it with patients, with me, but most often against himself. During his first analytic phase there were clues we were missing the sig-nificance of what lay beneath his jokes. M gave himself so fully to his work and his patients that he had nothing for himself. He loved and hated this addiction—when his patients were doing well, he did well, when they struggled with despair, he was in the depths as well, when they were smacked down by life's adversity, he bore their bruised impact. In this manner, he had taken on his loving Bubba's formidable character and indomi-table will, to heal, to protect, to feed, to prevent suffering—even towards psychopathic criminals—to care for others. He was committed to halt Crystal's pathological swallowing and rid her of her violent underworld links with Zeno. He hoped to reduce Blum's *kvetching*. M followed perplexing cases, a

Jewish-Russian-Chinese depressed gangster, Sam-Lee Yan and a Vietnam vet with PTSD who he called GC.

M elaborated a theory of neurosis based on the nature of grandparental influence—the *Bubba complex*. He spoke about the *complex* in Montreal, Toronto, New York, Boston, and Chicago—audiences were powerfully stirred up, many strongly disagreed with his views, yet M persisted. I heard from another patient about a presentation he had given. M was by turns compelling, hilarious, and melodramatic; he made people laugh or cry—no doubt as he had once felt. M infuriated the audience that evening—women argued passionately against him. He had this relentless need to help lost souls like Crystal and her boyfriend, Zeno, whom he had seen in couple therapy before his jail term. M argued that Zeno and Sam-Lee Yan could turn away from crime and be reformed. He told me that GC stockpiled weapons but would never hurt a soul. I confronted him about his therapeutic fanaticism. I questioned why audiences grew outraged by his *Bubba complex*. I became so involved in my quest to formulate M's condition that I missed what was happening outside his analysis. I failed to see the rising storm. M's dog walker, Crystal, called and left a third message. The dog walker wanted to speak to me.

I received a night call from my security manager. An intruder, obscured in a trench coat and hat, had been trying to pry open my front office door. The person evidently disappeared moments later. "Put a second dead-bolt lock on your office," the security manager said. "Put your valuables in a safe."

I questioned if I should believe what M recounted in analysis. He had this restless energy; his body shifted here and there, he twitched and swore in sessions. M swore that he spoke the absolute truth. He told me he had been diagnosed with a neurological disorder as a child.

CHAPTER TWENTY

A neurological disorder? Age five

Each morning, after my parents left for work in the drug-store, my Bubba came from Family Outfitters to watch me. I had a few minutes to myself before Bubba arrived so I cranked up the volume on the table radio and snapped my restless fingers to the music. The radio was my morning companion. I remember listening to *Be My Love*, by Mario Lanza. Bubba first kissed me then ordered me to wash and put on my clothes so we might study Yiddish. "Reuben. Turn down the radio. Stop snapping your fingers. Hurry up. What's the big fuss in the bathroom?"

"Bubba, I am combing my hair."

"Don't be such a movie star. Too much combing and your hair will fall out. *Hurry up.*" I listened to Tony Bennett singing *Because of You* and stared at my hair in the mirror. Was I going bald? I ran to the kitchen and sat down like a prisoner. I twitched and made a face. I snapped my fingers to the music. "Don't snap your fingers. Don't make a face. Your cheeks will twist up. *Now eat-it-up-all!*" Bubba referred to breakfast as *eat-it-up-all*. I stuck my tongue at the soft-boiled egg, steaming oatmeal, stewed prunes, and sliced oranges. Bubba reviewed some Yiddish words and oversaw me eat. "First, the cod-liver oil." This foul substance stank like diesel fuel—I gulped it down each morning. "*Eat-it-up-all.** And if you don't eat prunes you know what happens. *Constipation.* And then? We use suppositories and the enema. OK, Reuben. Be a big shot. Make a face. Stick your tongue out," she said. "It won't go back to your mouth. It will run away. And if you cross your eyes you'll end up like poor little Herbie Faust."

"I can catch my tongue. I can run faster. I won't be cross-eyed."

In kindergarten there were so many students we had half-day classes. A picture of King George VI perched over the blackboard. He wore medals and had a sword at his side and lived through the Blitz. I wanted to be in the royal family. In class after "God Save the King", we learned that his daughter, Princess Elizabeth, drove an ambulance and visited sick soldiers. Guess what—King George stuttered like my father! Marco Santoro was my friend in kindergarten. His family came to Canada from Italy in October. Marco didn't have a winter coat. He hardly spoke English. The teacher stuck a pencil into his right hand and showed him to print. The teacher stuck a pencil into my right hand; I switched it to my left. "Make the letters with your right hand."

"Reuben *knucked* his head falling down stairs," Bubba said. "His brain is not working. He never uses his right hand. He twists his face and snaps his fingers. I warned him to stop crossing his eyes!"

Everyone in my family was right-handed. Bubba ordered me to use my right hand. Because of my twitches Uncle Max sent us to the famous Toronto child neurologist Dr. Beryl Koffman.

---

*Eat-it-up-all: M often repeated his Bubba's phrase. Her words were a break-fast exhortation: "Eat-it-up, all of it." He recalled the phrase "*eat-it-up-all*" and later realized the phrase spoken quickly bore a resemblance to Oedipal—the struggle he had with his grandmother. —*O. Pinsky*

A diagnostic dilemma

"Here today you see a five-year-old boy who appears in good physical health. The history is at age two he fell down a flight of stairs, was knocked briefly unconscious, and is left-handed with a deviated septum and frequent nosebleeds. The patient has symptoms of insomnia, hand tremor, episodic facial tics, a slight stammer, nasal obsessions, and believes he will die of an incurable illness before the age of thirteen. The question before us is whether these symptoms are the first sign of a genetic neurologic disorder or are these transient psychogenic symptoms, for which, at this point, we are unable to find any explanation." Twice that year I saw Koffman. He paraded me before specialists—he checked my reflexes. I was too ashamed to tell him about my testicles. The students examined me—not one could tell me what illness I was suffering.

"Please, Dr. Koffman. What's the matter with me?" I asked.

"It's something between a neurological and psychiatric condition. We think there is a 60–65 per cent likelihood you will grow out of this," he said. Koffman, one of the finest child neurologists in North America could not reassure me. I had to live with this fucking condition whatever it was. Pinsky, you know what, those medical numbskulls should have interviewed Bubba and my mother for god sakes, they should have lined them against the wall and fired questions—believe me, they needed to have had a session with those two—to ask Bubba what kind of fucking *Bubba mysehs* she was feeding this poor kid, then maybe they would figure out the big picture. Like I said before, my father had a nervous stutter as well. Bubba made it worse. I appreciated Bubba's concern, undying love and fanatic persistence. I fought against her worries, threats, glycerine V-2 suppositories, and Lifebuoy enemas.

I didn't believe that shit about ending up permanently cross-eyed, like Herbie Faust.

Bubba took me on a Toronto streetcar to buy chickens at Leo's butcher shop and fish at Zapinsky's in Kensington Market. Ruthie-Annie, Herbie, and Josh Karp came with us.

October 15, 2007

I debated whether M had a neurological condition. I was unclear about his constant unease masked by bodily complaints and sarcastic humour. I had some inkling that his anxiety was tied to sexual issues and the birth of a younger brother which came up in the next session. Much was obscured. At some point I questioned whether analysis would fully reveal M's underlying problem. If matters did not become clearer in the next few months, I resolved to personally follow M.

CHAPTER TWENTY ONE

Birth-anxiety: age five to six

My parents went to Mount Zion Hospital. Mother's stomach was a colossal watermelon ready to explode. Her breasts were huge pineapples. She walked like a sagging fruit tree. Uncle Eli and Auntie Leah and Bubba kept me company. No one had a straight answer where babies came from. "The storks come to the hospital," Auntie Leah said.

"Show me a stork." I didn't believe her. "Show me!"

I asked Marco where babies came from. "D-Do storks bring babies?"

"Nope," Marco said "That's a *fucking big fat lie*."

"Then who brings them?"

"A man puts his *thing* in a lady's bum. They make a baby that way."

I figured out why ladies had zippers in the back of their dresses and skirts. It was so a man could put his *thing* in her bum. "It is called *fucking*," Marco said. "That's what parents do. Your dad sticks his *thing* into your mom."

"Marco, are you sure?"

Tell me, Pinsky, why was he confident about sex? Marco was born with *braggadocio*, which is why I became a shrink and had two analyses—I was obsessed and terrified about sex.

I had trouble grasping *shtupping*. To me this was the basic riddle of the universe.

"But where *exactly* d-does he put his *thing*?" I asked.

Marco told me he would find out. The next day in kindergarten Marco and I went to the washroom and had a pee together. We showed each other our *thing*. "The real name for this is a *braggiole*," Marco said. Marco had a little white *braggiole* and I had a little brown *braggiole*.

"Yours is like salami," Marco said. "When you grow up you use it for *fucking*."

I noticed mine had less skin than Marco's. I asked my father what happened to me. When I was eight days old a religious terrorist, a *mohl*, had beheaded my foreskin, he explained. *Chop-Chop*—like Leo chopped the head off a chicken. That was all I needed—more nightmares and constipation all over again. During an enema I was stupid enough to tell Bubba about fucking. She washed my mouth out twice with Lifebuoy soap. Pinsky, being circumcised altered my psyche. We Jews have a primal racial memory of genital mutilation, that sadistic slice that puts all Semites eons back to the *first big bang*. Can you think of a more barbaric act than circumcision—what kind of sacrifice is that? In medical school, before analysis, Pinsky, I saw a *Reichian* therapist— what did she say? I was blocked up—feelings were stored in my body memory. I had to make up for what was missing. What outlet did I have except listening to the radio hit parade and having *Ubermensch* fantasies? Captain Peacock said that if I had a dog, I could follow him around until he found a lady dog and then watch how it goes. That's the way it's done, Captain Peacock said. For the next few weeks I was busy checking dogs. Meanwhile, my parents brought back a baby boy. He had black hair and big brown eyes and his English name was Danny. I gave him a big smile but he cried whenever he laid eyes on me. Right away I had two ideas— first, Captain Peacock and I wanted to send him right back to the hospital and get a dog, and second, if I couldn't exchange him for a dog, I wanted to care for him so everyone could say

82

what a wonderful great brother I was. Mother was breast-feeding, carrying him everywhere.

"Don't touch. You might drop him," Mother said.

"You fell downstairs," Bubba said. "How do we know you won't drop him?"

I promised not to pick up Danny. On Sunday Mother fried up salami and eggs loaded with schmaltz, Father's favourite brunch—*delicious*—Father religiously ate it every Sunday of his life until he dropped dead of a heart attack. [Pinsky, they should have fed this shit to the Nazis and maybe the war would have ended sooner.]

Danny was busy sucking and holding onto her big breasts. I was envious. Mother made him bottles of sugar water. When she was gone, I made sugar water. Danny drank the whole bottle. He smacked his lips and gave me a toothless smile. I picked him up, breathed in his doughy sweet body and told him about myself. "I am your b-big brother, Reuben. Mom and Dad work in the drugstore downstairs. They were *shtupping* so you were born—Marco says."

When mother went to the drugstore, I gave Danny a bottle of sugar water. When he saw me he jumped excited and smiled. "Captain Peacock—should I tell mom what a good job I d-did?" Sure, Captain Peacock said. Go ahead, go tell your mom. So I told mom how great a job I had done. *You … what?* You did what? "I give D-Danny drinks," I said, proud of myself. You didn't boil the water or milk? There are germs everywhere! Bubba slapped me twice. "*You want to kill Danny?*" When I was older I was finally allowed to push Danny around the block in his carriage. Marco and I talked about sex, stared at the bikes in Rossi's Bike Shop and looked at hockey skates in Moretti's shoe and skate repair shop. Cross-eyed Herbie Faust skipped rope with the girls. Yasha took three streetcars to visit us on Sundays. When he bent down, I saw a scar on his neck.

"What happened to Zaide's neck?"

"He was hit by lightning in Poland," Bubba said.

Bubba warned me to stay clear of horses.

M's dog walker: December 3, 2007

Crystal calls me in a distraught voice. "Dr. Moses told me where to reach him."

"He is not here," I say. "Call him at his private office."

"Jaffe-Jaffe is afraid. We are being followed. I need to talk to you."

"I have to see a patient. I am sorry I cannot talk to you."

"*Fuck-you*, don't you get it, you *dumb fuck*. I told you about Fidel."

"I regret I can't talk to you right now. I am sorry."

"*Fuck-you*, so you see a patient." Crystal is in a fury. "Listen, idiot! Fidel was assassinated."

Assassinated? Unsettled by her anxious suspiciousness I hang up the phone.

CHAPTER TWENTY TWO

Blum's fury: December 4, 2007

Blum is late as usual and lies down on the couch. She doesn't say a word. She lies flat on her back. I wait for complaints—the couch, the lighting, constipation, the winter snow, heart palpitations, the temperature, smells in my office, traffic, her son Ivan who wants to help with business, or my ex-wife, Frieda the analyst, who is seeing Ivan the Terrible. I think she is going to complain about her employees. I wait five minutes, then ten minutes.

"You seem quiet today, Mrs. Blum," I say.

She lies still. I inspect her fine features. No longer does she look pleased to see me. She looks like she could kill. What am I supposed to do? This is analysis, right? She wanted analysis five times a week. I wait. I bend over and re-check her facial expression from time to time.

"What are you thinking, Mrs. Blum?"

"Dr. Moses, you are not here. Do you know? You are not here," she says. "You hide behind that dark *farshtinkener* suit but underneath you are a piece of stone." *Pinsky, this sphinx is accusing me of being stone, see?* She shifts, curls up, waits ten minutes. "You aren't listening at all."

"Mrs. Blum, you haven't said anything until now."

"You are not listening, Dr. Moses. You are not here."

"But I am here, Mrs. Blum. *Look at me*, I am here. See me. Turn around."

Blum turns on the couch. "I see you. But that does not mean you are here."

"How am I not here? You see me. I am talking to you."

"You talk to me—that does not mean you are here—you understand, Dr. Moses? Physically you are here. Words come out your mouth. Parrots talk. You say you are here. You are not emotionally here. If you were here, wouldn't I feel it? I would know. I feel alone."

"*Mrs. Blum I am here,*" I say.

"Dr. Moses, you are not here. You only think you are here. And you vandalized my car."

We argued back and forth for the rest of the session. Was I there? Was I not there? Had I damaged her car? Was it someone else? Could she trust me? Could she not? Was I awake? Was I asleep? *Pinsky, I was awake.* I was taking notes with my Parker 21—I have proof, goddamn it! Look. I was listening, I was talking; Blum was saying I was physically there but emotionally absent. I had a strange feeling in the session; I was floating. Because Blum says I was not there, do I believe her? This brought out my existential angst—even when I am by myself, how do I know for sure I am there. I may be asleep with eyes open. What per cent of *being there* am I? This is why I write to myself and sketch, to make sure I am there. Is all I am writing a dream? Pinch me, *Pinch-ky*. Am I alive in this moment? Could I have let the air out of her tires? This brings me to Bubba in dialogue with the past, with evil eyes and devils. As a *pisher*, I wasn't sure where I was.

Was I dead or alive, or somewhere in between? Are we all of us in-between?

* * *

December 6, 2007

Bernard Bayer calls me from his hospital office. I have mixed feelings about this *putz*. Bayer is young, smart, and successful;

86

when he has patient trouble, he calls me. Why? The truth comes out. A former patient's wife is harassing him. She won't leave her name. She threatens to break both his legs. Big deal! He saw her husband some twenty years ago, this borderline gambler *schmuck*. Her married name was Fine. But nothing was fine with Fine the dentist—the hospital chart is missing and it seems Mrs. Fine has changed her name and gone underground—his wife was never a patient. We have nothing to go on. I tell myself I am not going to get upset.

"Blum, you know, is giving me a hard time—it is a form of harassment."

"Reuben, Blum is not behind this. Blum is decent," Bayer says. "This person is vicious."

"*Blum is vicious.*"

"Stop clowning. You saw the husband over twenty years ago," Bayer says. "Remember the harassment case back then— you did a phone consultation. We called the police. Well, I think now maybe it's his wife, making threats. She saw Karl Guttnik from the borderline clinic; he put her on Prozac. She wasn't happy with anyone."

"You know, of course," I say, "for over fifteen years Guttnik puts all his patients on Prozac."

"That is not funny, Reuben," Bayer says.

"Did you speak to Guttnik?" I say.

"I did," Bayer replies. "He doesn't remember much except that she was a pain in the ass."

Big deal, Pinsky—am I supposed to remember the name of the wife of a patient that I consulted once on the phone over twenty years ago?

I walked by Moretti's shop and stared at the skates in his window. Moretti came out of his store wearing his leather apron with a pair of used hockey skates. He knew I was pining for the skates. He said they were mine. I was in heaven. *Thank you so much, Mr. Moretti.* I took them home.

Bubba said I had to take them back.

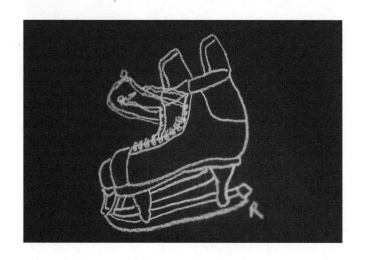

Crystal, the dog walker: December 7, 2007

The dog walker leaves a message. While out for a stroll Jaffe-Jaffe frees herself from her leash. Jaffe-Jaffe runs wildly along the snowy, icy sidewalk. Has the dog seen a squirrel or smelled food? Crystal chases Jaffe-Jaffe several blocks. Crystal catches up with the dog and re-attaches the leash. Before reaching Jaffe-Jaffe, Crystal has noticed something unusual. Breathless, sighing, Crystal sees that a car swerves on the snow closer to the sidewalk. The car brushes against the side of Jaffe-Jaffe, an accident narrowly averted. Crystal has been trying to keep her job as a dog walker.

Without Jaffe-Jaffe she would be without purpose, without a job.

CHAPTER TWENTY THREE

Existence or unconsciousness—O. Pinsky, December 10, 2007

The riddle of M's infantile neurosis preoccupied me since June 2007. What were its origins? The question of doubt and certainty which plagued M was deeply affecting. If I could have seen M when he was five, I might be clearer about what he was facing, but would he have been able to articulate his experience? I felt an odd stirring inside me. In 2007 I was sixty-seven, seven years older than M. I had grown up in Toronto in a second floor apartment on College Street above a delicatessen, one block from Euclid Avenue. I was raised by a strict Bubba. I spoke Yiddish as a child. I too never had hockey skates. M's childhood was similar to mine. My family had a Stromberg-Carlson radio. As M talked memories returned. One stood out. My Bubba was special although I didn't always agree with her. She was a tough loving soul and what a wonderful cook! What didn't she make? *Blintzes*, brisket, *latkes, borscht, tagilach, gefilte fish* (sweeter than M's Bubba's *gefilte fish*), she bottled her own herring, her strudel was amazing, and her matzo balls were as light as clouds. She had fled Vienna and valued her new life in Canada.

M looked familiar. I had no idea where or when I had seen him. I knew him as a committed Mount Zion psychiatrist-analyst; I worked at St. Luke's, the Catholic downtown hospital. M joked about Jews and Catholics. "What is worse to suffer—Catholic guilt or Jewish guilt?" I had no idea. "No difference—the Catholics go to confession and it is all over, *presto*, God forgives you. But us Jews go into analysis and it takes years."

M retrospectively returned to the past yet those early years were shadowed and blurred by overwhelming guilt and present dilemmas. I had seen patients who resembled M—narcissists, perfectionist characters, guilt-ridden souls, struggling to free themselves from their neurosis. M was different. He did not fit into a clear DSM diagnosis. I was unable to formulate his conflicts—I was troubled by elements which clung to the periphery of his narrative. Was he paranoid? What about the person who vandalized his car? Was there a connection to Bayer's harassment case? Should I believe what M told me? How about Jaffe-Jaffe? I told M about his dog walker's call. M said Crystal was recovering from a traumatic childhood; she needed Jaffe-Jaffe to settle herself.

I replied that her anxiety was affecting the dog. M rejected my idea.

I was sceptical. My doubts about M increased.

M presented controversial theories of childhood development—the influence of the Bubba on the child. Had he so angered his audiences that he had enemies? Could the vandalism be from a spurned ex-patient? What was the significance of the hockey skates sketch? In our next session M revealed *pyrophobia*, his fear of fire. M was getting under my skin.

If matters did not become clearer I planned to slip out of my office when he left and track M.

* * *

January 7, 2008

I call Dr. Sandor Gabor, my supervisor and consultant who shares the same brownstone as M and Guttnik. Many training analysts in Toronto see Gabor for their consultations. Because of his age, Gabor had given up a pure analytic practice, although he remains a formidable expert. Dr. Sandor Gabor had one foot in Freud's Vienna while the other was devoted to studying current advances in neuropsychiatry and psychoanalysis.

"Read Freud's early cases," Gabor said.

"I have read them all," I said.

"Read them again—read Little Hans."

"I read Little Hans."

"Read the Wolf-Man. He was Freud's most famous case." I read the Wolf-Man again. The case was difficult to penetrate and at times recalled my struggle reading Proust or Joyce. But as Sandor Gabor suggested, I could see similarities. The Wolf-Man had a close relationship with an older woman—his Russian nanny. The Wolf-Man was abused in childhood and terrified by the wolf in children's stories. Like M the Wolf-Man was preoccupied by sex and feces and his nose. The Wolf-Man was manipulative. He required many analysts to see him after Freud. The Wolf-Man was impossible to diagnose. The Wolf-Man lied. At times he was normal. At times he was paranoid. At times he was delusional. And what was I to make of M's fear of fire?

Toronto Analyst Argues for Bubba Complex

January 9, 2008. Special to the International Herald Tribune

> Dr. Reuben Moses, presenting at a winter psychoanalytic conference on the female body in Berlin, spoke on the erotic grandmother. Citing his own studies of the mature sexual object in literature and popular culture, from Jocasta to Marlene Dietrich, from Raquel Welch to Jeanne Moreau and Madonna, Dr. Moses argued for a "gender reversal" of the Little Red Riding Hood tale, suggesting that the female wolf, the she-wolf, the bitch, the alpha-female, or

as popularly called, "the cougar" represents a formidable sexual image for the young man. Some male analysts in the conference registered their support yet others proffered clear and vocal disagreement … a growing number of feminists have declaimed the *Bubba Complex* as a calculated slander against the mature woman and have formed protest groups. The largest protest to date was mounted by the *Bubba Bund* at a public rally of over three hundred male and female supporters in front of the Hotel Adlon, Berlin, where the conference took place … a few of the participants spoke in a threatening violent manner. Dr. Moses responded by saying that the primal mother was not entirely loving.

CHAPTER TWENTY FOUR

Fear of fire: pyrophobia, age six

Two doors away in Faust's Super Hardware what a fire I saw! Flames flew up to the sky. Little Herbie stared open-mouthed at his parents' store. Ruthie-Annie held his hand and shook her head. "Herbie, Ruthie-Annie, Reuben, stay far back, *back*," Bubba barked. "Your father's drugstore will be next. The entire block will burn down. Look out!"

Faggie Faust, the *koch leffel* [shit disturber] yelled some anti-Semitic arsonist had set the fire. She was sure of it. "Yes, the entire block will burn down, *God-forbid*."

In my child's eyes the fire devoured everything. The smell of burning wood, paint, and smoke was everywhere. The sidewalk was littered with pieces of wood, glass, and pools of water. Fire trucks, sirens blaring, came; the hardware store almost burned down. How did the fire start? No one knew. *Spontaneous combustion*, a fireman said—the paint, solvents, some combustible materials. Miraculously, the fire did not reach Rossi's Bike Shop or Moretti's shoe and skate repair—our drugstore was not touched. I smelled ash for days. A fire will start in the drugstore when I fall asleep, I thought—*spontaneous combustion*—what with the drugs and chemicals, or maybe it was Ruthie-Annie playing with matches. I developed insomnia.

My face twitched left and right. Uncle Max sent me to Koffman.

Hospital grand rounds with Dr. Beryl Koffman: age six

"The symptoms intensified," Koffman said. "The tremor is aggravated, the insomnia is total, there is slight head titubation, facial tics are constant; the stutter is still present." Koffman examined me, tested my reflexes, and checked my eyes. He presented me to more doctors. Physicians with flashlights in white coats looked into my eyes in the medical auditorium; beside them were medical students and interns taking notes. Koffman, the top neurologist in Toronto [so said Uncle Max] showed black-and-white 35 millimetre slides of me on a screen in front of the auditorium. My facial twitch was exposed—Koffman had captured the sudden muscular contraction; he demonstrated my EEG and asked me to step out of the wheelchair. *March*—one foot in front of the other, tandem walking—my balance was poor. He pointed to a twitch of my left hand, *look, did you see that?*—then a grimace of my lips and chin—involuntary perhaps?—an early sign of multiple sclerosis? Was it familial ataxia? What about my episodic constipation and my complex of phobias and insomnias? Father met Koffman in his office. Books, journals, awards were on the wall, a skeleton hung in a corner. I changed from my hospital gown into civvies.

"Will his nervous condition improve?" my father asked.

"Your son has a 55 per cent probability that he will grow out of it."

"But last year you said he had a 65 per cent chance of improving," Father said.

"That was," Koffman replied in a sober tone, "last year."

* * *

At dinner after listening to Al Jolson and then the Jack Benny radio show, Uncle Eli talked of the London Blitz and the terrible Toronto harbour fire in the *S.S. Noronic*. More than 100 people perished. The ship's hull glowed pink like the Rexall sign. My fire phobia worsened.

I play with little Herbie on top of his family's store. I sneak into Ruthie-Annie's room and find her diary. Now after Yiddish lessons with Bubba I can read some Yiddish words. I hear Ruthie-Annie coming up the stairs. I have a few moments alone.

I read that she blames her dad, Sam Faust. Why? What for? She hears her parents argue. She suspects her father knows who set the fire. Puzzled, I shut the diary. I flee from her room.

* * *

Marco and all my schoolmates were given Canadian flags. We stood beside a new highway that stretched from Toronto to Niagara Falls. We waved at Princess Elizabeth and the Duke of Edinburgh as they passed by in a black Cadillac convertible. Elizabeth was younger than my mother, slim, pretty with dark hair. Months later her father, King George VI, died. In *The Toronto Daily Star* were pictures.

"How did he die? Don't kings live a long time?" I asked.

"A king is also a *human being*," Bubba said.

My parents spoke of them like family. Uncle Eli was deeply touched. School closed one day for the funeral. The next day we sang, "God Save the Queen". When Charles was born Marco told me the truth. The duke stuck his cock into the queen and they made a prince.

Hurricane Hazel

Pinsky, remember a terrible storm called Hurricane Hazel—it blew wind and rain across Toronto. The Humber River beside our drugstore overflowed. It destroyed roads, bridges, houses, people. When Uncle Max drove me along the Lakeshore Boulevard hundreds of cars were under water. At the Humber and Lake Ontario, roads vanished. Outside our drugstore the wind was merciless. Rain pelted windows. Our roof shook. The Rexall sign flew off and flattened a car. Eighty people died,

Uncle Eli told me. Humber Bridge washed out. Customers could not cross it. Two feet of water sloshed in our basement. "*I am ruined. Look at my stock in the b-basement ...*" Father was sleepless. Business was sinking. "*D-Do I deserve such mazel? Does God have it in for me? First a fire, now flood, what plague will be next? D-Do I have to drown? Will I never pay off my d-debts?*" Fridays he argued with Bubba. He held a teacup over his head. He pitched it at a wall. He hurled a crystal glass at the floor, smashing it into glittering points of light.

"Watch where you walk, Reuben," Bubba said. "If a sharp piece of glass gets under your skin it can go up a vein and enter your heart ..."

I sobbed when Bubba made me take the hockey skates back to Mr. Moretti. When Mother was a child, Bubba got in a wild fight with *Yasha*, her husband. She ordered him to leave. That was the story Bubba told me. Mother and Father were misfortune's twins—my father lost his mother and mother had no one to care for her except her mother's mother, Bubba Reba.

"Reuben, you are named after Reba. She died when your mother turned thirteen."

Bubba feared I would come to grief at that age. Bubba was my first roommate. I remembered the scent of her perfume and sweat, her false teeth stored in a *Yahrzeit* jar with water above her night table. Her dentures had once been pearl-white but age yellowed them; the glass water was clouded. Bubba was toothless but had large full lips. I was put to bed in a tiny crib. I awoke with a door creak, light like flames streamed into my raw eyes, igniting the ceiling in a bonfire. Bubba pulled off shoes and stockings. She removed her work clothes. I watched her ebony silhouette as I lay silent in bed. I saw her great breasts like two charging horses, her dark mane of hair, her smooth buttocks. She lifted her slip and undid her corset with its straps that attached her stockings. The corset was hung on a rack—a suit of armour, shiny with whalebone stays and metal clips. Bubba slept in the nude. She was beautiful and terrifying.

Torture #4

Bubba breasts. I waited up for the two of them. I smelled the hairy savannah of her armpits, the sweaty mists rising from her body, the scent of her lips, her teeth, her shadowy pubis; I sniffed her dark anus and her puckered vagina. How could I not inhale that she-wolf? She made money to buy the Euclid Avenue house when my mother was a child. She built two stores in West Toronto. She lent my father cash for his drugstore. Mother told me if Bubba had luck, she would have built a department store. In daylight her polished satin skin was coffee. Five years she was my roommate with her *Yahrzeit* glass filled with teeth.

What lips! What breasts! What big buttocks you have! What a wonderful smelly place between your legs! My *schlong* stood at attention. I stared at her dentures.

I feared that they would grow legs, jump out the glass and bite me.

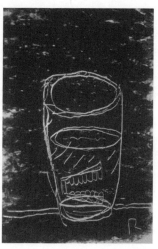

Bubba's false teeth in the Yahrzeit jar—they terrified me.
—R. Moses

I am sceptical of M's exaggerated account of childhood tragedies—the *S.S. Noronic* blaze, did it even exist? What about Hurricane Hazel [a hurricane I barely recall], surely M exaggerated? That night, after our session I check the local newspaper archives and google *S.S. Noronic* and Hurricane Hazel. I read the accounts. I feel a chill descend my spine. In the early morning hours of Saturday September 17, 1949, at Pier 9 in Toronto Harbour, a terrible fire broke out on the S.S. *Noronic* killing over 120 people. I check Hurricane Hazel—on October 15, 1954 the hurricane struck leaving thousands homeless and killing eighty-one people. I read a further note about a fire beside M's father's drugstore in 1950.

M has reported the truth. A child eyewitness he has impeccably recorded the tragic past.

CHAPTER TWENTY FIVE

Father's Remington: age seven

Little Herbie Faust, Ruthie-Annie, and I watched Father prepare ointments. He hated distraction. He put pills on a plastic pill counter, counted them with a spatula, and pushed them into the medicine bottle. He typed up a drug label on his typewriter. "Reuben, Herbie, Ruthie-Annie, d-don't talk and l-leave me alone. Play outside." I was curious about the huge dispensary bottles filled with liquid. They looked like water. "This one, Reuben, never touch," Father said. "This is called sulphuric acid."

"Why?"

"B-because it will burn your skin! Don't you dare drink it? You promise?"

"I promise."

"This here is Prussic acid. See the skull and crossbones, Herbie, Ruthie-Annie? Never—you must never d-drink these— they are p-poison. Remember, Reuben?"

"I won't drink that," I said.

"And this bottle here is c-caustic soda—sodium hydroxide."

I could blindfold myself and know *Moses' Drugs* scent anywhere—soap, perfume, Dustbane, and cod-liver oil. In the dispensary stood bottles of bark from trees, plant roots, leaves, white powders, and a locked narcotics cabinet with morphine, laudanum, and codeine. At the back of the drugstore was a special drawer of creams and ointments for ladies and small boxes for men. Men whispered to Father. He gave a solemn nod, walked to the dispensary, and reached into a drawer.

"D-Dad, what was that you gave that man?"

Father whispered. "They p-p-protect against pregnancy, *safes, condoms.*"

I checked dispensary drawers and searched the safes. They had exotic names—*Sheiks, Ramses, Trojans.* I opened up a woman's gel; I put a drop on my tongue. *Yechh.*

* * *

At night thieves broke into my father's narcotics cabinet. We heard them from upstairs kicking in the door. My father called the operator on a phone. "C-Call the cops right away. Goddamn sons-of-a-bitch made off with my safes and narcotics."

My father prepared powders with a mortar and pestle and ointments with a spatula—there were different size vials and brass avoirdupois weights beside his pharmacist's scale.

"D-Don't make a peep, Reuben," my father said. "I am w-weighing." He prepared zinc oxide ointment for baby rashes and burns. Father wore a spotless white jacket with big white buttons that went up one side to his neck. People came with cinders in their eye. Father found a cotton tip and rolled the eyelid back and took out the cinder. He dressed cuts and scrapes with tincture of iodine. He offered credit to families who lived across the road in wartime houses. He typed and delivered prescriptions by himself. The tapping of his old Remington was a constant rhythm in his store. I loved to be with Father. He was always careful and honest with everyone.

Sunday evening Father took us to Shopsy's deli for corned beef. It was a special treat.

* * *

100

Father caught Ruthie-Annie stealing matches and shoplifting chocolate bars. She denied it. The next week Ruthie-Annie did it twice more.

Mother called Faggie Faust. "Which jail do I send her to? Your red-head was shoplifting again." Herbie had a gentle disposition but Ruthie-Annie was a ruffian. Little Herbie had a sweet tooth so Ruthie-Annie stole chocolate bars for him.

She fussed over him like he was her own child.

I was curious about my father's special cough syrup. He made it using oregano, thyme, eucalyptus, liquorice, and honey. He put it in bottles—*Moses's Cough Syrup*.

It had an aromatic tarry smell. I gave a spoonful to my little brother, Danny.

He made a face, turned red and started to cry. He spit it out.

Then I sipped it.

I spit it out.

Yecchhh!!! It tasted terrible.

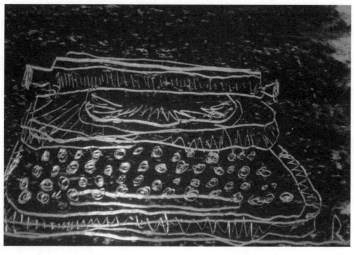

Father's portable black Remington typewriter—R. Moses

101

I sneaked into Ruthie-Annie's room when I played with little Herbie. I understood a little more of the Yiddish. Usually I got to peek at one or two pages of her diary. She was always a few steps away from her brother.

I learned something new. She was scared to death of red-faced Sammy Faust. She asked her mother to put a special lock on her door. She wanted to lock herself in her room.

Little Herbie told me that Ruthie-Annie hated her father. There was a line I could not read. Instead of writing these words in English letters Ruthie-Annie wrote the words in Hebrew. I took a pencil and wrote the Hebrew letters down. I had no idea what they meant. I decided to show the words to Bubba.

ער טוט שלעכט זאכן צו מיר

CHAPTER TWENTY SIX

More threats: February 6, 2008

Blum calls to cancel a session; she is depressed and angry. She threatens to sue me. I persuade her to come to the next session and discuss her grievances. *What happened since our last session? You told me you were feeling better on Celexa. Wait—you stopped your medications? You won't see your cardiologist. Your naturopath said to take fish oil? I am not pushing Celexa; Mrs. Blum, psychoanalysis alone can't cure all your symptoms. What do you mean I ruined your car?* Pinsky, I could go on about our therapeutic relationship. Let me sum up.

It started out like gold. It was now turning to shit.

"Once I respected you, Dr. Moses. I thought you were good."

"And now, perhaps, you have some doubts, I suppose?"

"After the first months you seemed disinterested. Now you have vandalized my car."

Blum turns on the couch and checks me. Her accusations are so absurd that I smile. Smiling has been a nervous tic since childhood. What do I do when she goes on her lunatic harangues? I smile and rub my nose; she talks about her toilet business. She feels alone. She turns around. Someone let the air out of her tires last session. It's twice now air has gone out.

What comes to your mind, I ask her.

February 6, 2008: my total respect for feminists

Pinsky, don't arch your eyebrows. I am a feminist, respectful of women—this is no cliché. I still love Frieda—I love her independent mind, her fine sense of ethical values, and her luscious body. My separated wife is an analyst; my three daughters are college graduates. Believe me, statistics point to the basic fact—women are more evolved than men, hands down. I accept that. You just wait, Pinsky. In a generation or two it will be women—grandmothers—who will demonstrate greater creative leadership than men. Look at Golda Meir, Hillary Clinton, Meryl Streep. I loved my Bubba. I am proud of my three daughters.

You think behind my admiration there lurks a sadistic misogynist?

Blum pushes her unconscious fears into me—on the outside she is super-strong, on the inside she is filled with hate, fearful, alone, and anxious as hell. What do I do, Pinsky? I fear a serious cardiac arrhythmia—I may drop dead any second—you see why I am here? I have redeveloped an identical case of constipation like Blum. I can no longer sit on my safe toilet and blast off. No more reading the *New York Times* when I have a shit—a soft stool is a thing of the past. I suffer vicious haemorrhoids. Is this an anal countertransference? I should have smelled it coming. An image flies to my mind—a sawdust floor, chickens, mirrors, and white shroud.

"Leo Rosen's butcher shop," Pinsky says. "Zlotnik's barber shop. You saw the butchery of bodies—blood, mutilation, and death fantasies."

* * *

Blum could pass for a thirty-eight year old. She looked ageless yet every disease known to mankind she had. And yet she projected her disease symptoms into me.

"Were you attracted to her?"

"Never—not on your life—absolutely not."

"Moses, you had erotic feelings! You likened her to Jane Fonda."

"How could I be attracted to her? She was a grandmother."

"*Grandmother*—did you hear what you said? Isn't this what you write about?"

I sit up on the couch, trembling, holding my head in both hands, hearing Blum's voice.

"Dr. Moses, do you know how much money I raise for psychiatry at your hospital? Have you any idea how many volunteer hours I have put in on the sisterhood and foundation committees so *you* have decent waiting rooms, an auditorium, and your fancy equipment? Do you have any sense how I have supported Dr. Bayer and his research department? Not only will I call your department chief, but I will launch a complaint to the College of Physicians and Surgeons about your incompetence. I will speak to my lawyer about a civil action. What do you have to say to that?"

Neuro-surgical grand rounds: age seven

In my seventh year, the symptoms remain. I am the subject of rounds at the university. And this time, my specialist, the legendary Dr. Beryl Koffman invites the entire neurosurgery division. Why? Because he poses the question—is some neurosurgical approach to alleviate persistent severe obsessions justified? The auditorium is filled with fifty-eight doctors, forty-four residents, forty-three medical students, and twenty-four nurses—how do I know? Because my obsession that year was to count whatever was around me—I counted people, cars, licence plates, colours; it began with counting my testicles. I was double-checking.

Frieda said I was obsessed by sex—a grown man in his sixties should be more settled. Can I help it that I had this hypertrophic sex drive? Frieda felt worn out. She had to protect her vagina. Before bed she dressed like a Russian doll, she wore a housecoat, under that she wore jogging pants, under the jogging pants were tights, under the tights were panties. In the dark it took ages to find and undress her.

* * *

After three operations little Herbie's lazy eye was better. In addition to Ruthie-Annie, Herbie found two girlfriends on the next block. He played with their dollhouses. I built a fort out of orange crates in the field for me and my friend, Marco. That summer we ran after the ice truck and sucked ice chips. Ruthie-Annie wanted to join our club—Marco said no girls could join. Ruthie-Annie punched his nose. I tried to read Ruthie-Annie's diary but she was always around Herbie.

I was planning to show Bubba the Hebrew letters from Ruthie-Annie's diary.

ער טוט שלעכט זאכן צו מיר

Marco's father was a construction worker from Calabria. There was always a truck or flatbed in front of Marco's place. We sat in our fort made of cardboard and tomato boxes. The fort was a good place to talk and share our secrets. We invited Herbie—he wasn't interested.

We talked about religion, sex, women, kidneys, testicles, and death.

Marco had his *nonna* living with him. In summer she picked dandelions in her black dress, sweater, and stockings. She spoke Italian. She told stories about her dead husband, *stregas*, and made curses. She was a cook, boss, and top-notch worrier just like Bubba. Little Herbie and Ruthie-Annie had no family except for themselves.

Their parents were always working and when they weren't working they were arguing.

* * *

Crystal, the dog walker: February 8, 2008

Crystal calls my office. "Dr. Pinsky, Jaffe-Jaffe refuses to go out. She flops on the floor and refuses to budge. She crapped all over the apartment hall. Can you put Dr. Moses on your phone?"

"He left my office two minutes ago," I say.

"The super won't be happy. Can you tell Dr. Moses to call me? Jaffe-Jaffe is out of control."

"I am sorry, I can't locate him now."

"Well, *fuck you*, Pinsky, I must speak to him," Crystal says. "Why don't you pop out and get Moses yourself."

"I have a patient in a few minutes, I can't do that."

"Get off your fat ass and look where he is, can't you?"

CHAPTER TWENTY SEVEN

The beginning of the end of the first analytic phase:
O. Pinsky, February 19, 2008

Pinsky—R. Moses

I reviewed my notes each session. I compared them to M's diaries. He gave me a sketch of Jaffe-Jaffe, Frieda, then a sketch
of myself. He baked poppy seed cookies from his Bubba's
recipe. I ate a cookie with him, tasting the poppy seeds, the
salty-citrus hints in its honeyed sweetness. He brought me *tage-
lach* and borscht, and of course, *gefilte fish*. M said his sketches
and Bubba's recipes brought back past struggles. I recalled my

Bubba's poppy seed cookies and strudel as if I had just tasted them. She baked *chala* Fridays and watched over me. She was firm, old school, from Russia, spoke three languages. Yiddish was our first language, our *mame loshon*.

I didn't learn English until I went to school.

M's mother lived two blocks from his apartment. Fridays he took her shopping. Sunday morning they went for coffee before he saw his grandchildren. He told her he was seeing an analyst. He repeated a question about his childhood. "Who set fire to Faust's Hardware Store?"

* * *

February 19, 2008

M mentioned his wife, her skills as an analyst, his youthful passion, and his ardent love. Not until later did we see his need to be loved and his guilt over self-acceptance. He repeated this pattern with the most difficult individuals. He attempted humour to deal with intractable patients when other treatments failed. His jesting was used on himself, a form of denial. It was, for the most part, impossible to penetrate. His reputation working with difficult cases spread across Toronto; his name was cited where I worked in the outpatient department at St. Luke's Hospital.

M was devoted to his three grandsons, Jason, Jonah, and Jeremy, each from a different daughter. He brought me photos. Sundays he made sure to visit family with Jaffe-Jaffe his beloved retriever. Jason was four months—a chubby dark-haired infant. Jonah at twelve months old was afraid of Jaffe-Jaffe and retreated to his mother's arms. M worried Jonah was terrified of him. Jeremy, the oldest, was five and adored M. They went to the playground, played ball, and M babysat Jeremy whenever possible. His daughters married well. He relished being a grandfather—wanting to resolve his childhood issues—he was afraid of his father's father, the rabbi-*shoicet*, Rav Natan. This life stage, now that M was a grandparent, became his area of research. He spoke to his aged mother, telling her about his analysis with me, trying to glimpse an unrecalled past. At one point he suggested I meet her. He sent me a transcript of one of his mother's phone messages.

Reuben, you never did a bad thing. I don't know who that awful lady was who called twice.

M devoted hours writing on the Bubba complex and its relationship to the child. He presented papers in London, Paris, and Berlin. I pondered M's theory of the Bubba complex. My childhood had been shaped more by my Bubba than by my parents who fled Poland as refugees—in Canada they were called DP's—displaced persons, two of the hundreds of thousands of refugees after the Second World War. I was a child in *Feldafing*, Bavaria, a displaced persons camp. Like M my childcare was left to my grandmother. What would have become of me if my Bubba did not feed me and watch over me while my parents struggled to find their way from war-torn Europe to the new world? When we arrived in Canada my Bubba guided me to kindergarten, gave me my evening baths, *schlepped* me shopping to bakeries and butcher shops. Zlotnik was the barber who cut my hair as a child; Lustig was our baker. It was uncanny—how our past was similar.

* * *

On two occasions M mentioned his car had been vandalized. The first time air had been let out of his tires; the second time feces were deposited on the hood and seats of his Volvo convertible. He dismissed this with a joke. Had the event happened? Had M made up a tall tale, like the tales Bubba told him? Although his memory appeared accurate I could not be sure. Was he dissociating? Was another personality presenting itself? His dog walker Crystal called me several times. At certain moments she sounded terrified. I told M that employing this anxious patient was problematic and un-therapeutic. M violently disagreed. When I told M that the dog walker suspected someone in a car followed Jaffe-Jaffe he dismissed my concern. M was not the only one experiencing this public mischief. Sandor Gabor shared the same office building. When Gabor returned from a holiday he found air had been let out of his tires. Guttnik was in the same brownstone and in February 2008 feces were smeared on Guttnik's car.

M giggled as he recalled these events.

M's Volvo convertible

Thursday February 21, 2008

Moses shrugged his misfortune away as a prank. M's car had its tires slashed; the front left headlight was broken. Feces were placed on the hood—smeared on the convertible top.

I questioned whether the same person behind this vandalism had damaged Blum's, Gabor's, and Guttnik's cars. When I reflected on this longer I was unable to cast more light on the matter.

I decided to follow M to get to the bottom of this mystery. I had time after a session. I waited as M departed and followed M on foot. He proceeded to walk in a direction away from his office. I traced him for eleven blocks. He stepped into a rundown apartment and disappeared.

CHAPTER TWENTY EIGHT

A restless kid: age eight

They *schlepped* me back to Beryl Koffman, head of pediatric neurological diseases, and this time, since Father insisted, Koffman told him the truth. Yes, I had a neurological condition—after three years it did not appear to be progressive and it was not degenerative. I would not die. It appeared in ten out of a thousand individuals. I had minor features, the grimaces, the neurotic smile, the stutter, the tics, and hand movements. I was restless with a tendency to think dirty. I had to live with it—there wasn't treatment then.

It had a fancy aristocratic French name. *Gilles de la Tourette's* syndrome.

Since the terrible fire the Fausts extended their hardware store hours 9 am to 10 pm each night. Sammy red-faced Faust yelled that our whole block would go out of business. O'Reilly's butcher shop went belly up. Who had set the hardware fire? Faggie Faust pointed a hateful finger to the yellow-and-black Loblaws supermarket across the street. "*They did it.*" The supermarket gobbled two stores on our block. While we waited for the next fire, plague, or catastrophe, Herbie, Ruthie-Annie, and I read comic books in my dad's drugstore. Marco got a new bike from Rossi's bike shop. "A bicycle is too dangerous. On a bicycle you can *plotz*," Bubba said. "*Davidel*, why not build a nice little garden for the boys to play in?" Father made a tiny garden with a swing behind our sunless store. I planted sunflowers. Danny, Ruthie-Annie, Herbie, and I played on the swing. In the drugstore Herbie read *Donald Duck* and Ruthie-Annie read *Little Orphan Annie*. I liked the gory horror comics like *Tales from the Crypt*. In the middle of the comics was an ad to change from a ninety-pound weakling to a body like Charles Atlas. Danny and I wanted to have muscles and fly like Superman. Uncle Max warned that comics led to juvenile delinquency.

I got eye-twitching from reading.

"*Temporary blepharospasm*—you will grow out of it," Koffman said.

Pinsky, our sunless garden was a disaster. Grass withered. Sunflowers perished. "Next year we will plant again," Bubba said. I never planted again until my rose garden. I studied Yiddish.

I wanted to find out what was in Ruthie-Annie's diary.

Ruthie-Annie's secret diary.—R. Moses

At night Bubba and I read Yiddish. We spoke Yiddish to each other. I wanted to ask her about Ruthie-Annie's diary. I found the paper that I had written the Hebrew letters.

In those years in Toronto nothing remained open Sunday. Shops and department stores were shut, most drugstores closed, and restaurants were sealed tight. It was impossible to see a movie. People ate at home and never went out except to church. I recall Sundays, walking block after block, seeing nothing move, as if an epidemic of sleeping sickness had overtaken the city. Mother and Father stayed in bed all morning. I heard them laughing. When Father was not *shtupping* Mother, our family went for a bus ride, listened to Mr. Moretti play the accordion or Yasha visited. For a treat we went to Shopsy's deli for a corned beef sandwich.

I wanted to be a cowboy like the Lone Ranger. I wanted a gun. A shotgun, why not? A bowie knife, a slingshot, a BB gun at least, please? *Goyische* kids had guns, pistols, rifles, machine guns, machetes, spears, tomahawks, and cowboy outfits. I would settle for a red cape and blue tights. I wanted a big S on my T-shirt—a basic Superman outfit.

"Please Bubba—why can't I play like other kids?"

"Little Jewish boys don't play with guns and knives."

"Why not?"

"You will get hurt."

"Why can't I have a Superman outfit?"

"No."

"Why not?"

"You will run like Superman."

"*Great!* What's wrong with running like Superman, Bubba?"*

"You will think you can fly like Superman."

---

*A boy often requires identification with a male heroic figure. In this case M surrounded by women used comic books to expand his omnipotent male fantasies.

"*Super!* So what's wrong with that, Bubba? That's called make-believe."

"Then you will make-believe and jump around," Bubba said.

"*Fantastic!* So what's wrong with make-belief and jumping around, Bubba?"

"Then you will jump out the window and break both legs."

Late at night I heard people talking. Leo, the butcher, Sammy Faust, Zlotnik the barber, Faggie Faust, Bubba, sometimes even Karp, the *ganif*—I couldn't make out what they said. They had come from Poland near the town of Bendin; they were in the *Zaglember* Society telling stories about the war. They spoke softly. I remember the darkness of the night and their sad voices.

I understood more Yiddish. Sunday afternoons I played with little Herbie in his room.

I looked for the chance to snatch Ruthie-Annie's diary and read what she had written.

CHAPTER TWENTY NINE

Blum opens up: March 5, 2008

B lum curls up on the couch. I see she is grimacing. She rocks side to side. Are you all right? She stopped her Celexa; she stopped her heart medication. Blum doesn't look well. I ask myself is this a drug withdrawal reaction and wonder if I am missing something.

I have this terrible pain in my heart, Blum says.

I worry about her last attack of palpitations—the cardiologist said nothing was wrong—you can't be sure, Pinsky. Heart doctors can be wrong. Blum starts to cry softly.

"What is the matter, Mrs. Blum?"

"I feel all alone."

"You mean *now?*"

"No," she says. "I mean then." She takes a cushion from the couch; she clutches it like a baby. She rocks side to side with this cushion.

"You are safe. You are a little girl; you are holding your teddy bear—"

"My dolly—"

"Your dolly, yes—you are holding your dolly. I am beside your dolly. I don't want you to be afraid. Tell me what you are afraid of."

Blum whispered of childhood arriving after the war in Montreal with her mother living in a tiny apartment over a depanneur shop. After school Blum returned to an empty apartment. Her mother worked as a seamstress on the Main in Montreal. She added that there was a tenant who lived down the hall. "If I am not safe something terrible will happen."

"You are safe here. The little girl can say what made her afraid."

She turns around. It is the first time she looks at me in this way. It is the very first time I have seen her eyes, so beautiful, so innocent, so pleading and terrified. "Dr. Moses. I don't trust you."

On call at the hospital at 2 am: March 10, 2008

"Why does ER call me at this ungodly hour, Pinsky? I drive to the emergency, bleary-eyed. Crystal, the dog walker waits for me. I check her out."

"Why hire her as your dog walker?" I say. "She is your patient. Are you a welfare worker?"

"She has no one."

"That's untrue," I reply. "She has her boyfriend, Zeno."

"Zeno is in jail."

"He will be released soon. Meanwhile Crystal calls me daily."

"She is worse since Fidel was run over," I say. "Was his death an accident?" I repeat my question. M does not answer. My head is tight.

"I have news for you, Pinsky. Since her job, Crystal is not depressed."

"Maybe, but she calls me in a panic looking for you."

"She feels better knowing where I am. She has separation anxiety."

"Do you realize that your patients have become your family?" I say. "Do you see that they have moved into your personal life? You realize that this was why Frieda left you? You

118

have many difficult patients. How can you keep track of them? Your patient, Crystal, calls me in tears."

"Crystal is feeling better."

"Feeling better? I would appreciate if you would ask her to not phone this office."

"Crystal knows I come here. It makes her feel secure."

"Please, do not inform your patients that you come for analysis here. Tell me, why does Crystal go to emergency?"

"She has this symptom."

"What symptom?"

"Her anxiety turns to swallowing. She swallowed something big—a knife, bedsprings, more batteries? I call the GI guy again to take out her stuff. He is not very happy."

Sam-Lee Yan, the depressed Jewish-Chinese-Russian gangster: March 13, 2008

Sam-Lee Yan is originally from Vladivostok with a Chinese-Russian mom and a Jewish father. The family immigrated to Israel. Sam-Lee joined the IDF to become a paratrooper. In Toronto he is a builder, a go-between with the Russians and Chinese. Like them he doesn't believe in strict rules. He builds shopping centres in Iraq. His full name is Samuel Leopold Yanovsky. He has two bodyguards and suffers from nervous insomnia. He likes Jaffe-Jaffe. He is calmer around my dog.

Lippman, my first analyst: M's notes to himself

Have you figured out the big question, Reuben? Why are you such a hero? Why let them get you in the corners and kick the shit out of you? Why do you run that goddamn borderline clinic? Why go into the emergency at all hours? Are your patients your family? You think you are working through their conflicts? You believe you alone have the answer? I got

119

news for you. Reuben—you are a chump, a sucker, a dupe, a blockhead, a fucking human toilet seat—the more I point this martyr role out to you, the more you joke and shake your head and show both of us that you are a glutton for punishment. Go on and let them all shit on your head! That's why Frieda left, isn't it?

"*Please*, Mr. Moretti said, why not take my secondhand pair of hockey skates? Reuben, I give to you for free."

It's no use—my Bubba says I will get hurt playing hockey. Pinsky, it wasn't only Bubba who was a worrier—all my family were worriers. So was Ruthie-Annie, she worried something terrible was going to happen to little Herbie.

CHAPTER THIRTY

Polio: age eight

Bubba said there was no safe place to send a Jewish kid in the summer. I was too young for camp. "Take him to Sunnyside Beach," Father said. "Cool him off in the water. Look—he's fidgety—he rides his tricycle in my store. I can't count p-pills with him—what if I send the wrong p-prescription? And Herbie and Ruthie-Annie come. Ruthie-Annie—she shoplifts. And Reuben, one day, I swear, he will drink acid. He's driving me *meschugge*. Take him Sunday with Danny to the b-b-beach. It will settle him and he'll sleep."

"Sleep—that's what worries you?" my mother said. "*Polio* lives in the water."

"Reuben and Danny won't get a chill. Let them *b-b-be normal*."

"*Be normal*? It takes a few drops of water," Mother said. "*The two of them don't know not to swallow*. It goes to their mouth and nose and stomach."

"Then their lives will be over," Bubba said. "*It should be on your head*."

No one knew how you caught polio. No one knew what to do when you got sick. One day you were fine. The next day you felt sick with a headache, a fever. Two days later you couldn't move your arm. Then, you couldn't breathe. Then you died.

The basic truth about polio

Whenever Bubba recited Little Red Riding Hood, she added, in the next village there was, *nebach*, a polio epidemic. I knew polio symptoms by heart. If you recovered you wore special metal boots, walked with a cane, or one arm ended up shorter than the other. Doctors locked you into an iron lung. You lived the rest of your life there. The iron lung looked like a steam engine; it wrapped around your body to help you breathe. Bubba taped a picture of a kid inside an iron lung to our fridge. One hot day Bubba felt sorry for me and Danny. She bought us bathing suits. She took two huge *shissels* to the porch, the kind you roasted chickens in. She filled them with water; put my *toochas* in one, and my *fesilach* in the other. "*Gay gesundt*," Bubba said. "Make like you are swimming, Reuben. Go. Swim. First you go, then Danny." It was no pool. When I splashed, water vanished. "Bubba, the water's gone. Bring us water." Bubba got fed up with filling the *shissels*.

* * *

Friday night dinners the family discussed polio, TB, and doctors. As usual, there was a big *megilla* about death. Who died? Who was going to die? Who already looked dead but was alive? Who was alive but worried that they were dead? Who was dead but had not paid the undertaker? Who should have been dead but kept on living and had left their wife and children and was staying in another part of town with a *shiksa*. In the *Toronto Daily Star* that June was a big picture of Manny J. Karp, on trial for working with the Jewish-Italian gangs, tax fraud, and carrying a loaded gun. Can you believe Karp was a gangster? I played with his son Joshua. Meanwhile the polio epidemic peaked in summer. Like flies people dropped. My father's close friend, a doctor down the street, caught polio and died in two weeks. My dad was stunned; he could not accept his friend had succumbed to the epidemic. Then we heard Josh Karp's little brother caught polio and died. Frantic radio announcers warned polio spread in pools, movie theatres, parks, beaches—any place kids congregated, polio lurked. My parents were traumatized by my fall down the stairs, my double pneumonia, not to mention Tourette's syndrome, and now, in the summer, *polio*. Father wanted Danny and me to play baseball and swim. "Reuben, my father, *Rav Natan* was a rabbi who knew Torah—*only Torah*. Everything else was not his business. You want to know Torah b-but b-be scared of water for life?" Father was dead serious. "Suppose Hurricane Hazel comes back and you can't swim. Be normal, Reuben. *Swim*. You want religion and women to take over your life?"

"Look at FDR. He caught it swimming at Campobello," Mother said. "He's in a wheelchair the rest of his life. What will polio do to Reuben?"

"A *b-boychik* has to live," Father said. "It's summer. He needs water—a b-beach, right?" When I went to bed, my sheets turned wet from fear. My family argued. It ended with Father throwing a plate at the wall. "Let him b-be normal," my father yelled.

"*Be normal?*" Bubba warned. "You want *polio* should paralyze Reuben?"

"*You* will p-p-paralyze him into a bedridden hypochondriac!" Father roared.

That night I dreamt I was locked in an iron lung for the rest of my life. I had to eat strained prunes through a straw. The following Sunday my mother, Faggie Faust, and Bubba threw caution to the wind and took Danny, me, Herbie and Ruthie-Annie by streetcar to Sunnyside Beach. Bubba, Mother and Faggie Faust, like my father, didn't know how to swim. They stood guard over us on a beach towel the whole afternoon like water police. When can we go to the water? Not yet. Sit still. When? When we say you can. We had to sit still on the beach towel at all times, and then suddenly, two hours later, they said we could get out feet wet. They didn't take their eyes off the four of us until they saw a fat lady drinking Honey-Dew with her fat husband, ready to go in the lake. "Would you keep an eye on our little ones? They can go out a little—just to their knees."

"I won't go out far," I said.

"You stay quiet beside those two nice fat people," Bubba whispered.

"Why?"

"Fat people don't sink—*Farshtaste?*" They asked if we wanted a hot dog. I told them we were Jews. We didn't eat pork or ham—that was *traife*. They got the idea. They let us go into the water to our neck. When Bubba came, they said someone should teach us to swim. Danny and Herbie slipped under the waves. Ruthie-Annie tried to drown me. Bubba slapped me until I saw stars. She towelled water off me like she was cleaning candlesticks. Pieces of my skin flew off. "*Reuben be honest. Now, tell me the truth.*" Bubba shook me. "Did you swallow water?" I shook my head. "He's lying," Bubba said. "Look at his lips quivering." Okay, I slipped. [Ruthie-Annie pushed me.] "You slipped? So that's the truth?" I sipped some water, I said. Bubba wound up and gave me a left hook to the cheek like Rocky Marciano. "*Be honest.*" I looked at the beach through my watery tears. Hundreds of *goyim* were having a wonderful time running into the waves. They jumped headfirst into deep water or had piggyback fights. They swallowed beach water and spit it out, making fountains. No *goyim* died as far as I could see. Meanwhile, I was getting annihilated by Bubba. The *goyim* ate foot-long hot dogs. They nibbled French fries; they sipped Honey-Dews and Canada Dry. They smiled. They lived life. We had to sit an hour after eating a boiled egg before we moved one foot. "*Don't go fast to the beach, Reuben,*" Bubba said. "You'll get cramps. Sit on the towel quiet like Danny." Bubba—sitting, I get worse cramps. Bubba *knucked* my head until I saw pinwheels. Why was it that *goyim* knew how to have a good time at a beach while Jews watched, argued, slapped each other, and worried? Pinsky, next day Herbie and I got sick with a sore throat. My ears throbbed. It hurt to swallow. My neck puffed up. "See what you did sipping Sunnyside water? Who knows what will happen?"

"Nothing will happen," Father said. "It's just a summer throat."

A summer throat

Father and Bubba argued at my bedside. Mother took my temperature. "Please, *Davidel*," Mother said, "Let's not fight." Something will happen, *nebach*, it will get worse, TB, maybe polio? Bubba said. Look—does he look healthy? With pneumonia he goes blue. Now he turns red with a new disease. Father advanced, his finger stabbed the air in front of Bubba. *Are you a doctor?*

"*Davidel*," my mother said, "Max should come over and look in his throat."

Bubba scrubbed me top to bottom with Lifebuoy soap.

My fever rocketed to 103. Max came over and opened his black bag. I could hardly open my mouth. He pulled out a tongue depressor. Was it lockjaw? Was it strep throat? Was it polio? Uncle Max said we treat this with antibiotics. The tonsillitis should settle with daily penicillin shots. Later we pull out the tonsils. Marco already had his tonsils yanked. For three weeks he spat phlegm, blood, and flesh. Uncle Max injected penicillin. I had to turn over on my backside and get this huge spear in my *toochas*. Within days my fever abated, my throat shrunk.

Pinsky, when I pick up Mother for shopping I tell her about my sessions. Mom, you recall Bubba punched me because I swallowed water? And then Herbie got sick. Do you remember?

"Reuben, you were always a good boy," my mother said.

"Mom, who set fire to Faust's hardware store?"

* * *

When I went to bed I heard Bubba, Zlotnik the barber, Sammy Faust and his wife Faggie [when they weren't arguing], Leo the butcher: they spoke in hushed voices. Bubba had lived with her parents and little brother in a tiny wood house in Poland. The house had an earth floor. In winter the house froze. Her father brought in a cow during winter. Bubba slept near the cow to be warm. They fled Bendin. They were refugees, displaced people, they were sent to a resettlement area in Bavaria, Feldafing. They were happy to be alive but nothing was ever the same again.

* * *

March 18, 2008

Sam-Lee Yan, aka Samuel Leopold Yanovsky, my patient with nervous insomnia, is in land development. He dropped out of the borderline group. He didn't trust anyone. He is uneasy with his Russian partners who want to buy out his share of a condo megaproject north of Toronto. His eastern business partners, the Chinese, tell him to stay in the deal and play hardball with the Russians. There is no love lost between the Russians and the Chinese. Sam-Lee Yan has another deal with the Russians and Chinese, building shopping malls in Iraq—an Iraqi middle-man, the one who handled the real estate outside of Basra, agreed to accept a cache of arms from an ex-government dealer, an incentive. The Chinese have not been told. The Russians want the weapons to give to their "friends." Sam-Lee Yan is not sure what to do. He says in business you must be open with your partners or else something bad happens. Yanovsky feels a vice closing around him. Each session he nervously pats Jaffe-Jaffe.

A Serbian-Russian arms dealer, a middle-man, Luka, living in Toronto, tells Yan that he will take the arms "headache" off his hands and give him cash in an offshore account. Nothing can be traced. The Russians will be happy. Our "friends" will be happy. The Chinese won't know. The Serbian-Russian, Luka, who has a Forest Hill mansion, with three kids and a gorgeous ex-stripper wife twenty years younger, tells Yan that no one but the two of them will know.

You mustn't tell a soul.

Sam-Lee Yan, aka Samuel Leopold Yanovsky, says his nervous insomnia has increased. He pats Jaffe-Jaffe again. Jaffe-Jaffe nuzzles Sam-Lee. The two have become friends. Sam-Lee looks out my office window to check if he is followed.

Following M: March 20, 2008

I follow M as he exits my office. I make sure that he does not see me. He has a brisk stride, despite a limp from his jogging. He leans forward, his head straight ahead, his back slightly curved. Snow and ice lie on the sidewalk but M seems to fly over the surface keeping his balance. I am not sure why I follow him except to see if he is the instigator of the vandalism he complains of. I wonder if M is himself being followed. He skirts furtively along the sidewalk and disappears into a faded apartment building. It is the same apartment building where I lost trace of him. I hear a dog barking, not Jaffe-Jaffe, but another dog; the bark is deeper, louder, more menacing. I push the residents' entrance and find the door is not securely closed. I enter the foyer. The sound is coming from the second floor, a door closes. I scramble up the stairs and search the hallway. M has disappeared. I pause to write down the name of the apartment, the address, the floor area.

Excelsior Apartments, 240 Dumont Street, Suite 21 or 22.

I wait several minutes in silence. I pick up the low bass growl of the dog; it must be a large dog. The sound comes from Suite

21 mingled with two voices inside. I lean my ear against the door but I cannot make out words; someone is talking softly and then the growl again.

One voice is sonorous and deep, baritone, almost as low as the dog. The other voice is higher, quicker—scolding and sharp in tone. There is no mistake, I know that voice.

And then a third voice, a woman. I am unable to follow more.

After some minutes I hear steps approaching the door.

I rush away and slip down the stairs.

PART TWO

LATENCY
MARCH 2008–JULY 2008

CHAPTER ONE

The second phase of analysis:
O. Pinsky, March 2008

Mdeveloped a more trusting relationship with me in analysis. I did not confront him about the death of Fidel or the riddle of his excursions to the apartment of the growling dog. M recalled his first analyst, Lippman, an *enfant terrible* in analytic circles, opinionated, blunt, bellicose, cocky.

Lippman had a try-out with the Toronto Maple Leafs— Lippman's exhibitionistic phallic narcissism fascinated M. The *Toronto Daily Star* recorded Lippman played six games with the Maple Leafs—he got into two fights, received a game misconduct and punched out a linesman. The reader will note M was refused skates until adolescence. This affected his male identity and accounted for M's frustration with his Bubba and his sexual preoccupation with Estella, his best-friend's stepmom.

As an immigrant kid, the son of refugees, I was bookish. My sport was baseball—my hero, Hank Greenberg. When I asked my Bubba for skates she said hockey was not for a Jewish boy.

I understood M's past as if it was part of my own.

* * *

Acts of vandalism reported by patients who parked their cars in M's parking lot hinted he was acting out his repressed

131

delinquent self. Outwardly M presented himself as scrupulous, conscientious, and correct. For this reason I had followed M outside my office on two occasions but uncovered no clues. M was fascinated by individuals who lived outside conventional rules and the constraints of law. M was seeing a Vietnam vet referred to as GC. He followed Sam-Lee Yan, alias Samuel Leopold Yanovsky, the gangster, and Crystal who had ties with the drug gangs. These patients gratified his unconscious wish to be an arch-criminal or militant vigilante himself. Two more patients had feces spread on their windshield. When M reported this he broke into laughter. One patient had a dead chicken tied to his bumper—he laughed so hard that he had to excuse himself to go to the washroom. What was so comical? M could not say. He reported that his aged mother received hostile phone calls. M noted that he had blocked again on a patient's name—psychogenic forgetting? I said nothing of this—it was not appropriate for an interpretation. M lectured on grandparents' role in child development and had become an international expert. Two sides of his mind, the academic self, sure and in control, and the rebellious adolescent self, appeared at some distance from each other. M finished his text on *The Bubba Complex*. He received growing recognition for grandparents' role in child-rearing yet some academics objected to the critical role M placed on the grandmother. Groups in Berlin, London, New York, Boston, Montreal, and Toronto protested against M's work. They formed local action groups called *Bubba Bunds*. After a Toronto talk, one irate social worker confronted him. "How dare you insult my Bubba," she had said. But M did not mention these threats until later.

* * *

Two months later, in May 2008, as I was walking down a Toronto street in front of Mount Zion Hospital I noticed a large protest group, perhaps 200 individuals. The group marched silently carrying placards, banners, and flags. I looked closer at the large black flags which had a central white circle on which was written in bold red letters—*BB*—*Bubba Bund*. I saw the protest members wore similar armbands on the right arm. Many were elderly women, although there were some men and young children. The group repeated a phrase, or perhaps it would be more correct to call it a rant, *Ban Bubba Bashing*. They came to a halt in front of Mount Zion Hospital. They closed ranks and I noted that they had divided into two phalanxes of about 100 protesters each, raising and inclining their placards forward like spears, chanting *Ban Bubba Bashing*. Their protests rose in volume. I heard the words *Bernard Bayer* recited in chorus. After several minutes of this raucous refrain a man wearing a suit appeared on the front steps of Mount Zion Hospital. It was Bernard Bayer, the head of its Department of Psychiatry. He raised one hand and spoke with a portable loudspeaker, unsettled by the protesters.

"I assure you our Psychiatry Department recognizes the importance of the Bubba and women in the lives of children. We believe in the centrality of grandmother in child-rearing."

Bayer repeated his brief message to jeers from the crowd.

Security guards were at the front door. Plainclothed personnel joined Dr. Bayer. I gathered that the protest march had as its goal Mount Zion Hospital. To be more correct its target was the Department of Psychiatry, specifically Dr. Moses, or M as I referred to him. The protest group was heated. I cannot over-emphasize my apprehension as the group grew unruly when Bayer left. A stone was hurled at the plate glass doors of Mount Zion Hospital.

A glass door shattered.

Myriads of sharp fragments scattered violently outwards.

The police were called in and dispersed the crowd.

* * *

I followed M in the next few months. Much of the time it was just to see what direction he took upon leaving my office.

I watched to see if he left by himself. I looked across the street and down the block. I wondered if there was anyone waiting for him. Call it a sixth sense, but I sensed a crucial piece of information was absent. Despite my questions M did not disclose what was missing. Perhaps he was suffering a mental block. Perhaps this information was repressed.

CHAPTER TWO

More catastrophes

Pinsky, one week after Sunnyside Beach, Herbie Faust got a sore throat. I had recovered from my tonsillitis. I went to see Herbie. He was such a dreary, quiet child. I wanted to make him feel better. His sister was out for some minutes. I found her diary. She wrote that Sammy Faust lost his temper. She wrote that he shut her in a room and beat her black and blue.

I brought Herbie my father's cough syrup, Moses's Cough Syrup—he took two sips and threw up. He was feverish.

"Look, you made him sick! It's not a sore throat," Faggie, said. "Yesterday, *nebach*, his neck was stiff. He had trouble moving a leg. *And it is all because of you, Reuben.*" The next day Herbie Faust left on a stretcher. Bubba slapped me for visiting him.

He went to emergency and was transferred to the pediatric ward. Guess what he had, Pinsky?

Polio. Ruthie-Annie's family blamed me. They put him in an iron lung.

"What did you do to poor little Herbie?" Bubba demanded.

* * *

Fed up with Bubba and Mother, my father sent me out of the city with Auntie Leah and Uncle Eli, who had no children

135

and were not big-time worriers. During August, Leah rented an apartment on Erie Road in Crystal Beach. The apartment was a single room with a gas stove, icebox, and curtain in the middle separating the kitchen from a bed. Ruthie-Annie got worse after her brother caught polio. She broke her dolls. She stopped sleeping.

She hated doctors and never forgave me.

* * *

Crystal Beach in the evening—R. Moses

In Crystal Beach my guilt, constipation, stutter, obsessions, and insomnia vanished, my tics melted away. I slept like a top while Auntie Leah and Uncle Eli snored in the other bed. Uncle Eli smoked Black Cat cigarettes first thing in the morning. He said it assisted his indigestion. After breakfast we crossed Erie Road to Crystal Beach Park. There was a playground with swings and a huge slide that spiralled down. A train took you around the park for a quarter. Morning to night you smelled French fries, waffles, popcorn, donuts, hot dogs, and hamburgers. At night the sky filled with lights and music. People danced, jived, or roller-skated in the covered pavilions. Auntie Leah wasn't afraid of polio. She didn't keep kosher. She gambled for real money, played bingo, and stayed up late. Whatever she liked she ate. She let me do the same. Carloads of Jews from Ontario, New York, and Pennsylvania came to Crystal Beach. They acted like Aunt Leah and Uncle Eli—staying up late, playing cards, strolling in bathing trunks all day. Some played the horses at Fort Erie; others drank beer and slept in hammocks. Nobody looked worried as far as I could tell.

Uncle Eli promised to take me on the roller coaster. Reuben can't go there—he will fall out, Auntie Leah said. But Uncle Eli had a perfect answer. He pulled out a belt from his old steamer trunks. He tied it around us—a perfect fit. He will be tied to me, Uncle Eli said. They won't let you do that, Auntie Leah said. Reuben is too young.

At Crystal Beach you sat in the shallows and felt the waves push you side to side, over the bumpy ridges of sand below the water. Bathers sprinted full speed from the sandy beach into the shallow water, splashing spume on all sides until waist-high they dove forward and disappeared under the surface. Uncle Eli taught me to lie still—to float. We drifted to the long pier where the boat from Buffalo was moored.

"Look—the roller coaster," he pointed. "Let's go later. I'll talk to the manager."

After my afternoon nap, Auntie Leah and Uncle Eli took me on the bumper cars, the caterpillar, and for a special treat, the roller coaster. Most riders looked happy to be back on earth. Some were unsteady on their feet and others clutched the railing; a couple staggered. People giggled. Then a young kid with the whitest face you ever saw threw up two feet away. He must have had a three course Italian meal—it was there to see—pizza, spaghetti, and meatballs—food you shouldn't eat before the world's biggest roller coaster. It came out in two puddles and he wasn't four steps away from me when he made an awful retching sound and deposited another fresh mound.

Uncle Eli was beside the gate chatting with the manager, a man in overalls and a T-shirt. "The boy's with me," Uncle Eli said.

"Is this your kid?"

"My flesh and blood," Uncle Eli said. "He's my boy."

Pinsky, I felt proud Uncle Eli called me his boy, even though I had second thoughts about the ride. The manager looked me over. "Young man, come here. I want to measure you." He made me stand against a wall beside a picture of a clown. If I was as tall as the clown I could go on the roller coaster. I stretched myself as tall as possible.

"Try next week, sonny," the manager smiled, "—or maybe next year."

To make me feel better Auntie Leah bought me a glass of *Cronfeldt's* loganberry. *Cronfeldt's* was tart yet sweet—the best drink I ever tasted. Uncle Eli said the boss was ten feet away checking on things. That was why the manager said no. Next time we will get the front car. What if the roller coaster goes too fast? "There's a button," Uncle Elis said. "It slows the roller coaster."

The next year our entire family—Uncle Eli, Auntie Leah, Mother, Father, Danny, Bubba, Auntie Sadie, Uncle Max, and cousins Robert and Sheldon rented a cottage for two weeks. Everyone but Yasha came. Beside us was a cottage with a pool. The lady next door had a cuddly poodle, Zsa-Zsa; she invited her neighbours over to swim. There was a gorgeous dog walker by the pool, Polly. I never found out her last name. A sixteen-year-old muscle-bound kid was lifeguard at his aunt's pool, *Sid the Stick*, we named him, a hotshot hockey prospect. I was crammed into a tiny bedroom with cousins Robert and Sheldon. Each morning my cousins and I hung out at the pool and in the afternoon I went to the beach with Uncle Eli. At night my parents played canasta. When Uncle Eli and I floated at the beach he said that my mother had an older brother she never talked about. "Who was her brother? Why did nobody tell me?"

"Much of your family fled the war and wanted to protect you. I will tell you later."

That year Uncle Eli finally took me on the roller coaster. The manager looked the other way. We jumped into the first red car. I was tied tightly to Uncle Eli's waist. The roller coaster clicked and inched up the incline. Gravity pushed me back in the wooden roller coaster seat. I saw sky above and bathers like tiny ants below. I felt the wind across the lake. Two seagulls floated in the air. *Everything froze—the gulls, the roller coaster, the boats, the bathers.* Instead of gazing at the sky I stared at the roller coaster track. We flew a mile a minute. Everyone hollered. Uncle Eli put one hand around me. We fell straight down; yanked, left, right, down, and up again. "Push the button," I said. "Slow it down. Where is the button?"

"I can't find the button," Uncle Eli said. At the end we staggered out. I leaned against a wall. I vomited three times. Uncle Eli lit a Black Cat. "That's the roller coaster for you—it goes up slow and comes down fast—like life. Reuben, I want to tell you who you are named after. It's not only Reba, your mother's mother. There was someone else; no one wanted to tell you."

Later that month, after we returned to Toronto, Uncle Eli was taken sick.

"Uncle Eli passed away in his sleep," Father told me. My parents wore torn black ribbons on their lapels. Their faces were heavy, their eyes red. In the Fifties no children went to funerals. The s*hiva* was at my parents' apartment. Yasha was not invited. Auntie Leah was inconsolable. Ruthie-Annie and I were the only children. She didn't say a word. I saw the rich lady from the cottage next door come with her nephew, *Sid the Stick*, and Polly, who watched Zsa-Zsa; even Karp came—his lawyer got his charges dropped. I saw the roller coaster manager—he wore a suit, a countryman of Eli's. He had no recollection of me. After Uncle Eli died Auntie Leah rarely went out except to play cards or babysit. She was in her mid-forties but never met another man. She was our tiny aunt with a high voice. She lived with Bubba. Later she lived in a tiny apartment, growing tinier each passing year. She was four foot ten. When I was eleven I was taller than her.

Uncle Eli was my buddy—we caught grasshoppers. We played cards. We floated together at Crystal Beach. Ruthie-Annie said Danny or I should have got polio and walked with a limp. She had rings around her eyes. She stopped taking care of all her insect friends. I missed Uncle Eli. I was curious about my mother's older brother. Except for the button on the roller coaster, Uncle Eli always told the truth. In his eyes I never did anything wrong.

Herbie Faust went into the iron lung,
He wasn't able to breathe.—R. Moses

* * *

I remember Cronfeldt's loganberry. I drank it at Crystal Beach, sweet yet tart, just as M said. The long white sandy beach beside the amusement park was filled with families and young people.

I was there with my family. But although M looked familiar I did not know him at the time.

CHAPTER THREE

Pain: April 3, 2008

Next session Blum enters my office nine minutes late which for her is one minute early. She sits up in a swivel chair opposite me. "I had an argument with Ivan, my son."

I nod and motion her to the couch. "No—I am not lying down. I get tearful."

"Isn't that what you avoid—your tearful feelings, your vulnerable side?"

"My back has been hurting. The pain runs down my legs. I've stopped all drugs. Lying on your Wal-Mart couch makes it worse. You should get an orthopedic couch."

"Mrs. Blum," I say, "what has been happening the last few sessions?"

"Dr. Moses this has nothing to do with you."

"I received a notice from my college."

"Yes, *that*. I made an official complaint, a copy which I sent to Dr. Bayer, your boss. He asked me to forget about the complaint. What do you think?"

"You are frustrated with me, Mrs. Blum—we should talk about *your frustration*. You intimidate others. You want to strike out against me."

"You already have three strikes against you, Dr. Moses. *You have struck out*."

"I know there is a part of you that is afraid of closeness—you are telling me how it is difficult to remain in a relationship with anyone—you dismiss them."

"I knew you'd say that. Even if you are right, Moses, you are not right."

"I am not always right. I have to accept that. Mrs. Blum, I know you are angry with me. Did you express your anger by doing anything to my car?"

"You are asking me about your car? Why in the world would I touch your car—someone trashed my car *again*. I should ask you the same question."

"I didn't do anything to your car, Mrs. Blum."

"You are odd. I see you doodle during sessions. You jog by yourself. You live with your dog. Your wife left you. She grew bored. It is common knowledge—she had an affair with Karl Guttnik. You work at a Jewish hospital, word gets around."

"Why are you trying to hurt me, Mrs. Blum?"

"Because I won't let you have power over me," she says. Instantly I am erect.

Pinsky says: "So, you feel erotically attracted to an older abusive woman?"

Karl Guttnik, colleague and traitor

Urbane, sophisticated, good-looking, witty, and charming, a fellow analyst at my hospital, Guttnik worked in our borderline clinic. I knew Guttnik from Euclid Avenue—he was four years older. My Bubba did not stop talking about how *shain*, how handsome this little Lothario was. Guttnik stood first in class, we attended the same Jewish camp, he took out the camp sweetheart, Sabrina Lustig. Guttnik went to med school and won the gold medal. He married Sabrina—I had a crush on Sabrina—why did he always get what he wanted? Guttnik had a wonderful practice, a beautiful wife and became a drug expert so whenever there was a problem patient we sent the person to Guttnik. I kept up our friendship, I liked him too—he was my regular jogging partner. Guttnik was genial, polished, adored by his patients—a total success. Pinsky, I am ashamed to tell you, I felt colossal envy for Guttnik—it was eating me up inside, killing me. Of course, I consoled myself that I was two inches taller than Guttnik and since age thirty-five he had lost his golden locks and was bald. A few years ago, his lovely wife Sabrina developed a brain tumour and died. I felt guilt for my envy. Frieda and I had him to the house for dinner. I invited him to debate my *Bubba Complex* paper. What does Guttnik do? He shits all over my work.

For years the two of us jogged together. Why did he savage my work on the Bubba?

Worse, how was I to know he was *shtupping* Frieda?

What if Guttnik vandalized my car in the parking lot?

Little Herbie was put in the iron lung. I wanted to visit him in hospital, but his family refused to let me see him. Father and Uncle Max said it was not my fault that Herbie caught polio. That summer Mr. Moretti, the little shoemaker, fell ill with a fever. He stayed in bed for two days. And then his poor wife took him to hospital. Mr. Moretti died of polio.

I did not go over to the Fausts' hardware store. Herbie's illness put an end to my visits to his apartment. His sister refused to talk to me and wrote notes in her diary to herself.

April 7, 2008

I ask M if he retained a copy of the Hebrew letters from Ruthie-Annie's diary. He does not answer me. In our sessions he has not spoken the Yiddish phrase from the diary transcribed in Hebrew. I understood and spoke Yiddish as a child. I studied the language together with Hebrew at cheder (Jewish school). The two languages are different, Yiddish being derived largely from German yet written in the Roman or Hebrew alphabet. Hebrew, by contrast, is written in the Hebrew alphabet.

For Jews from Germany, Austria, Poland, Russia, and the Baltic States, Yiddish was their first language—the *mame loshon*—the language spoken at home. It is a rich visceral tongue; when I hear it now it reminds me of my Bubba, of my parents and lost childhood.

* * *

I follow M for a few blocks. He returns to the same apartment. Excelsior Apartments, 240 DuMont Street. This time M takes Jaffe-Jaffe to the apartment—he had earlier brought the dog to our session claiming Jaffe-Jaffe seems more unsettled. I walk up to the second floor and hear the high-pitched barking of Jaffe-Jaffe and the low sonorous growl of a large dog.

The sounds come from #21, closer to the stairs. I descend and check the address roster. #21 has two letters beside it. GC—the initials of his Vietnam vet patient, I wonder.

CHAPTER FOUR

The rules of interpretation—O. Pinsky, May 9, 2008

One afternoon in May, after M had left our session I received a call from my building manager. He asked me to come down and take a look at my spot in the parking lot.

When I arrived I saw nothing except for a few scattered feathers. *Look here*, the manager said. I walked to the edge of my parking spot. The front left headlight of my car was splattered with blood and entrails. Did you hit anything driving here today?

Not that I remembered.

In the corner, the manager pointed to something he had not noticed before. When we stepped closer I saw a dead bird. A mutilated capon—the head had been severed. The body was eviscerated. My first association was odd—the capon was placed there by M—or was it Blum? I was shocked and dismayed. I did not believe M would commit such a macabre act. He was polite, kind to everyone, especially his difficult patients. He had a reputation for tolerance. I recalled his memories of Rosen's butcher shop and Zlotnik, the barber—his morbid fascination for death. M portrayed himself in his analysis as an innocent victim and a healer. How would I investigate the acts of smearing, the vandalism, or the meaning of the headless eviscerated capon?

145

I was disturbed and irritated. I wanted to find out who was behind these cruel and vicious pranks. A week later I received a call from the night security officer. Someone had been seen outside my office wearing a trench coat and a hat. The person disappeared into the night as soon as the security officer approached. Our office building is installing a new closed circuit television camera with sensors that follow motion. The next time we will get a clearer image of this mystery intruder.

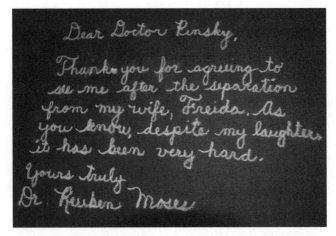

Dear Doctor Pinsky; Thank-you for agreeing to see me after the separation from my wife, Frieda. As you know, despite my daughters it has been very hard.
Yours truly, Dr. Reuben Moses.
M's original letter to me requesting analysis in June 2007

At one point M suspected Guttnik was the instigator of the parking lot attacks. We later learned that Guttnik's car had been vandalized. Guttnik phoned M and accused M of retaliation after his affair with Frieda. M vigorously denied any wrongdoing.

* * *

Crystal, the dog walker, May 15, 2008

Crystal, the dog walker calls my office. "Listen, Dr. Pinsky, this is an emergency."

"I can't exactly speak with you now."

"How is it that when I call you, you won't speak to me."

"Look, Crystal, you call six minutes after my patient leaves. I have ten minutes between patients. You are not really my patient. I can only talk for about three to four minutes."

"Well, fuck you, *Dr. Three-to-Four-Minutes*. What kind of crazy life do you lead that you can't talk to a person who is suffering a serious panic attack? If sick people had to depend on doctors like you with your goddamn three to four minute break they would go off the fucking deep end! What kind of screwed up compassion do you have? I am struggling with a major problem and I want to speak to you because you know my doctor and he tells me he sees you. I can call and see him whenever I am scared. And you, *you piece of shit*, won't give me the fucking time of day."

We argue for another minute which leaves us less than two minutes to talk. I cannot speak at length with her; she informs me again that she suspects her movements are followed.

"Perhaps it is your boyfriend Zeno who has sent someone to watch over you?"

"Zeno and I had a fight," Crystal replies. "Drop dead and leave me alone, I said. Zeno is going to be released from jail in 2008. He doesn't like that M is the only one I trust. Pinsky, I am not being followed when I am alone. It is when I walk Jaffe-Jaffe. Now you understand?"

* * *

A text message from Sam-Lee Yan May 16, 2008

I get a text message from Sam-Lee Yan. He has figured out I am M's analyst. He would like to talk in person. Security concerns. I discuss these inappropriate calls with M at our next session.

* * *

M tells me he is used to misunderstandings and protests. He recalls that when Stravinsky first presented *The Rite of Spring* the audience failed to appreciate his music and stormed out of the theatre. M goes on and tells me few people accepted Freud's idea of the unconscious.

A few days later I see another group of marchers, this time larger, perhaps three to four hundred protesters carrying placards and banners. They wear the black, white, and red armbands.

They walk towards the Mount Zion Hospital and encircle the front doors.

* * *

M is limping and has been running sixty K a week preparing for a marathon in a few months. He tells me that the drivers in Toronto are the worst in the world.

"Have you tried running on a track?"

"I prefer running on the sidewalks or road. Some blind kamikaze in an SUV almost hit me."

"Do you think you can outrun a bad driver?"

"You are acting like Bubba again."

"You are re-enacting childhood. You do not recall it, you repeat it in action—you followed Bubba's orders but there was a side to you that disobeyed her. That is in full display."

CHAPTER FIVE

Bayer's error: June 2008

Blum writes Bayer about how inept my treatment has been. Over twenty years ago I supervised Bayer when he was a resident-in-training. Bayer was a therapeutic ignoramus, wet behind the ears—the *schmuck* didn't know his ass from a hole in the ground. After graduation, he followed a borderline dentist with a gambling-drug addiction. The patient gambled away a fortune then lost his licence. He was forced to sell his house. Bayer called me up for a phone consultation. Bayer had made a major error—he should have had the patient's banking and credit cards halted and arranged for the wife to have power of attorney. The wife was enraged—the couple lost everything—the dentist-husband gambled to pay a loan shark debt. He went psychotic on drugs. A week later he committed suicide. His wife accused Bayer of malpractice. Bayer received threats. Someone slashed his tires. Then I received threats. At the time the police couldn't prove it was Mrs. X. The anger and threats faded away. Bayer put the disaster behind him. He got busy with being a success. Last week I spoke to Bayer. He was receiving threats again. The police re-opened the file.

* * *

Bayer's short-term therapy offered hope for difficult patients. He had a core of devoted clinical co-workers. I agreed to be a program consultant—the drop-out rate was 40 per cent. Six years later he published a monograph on evidence-based short-term therapy and was made associate professor. Eight years after that he was promoted to full professor. Then, with two more books to his credit, baby-faced Bayer became an expert on depression and anxiety. Did research make him a good therapist? Guttnik and I were delegated to see his mess-ups in the borderline clinic. Years later the failures started coming back to the clinic. Patients were infuriated by Bayer. I recall that I spoke to Mrs. X by phone. Should I recall her name? Maybe I don't want to remember the past. Over the last four decades my psychoanalytic colleagues have left the hospitals. We used to chair psychiatry departments, run hospital wards, and teach psychiatry residents. We received respect in those days. Our star has fallen. Why did this happen? Who remains to fathom the unconscious, Pinsky? Why did psychoanalysis get such a lousy rap—we were plumbers of the psyche. We had years of intense training and study. We explored the stench of life to its source. Who first saw and named the borderlines, the depressive-masochists and narcissistic characters? Who wrote about these conditions? Who first studied suicidal patients and their dark interiors? Who explored the swamp-infested regions of perverts, fetishists, and psychopaths? Who unearthed the psychological stress of war or understood childhood terrors and separation anxieties? Who took on these patients when no one would see them?—psychoanalysts—we laid the groundwork. Guess what?—hospitals and patients got fed up with complexity. They wanted quick fixes and discharge in ten days. Patients want relief without understanding how they develop symptoms in the first place.

I have sympathy for M's view but it is a lament anchored in the past.

* * *

Pinsky, I do not speak lightly of Blum's symptoms—headache, palpitations, vague chest pain, rapid breathing, shortness of breath, swollen and painful joints, pins and needles in her extremities, bladder sensitivity, fatigue, malaise, difficulty concentrating, lowered mood and episodic rages, and decreased sexual enjoyment. Through all this she worked in her business like a horse. She found a younger man, forty-five; she complained of the classic in-out—not a bang, but a whimper. The guy had performance anxiety—*like all you men*, Blum added—but better than nothing. Pinsky, she was referring in the transference to me.

I was the metaphor of in and out, *boom*.

I was the incompetent nincompoop, the nothing guy who went soft, the cuckold.

Blum heated up sessions engaged in feelings and lots of anger. She wanted to continue the session but our time was up. I got a baleful look. She blamed me for *analysis interruptus*. During Passover Blum asked for a double session. I pondered this for half a nanosecond—had I *sitzfleisch* to bear hours of her toxic farting about how difficult everything was outside her ass-hole? She started with the exodus from Egypt and how it brought back her persecuted family's flight from Europe. Blum, has it crossed your mind that you replayed the same set of persecutions here? I said this nicely six different ways; Pinsky, no sooner did I give a deep penetrating interpretation than she *kvetched* about her body. This colossal embodiment of psychic conflict—this *farshlepter krenk* wrapped in the dark continent of her seething enigmatic bowels. Inevitably we returned to the Gordian knot which no doctor, no analyst, no lover, no conquistador, was to unravel.

Constipatio permanens—chronic constipation.

The Passover Seder was upon us. Blum persisted with her matzo tortures, out of sheer obstinacy, out of self-proclaimed masochism, at the same time complaining of swallowing vast quantities of prunes and mineral oil to no effect. Pinsky, I swear your face reminds me of someone from the past. Do I know you from somewhere?

* * *

For six months from Passover until Rosh Hashanah my Bubba ate matzo. She ate it for breakfast. She ate it nightly. Was she guilty for sins? What sane person ate matzo after Passover [unless you had traveller's diarrhoea]? After one helping you developed constipation. After two days you became impacted. After a week your guts turned into the Great Wall of China.

Bubba *shlepped* Ruthie-Annie and me to Gershon Zapinsky's fish store on College. Herbie was in rehab hospital. Ruthie-Annie gritted her teeth and hardly spoke to me. Zapinsky pulled out a big carp, *knucked* his *kop*, wrapped him in paper. Since we lived miles away we took the carp home on the streetcar. White-fish. Carp. Pickerel. Sometimes a piece of salmon went into *gefilte fish*. Bubba said this recipe went back centuries to our Russian relatives. I had sharp eyes and quick fingers, I worked the *machinka*. "Watch your *fingerlach*, don't get *chupped* inside. Careful."

Torture #6. A *machinka* was a heavy metal hand-mincer you bolted to the table. Poor Jewish families had them. You had to be a soldier to make *gefilte fish*. Inside the *machinka* was a metal screw. You *areingeshtupped* the fish and onions into the *machinka*, but not too hard, while you turned the screw handle with your other good hand like a Gatling gun. "Turn," Bubba ordered. I can't see. *Onions*. I'm blind. "Reuben. Don't panic." I can't breathe. I can't see. "Get used to it," Bubba said. Bubba warned to keep your eyes open with onions. Never talk when you worked the *machinka* or *ribeisen* in case you got distracted and lost *fingerlach*. On the other side of the *machinka* was a wooden chopping bowl. I chopped fish and onions with a *hackmesser* [torture #7]; Bubba threw in eggs, matzo-meal, salt, sugar, pepper. With the *reibeisen* I scraped carrots. People collapsed and died making *gefilte fish*. If you didn't catch fingers in the *machinka*, you cried, you went blind, you left your flesh on the *ribeisen*, and you could maim your entire body with the *hackmesser*, a weapon from the Crusades, a huge blade that curved around your hand like brass knuckles. There was also *chrain*—a lethal concoction of ground horseradish and beets used to season *gefilte fish*. One tiny spoonful brought a grown man to his knees. If you were unfortunate enough to inhale *chrain* [torture #8], the vapour [like mustard gas] more or less stunned you for an hour before you came to your senses. Bubba sat me on a stool with a wooden bowl on my thighs—I *hucked* in time to the radio—*Mambo Italiano* by Rosemary Clooney. "Reuben. Stop with the music. You'll *huck* your *polkas* off." I *tzaclapped* eggs. Bubba fried chicken fat for *grebenas* [chicken skins fried into chips]. She made bottles of schmaltz for frying: eggs, onions, and matzo-*brei*. In those days, people threw schmaltz [Jewish Crisco] on everything. Bubba, Auntie Leah, and Mother made *tzimmes*, *knaidelach*, *flumen*, *potatonik*. Downstairs Father counted pills and filled prescriptions. Upstairs, I chopped, sliced, and bled to death in the kitchen.

Bubba yelled at Father that Sammy Faust, the only self-respecting Jew on the Queensway, sent his kids to *Talmud Torah*, built a third hardware and soon would have a fourth. Another of his stores burnt to the ground. How did Faust make money to send Herbie, the polio cripple, and Ruthie-Annie to violin lessons and Jewish school? Incensed, Father hurled a precious vase to the floor—the gift from Bubba shattered. Eyes bulging he took a seltzer bottle and threw it. The seltzer bottle refused to break. "Don't you see how I sweat for our living?" Father said.

"Is it ever easy?" Bubba said. "We try to make it better for our children."

Father, feeling sorry for his outburst, went to hug Bubba. She turned away.

I invited my colleague, the widower, Karl Guttnik, to our home for Passover. I should have sensed something when I saw Karl pinching Frieda under the table.

* * *

Rav Natan, my father's dad, had a beard and eyes the colour of old iron nails. He sat at our Seder wearing a skullcap, a rabbi from Riga who knew Torah backwards. My father and Rav Natan hardly spoke. As a *shoichet*, a ritual butcher; he slaughtered animals. "Reuben," Rav Natan said, "*Nem a kish*." I kissed him. His beard was as gentle as rusted steel wool. Pinsky, I see their faces in a haze—my father, beside his father, Danny, Bubba, Aunt Leah, and Mother, her face flushed, her stomach growing larger. The round Seder table faded. We rotated around, until the youngest was no longer young and moved to the middle along the table, and became the oldest and then joined eternity. At the end sat Yasha, staring still and silent as a statue on Easter Island.

* * *

For a month in June 2008 I received no further calls from M's patients. I began to feel more relaxed and assumed that the analysis was having a positive effect. In other words, M was alert to the immense burden he had placed on himself with his busy schedule of problem patients. I further believed that my interventions were finally reaching M and that he was taking the necessary steps to reduce his neurotic workload. There were no reports of vandalism and no calls from Bayer or the police. However, the security cameras in my office building picked up an image of a person in a raincoat and umbrella wandering by the front door on a rainy Friday afternoon. The super wondered if this figure was similar to the previous trench coat intruder. On a frame by frame digital review, the second set of images revealed a stooped individual who used the umbrella as a cane. My first inkling of a visitor was a knock and a buzz from my waitingroom. Like most analysts I had no receptionist. I was finishing a session with M. I excused myself to open the door. "Is my son here?" An aged woman in a raincoat leaned forward on her umbrella. Over her other arm was a shopping bag. I had no idea who she was. "My Reuben, is he here?"

M informed me that he picked her up to go shopping on Friday after he left the session. M had given her my office address but only for emergencies. She was unsteady on her feet. He worried about her health.

She took me aside in the waiting room. "Doctor Pinsky, my son makes me nervous."

"What makes you nervous about your son, Mrs. Moses?" I asked.

"A grown man should take care of himself."

"You came here to tell me this?" I asked.

"Like a *meschugge* he runs on the road. He doesn't listen to his own mother, doctor."

The dreaded machinka—R. Moses

CHAPTER SIX

Further comments on latency—
O. Pinsky, June 2008

M swore incessantly—his stories were amusing; his jesting rant was a defensive tactic, a *diversion*. From time to time he returned to speak of his first analyst, Lippman, whom he had heroized. During M's analysis Lippman had bought himself a motorcycle—a Russian model with a sidecar. Lippman offered M a lift in the sidecar to an analytic meeting. Lippman drove the motorcycle at breakneck speeds. The ride was fearful but enjoyable—this brought back M's cherished connection with Uncle Eli, who had taken him on the roller coaster against the wishes of women like his Bubba and mother. What was this about? *Father hunger* was an essential issue in M's struggles. The child, in the oedipal period needs the father to modify female intrusion—M's father, like Sammy Faust, worked night and day to support his family. Faust was a cipher, fiendishly busy. During latency the presence of male figures was essential—Uncle Eli died, Uncle Max was a busy doctor, M's two grandfathers were absent. Rav Natan, a rabbi, a *shoicet*, a ritual butcher, slaughtered animals and spoke Latvian, Russian, Yiddish. M was terrified of him. Yasha spoke Polish, Russian, and Yiddish—neither spoke English. M was perplexed about his mother's father and his past and felt neglected by men—hence his comic book superheroes, *Superman*, *Spiderman*, *Captain America*, who served as idealized alter ego figures for his vulnerable ego. M spent his lonely times with an imaginary companion. Play outlets were denied—Bubba forbade *Superman* outfits. He was not given a bicycle until before his bar mitzvah. He was refused hockey skates, a staple for a Canadian boy. I noted his Bubba's concern about M's health. He had a frightening fall down a flight of stairs at age two, sustained a scrotal hematoma, was left-handed, contracted pneumonia at age four, suffered purulent tonsillitis after a swim at Sunnyside Beach and was later diagnosed with a minor variant of Gilles de La Tourette's disorder. To this must be added the constant threat in the early Fifties—epidemics of TB and polio. Polio peaked during summer—anywhere crowds of people gathered.

When I was a child two of my schoolmates contracted polio. My family was petrified.

I understood the struggles of his refugee family, the threat of illness and death, and the vulnerability of strangers in a strange land. This anxiety may appear risible to those born after the Salk/Sabin vaccines, but Moretti's death and M's childhood friend, Herbie, falling ill with polio* struck terror into the hearts of families. M was accused by the Fausts of causing their son's polio.

From a medical perspective this was doubtful.

* * *

To hear M talk about clinical cases one fell under his spell. He appeared witty, confident, entertaining, thoughtful, and intrepid about the most difficult patients. Some patients were severely depressed; others were regressed, chronically suicidal, traumatized, grief-stricken, hypo-manic, paranoid, and anxious. M presented with his invariable pleasant grin at scientific

---

*Manny Karp's youngest son also contracted polio and tragically died within a week.

meetings in a charming, convincing manner—no one would guess his internal torments. M's reputation for working with and supervising intractable cases was well known. Why work with intractable cases that failed therapy? I struggled to explore his motivation, aware that, like Icarus, he was flying close to the sun. Blum, his patient, appeared dead-set on rendering him impotent, defeating him. Crystal, *deep-throat* caused him to be reviled by emergency staff. Sam-Lee Yan, the depressed gangster, had ties to violent underworld figures. And with his mystery patient GC (who I supposed he visited in an apartment), I was in the dark. Interpreting M's sadomasochistic tendencies had no effect. He laughed at me. I sought consultation from Sandor Gabor. He warned that I did not actively challenge M's massive denial. I needed to penetrate his primal anxiety—his fear of death.

I return to my first comment—M's analytic banter was a comic camouflage, a detour from a specific situation, which ultimately proved disastrous. A complicating factor was his attachment to Jaffe-Jaffe, his neurotic retriever. The dog was restless and misbehaved. In two sessions the dog had the audacity to urinate on my oriental rug. M was apologetic. He immediately paid for the rug to be cleaned. The next week the dog shat in the hallway and repeated this in the parking lot. I reflected that M was exploited and abused not only by his patients but by his pet. Crystal continued to call me with her anxious attachment to the dog. One of M's patients, Sam-Lee Yan requested to meet with me. I refused. I questioned if M's unconscious colluded with Jaffe-Jaffe's unruliness and his psychopathic patients since it allowed M to secretly relate and express a hostile aspect of his character. Was this why he saw GC, the Vietnam vet?

Neither M nor I could formulate the danger at the time—yet the signs were there.

M's mother stated his dilemma clearly when she arrived at my office.

"Reuben doesn't take care of himself. A grown man should take care of himself."

M stated that his mother was mistaken to come to my office—he was going to pick her up and go shopping immediately after our session. M mocked me and made light of the warning signs I had touched on in his analysis. His joking reduced my vigilance. What were the signs? I refer to the acts of vandalism to his property, the unseen intruder outside my office, the veiled phone threats his elderly mother received, car damages his patients sustained while parked at his office.

Lastly and not least, I refer to the *Bubba Bunds*, protesting M's *Bubba complex*.

* * *

Uncle Eli had hinted that M was not only named after his mother's mother, Reba, but another nameless refugee figure, her lost older brother. This enigmatic identification had an unsettling effect. M was forbidden to play or dress like *Superman* as a child. His inclination was to turn his intelligence to grandiose mental powers. M worked with impossible patients.

If Superman took on Lex Luther and Batman faced The Joker, M had his own fiendish villains.

I set myself thinking who was M's arch-enemy.

CHAPTER SEVEN

Escaping Bubba

"... for the grandchild, the necessity of child care is provided by the Bubba ... prevailing Western notions of the nuclear family oppose the traditional middle-European socio-centric model ... we see heightened anxiety and guilt over loss, abandonment, and migration to the host country ..."

R. Moses.

Father downed Crown Royal, smoked incessantly, and paced the floors at night. When I looked at his dark wavy hair, I saw strands of silver; his forehead was creased; his eyes inflamed. He worked seven days a week. Mother expected a third child.

"You are stressed," Mother said.

"It's your goddamn *balabusta* mother." Father hefted a cup like a projectile. "*D-Do this. D-Don't do this*—a five star general. She orders me and you. I need her out of my hair."

In late spring Father drove us east across the new Humber Bridge. Since Hurricane Hazel the destroyed bridge had been rebuilt. Where is Bubba? I asked. "*Ssshh*. I don't want her here—over my d-dead body—*understand*?" Father lit a cigarette. He pulled the car to the curb and slammed on the brakes. We came to a dead stop. "Nobody b-breathes a word to Bubba. *Where we are going is Ground Zero ... it is strictly confidential.* Is that clear?" My query nettled him.

"You almost went past a red light and hit that car," Mother said.

"It's his dumb fault." Father pointed out the side window. "See. See that *nitwit*."

"Please, be nice. You don't have to get us killed."

Father lit a third cigarette. He drove through a red light. He muttered about the supermarket, his business rival. He was furious with Bubba since an argument the night before.

"Bella, with you who needs enemies?" Father had said.

"*Davidel*, you never got along with your father," Bubba had replied. "You ran away. You ran from religion and your people. You run from me. You never had a mother to tell you what to do. Your mother died when you were a child. Don't blame me."

* * *

Father was taking us on a secret mission. I worried Bubba with her X-ray eyes would find out what Father was doing—she seemed to know these things. He drove east along Lakeshore Drive to downtown Toronto. Mother pointed, "See the *Palais Royale*—we danced to Tommy Dorsey there. Father pinned me at the CNE after a dance to Glen Gray's band." Mother clasped his hand. We drove past the CNE. On the Prince's Gates a beautiful winged goddess watched over our city. Father swerved north on Bathurst Street and then turned onto College. It had been years since I had seen Euclid Avenue. An Italian family lived in our house. Instead of Jews we saw Italians, Greeks, Portuguese, African refugees, who had come to College Street. Father's eyes brimmed. He drove up Bathurst Street. The farther north he went, the larger the houses. Danny woke, frightened. M-mommy where are we? I want to g-go home, Danny cried. We overheard our parents talking about how much each house cost—in 1954 a good house cost between twenty and forty thousand dollars—a fortune. "Sammy Faust is building

161

a fourth hardware store on Lawrence Avenue," Mother said. "He's looking for a house in Cedarvale. He never stops working."

"How is Herbie?" I asked.

"Herbie is in leg braces," Mother said. "We don't know if he will walk again."

"It wasn't my fault," I said.

Mother didn't hear me. She talked home prices. Father vowed never to ask Bubba for a dime.

"I will personally hold up a bank. Will that make you happy?"

"*Davidel*, you owe ten thousand for the drugstore. How will you pay her back? I don't like that you play cards with those players. Is the *ganif* Manny Karp in your card club?"

* * *

Pinsky, my parents put a deposit on a two storey red-brick house near Cedarvale ravine. Father's mood was expansive, his eyes twinkled. Behind our house was a forest.

"See the nice ravine," Father said. "Reuben and Danny can play there. *Listen*; there are so many Jews here that Friday afternoon the sky gets misty—from chicken soup."

"Daddy, have you money for the house? Are you playing cards with Mr. Karp?"

"I have money," Father said. "D-Don't tell Bubba. We move in August." Danny, my brother, was five, and mother's stomach was the size of two huge watermelons.

If she bent over she might explode.

"Can I get a bike now," I asked.

"If I get you a bike, Bubba will be *suspicious*," Father said. "Be patient."

The first day Bubba arrived at the new house, I saw her faraway look. Was it because Father bought the house without her advice? Was she worried he had spent too much money and made a mistake? Was it because he had not paid back her $10,000? Auntie Leah and Bubba, my father boasted, were *always welcome*. He showed us our parents' room, the room Danny and I had; the baby's room, and Bubba's room that she shared with Auntie Leah. Father took us aside.

It's time to be alone, he whispered. They will come on weekends. This is the Fifties. We have to be modern like everyone else. I begged my parents to invite Marco. The next week he came for lunch. I told him we were moving up in the world and becoming modern. Father bought a new GE television with a twelve inch black-and-white screen—it cost over $500. The TV picked up CBLT and WGR and WBEN, from Buffalo. My parents went nuts for *I Love Lucy* with Lucy Ball and her Cuban bandleader husband, Ricky Ricardo. Feeling modern I showed Marco our house and driveway and demonstrated our television. Marco's family moved to Woodbridge. His father constructed an Italian castle, Marco explained, with parking for six trucks. Marco had a seventeen inch television with an aerial that sucked in TV stations across America. His father built a swimming pool. Marco invited me to watch *Howdy-Doody*.

"Are we rich now, Bubba?" I asked.

"Stupid questions, don't ask," Bubba said. "Where did your father find the money?"

* * *

Crystal, the dog walker, July 3, 2008

Crystal is back in emergency. Why come at 2 am? She is accompanied by a group worker and two burly policemen. She wants to talk to me; her voice is raspy, inaudible. An object is lodged in her throat—a large nail. Crystal can hardly whisper. We write back and forth on case history paper. She is anxious but not suicidal or severely depressed. *The irony is she wants to talk*. It is not about Jaffe-Jaffe. Something happened years ago in foster care; she wants to talk tonight, except she cannot talk. Why must you swallow such hurtful objects? Crystal is in pain. I call the GI service, to "scope" her, that is, do an endoscopy, a special medical intervention, to enter her esophagus, find, and remove the foreign object. The ER is not overjoyed with Crystal.

The gastroenterologist on call shows up furious with me.

* * *

Pinsky, these days everyone is into BlackBerries or iPhones—our analytic notes are going digital. But the summer we moved to the new house, I was learning to use ink. Bubba gave me a Parker 21. There were no busy streets in front of our house; the roads and sidewalks were quiet. Beside the houses were manicured lawns, hedges, and flowers. I had duties—to watch Danny. I took out the garbage Tuesdays and Fridays. I made my bed. I helped clean the kitchen. Danny and I explored the ravine behind our house, a jungle of bush and small ponds.

We had no friends. I had no bike. But we had a modern home and a new TV.

Where did Father find the money to buy all these things?

Frieda and Guttnik: a few months before June 2007

After our three daughters married and left home, after thirty-six years of marriage, Frieda said to pack my bags. Reuben, stay in one place and stop pacing. Be still. Pay attention for five minutes. I want a separation. I don't hate you. And then she told me about Karl, my old buddy from Euclid Avenue, the analyst, yes, they had had an affair for two years. Guttnik, for whom I felt compassion, had lost his beautiful wife Sabrina to cancer. Guttnik, that *ligner*, lied to me that he was impotent. Was it a ruse so he could get his *shmootzik* hot hands on Frieda?

164

What a schemer! This hit me like a truck. It killed me, Pinsky, and then Frieda told me she wasn't leaving me for Karl.

No. The affair was a symptom of a deeper conflict.

Honey, we are analysts. Let's analyze this.

We'll work on it. We have three beautiful married daughters.

Reuben, she told me, you're not listening. I am asking *you* to leave. I've been warning you that I would leave for years. She was fed up with my borderline clinic, my crazy on call schedule, being the perfect analyst for everyone.

And so why was she with my jogging partner?

The answer: Guttnik had time for her.

I was busy at work.

That was her official reason. How many meetings did you go to? How about junior staff you helped to write papers? How many analytic conferences do you attend? How about that crazy wife of Bayer's patient? She threatened your life. You can't even remember her name. Why supervise residents? Why see crazy patients and relatives of hospital staff? Why sacrifice yourself but not take care of your family and yourself?

Pinsky, this was why I came to you.

The return of the kalika, the cripple, Herbie Faust

Workers plastered and painted the windows and doorways of a large empty Cedarvale house beside us. Two weeks after we moved in, Danny and I saw Sammy Faust park his hardware van next door. He carried in boxes and waved to us with his free hand. Faggie Faust stepped out of the van with her little Toulouse-Lautrec in shorts. He wore braces and limped with two walking canes. "Herbie, it's good to see you," I said. Herbie's convalescent face was pallid and drawn. One leg was smaller than the other. Ruthie-Annie marched over to Danny and me and gave us a hateful stare. As pale as Herbie appeared,

Ruthie-Annie had flowered. Her hair bloomed into rosy curls; her breasts had budded. She focused her sour cherry eyes on me. She was in her gorgeous puberty, but seemed angry about it. Herbie hobbled with his walking canes to open their garden gate. Inside were fragrant peonies, roses, and day lilies that little Herbie sniffed and sketched.

"It's our *private* garden," Ruthie-Annie announced. "Not everyone is invited."

"You guys are welcome," Herbie said. He was happy to see us.

"Herbie, you got a bad limp," Danny said. "You go this way-that way, sideways."

Herbie wore special boots that had a metal rod from the heel to above the knee.

Danny stared at the boots. "Are you going to d-die, Herbie?"

"The polio only went up to my legs."

"Will you walk again?"

"I don't know," Herbie said. "I have to do exercises every day."

"Can we catch p-polio from you?" Danny asked.

"*Stupid!*" Ruthie-Annie said. "Herbie caught polio from Reuben."

Danny turned to Ruthie-Annie. "Reuben didn't give Herbie polio."

"Yes he did."

"No he didn't," Danny said. "Herbie gave it to himself."

Ruthie-Annie glared at us as if we were public enemy #1. I led Danny from the Fausts' garden. "Ruthie-Annie blames me for Herbie's polio. Talking does no good. You upset Ruthie-Annie. Now she will be angry at me all over again. She gets crazy angry, Danny."

"I d-don't want to be nice *like you*, Reuben."

Pinsky, I tried to be nice all the time since little Herbie got polio. I was getting more superstitious. Bubba warned us about

166

an *ahora*—an evil eye. Bubba pointed to Herbie—if you are not good, Reuben, you will end up a tiny *kalika*, a cripple.

Bubba lived in a demon and spirit world of past and future merged. And I was joining her.

Sam-Lee Yan, July 9, 2008

Sam-Lee Yan enters my office unsettled, dressed impeccably in a charcoal Armani suit, Berluti handmade leather shoes, a Zegna tie. He is sweating profusely. A bodyguard stands in the waiting room. The other bodyguard sits in a parked black Hummer on the street. Sam-Lee points to him through the window. "I have not slept … for days." He paces in my office and again checks my outside window. "I don't think this is such a good idea."

"What are you talking about?"

"Coming here and talking—it is not a good idea."

"What makes you think so?"

"*Look*," he points, "look who is outside."

I walk to my office window. I see Sam-Lee Yan's bodyguard in a black Hummer parked on the curb. A block away, a small silver foreign car pulls up where the driver can keep an eye on the Hummer and my office.

"See now?" Sam-Lee says.

"Who is watching you?" I ask.

"Who is in the silver car? I will tell you. I am followed. The arms deal went through—the Chinese found out. They do not like that. The Russians are not happy either. So now I am watched. The Serbian-Russian fellow is in hiding. The Iraqis are not happy. The Russians are not happy. The Chinese are not happy. The Iraqis are most unhappy. This unhappiness is not something you improve with antidepressants or psycho-analysis. I don't sleep well at night. Any noise, any move-ment, any slight change and I have terrible insomnia. This is a difficult business; it is an impossible profession being a

167

part-time arms dealer. You, as an analyst, appreciate this problem, Dr. Moses? This is an angry unhappiness. And all of these unhappy angry people know that I come to see my analyst, you, Dr. Reuben Moses. "

M chortles, points two fingers to his eyes, and offers a forlorn chuckle.

CHAPTER EIGHT

The end of latency—O. Pinsky, July 11, 2008

The unconscious does not know of its death, Freud tells us. M in his consciousness was struggling with life's meaning. Following Jewish tradition he believed he was named Reuben after his maternal great-grandmother, Reba, who died when his mother was thirteen. Bubba did not tell him the true source of his name for years. She felt concern for the Fausts' neglected children, M said. Twice a year M's parents, Bubba, and Auntie Leah joined Sammy and Faggie Faust for a city-wide meeting of those who had fled Poland. The group was the *Zaglember Landsmanschaft Society*, recalling the region where they had once lived.

At this meeting they shared stories of Poland. Yasha was not invited.

Yasha's story remained untold. M joked that Yasha's impassive brooding face reminded him of statues on Easter Island. I debated if M knew more of his enigmatic silent zaide but he deflected my questions at the time. M spoke of his delight visiting his three grandsons, Jason, Jordan, and Jeremy. He was stung that only Jeremy seemed to know him. In this analysis, he saw that he pushed Frieda and his children away by dint of hard work, driven by his ambition to help others. Being a grandparent offered him a chance to rework adulthood and childhood. M saw his ninety-three-year-old mother each

Friday when he took her shopping, had dinner, and delivered her to his daughters' families on Sunday. He spoke regularly with Frieda. Throughout our analysis he relished family time—his depressive symptoms faded—save for the abusive quality of his work with difficult patients, Blum, Crystal the dog walker, her prison partner Zeno, GC the Vietnam vet, and Sam-Lee Yan, to mention but a few. This was his oppressive Herculean labour, to cure suffering, a form of superego punishment for his powerful instinctual side—his sexuality and aggression. Now our analysis left M's latency and entered his adolescence. M's notes, diaries, drawings, recipes, and my written sessions expanded to three thick manila folders. At the end of each session I locked the folders in my filing cabinet.

While M's files were taking over my office space, his conflicts were taking over my mind.

* * *

My door—someone prowled outside my office—R. Moses.

170

M received a note from his building manager. Someone had been hanging around his office at night. The outside closed-circuit television camera showed a person, bent over, wearing a broad hat and trench coat, standing in front of his entrance. Was it his mother or the other intruder?

Two more of his beloved red rose bushes had been deflowered.

One evening, a few days later, a similar person was seen outside my office door.

PART THREE

A BORDERLINE ADOLESCENCE
JULY 2008–DECEMBER 2008*

> *"The eldest child bears the struggle of the refugee grandparents, the deracination from the primary culture, the relocation to host culture, the stigma of prejudice, fear and hate, the brunt of resettlement and neurosis."*
>
> (From Reverence to Rage: Failed Resolution of the Bubba Complex, R. Moses MD, *Analytic Journal*, Vol. 9, No. 1, p. 20.)

---

*By July 2008 M completed his first year of analysis. Because of the warm summer that July of 2008, M recalled his first summer at Jewish camp, *Camp Hello-Goodbye*. Jewish camp marked M's longest separation from his Bubba and family, the onset of puberty, and his initial foray into sexual desire and anxiety.

CHAPTER ONE

Camp Hello-Goodbye

When we moved to the new house Father told me he had saved enough money to send me for three weeks to Jewish camp. No more *plotzing* in heat with Bubba shrieking polio if I swallowed lake water. Finally we got rid of Bubba. At last! My mother's pregnancy depleted her energy. My father hired young girls to look after us. No one stayed more than a month. Danny and I exhausted them. In desperation Father called Bubba and Auntie Leah. They slept over and bossed us around as usual. We were back where we started from. Three blocks to the north were shuls, cheders, Zapinsky's fish store, Guttnik's grocery, Greenbaum's dairy and Lustig's bakery. The stores in Kensington Market shifted north to Eglinton Avenue like a tilted Monopoly board. Herbie Faust walked without a cane. He knew each flower. He sketched them as he hobbled. Ruthie-Annie stood guard. Manny J. Karp moved to the next block and Josh joined us. The Guttniks, Greenbaums, and Lustigs relocated their stores to Eglinton and bought homes in our area. Herbie's left leg remained smaller than his right. I saw bruises on Ruthie-Annie's shapely legs—was it the shock of Herbie's polio? I wondered if she hit herself.

Herbie said she still kept notes in her secret diary hidden in her pillow.

March 2007: Frieda gives me the ultimatum

Frieda was dead serious, Pinsky. In March 2007 she wanted me out of the home by June—three months flat. She was firm. How do you expect me to leave? Frieda, we were to be together for life. I bought us plots, side by side, in Beth Jerusalem cemetery. By June, empty and alone, I fell apart.

* * *

I had never seen a stomach so colossal. "Rivkah will have twins," Auntie Leah said. Bubba warned: *Triplets*. Bubba ruled the house again. She baked, cooked, and stuffed us with food. Bubba invited our neighbours, Herbie and Ruthie-Annie for dinner since their parents were busy. Late at night I heard the Fausts fighting next door. Herbie didn't play sports. He talked about flowers. Ruthie-Annie watched Herbie and her pets.

Danny whispered. Can I c-come to camp with you, Reuben? Sure, I said. I'll put you in my trunk. Danny believed me. Three days before camp, I went for a physical. Uncle Max's office was filled with sick patients. They wore bandages, coughed, had crutches, or were on so many drugs they leaned sideways. Uncle Max wore a starched white coat. He had a pencil moustache and marched ramrod straight like Alec Guinness in *The Bridge on the River Kwai*. On his walls were bayonets, grenades, and bullets from the war. "Reuben, what's bothering you?" To calm myself I stared at his bullets. I'm fine. "Fine is no answer," he said. "People have symptoms. What hurts?" Nothing hurts, I said. "Nothing hurts is not an answer. Something always hurts." My stomach hurts, I said. Uncle Max examined my stomach. He shook his head. He weighed me. He listened to my heart. Is it cancer? I asked. "Who is stuffing you like a *gans?*" Bubba d-does it, I said. She's got it in for me. Uncle Max wrote a prescription. *Rx = Get Exercise. Fresh air. No noshing*.

Two days before camp, Father brought bug spray, tincture of iodine, aspirin, Noxzema, bandages, and calamine lotion. Danny watched everything shoved into a trunk.

Bubba pushed in a winter parka. Reuben. Look, Danny said. There's no room. I'll put you in the trunk later, I said. Bubba threw in *kuchen* and *mandelbrodt*. My trunk grew like Mom's belly. Dad cinched it with a thick belt. The night before camp we couldn't sleep. Next morning Mom and Bubba *schlepped* Danny and me to the bus station at Bay and Dundas with kids from Timmins, Hamilton, St. Catharines, Niagara Falls, Sudbury, and Ottawa. Bubba stuffed food in bags so no one would die of starvation on the bus. In the Fifties most of us DP kids were fat enough to live six months without food. It was déjà vu *Exodus*. Families shoved, yelled, and moaned. *Reuben. Put me in a trunk. D-Don't leave me.* Bubba held Danny back. Reuben, why can't I go in the trunk?

"It was a joke, Danny. You can't leave and go to camp. You're not big enough."

Bubba pushed me forward in the line of children entering the bus. When will you write home? First I have to get off the bus, I said. Don't be *tzugeshvitzed*, Bubba said. If you need clothes, write. Watch out for *schwartzfliegen*. One smart aleck, pimple-faced Melvin Sax, shouted dire warnings about camp. We drove into a dark forest. Huge bugs flew up from the road. A dirt playground and a huddle of lopsided white cabins nestled in a semicircle beside a tattered Israeli flag. This was the bargain basement of camps where poor socialists dumped their kids. I was in cabin 5, along with Josh Karp, Herbie Faust, Ari Mazer, and Melvin Sax. Our senior counsellor was Ozzie Zapinsky—his uncle owned Zapinsky's fish store. Ozzie tried to settle us down. He told us bedtime stories about dinosaurs and antimatter.

Come to think of it, Pinsky, you look a bit like Ozzie, minus the hair.

Don't listen to Zapinsky, campers get tortured and die, Sax said. I found a top bunk. Sax, a *Galitzianer*, the camp *kvetch*, with premature acne vulgaris, sported the hairiest most enormous testicles and had the bunk beside me. He told terrible stories of rattlesnakes, fatal insect bites, and bottomless cesspools. The food was awful, campers got typhoid, and counsellors were morons. The director was a pervert. Three years straight Sax came to *kvetch*. Sax, if you hate it, why come back, I asked. There's nothing I like, Sax said, viciously picking a blackhead on his nose. I hate everything. So, why do your parents send you here? *They* need a holiday *from me*. Nightly counsellors recited bloody stories of massacres and Jewish martyrs. Herds of bigfoot lived behind cabin 14, SS troops and Nazi U-boats waited for us in the dark Muskoka night. We slept with baseball bats and slingshots under our blankets. We rehearsed pressure points and death holds. At night, under flashlights, we compared the size of our testicles: Sax's testicles won hands down. I felt homesick. Still, camp was not as bad as Sax predicted. No one died of food poisoning. I learned to swim, canoe, make campfires, climb rocks, shoot a bow and arrow, and play chess. Ozzie Zarpinski taught us about dinosaurs and Mendeleev's periodic table. He was a *Litvak*, a bookworm. Roxanne Greenbaum and Sabrina Lustig were bunkmates in cabin 14. Roxanne was my age from Toronto. Her dad, a DP from Hungary, ran the local dairy. We danced at socials. Guttnik, a senior and Mr. Cool with his wavy blond hair was seeing Sabrina Lustig, the most beautiful girl in camp.

Guttnik had his own transistor radio. He splashed on Old Spice before each camp social.

I was not a great dancer because of my constant erection. Roxanne Greenbaum already went through premature puberty at age nine and had big breasts and curly auburn hair like Brillo pads. We kissed under pine trees. Electricity went up my spine. My penis shot sparks and stuck out like a car door. I folded it into my side pocket. All the guys in my cabin were experienced masturbators, Jewish neurotics. Pinsky—did I tell you Ruthie-Annie was at the same camp? Ruthie had grown lovelier. My cabin lusted after her. Sax made fun of Herbie.

Ruthie-Annie kicked him in his testicles. I don't mean a tap either.

I stayed close to Roxanne Greenbaum, for protection; even though I wasn't sure I liked her.

The last day of camp we had a bonfire and held hands. Roxanne bent over me with her fabulous boobs and russet hair. To tell the truth, Pinsky, I had a love-hate relationship with boobs. Some days I wanted them around me; other days I wanted to be in the wild blue yonder—nipple-free. That last night we had a farewell banquet. Everybody cried.

I kissed Roxanne. I felt her tongue at the back of my throat. I almost choked to death.

July 2008: Pinsky's question

Pinsky sits forward in his chair and asks me this dumb question. "Are you sure you went to Camp Hello-Goodbye, not some other camp?"

Camp Hello-Goodbye—R. Moses

"You think I am making this all up, Pinsky?"

"Herbie Faust, Ari Mazer, Josh Karp, and Mel Sax, they were all in cabin 5 with you?"

"Yes, that was the way it was."

Pinsky has this perplexed look on his face. "And Sabrina Lustig was at your camp?"

"Yes, why do you ask?"

"And you said Ozzie Zapinsky was your senior counsellor?"

"Yes—that's what I remember. Is there something wrong?"

CHAPTER TWO

Blum confesses: August 2008

In August I received a notice from the college that Blum had sent a third official complaint about my case management. In the first she accused me of incorrectly diagnosing her medical condition; in the second letter she wrote that she should not be receiving an antidepressant because of *anorgasmia*.* Against my advice she took more oestrogen to feel normal. In her third letter she added the antidepressant wreaked havoc with her bowels. My first reaction was that I did not want her to step into my office. I worked hard to help her. I felt exploited. Now I wanted out.

Exploited was how I felt with my wife, with my colleague Guttnik, with my patients, with my Bubba. All I do is *repeat life*—you tell me that, Pinsky. *We repeat life*. Isn't that brilliant?

And yet there is a modest wisdom to this interpretation— our lives are but a repetition. Everything we do is repetition, the way we walk, the way we talk, the way we love—if we see our repetition we understand ourselves. I know you are trying to tell me that, aren't you?

---

*Anorgasmia: an inability to achieve orgasm. This is not uncommonly seen in women (and men) taking antidepressants, particularly selective serotonin reuptake inhibitors. —*O. Pinsky*.

181

Is that why I lose and forget names, Pinsky? Is it because I was lost and forgotten?

* * *

I was not going to lose my temper with Blum. I left the college letters on my desk—she could see them. I said nothing. Blum lay on the couch. She complained about my suit, my dark tie, my déclassé hush puppy shoes. She didn't like the colour of my office, my clothes, she blamed me for her car vandalism, and I sensed she was behind all my problems. Her son Ivan called me. She was not caring for herself and we were both fed up with her. I had Ivan come to my office.

Blum the mother and Ivan the son entered the office. I sat in the middle.

My mother's daily weather report: August 7, 2008

Reuben, Frieda calls me. How is it you two don't make up? Frieda came over with little Jonah—he is adorable—the other two as well. That lady phones me—she says the most awful things. How do people get so angry with you? I hear Herbie Faust is in a wheelchair at Zion Rest Home. He has that fagele disease. Reuben, this August is too hot to jog, so please walk.

Pinsky's apology: August 8, 2008

All right, I am sorry. I am sorry. What can I say? *I made a mistake; I forgot, Dr. Moses.* You recall from previous sessions you said you knew my face from somewhere—well, you were right. You did know me. I had not remembered where we had met—it was foolish of me—I was unsure until you told me about camp days. You see, I saw you in my Uncle Gershon's fish store, Gershon Zapinsky. You went there with your Bubba and your neighbours—Herbie and Ruthie-Annie.

It was a dim memory—maybe sixty years ago. It's coming back. Ruthie-Annie was the cute one with the curly red hair and braces. I remember you from camp—I was your senior counsellor—Ozzie Zapinsky, before my father, Gershon's partner, changed our name to Pinsky. I taught campers about the periodic table, I remember. Sax, that pimply *Galitzianer* shyster with dinosaur testicles; he hated camp and insulted little Herbie—he became a multi-multimillionaire from waste disposal. I remember Guttnik from camp. I am sorry.

* * *

"So my memory is better than yours."

"In this case, yes."

"You went to my school, Pinsky. You were friends with Guttnik, right?"

"I knew Guttnik, yes."

"I had mixed feeling to Karl. He was too good-looking and too smart for his own good."

"He was two years behind me. He dated Sabrina Lustig, the prom queen."

"*Sabrina Lustig* from cabin 14 at camp—he was already dating her. I hated him for that."

"Well, you have some hate to talk about."

"I am pissed as hell with you, Pinsky. You don't listen. You don't remember."

"I am listening as best I can."

"Maybe your best is not good enough for me."

"Our time is almost up for the session today. One thing—there has been someone snooping around my office. My surveillance cameras have picked up images. Nothing definite—it seems to be a person wearing a hat and trench coat. You've told me about an old harassment case—could it be that person? Do you have any thoughts about that?"

"Nothing."

"Surely you must have thoughts."

"I don't remember like I used to either. Ageing? I forget what I ate for dinner last week. You don't remember so shit-hot yourself, Pinsky. Or should I call you Zapinsky?"

"My father disliked his last name; he shortened to Pinsky. Please refer to me as Pinsky."

"What the fuck is the difference between Pinsky and Zapinsky? You wanted to anglicize?"

"I had nothing to do with it. It was for business."

"What do you mean business?—Pinsky or Zapinsky? You weren't joining some golf club?"

"It was for the fish store. Pinsky's pickerel, perch, Pacific cod, Pacific salmon, pompano, and pike. We pickled and bottled fish. *Pinsky's Pickled Herring* was a big seller."

"*Pinsky's Pickled Herring*—that's rich."

"Hardly any fish begins with Z, you see? It was strictly for business. *Seriously*."

CHAPTER THREE

Father's lament

When I returned from camp I saw Mother's weary bloodshot eyes and a new brother in his blue sleeper in my crib from Euclid Avenue. "*Don't breathe loud. Benji needs rest.*" Instead of triplets, she had an eleven pound boy who slept like an unstable landmine. Any movement, any vibration, he exploded. Each night Father came home exhausted, bent over, eating late with Mother, playing rummy to unwind. Mother had no energy. She ate little. She slept poorly. She was lifeless. I think she was depressed post-partum. Uncle Max ordered her sitz baths and bed rest. To keep her energy up she drank *Lucozade*, a fortified tonic. Father was preoccupied with debt. Since Hurricane Hazel, as Bubba warned, business went south. Father had many expenses—the house, Danny's Jewish school, Jewish camp, and Beth Jerusalem, the local shul. Nightly he paced in the kitchen. Danny and I listened to his lament from upstairs.

Crystal the dog walker: August 11, 2008

Crystal finds out that I am on call and at 2 am she appears. She tells everyone I am her doctor. Is she the toilet mouth calling my mother or leaving shit on my car? From prison Zeno blames me for her swallowing foreign bodies, can you believe?

My buddies, the GI boys "scope" Crystal and pull out spare change, a ball point pen, and paper clips. She talks about foster home years—she never told a soul—abused as a kid—forced intercourse and oral sex galore. Again and again she submitted to these horrid men—she dissociated from the abuse but her body kept a tally of what went on. She punishes her throat for what she had to swallow. Maybe now, Pinsky, she won't swallow and hurt herself with the secret out? But she has another fear. Crystal tells me that whenever she walks Jaffe-Jaffe she is followed.

Father's lament

I'm not going to let Bella, your Bubba, that balabusta, run my life. Ten thousand—I will pay her. Should I expand like Faust? What about shoplifters and fires? Who the hell is stealing my expensive perfume?—I have to call a private investigator. It will cost me a fortune.

No one knew how to work the new GE TV. Our set made noises and the picture went haywire. Mr. Watanabe, the Japanese TV repairman, instructed us to set the volume, contrast, horizontal and vertical hold buttons. He extracted tubes from the back. Never touch the back, Mr. Watanabe said. What about that *b-black thing* at the back? Danny asked. Never touch that *black thing*. It has 500 volts of electricity. Mr. Watanabe came monthly—as wonderful as the GE TV was, something went snafu. Tiny capacitors burned, the picture tube died, knobs stopped working and gave shocks. Never touch the knob when it gives you an electric shock. Never touch the back of the TV set. There is voltage there to kill a horse, Watanabe said. Special TV warnings came on each day about bomb attacks. *Civil Defense Alert. Do not adjust your television set.* We were to go into the cellar during an enemy attack and stay until the fallout cleared. Nightly Captain Peacock came down from the ceiling. I asked if Russia would drop the

H-bomb. *Yes*, Captain Peacock said. I made close friends with Ari Mazer the shul caterer's son. Mazer, whose refugee family escaped with their lives from Austria before the war, lived in a semi-detached hovel in downtown where his dad worked day and night as a hotel cook. Mazer opened a deli and restaurant, became the shul caterer, divorced his first wife, and moved to Forest Hill. Lenny Loeb lived across the road. His dad, Noah, the shul undertaker, wore a perpetual black suit. Three years passed. I was eleven. Benji was three—Bubba somehow toilet-trained him at one year old. I was promoted to Benji's official full-time babysitter. As restless as Danny and I were, Benji was more restless with no fear. Benji climbed, ran, slid down-stairs, and hardly slept. He wandered to my bed before six. *Woo-bin? Wake up*. From the start with Benji, everything was mixed up. Dessert started a meal. Ice cream was an appetizer. *Passghetti* was his staple. *Strollybears* were his fruit. Benji had ebony eyes and blue-black hair. In summer, his skin tanned brown. A *Schwarzekind*, Bubba said. Like reveille he woke early. *Woo-bin*, I want food. The birds are asleep, I said. *Woo-bin*, I want French toast. For French toast you go to France, I said. Benji never stayed still. I had to watch him all day. He was very proud of his shit. He not only shit in the toilet, but outside the house in our neighbour's garage, all over the place. Sometimes he hid at our neighbour's house, the Fausts'. During the summer my friends Karl Guttnik, Ari Mazer, Josh Karp, and Lenny Loeb had a pickup game at the baseball dia-mond. Lenny and Ari asked me to hit flies. Karl had a Louis-ville Slugger. You touched the ball and it flew. I threw the ball in the air with one hand, pulling the bat back, and drove the ball deep to centre field. Benji, I'm hitting, I said, stay still. He wanted to play with me. Sit still. I threw the ball up high and gripped the bat. There was an odd sound as if the ball was softer. Lenny yelled. I dropped the bat. My brother stood still; his lips spread apart, eyes unfocused. Blood spurted over his forehead. I took off my shirt and pressed it to his head,

187

running with him along the fields. Blood soaked my shirt. A cop car sped us to the children's hospital. Between sobs I told an emergency nurse my story. I phoned home. Bubba answered. Benji had an accident, I said.

"Where are you? The hospital—*Gevalt!* Don't leave. I will call Uncle Max."

The doctors put bandages on his head. Did my brother speak? Did he complain of pain? Was he unconscious? Did he vomit? Doctors checked his reflexes. They looked into his eyes. Pinsky, it was the worst day of my life. I feared his eyes might close forever. The doctors stitched up his head—more X-rays. Benji stayed in hospital two days. When he came home Bubba cradled Benji. *Poo-Poo-Poo.* How can a big brother hit a little brother in the head with a bat?

Ruthie-Annie visited Benji. She read him stories and brought him treats. I hadn't meant to hit Benji. "You never look after your little brother," Ruthie-Annie said.

To this day, I worry I ruined his mind forever.

Benji—R. Moses

CHAPTER FOUR

Insomnia

For a month I woke in the middle of the night, my nerves shot, to check if Benji was alive. After several sleepless nights Father took me to see Koffman. We sat in his hospital examining room while the great white one checked my cranial nerves, my muscle tone, asked me to walk a straight line, pounded me with a reflex hammer, looked into my eyes, asked me to reach his index finger on his right hand and touch my nose in quick succession. "You say Reuben was fine until three weeks ago?" Yes, Dr. Koffman. "No tics, no stutter, sleep was good?" Koffman waved the residents closer. Yes, Dr. Koffman. "His obsessions were not noticeable? He had no tremor?" We didn't put him on the pills. "He was fine off medication?" Exactly. "Then if his symptoms resolved—more or less," Koffman said, "what happened that his symptoms returned. Did he suffer a head injury?"

"Yes," my father said. "He hit his brother in the head with a baseball bat."

* * *

When I had three daughters I lay awake at night, perturbed that they might asphyxiate during sleep. I checked once or twice nightly. I woke Frieda—a light sleeper because of her own childhood demons. It wasn't sex—I mean it was, but it was soothing I needed. Frieda got it—she knew my analysis with Lippman had given me balance, but I was far from stable. Lippman did not go far enough back to my primal anxiety. I worry about Jason, Jonah, and Jeremy. On call for the hospital, I am certain calamity will occur. Pinsky, I don't want to exhaust you with how I talk patients down from jumping off balconies, shooting themselves, leaping into subway trains, or committing murder.

Here's my point. Why did no one let me be the little savage I wanted to be for a few years, running free and wild, with a load of crap in my diapers, enjoying myself, peeing, farting, shitting, smearing, yelling, and whatever?

Why did I have to be such a precocious decent civilized *mensch?* Why did I grow my special sense to pick up other people's worries before they put them into words? Why am I in the firing lines with my fucking empathy? This started with cod liver oil and toilet training—to know exactly what Bubba wanted. I was her loyal subject and swore allegiance *before I knew myself.*

* * *

Ivan Blum, my patient's son, wears a dark suit and tie and is soft-spoken; he is in his early forties, clean-shaven, a nice-looking fellow, who sits opposite his mother, the toilet czarina. She is under the weather weighing what her son says and what I will do with it. "Dr. Moses, I have heard about you from my mother. She is disappointed with her treatment; she tells me you frustrate her. I ask her if she can say precisely what is so unsettling in her analytic work, because, as you know, she has complained to Dr. Bayer, your hospital chief, and sent off some nasty complaint letters to your college. Mom, as you probably know, is a perfectionist, hard to satisfy."

Oh? Really, she is hard to satisfy, I say. Is that so?

Ivan goes on. I can't tell you how many times she has sent food back in restaurants, fired a hairdresser, walked out of a meeting, dismissed an interior decorator, or turned her back on suppliers. Mom is sensitive and critical. You are not the only one who hears her snarl. She blows up at me too. She is a great entrepreneur with an eye for new ventures. But when it comes to being with people, Mom has her hands full. She can't relax. It is impossible for her to take holidays. She is always on the go. Mom, I tell her, you don't have to work as hard. Let me help—she refuses. *SHE RELIES ON NO ONE*. Dr. Moses, I am independently wealthy. Mother tells you I live with her—a lie. I visit her daily. She is alone. My wife and I have her come to our house during weekends. She can't resist telling us or the children what to do. If it wasn't for me checking on her, apart from her accountant of many years—whom she has fired as many times—she would be truly alone. Her accountant won't abandon her because as we all know deep down, Mom needs company. She talks about her forty-five-year-old lover. He refuses to live with her. *No one lives with her*.

Why am I in analysis? I can give you one guess.

* * *

August 19, 2008

Pinsky, we are going nowhere; this is a rehashing of Blum's life with the added irony that Ivan is seeing my ex, Frieda. Up to now, Blum, the mother, is silent. Then Ivan turns to his mother, taps her lightly on the shoulder. Mom, I think the analytic work is actually helping you out. Blum scowls at both of us, huffs, but says nothing for the moment. "Let me finish," Ivan goes on. "You say how upset you are with Dr. Moses like everyone you have been with in life, but there is a change, Mom. You talk about feelings. You see life as empty. Without your complaints, what do you have? Mom, I want you to continue to see Dr. Moses."

Blum storms from my office. Ivan comes to me to shake my hand. "Thank you, doctor, *thank you*, you have gone farther than anyone." (I feel like Franklin at the North Pole.) "You are all she has. You are everything."

I am everything and nothing. I stare at Ivan's nose, a prominent nose, but not as big as mine.

My mother's daily weather report: September 3, 2008

You work too hard like your poor father. Work KILLED him. It was no mistake I went to Doctor Pinsky … he should talk sense to you. You never take holidays. Who takes care of you? Patients are not family. Reuben—that person has phoned again—she won't leave her name. She is very nasty. Please call me. And call Frieda. Reuben, remember, it is still too hot to jog.

The Camp Hello-Goodbye reunion: circa 1970

Pinsky, it was around 1970, we had a camp reunion. My old camp buddies came to Shopsy's deli on Spadina, Karp, Mazer, Guttnik, Sabrina, Roxanne, Herbie, and Ruthie-Annie. We talked of old times. Roxanne Greenbaum and I had a fling in grade 9. Melvin Sax showed up. He had nothing good to say about camp. Herbie and Ruthie-Annie sat by themselves. By this time beautiful Sabrina was engaged to Karl Guttnik. Ruthie-Annie was marrying some doctor or dentist whose name I can't recall. She seemed happier though.

CHAPTER FIVE

Father's addictions

My father was addicted to cards and nicotine. In his spare time he chain-smoked cigarettes at a gaming club. Cards relax me, Father said. Cards take my mind off work. Mother, the most taciturn and soft-spoken in our home, for once let loose. "I hate Karp, that low life, that scumbag, that criminal bookkeeper with Jewish-Italian gangs. I hate that he is a member of your club. How can a *Zaglember* from a concentration camp, no less, be such a *trombenik*. Stay away from him. He carried a gun when he lived on Euclid. He is a rotten apple."

First thing Father did when he came home was to pull out a purple bag where he kept his Crown Royal and pour a half-tumbler. Father debated opening more stores like Faust—you increase volume to turn profit, he told me—but there was risk in new locations. Faust continued to have problems with theft and store fires. In those years father was a blur, rising early, managing family expenses, staying late at his drugstore, fretting about his profit-line, muttering over his money worries to himself, and in spare moments, playing cards with Karp and drinking Crown Royal. Mother was exhausted. She could not work each day. When father had his head down at the dispensary and mother was home, shoplifters had a field day.

Father's lament

Imagine, Reuben, if I had two stores—what d-do I do with shoplifting and in-store theft or a fire? It would be twice as bad. If I had a third store—d-do the math. Danny, Reuben, you know an interesting fact? Since we moved away from Bubba Bella, she spends more time here. And Mom is exhausted. How about a house-helper? A young woman, to help, you know, a maid.

Instead of a maid, Father brought Malka, a female spaniel, fun-loving and high-strung. Danny was overjoyed. Captain Peacock and I were in heaven. Even Herbie and Ruthie-Annie seemed pleased. Father, as usual, made a snap decision: a customer offered him the dog, and what did Mother do? She locked Malka in the basement. At night poor Malka moaned. We wanted Malka to sleep with us. Mother said a dog was not a person. You treated a dog differently. Malka ran off into the ravine after rabbits or squirrels and made a mess in the house. We searched for Malka and brought her home. I worried she would get hit by a car. We had Malka six months. One day when Danny and I came home from school, Mother said Malka ran away. We put notices in the paper.

Lost cocker spaniel—sandy coloured. Answers to Malka

We searched the streets but came up empty-handed. When I was fifteen, Benji confided to Danny and me that Malka had not run away. Mother and Bubba had sworn him to secrecy. The truth was that Mother, who was exhausted, called a farmer to take Malka to his farm. She was overwhelmed by Benji, making meals, washing, cleaning, and cooking. Pinsky, if Bubba said never lie and Bubba and mother lied to us, how could we trust them? After Benji told me the truth, I felt furious with Bubba and Mother and closer to Father. Years later, at father's *shiva*, the story changed. It was Mother and Bubba who called the farmer but it was not their idea.*

The true story

Faggie Faust protested that Malka wailed nightly. Faggie couldn't sleep. Ruthie-Annie loathed wailing—the dog reminded her of Herbie crying with polio. Faggie complained to my mother. Ruthie-Annie barked at Malka to be quiet. Malka barked back. Ruthie-Annie tapped Malka on the nose. Malka decided to bite Ruthie-Annie's cheek. Ten stitches later Malka left our home forever.

Ruthie-Annie hated all dogs after that.

* * *

Sam-Lee Yan: September 10, 2008

My insomniac patient Sam-Lee Yan, aka Samuel Leopold Yanovsky, considered moving back to Russia, perhaps Vladivostok, or Tel Aviv, or Miami since in these cities he has contacts where he can feel secure. "Toronto the Good," by contrast, is too democratic, too open, and too honest, which is fine for the general populace, but in his business of Iraqi construction and an arms deal that has gone sour, it means that he feels unsafe. There is an advantage to hiding in shit when you are shit yourself, when everything is shit. Here, in Toronto, it is clean and smells good and the Chinese and Iraqis and Russkies can sniff me out. "Luka received a threat—he warns me not to

---

*Malka, M's adored dog, was never forgotten. When M bought Jaffe-Jaffe, she became a replacement for his lost pet. Jaffe-Jaffe appeared to share the same sensitive unruly nature as Malka. Fidel, his previous pet, despite his name had been a placid conservative dog.

see you because they may target me: they know you, Dr. Moses. I haven't told you the whole story but they don't know that. I need to talk but maybe I should go to Miami?"

Miami was where Bubba took her winter holidays. She resided at the Di Lido on Collins Avenue. Sam-Lee had properties in Key Biscayne, Bal Harbor, and Coral Gables—he invited me to stay. The Russkies, Chinese, Iraqis had grown more unhappy with him and possibly with me, his analyst. Maybe we should both take off, he tells me.

I feel too much heat here in Toronto.

Take your dog, come with me; you can swim in my pools or jog at a park beside the ocean.

Pinsky, I think it over. I think of swimming in the ocean and reclining on a lounge chair in the sun. I think of the swaying palm trees and closing my eyes and finally relaxing. I think Jaffe-Jaffe would enjoy the holiday. But I say no.

CHAPTER SIX

Medical files: September 17, 2008

A week later, in mid-September, Ivan arrived with a pile of medical files—reports from Blum's past family doctors (she fired them all). That evening after my patients I read the files. Ivan left a summary detailing his mother's treatments. She never talked about her past medical issues—big-time denial. She complained about bowel and cardiac problems, which I attributed to her hypochondriac nature and the fact that she had to attack her former doctors.

Ivan wrote me that Blum's father ran a hat factory in a border town between Germany and Poland. Her parents fled for England at the outbreak of the war. Blum was born in London. Her father returned to what was left of the border town between Germany and Poland at the war's end to check on his factory and search for his lost brothers. He was shot and murdered. His entire family was killed, Ivan told me. Blum had difficulty sleeping because of pain. Ivan noticed that she had left food on her plate—something she did not usually do. I looked through the specialist reports.

Twenty years earlier Blum had cancer.

* * *

I take Jaffe-Jaffe to the park. Jeremy loves the sandbox—he gets sand in his hands, his hair, and his shoes. Jaffe-Jaffe digs a hole beside us. We make sandcastles; I get on my hands and knees: it is pure pleasure, digging, swirling sand through my fingers.

Jaffe-Jaffe appears to be enjoying herself but then she starts to bark and tremble.

I am not sure what has come over her.

Don't worry Jaffe-Jaffe. Everything is OK.

Jaffe-Jaffe continues to strain on her leash. She is barking at something I neither hear nor see. Crystal has told me that Jaffe-Jaffe has these sudden changes of mood. I look around and Jeremy begins to cry.

Psychoanalyst attacked at meeting—Boston Globe, September 18, 2008

Speaking in Boston at a conference on migration and child-care, Dr. Reuben Moses, an expert on grand-parenting, was physically attacked by a furious audience member. The woman, later identified as a senior occupational therapist, argued that Dr. Moses was hate-mongering. Dr. Moses laughingly stated that he was exploring the nature of human attachment and refuted her accusations as "wild and uninformed" on *The Bubba Complex*. A mob of angry women protested against Dr. Moses' findings. Across Europe and North America groups have formed, Bubba Bunds, largely composed of women who view The Bubba Complex as an inquisition against older women.

M proudly reads me this press clipping during a session. He breaks into peals of laughter—it is the utter ridiculousness of audience response—how did these people not see the truth? Why do they continue to misunderstand him? He passes me the clipping. He seems pleased with notoriety.

I question M. Have you an unconscious need to make women angry? I tell him I have seen protests in front of Mount Zion Hospital.

* * *

September 19, 2008

Sam-Lee Yan debates whether he should go to Miami. If he wasn't such a gangster I would ask him to take my mother with him. My mother could see her old friends. Instead, I refer Sam-Lee to Karl Guttnik, for severe insomnia. Psychotherapy has been useful for Sam-Lee. Now he asks for stronger meds to help him relax, close his eyes, and get to sleep.

Nothing I prescribe touches Sam-Lee. Guttnik gives him 2000 milligrams of chloral hydrate—an ancient hypnotic—nobody prescribes it. Specialists refuse to offer the drug—it can be dangerous. Guttnik boasts that he has solved Sam-Lee's insomnia. The chloral hydrate works.

Listen, Pinsky, I have nothing against Guttnik and his narcissistic drug rap.

Guttnik trained as an analyst but he threw out his couch and took the easy way out—drugs. Sure, sometimes we need a drug. But you see what happens? *Patients are all on drugs*—not just one, but two or three or four. And, tell me, for what goddamn reason?—a touch of anxiety or depression? I am not talking severe anxiety or clinical depression. Who doesn't have worries or fears or sadness? Who doesn't have difficulty concentrating or finishing assignments? Should I put a patient on Ritalin or Prozac just because they have a work conflict or trouble concentrating? Look at the studies—drugs don't make a hell of a difference. Feelings are part of life—you don't give patients drugs to numb and anesthetize, to remove emotional experience, do you? Twenty or thirty years ago if you had a problem, you went to an analyst. You talked. You associated.

You lay down on a couch. You talked about your problems; you analyzed your dreams and feelings.

You went back to childhood. You had time to reflect in sessions. You figured it out.

Pinsky, you must see the same thing at St. Luke's—how patient are your patients? Do people carefully review their life to see how they got to where they are? People are not interested in the past, in sorting out their distress. They live in this bubble called the present. They want the *now*.

These days who has time? Who lies down on a goddamn couch? People are busy with smart phones, video games, computer tablets—they take *medication tablets* for a quick fix. They use microwave ovens to cook their meals and gorge themselves on fast-food crap. They get fat and suffer from diabetes and cholesterol problems and high blood pressure. They drink Red Bull, pop uppers and stimulants to cut down sleep. They take downers. Drug companies are filthy rich. Doctors line up patients to fill out anxiety or depression scales or do online surveys. Who talks? Who reads? Who writes letters? Everybody is running around, multitasking, sleeping less, dreaming less, thinking less, mind-less. This world is going to hell and no one cares. Pinsky, here's the scoop. There is no goddamn short cut. You can't turn away from problems. There is no quick fix. Bubba picked out her chicken at Kensington Market, plucked off the feathers, and made chicken soup; she bought carp and pickerel and salmon, seasoned and chopped them up and made *gefilte fish*; she bottled plums and marinated herring and pickled tomatoes; she baked her *mon* cookies, strudel, *blintzes*, and borscht. I helped her in the kitchen. Everything took time.

Life is a kitchen.

CHAPTER SEVEN

The German maid

"The young are protected from external danger by the Bubba. When past narratives of physical and psychic trauma are revealed, the child's fragile ego is overwhelmed ..."

R. Moses.

Ursula slept in a tiny basement room with her postcards, pictures, alarm clock, and teddy bear beside her cot. She arrived in October. Why can't she talk? Danny asked. Is she dumb? No, I answered. Danny's brown eyes dilated. Mommy needed help with the house, Ursula's not from here. *Shtill, Shveik*, Bubba whispered. She's a German. She has blood on her hands. A German—what's wrong with N-Nursula's hands? Danny stammered as he rubbed his forehead. His stammer came out when he was tense. Germans killed Jews. Bubba made a fist. *"Murderers! They killed my family."* Bubba's words were sharp. "Your mother needed a *dienst*, a maid. You are seven. Reuben is eleven," Bubba said. "You are big enough to know from truth."

Father wanted Mother in the store to keep an eye on his help. It was too exhausting for her to work each day, to come home, to do laundry, cooking and cleaning, and care for us. Bubba tucked us gently into bed and told us Little Red Riding Hood stories. Danny dreamed of wolves in the ravine that came to eat him. I told Danny that Captain Peacock protected us.

After Bubba's talk about Germans who murdered her family, Danny was scared that the German maid would kill us. Who talked about the black-and-white pictures of our families in Europe? Bubba spoke about *Bendin*, a town in Poland, and the *Zaglember Society*.

Finally my mother admitted she had lost relatives in the war. "Mom, what was it like growing up? Was there a brother in your family?" Don't ask me questions. "Why can't I ask questions?" Reuben, it upsets me. "If I don't ask questions, how will I know anything?"

When I was eleven Ursula came and we started to ask more questions.

* * *

In the Fifties young *frauleins* arrived from war-torn Germany to work. Canadians gave them room, food, money, uniforms, and they watched over their children. Our Cedarvale Street had many German maids—the Fausts, the Guttniks, the Loebs hired German maids. They had coffee with strudel in our kitchen, and talked of old times. Yiddish was close to German. I could understand some of what they said. It was as if we were cousins, related somehow. Did Germans kill Jews? Danny asked. Not all Germans, I said, just bad Germans. How was a child to know good from bad? On TV, they showed war movies. Senator McCarthy searched for communists. Russians were bad. Americans were good. Danny asked questions. Is Superman good? "Yes." Howdy D-Doody—he's good? Yes. Reuben, what is a Cold War? C-Can it come to Canada?

* * *

That year our father bought a new seventeen-inch General Electric black-and-white TV. You couldn't pull Danny away.

202

He wore out the sofa. He ate Cheerios staring at test patterns, civil defense warnings, and profiles of Indians with Benji. Bubba said that watching TV we would all go blind. Benji was too young to understand but Danny said he was looking for the truth. Danny watched Walter Cronkite on CBS TV. Reuben, does Cronkite tell the truth? Was Hitler b-bad? Reuben, why d-did Hitler kill so many Jews?

Like rain it came. A drop fell here, another fell there.

Bubba told us Germans killed Jews. Then Mother said we lost relatives during the war. We saw TV with Walter Cronkite talking of WWII. We saw pictures of Adolph Eichmann on trial in Jerusalem for the murder of European Jews.

At cheder, which I had just begun, a teacher spoke of the concentration camps.

Why hadn't anyone told us?

* * *

Uncle Max had been a doctor during the war. After three shots of Scotch, Danny got him talking one night. What was war like? Danny asked. Don't ask. Was it hot during the war? Danny's lower lip dropped. In summer it was hot. *Hot*. Don't ask. Was it c-cold? Cold? Uncle Max said. Don't ask. Will the C-Cold War come to Canada? *Freg mir nisht* with questions, Uncle Max said. D-Did you kill Germans? Danny's eyes darkened. No, Uncle Max said. A doctor doesn't kill people.

You kill germs, Danny said.

Germs are not the same as Germans, Uncle Max said. This was big news to Danny.

Why d-didn't anyone tell us about Germans? Is N-Nursula bad? Danny rubbed his forehead. Stop calling her Nursula, I said. Her name is Ursula. Uncle Max—are the Russians good? Go ask the Russians, Uncle Max said. Friends, enemies—our universe split into two, into a before and after. We were blind. Then our eyes opened. Then it hurt to see the light.

I asked Mother about Yasha. *Please*, don't talk anymore.

I stared at the faded black-and-white family photos in Latvia, in Russia, in Zaglembie and Bendin, Poland. When Yasha came, he rolled up his sleeves, to clean furniture.

On his left forearm was a blue-black tattoo. I started joining up the blue-black dots, Yasha had a tattoo, Sammy Faust had a tattoo, Karl Guttnik's dad had a tattoo. Leo Rosen the butcher had a tattoo; Zlotnik the barber had a tattoo. Karp, the *ganif*, had a tattoo.

* * *

Mother ordered Ursula to tidy up, iron clothes, carry out errands, or to help the Fausts next door. Mother was inspector-general. Even though she was exhausted with us, to Ursula her soft voice became harsh. "Stop ironing, Ursula. Take Danny and Reuben shopping to Eglinton. Ursula! My list—can you read it?" Ursula found her glasses. How pretty she was! Blonde hair and Prussian-blue eyes sparkled over ruddy cheeks as if she had been in a winter wind. She wore a white uniform that accented her slim waist and shapely bosom. Sometimes she helped out and babysat little Herbie and Ruthie-Annie next door. I couldn't take my eyes off her. Ursula smiled, her head cocked bird-like, to one side. When Mother was unsure, she spoke Yiddish. Ursula spoke German.

Ursula learned faster than all of us.

* * *

The wolves left. They were replaced by alligators that lived in the basement. Danny said Ursula let them loose and they slithered upstairs. Danny turned on the light. "They almost ate me last night." Look. Nothing is there, I said. You can't see them in the light. N-Nursula has knives too. She looks pretty but she kills people, Danny said. Ursula is from Germany. Bubba says Germans have blood on their hands. We crept downstairs.

Father's car was gone. I turned on the kitchen light; I saw the clock, the melted Menorah candles. Ten o'clock, Danny. Dad's closing the drugstore. Danny rubbed his nose on his pyjama sleeve. So late? It's before Christmas. Look, it's snowing, I said. Danny squinted at the falling snow. First it snows then Cold War comes.

Danny's restless feet scampered over the kitchen floor.

"Where are you going?"

"To see N-Nursula." He ran to her cold small room. A single light was on. Ursula held a letter, her back to us. She wore a sweater over her uniform in the draughty room. A weak scent of perfume hung in the air. Ursula opened a box and sneezed.

"*Gesundheit!*" I said.

"You surprised me!" Ursula blew her nose. "Come in."

Pinsky, she had been with us four months and spoke perfect English. Ursula's blue eyes moistened. "A present. See." In a box was a picture of her mother, father, baby brother, and *Oma*, an elderly woman with grey hair and twinkling eyes. "*Oma* sang me lullabies before bed." Ursula sang us a German lullaby. Her eyes moistened. "*Oma* died last year." There were German letters and chocolates. "Here." She offered us her chocolates. We sat on her cot, munched chocolates, and waited as she stroked her teddy bear and read letters. "It is nice you visit me." She folded a letter and looked away.

"Are you crying?" Danny asked.

"I write home that I am fine. I miss *Oma*."

Ursula reached for us. I felt her rough wool sweater and cold hands. She kissed Danny's cheek. She kissed my cheek. She held us tight. She trembled and sighed. Her breasts lay against me. A wave of desire rose through my body. "Next week is Christmas. They sent me perfume." She sprayed a cloud of sweet perfume into the air.

"You killed Jews," Danny said, pushing her away.

"No." Ursula kissed us again. She kissed my cheek. I ached for her to touch me. My eleven-year old sapling penis sprang

205

to life. "Please, *please*. Since I come, everyone hates me—*please, you do not hate me too*." She pressed her hands to ours.

"You have b-blood on your hands," Danny said.

Ursula took a breath. I couldn't believe what Danny said to her face. Ursula was stunned. "I was a *kind* during war like you. *Juden* were taken. Did I know? I was afraid—be *still* mother warned. We were afraid to talk. Once, my aunt said, Germans and Jews lived happy together."

"Is that true?" Danny asked. "When was that?"

"That was before the war."

"I will tell B-Bubba," Danny said. "Bubba knows everything."

Her family was poor. Did her father do bad things during the war? No, she said. Her father almost starved to death. Danny stood up and his small dark head inspected Ursula on her cot. "D-Did you kill Jews?" Danny asked.

"No, I was a child."

"Was your father a Nazi? Germans have blood on their hands."

Perhaps it was what Bubba had said. Danny's face hardened. Danny was an inquisitor. Like Bubba, he was stern. I was sensitive like Mother. I felt shame, doubt. I did not want to hurt others. Was Danny saying what we thought but were hesitant to say? If a child spoke truth it came from a higher place. I was in a haze. I heard our parents arrive, the spell was broken; we rushed upstairs. We never talked to Ursula about Germans again. If not for Danny, I would have said nothing.

* * *

The Fausts were unable to keep their German girls. Every few months a new girl would arrive. It must have been Ruthie-Annie driving the poor girls away. Ursula would go over to help out. Each time Ursula came home from babysitting little Herbie and Ruthie-Annie she had tears in her eyes. When my parents were away I heard moaning softly at night. Once I went downstairs after she had returned from the Fausts and saw her lying on her small cot, her face to the wall.

"Are you all right, Ursula?" I asked.

She turned around. She dried her eyes. "I must leave soon."

I didn't follow her. "What is wrong?"

"There are bad people in this world, Reuben. You are too young to understand."

* * *

That year I got a two-wheeler. But it wasn't new, and it wasn't one of the racing bikes from Rossi's bike shop. It was a CCM Glider that Cousin Robert passed on to me. Ursula taught me to balance myself. She held me by the seat until I learned how to ride the bike. Ursula stayed six more months and fell in love with Jean-Pierre, a burly French-Canadian soldier from Quebec. In his uniform he seemed an overstuffed teddy bear. I dreamed of Ursula's flaxen hair and shining Prussian-blue eyes. I wanted Ursula for myself; she was so gentle and kind.

Our parents made her a tiny wedding in our basement. The Fausts were invited and spoke fluent German to Ursula. When Sammy Faust danced with Ursula he held her tightly and she sobbed. I could not tell whether she had tears of sadness or joy.

Father said we might have a glass of wine. We sipped *Liebfraumilch*, Father kissed Ursula goodbye. He had hoped for a daughter. Later I learned that Ursula was only eighteen. After Ursula, we had Rosa and Monica. Mother said they were nice German maids but not as pretty as Ursula. Mother moved them from the basement to a room with a decent bed beside the kitchen.

Was it true Germans and Jews lived happy together?

Bubba grumbled you could never be sure.

* * *

Pinsky, I take my mother shopping each Friday. We go to Loblaws, the supermarket chain my father hated, the one he swore to fight to the death. My mother reads the weekly flyers and shops for specials—vegetables, milk, All-Bran, cheese, bread—Loblaws has a kosher section—she buys her weekly supply and after shopping I drive her to her apartment. She walks with a cane, partly deaf, bent over, grey-haired; I hold her hand as we cross the street to my Volvo.

"Reuben, once I held your hand across the road. Now you hold my hand—*that's life*."

"I know."

"All my friends have died or live in Miami. I have no one. Danny and Benji have left the city. Your father died so young."

"I know."

"Mom, why not go to Miami yourself? In December you can get away from the cold."

"I am too old. I am alone. How is Frieda? Why don't you see her anymore?"

"We separated, Mom. I see the kids. They are fine."

"Why don't they come and see me more often? How is Ari Mazer?"

"Ari moved away, Mom."

"Are you still jogging, Reuben? You have to be careful on the street with all the cars."

"I still jog, Mom. I am careful."

When we get back to the Volvo my mother halts. "What is that?" She points to the hood and the bumper. "What is that?" I open the trunk and put in her groceries. I don't want to make a scene in the parking lot. I drive her to her apartment. I take the elevator with her bags of groceries up to her kitchen.

"Reuben, what was that, that pile on your car hood? You never answered me."

* * *

When I was eleven, the day after Ursula's wedding I went to Herbie Faust's house. Ruthie-Annie was at the dentist getting new braces. I found Ruthie-Annie's diary. I read more Yiddish. I knew a tiny bit about the Second World War and the refugees and what happened to Jews. I figured why my parents never talked of the past. I understood why Bubba said Germans had blood on their hands. Ruthie-Annie wrote her mother and father had escaped their small village to flee the Germans.

Her parents hid outside the village. They lived in a farmer's barn. On moonless nights they would go out to search for food. They lived this secret life for years. And then one day they had to run from the farm to the forest. They lived in the forest for a while and then they had to run from the forest. The Germans caught them. I searched for the Hebrew letters in the diary.

ער טוט שלעכט זאכן צו מיר

CHAPTER EIGHT

Cheder atrocities

"Often the nominal head of the family, the father, is absent— forced to work long hours to support family needs. The Zaide factor—the presence of a reliable senior male [wisdom figure] is essential for the youth's well-being … in its absence we see acting out against the female imago …"

("Narcissism and the Fate of the Bubba-Complex in Refugee-Migrant Situations Revisited", Reuben Moses MD, Analytic Books, New York and Toronto, 2007).

In the 1950s everyone was afraid of Miss Blot, our cheder teacher. Miss Blot carried a yardstick like a bat and swung at our heads when we didn't listen. Who could sit after a day of English classes? In early fall our third-floor classroom reeked of stale air and was warm as an oven. Studying Hebrew and Jewish history in a small hot room made us into wild animals. "Sit," Miss Blot said in her thick foreign accent. "Stay down. Don't move. *Schweigen bitte!*"

"But it's hot in here, Miss Blot," I said.

"Reuben, Lenny, don't talk when I'm teaching Torah."

Lenny Loeb said already he had heatstroke. My buddy, Ari Mazer, pointed to the thermostat. "It's over 90 degrees. My buttons are melting. Can you turn down the heat?"

"Jews lived in the desert forty years. Did they complain? Why can't you boys sit still?" Miss Blot said. Her classes began with threats. She said she taught *nudniks* at *Talmud Torah* earlier that day. She pointed to the 1948 wall map of Israel and ordered us to memorize it. She had been a nurse in the Israeli army. She never smiled.

Pinsky, the best we hoped for was that she would get a terminal illness and die.

Miss Blot was fluent in six languages—German, Hebrew, English, Yiddish, Polish, Russian—none of which I listened to. If she yelled in Hebrew, I laughed. If she spoke English, I snorted. With Russian I doubled up. In English she called us idiots, good-for-nothings, and spoilt Canadians. In Yiddish she called us *vilde chayas*, and *puskudnyaks*; in Polish she said I was a *paskudzić*, in Russian she called me a паскуд—I think the words mean that I was a wild, terrible, stupid person. Herbie Faust, who transferred from *Talmud Torah*, was the teacher's pet. Karl Guttnik, a few grades ahead of me, was held up as a model student. Lenny Loeb, whose dad was the undertaker, was sober-faced. "My dad has a reputation. I can't act like you dumb idiots." Josh Karp, who believed in law and order, refused to joke. Josh vowed to follow a path of truth and justice unlike his dad, Manny J. Karp, the local bookie. Josh's hero was Eliot Ness. We figured Josh worked as an undercover agent for Miss Blot. We named Miss Blot, Blot-bum or Polka-Blot. With her back turned Ari Mazer and I impersonated Stuka dive-bombers. I made clucks and honks. Ari threw in some farts. Why was I such a *shmuck* in cheder, Pinsky?

"You deceive yourself now as you talk," Pinsky says. He has been listening and waiting for months. "Blot was a re-enactment of your relation to your Bubba. You repeated the antagonism and rebellion. Blum, your patient, relives your past, Dr. Moses. You treat me like Blot. You hardly listen. You plead suffering; you fart and urinate out your great misery. You are a shit-faced rebel like your dog—that spoilt disobedient

shit-dispenser. Moses, you have not grown up. You are constipated in childhood-adolescence. You want to enrage me and be
put over my knee—"

"Over your knee—for what?"

"To spank you. To give you an enema."

"Spank me? I want you to spank me? I want an enema? Fuck
that! *Fuck you, Pinsky!*"

"You are trying to be punished for your past and present
perceived misdeeds. Why did you marry Frieda, a blue-eyed
pure Aryan German, after all the warnings your Bubba offered.
You are looking to transgress and be beaten up by me and the
world. Look at the intractable patients you see. Look at the
reaction you are getting from *The Bubba Complex*. Do women
idolize you? I read the press clippings—you have developed
notoriety, quite a reputation. People see you as an *agent provo-
cateur*, a rabble-rouser, an iconoclast—you took your lessons
from Sax, that testicle-brain *Galitzianer* shit-disturber, your
camp bunkmate. You will end up isolated and alone, beaten-up
in your little blue plastic potty with Captain Peacock, just like
you complained about in childhood."

"But I was isolated. In my fucking potty *I was isolated*."

"You had Peacock. Do you know why you called him
Captain Peacock?"

"I have no fucking idea."

"He was your buddy during your *pee* and *kuck*, you unconsciously enjoyed peeing and kucking by yourself—erotic
pleasure—that was where Captain Pee-kuck came in. Instead
of permitting yourself this satisfaction, you projected your
guilt-inducing persecuting superego to your adoring Bubba
and made her into a nasty Nazi bully."

"A Nazi bully? I made her into a fucking nasty Nazi bully?
Me? I loved her."

"*You had it too good*. You were firstborn. Your family doted on
you. It was postwar. You were your family's golden boy. Your
Bubba devoted her life to you."

"Devoted? That's a pile of bullshit," I say. "Let me tell you about Blot. Miss Blot was an appalling, disgraceful, tormenting teacher; I struggled with her all year."

"*She was a Jewish transference figure, Moses*. I am a transference figure *too*."

* * *

I recall Moses at camp and his bunkmate, Sax, the camp *kvetch*, the pimply camper with oversize elephant testicles who hated everything—food, counsellors, the camp director. Sax, the sadist, was a Jewish hate-monger, a rotten camper who became rich from garbage.

* * *

Pinsky, we had cheder Monday, Tuesday, and Thursday from 4:30 to 6:30, and Sunday from 9:30 to noon. Ari said cheder was brainwashing for Jews. We prayed for a cargo plane to crash into cheder when we were away or a fire to burn it down with Miss Blot inside. We waited patiently. Nothing happened. Miss Blot ordered us to go to synagogue. Her hawk eyes took attendance. "So, Reuben," she said, "did I see you in synagogue?"

"Ari and I studied the Old Testament," I said.

"Which portion?"

"It was deep," I said. "Very deep."

"You take me for a fool?" Miss Blot's eyes narrowed. "Do I call your parents?" She stared at me. I stared at her. We had a staring match. Two minutes passed.

"Miss Blot," I blurted out, "OK. I will tell you the truth. I did not study the Old Testament."

"As I thought, Reuben, don't lower my opinion by lying."

"You mean—you have a good opinion of me, Miss Blot?"

"Of Karl Guttnik three grades ahead of you in cheder, I have a good opinion. Of Sabrina Lustig who is in this class I have a good opinion," Miss Blot said. "She studies. Of Herbie Faust I have a good opinion. He listens. A liar, a *ligner* is what you are. Get into the hall."

Sabrina Lustig, who I knew from camp, was a top student. She was kind. She did homework and helped Herbie study. I stared at her dark hair eyes and hair. What a figure! When I made her giggle, I levitated. Sabrina was perfect. A new boy, Tzvi Biro, arrived in October. He was a ruddy-faced, long-haired, six-foot Hungarian with a nervous tic and a hoarse voice. His lips and nose twitched one way, his eyebrows and cheek twitched the other. His forehead and eyes convulsed, his size twelve feet wiggled. His fingers were busy. Like me, he was not one to sit still. Tzvi was almost fifteen, two years older than me. He spoke almost no English. His father fled Hungary before the revolution. The principal, Krafchek, figured Miss Blot, fluent in six languages, would help Tzvi. "Go ahead, Tzvi. Read." His forehead twitched. Miss Blot paused. "*Chanukah*, try to say that." She tried to be patient. Tzvi fumbled a second time. Beads of sweat broke out. Miss Blot repeated, "*Chchch*." How do I do the *Cccch*? Tzvi asked. My mouth doesn't go like that. Tzvi trembled. His shirt was drenched with sweat. I kept a straight face.

"It is difficult for him to say *cchhh*," I said.

"Reuben. Mind your business." I got sent into the hall. Miss Blot hated me.

Crystal, the dog walker: October 1, 2008

At night on call I cover the locked ward, the emergency, psych patients on medicine—people recovering from overdoses, post-operative delirium, dementia, depressed post-partum women, emergencies, and patients deciding to leave ICU with tubes and wires strapped to their body. I have my share of suicidal patients. Crystal returns each night I am on call— *surprise. Pinsky*, it is 2 am. What has she swallowed? I think

214

of Little Red Riding Hood—why? Because a child believes in oral impregnation—the baby gets inside the tummy by swallowing, see? Crystal's tummy has something painful inside—the foreign body represents an unwanted baby. I ask about pregnancy—she was pregnant two years ago. She won't say more except it was a family member. Crystal tells me her boyfriend, jealous Zeno, will be released from prison shortly. I can't wait.

* * *

In six months Tzvi Biro was to have a bar mitzvah. Miss Blot tried to give Tzvi lessons after class. They ended up yelling at each other. Krafchek, the cheder principal had to intervene. Cantor Schwartz spent evenings teaching Tzvi to sing Hebrew. By mid-October Tzvi knew eleven Hebrew words. At that rate he would learn his bar mitzvah by age thirty-four. Tzvi had a tin ear and did not carry a note. Unable to understand Hebrew, he lapsed into a Slovenian-Hungarian dialect. Miss Blot, exasperated, sent Tzvi into the hall. Now we had company. The hall was where we spent most of our class. When you forgot homework, or did not understand the Old Testament, or could not figure out what Blot said in English, you moved on to higher learning in the hall. If you looked at Blot the wrong way you were ushered to the hall. The hall was a long corridor on the third floor that was five degrees cooler than the classroom. At recess students played blackjack and slept there. My full name that year was *Reuben-go-to-the-hall*. "*Me*? What did I do?"

"You did what you did. Don't ask, *Reuben-go-to-the-hall*. Get out."

"I was studying, Miss Blot—since when is study a crime?"

"Get out. *Reuben-go-to-the-hall. Out*."

"Miss Blot, he *was* studying," Ari said. "I swear on the Torah. I am his witness."

"Ari. You go out too. Witness him in the hall."

215

You never knew what you did wrong in Miss Blot's cheder class. You could study Maimonides and get absolutely nowhere but the hall. Once, during recess, I had a horseback fight with Ari and Tzvi. Ari was the enemy rider and Tzvi was the horse. I persuaded Herbie to get on my back. I felt sorry for Herbie. I wanted him to have fun and be with the guys and join our horse back fights. "Herbie—don't let Ari push you off!"

"I don't like this," Herbie said. "This is too vicious. I don't want to fight."

"I am the horse. You *be* the man," I said. "Don't get knocked off. It's fun."

Two seconds later little Herbie went flying sideways. He fell to the hall floor in a lump and landed on his head. He split his lip and chipped his tooth and there was blood galore. Believe me, it wasn't my fault. I cleaned up all the blood. For the rest of the class Herbie writhed in pain. "Miss Blot, my left leg is *killing* me," Herbie moaned.

"Herbie, wait until the end of class," Miss Blot said.

"My left leg is *killing* me—my polio leg. I think my leg is broken," Herbie said.

"Nobody breaks a leg in cheder," Miss Blot said. "That is impossible."

"It happened at recess, Miss Blot," Herbie said. "Tzvi pushed me off Reuben's back. I fell on my bad left side and busted my lip and leg. They had a horseback fight."

Josh Karp, the undercover agent piped in. "Herbie Faust is speaking the truth. Tzvi pushed Herbie. I was there, Miss Blot. I saw it with my own eyes."

"Did I say, no fighting? Do you *nudniks* have to kill each other? All of you, Herbie, Tzvi, Ari, Reuben—go to the hall. And don't fight." After class Herbie stooped like the hunch-back of Notre Dame. He spit blood. He dragged his left foot sideways home through the cold snow. Next day we learned Herbie's left leg was broken in three places and required a steel rod with eight screws. He needed dental work and two stitches

216

in his lip. His parents wanted to sue Krafchek. Ruthie-Annie told me her parents had lost everyone in the war. In her diary I read that her father had a terrible temper and didn't trust a soul. Ruthie-Annie threatened to break my leg in three places.

* * *

Blum's GP: October 6, 2008

I get a call from Blum's old GP—he treated her when she had her two bouts of cancer. What a piece of work, this woman, she doesn't listen. She's the expert. She tells me what drugs to take. She stopped seeing me—why—because once my receptionist double-booked her. Dr. Moses, as far as I know, she has not seen doctors for years. Her son phoned last week—I understand you are her analyst—at least she is seeing someone.

* * *

Herbie Faust limped with crutches. His left leg was shattered. No one knew if he would walk again. Faggie Faust, his mother, accused me of being a bully. Overnight, as a punishment for what I did, hair sprouted on my armpits, face, and groin. My testicles expanded. My feet grew two sizes. I was going through some weird metamorphosis like a werewolf. I felt terrible. I visited Herbie as he lay in bed. I said I was sorry for his leg. Herbie at five feet was still waiting for his growth spurt. He didn't blame me. Ruthie-Annie was away at the dentist getting her braces adjusted. I went to her room. I found her diary. I struggled with the Hebrew words.

ער טוט שלעכט זאכן צו מיר

I decided to write more of the Hebrew letters down and take them to Miss Blot. When I showed the words to Miss Blot she shuddered and put a hand to her head.

"Reuben, did you write this?"

"I found them in an old diary."

"This is Yiddish written with Hebrew letters," Miss Blot said. "What does it mean?"

"It says, 'He does bad things to me.' Whose diary was it?"

"It was an old diary—I don't know whose it was."

Miss Blot shook her head. "This person was beaten, perhaps worse. Was it a woman?"

"I have no idea," I said.

* * *

"In less than two years most of you *nudniks* will start bar mitzvah lessons," Miss Blot warned. "Imagine your sick minds let loose on the world. What do you do during recess? You fight, you lie, and you break legs. Fugitives! None of you read Hebrew. You don't sing. You can't count. You don't think. What will become of you after bar mitzvah?" Some days Miss Blot had half the class in the hall. We joked, we had water and piggyback fights; we ran races down the hall and placed bets. This was cheder— running around in circles. One day it dawned on me. We had no respect for her. She had no respect for us. How was she to teach? How were we to learn? The two boys she had compassion for were little Herbie Faust, who played with girls, and Karp, the class informer. She told us after King David the Jews split into two kingdoms; they ended up fighting and worshiping idols like the bunch of us.

Miss Blot was two inches over five feet. To me she acted like a bully, but she was thirty-five with dark hair, a nice figure, and pretty. No one knew if she had a boyfriend. Esther said she had been a refugee child in Poland, lost her family and had run away to Russia during the war. Miss Blot taught Hebrew, history, Torah, and ethics. She warned that we didn't use our Jewish *kop*. To get our brains working, she shrieked: *Life is no joke*. She said I was a mental case. Desperate and irate with me,

Miss Blot phoned home. Bubba answered. "Reuben, you give me angina." Bubba popped a white pill. How was I to know that my Bubba had a heart condition, Pinsky? My parents met with the cheder principal, Kraftchek. In his cramped fetid office were propaganda leaflets, maps of Israel, pictures of army tanks, and photos of Jerusalem. The office was in Zionist chaos.

Miss Blot stared at me, grim-faced. Krafchek greeted us. *Shalom*, peace to you.

Father was slit-eyed, wary. "What is the p-purpose of this meeting?" he asked.

"We are meeting to discuss Reuben's progress." Krafchek shot a glance to Blot. She scratched her knuckles. She was waiting to pounce on me.

"My son Reuben is a nice quiet boy," my mother began. "He keeps kosher. He studies. His *Zaide* was a *Zadek* rabbi—he knows about being Jewish."

Krafchek nodded several times. "We all know he comes from a good family."

"Let's have it." My father was impatient. "What has he d-done?"

Miss Blot could not endure the silence. "Reuben, your son, is the class clown. He disrupts the room. He may look mature and act an angel at home, but here he is a devil, a rabble-rouser, a rebel, a terrorist—*a criminal instigator*—he is on a mission to destroy the class."

"Is it true?" mother, aghast, faced me. I burst into laughter. What else could I do?

* * *

I visited little Herbie each week. He was getting better and told me that Faggie had found Ruthie-Annie's diary and was on a rampage. Ruthie-Annie hid her diary in a school bag. When Ruthie-Annie was out for her violin lesson I read her diary again. I couldn't believe what she wrote.

219

Several pages were ripped out. I found Ruthie-Annie's last note.

He did it to the German nannies. He tried with Ursula when she came to babysit.

* * *

After February we never saw Tzvi in class. He spent each afternoon locked up with Cantor Schwartz studying bar mitzvah. We heard Tzvi's hoarse voice rise, fall, and crack. We heard Cantor Schwartz repeat the words slowly. He helped Tzvi, one word at a time. It was like pushing a blind man up a steep mountain. Esther told me Cantor Schwartz was a DP who had lost his family in Europe. Miss Blot spoke of how entire Jewish villages were destroyed in the war. I found out Rav Natan's family were murdered in the Holocaust. I was the class clown. We barked in German and clicked our heels. We marched goose steps to class. We put pencils on our lips moustache-like and gave Heil Hitler salutes. We yelled: "*Raus, alle Juden raus.*" The truth was none of us wanted to be Jews. Why were we always on the losing side? Why study Hebrew, the Bible, and history if the rest of the world wanted to kill us? Who in their right mind hoped for martyrdom? What sane kid wished for circumcision? We wanted to play hockey, eat pizza, and have a normal childhood. What kind of screwed up life was it to be a Jew?

In April Rabbi Spiegel came to class and gave us a sermon on the book of Exodus. "I gather Miss Blot has concerns about some of you boys." The rabbi looked at me, so I giggled. "What's so funny?" the rabbi asked. "You have a joke to tell?"

"I don't know," I smiled. The rabbi wore a suit, tie, and fedora. He looked the spitting image of Dutch Schultz, the gangster. I held my breath and burst into laughter.

"This wild hyena—" Miss Blot pointed to me. "*This one* is Reuben."

"Reuben. Tell me; please explain to me, what is the joke?"

220

"I don't know. To me everything is funny. To me life is a joke."

Spiegel nodded. "Life is truly a joke—a sad joke, Reuben. Our history of oppression teaches us in times of sorrow humour comforts us. Somewhere, you are filled with sadness. Why do Jews laugh—out of happiness? No—we feel life's suffering." The rabbi peered into my heart. My smile vanished. "Remember we were slaves in Egypt."

A second later I did a flip-flop. I was smiling again. I had figured out what Rabbi Spiegel was saying. During Passover we had seen families in China House ordering egg rolls and won-ton soup, gulping pepperoni pizza at Monte Carlo Pizzeria—Jews from our synagogue—infidels. They broke kosher rules. Blot told us there were Jews who drove on the Sabbath. They married non-Jews. They did not give to charity. They gambled and stole money. They joined synagogue but on *Yom Kippur* they ate Chinese food. I envied the Jews who were not Jews, Pinsky.

In April, Tzvi was called to the Torah. This raised questions for me since I was not capable of holding a straight face for more than ten seconds. In those days when Ari and I went to shul, we crashed bar mitzvahs. We dressed in our finest, walked to the welcome line, acted like semi-literate Polish relatives, shook hands, stuffed ourselves, filled our pockets with cookies, and left.

Twice Josh Karp followed us in to a reception and denounced us as impostors.

Tzvi's bar mitzvah was a small affair. His parents and young sister were his only family. There were no fancy clothes and no lavish food. Tzvi's voice was flat but he did not once falter. Like one of Hannibal's elephants he ploughed through everything—Cantor Schwartz sang behind Tzvi. I saw Blot after the service. I didn't laugh once, although I had two close calls and nearly passed out holding my breath. I was getting mature. The Biros had a tiny Kiddush. Sandwiches, dill pickles, *gefilte fish*, herring, *chala*, wine, and honey cake. My classmates sat in a corner.

"Did you know Tzvi's family ran from Europe?" Sabrina Lustig said.

"Listen, everyone runs from Europe," I said. "It's a Jewish relay race."

Esther sat beside me. I was in heaven. I planned to ask her out and later, when the time was right, I would marry her. I looked around the room. Blot sat with Cantor Schwartz, Kraftchek, and Rabbi Spiegel. It was the first bar mitzvah of our class. Tzvi gave a speech. He thanked his teachers. He thanked his parents for fleeing Hungary. He looked our way to thank his Canadian friends. His family had lost everything— friends, money, possessions. Esther was so gorgeous I could not bear to have our eyes meet. Her dark hair fell in ringlets over her neck. Her ebony eyes sparkled with joy and sadness. When I made her laugh, her lips quivered. I felt my penis grow hard. I worried it would fly out of my pants like a wild dog unleashed.

"In Canada we newcomers are free as Jews," Tzvi said. "It is a new beginning."

Sabrina looked at me. This time, for no reason, my eyes were burning. I pined for her enchanting eyes, tormented by desire. After cheder Sabrina invited me to walk her home. What should have made me delirious filled me with fear. My comic banter had dried up. Sleepless I composed her telephone number. Heart pounding I dialled her home, my chest tight. *One ring. Two rings. Three rings.* "Hello. Hello, who is this?" Sabrina asked. Overcome I said nothing.

Two months later, Cantor Schwartz had a stroke and lost the power of speech.

He died a week later, buried by Lenny's father, the shul undertaker.

CHAPTER NINE

Relativity: October 2008

Pinsky, it is October 2008, everything is still in boxes. I couldn't bear to unpack since the separation. I didn't want to think how long ago it had been—since June 2007. When Frieda and I said goodbye I rented a lousy bachelor apartment. Jaffe-Jaffe was insufferable when I left for work. Crystal took her for long walks but Jaffe-Jaffe was a basket case. Crystal herself was a wreck. I took Jaffe-Jaffe to my vet who says Jaffe-Jaffe has anxiety and gives her Prozac. I don't believe in antidepressants for dogs but the drug helped. My super said the tenants were furious with me for her yelping and moaning. I tried to take Jaffe-Jaffe jogging with me.

She hated running.

I doubled her Prozac to calm her. Crystal said a bowl of dog food was left outside my place.

Crystal didn't like the smell of it.

* * *

One year before my bar mitzvah, Rav Natan died. Father stopped taking Danny and me to Saturday Maple Leaf baseball games. Instead of baseball we went to shul. We sat in row nine, behind Noah Loeb, the undertaker. Lenny was my cheder buddy. Loeb was a hairy bison with no neck who took up two seats. His brother, Seymour, a tall thin man, sat close to Noah. Loeb was nuts about baseball. "*Good shabbas.*" Noah shook our hands.

"The Leafs play Havana today."

"Rochester is the one to beat," Father said. "Sunday is the double-header."

"And how is the drugstore business?"

"People get sick," Father said. "They need drugs. And how is your business, Noah?"

"My business is death," Loeb sadly patted his beard with a hanky. He motioned to the left of Sam Faust to a lady and young boy two rows behind us. "Glick died, Thursday." I turned to see their leaden faces. "Thirty-nine—they said it was a heart attack."

Rabbi Spiegel spoke of Glick, the dentist, a *gutte neshumah*, a good soul; he helped the poor and visited the ill. Behind Loeb's bison shadow I saw darkness. I stared at Glick junior. His head leaned against his mother's shoulder. He was unable to bear the weight of *Kaddish*. Mourners recited the ancient Aramaic words. *Yisgadal, ve-yisgadash, she-may, rabah.* The shul divided in two—mourners on one side, the rest of us, waiting. Life was a baseball game; the mourners' side was on the field. One day, destiny would put me in their place. I wanted to flee. I wanted to huddle by the grassy third base at Maple Leaf Stadium, smell Shopsy hot dogs, and be blessed by the sun. I wanted to see the Leafs play the Havana Sugar Kings and feel life's pulse.

"Dad, how long do you have to say *Kaddish*?" I asked

"A son has to say *Kaddish* for one year after his father dies."

While Loeb snored Rabbi Spiegel gave a rambling sermon. Spiegel warned of past massacres—the Cossacks, Polish and Russian pogroms, the Inquisition, Hitler and the Nazis. As Spiegel spoke, Loeb snored. Obsessively I counted the congregation. "Look what's happening," I said. My father opened his eyes. "Dad, if Spiegel talks of pogroms, people sleep. Ninety-four people have their eyes closed. Ninety-three have their eyes open. Why?" My father shut his eyes. Two seniors whispered. From this rabbi have you heard one happy word? The other said: It's the same story. Jews are in trouble—if they're not in trouble—that's trouble. If they get happy, more trouble. It's safer to be miserable.

It was a torrid Saturday in July—no fresh air, not even with windows open. Spiegel's forehead gleamed. Someone said it was hotter than the Sinai desert. The rabbi hit the pulpit. He yelled to the back. "Will you stop Colonel Nasser?"

I pointed to myself. "Me?"

The rabbi directed his hands across the shul. "*You!* Are you soldiers?"

"*Dad*? Rabbi Spiegel is speaking to us. Who is Nasser?"

My father opened one eye. "Nasser runs Egypt. He's against the Jews."

Noah Loeb had a habit of snoring and not breathing for ten seconds. The shul shook from thundering snorts. Lenny pushed his father to waken—Noah had become lifeless. Our rabbi talked of *fedayin*—commandos infiltrating from Gaza, Sinai, Jordan, to attack Israel. More people slept.

I imagined *fedayin* with grenades sneaking into shul.

* * *

"Dr. Moses, I am trying to gather why each session you return to the past, to old friends, to Jewish school. You smile and laugh at your many setbacks," Pinsky says. "Why avoid the present?"

"There is no present. We live in the past. When we think, we are already in the past."

"How about *now*? October 2008. What happened just before now—before this moment?"

"That's why I'm here. You tell me, eh? That's your fucking job isn't it?"

"Wouldn't it be best to face your wife's separation, your difficult patients, and talk about Blum's complaint to your college?

225

How do we understand this issue of vandalism and shit? What about the women's groups angry with you? Why laugh and change topics? Even your dog, Jaffe-Jaffe seems to be the target of retaliation. Could one of your difficult patients be angry with you?"

"Nobody is that angry with me—only me."

* * *

Pinsky, the big deal in the Fifties was dance parties. Parents dressed in gowns and tuxedos like aristocrats. They sipped champagne, smoked cigars, and handed out monogrammed cigarettes. For years they slaved to have a party that lasted for one lousy night. It was ridiculous, having a stinking bar mitzvah. I was dead against dancing. Monday night my parents and Auntie Leah took dance lessons. They went nuts about Arthur Murray. "A millionaire—a nice Jewish architect, *Teichman* is his real name—studios everywhere, such *mazel*, Reuben. He has his own party on TV. Mambo. Rumba. Cha-cha, tango. *Dance*," Auntie Leah said. She was a Jewish pygmy. I was careful not to step on her feet. "Reuben," she said. "You have no rhythm. You have no direction."

Ari Mazer's dad, Ben Mazer, the shul caterer, lived on the rich side of Bathurst Street in a Forest Hill mansion with a circular drive, a pool, and a pink Cadillac convertible. Ari was the first one to get home air-conditioning. Mazer and Loeb referred clients to each other—*relativity*, life and death. Grim Loeb wore black; Mazer wore a Panama and smiled. Loeb was sober, Mazer was cheery. Mazer married a hot Cuban gal, Estella, half his age. Loeb's wife was an actuary.

Several times a year Mazer flew to Cuba to do business and see his wife's family. Guess who went with him to Havana? Sam Faust who was trying to open a hardware chain in Cuba and Manny J. Karp—he was Mazer's accountant. The three of them stayed at *Hotel Nacionale*, owned by Batista. Behind Batista were Italian and Jewish mafias. Mazer's dad loved Cuban high life, music, partying in Vedado and Varadero. Soon there would be a civil war. Senator McCarthy warned America was hiding enemies. Cuba prepared for revolution. Nasser threatened to wipe out Israel. In Toronto there were air raid sirens. Loeb took us on a guided tour of his bomb shelter.

Loeb's underground bomb shelter—note stairs to cellar surrounded by two foot concrete walls.—R. Moses

"See—two foot thick concrete walls—see the ventilation— this bunker has a working toilet. If Soviets drop a ten megaton bomb Seymour and I and our families live here, no problem. See the canned tuna, juice, matzo, a transistor radio, and a Geiger counter—just in case."

* * *

October 14, 2008

"Look," Pinsky says. "It's been months now, aren't you tired of the past? Let me put it another way—you came here June 2007

227

because your world fell apart. Your wife left. Fidel, your loyal dog died. You felt alone except for your patients, your mother, and family, your rose garden and your new pet beagle—"

"*Pet retriever*, Jaffe-Jaffe, you forgot her name and her breed didn't you? *Hah!*"

"I am confronting your denial and joking. You are depressed and alone—apart from your work or compulsive daily jogging you never socialize, you laugh but you feel anxious, you complain of bodily concerns, you tell me someone has put shit on your car and let the air out of your tires. Who would commit such acts of vandalism? Has it occurred to you that you are in a state of regressive dissociation—you recall the feces incident?"

"So, I dumped shit on my car and complained to you someone else did it?"

"Exactly—that is what you did. Isn't that right?"

* * *

Rabbi Spiegel told us the Jews were in trouble again. The three of us, Lenny, Ari, and I prepared for war. To toughen our bodies we ate tons of protein, chopped liver, hot dogs, and hamburgers, and worked out at the local gym. Each night I dreamt of war, becoming a commando, or heading off to some remote place in South America. It could be the Russians, the Cubans, the Koreans, or the Arabs—who knew? In sermons, Rabbi Spiegel yelled Nasser was going to attack. Often the air raid sirens went off during Saturday services. Ari's stepmom, Estella, paid me two bucks to wash her Cadillac and scrub her whitewalls. She had long hair, wore toreador pants, and spoke Spanish. Ari told me she couldn't have kids. She was the sexiest mother alive. Looking at her gave me wet dreams. At Loeb's bar mitzvah, my parents, Bubba, and Auntie Leah sat at the same table. Faggie Faust, her husband, Ruthie-Annie, and little Herbie still on crutches sat beside us.

"One day I will break your legs in three places, I promise," Ruthie-Annie said.

"That's your way of saying you got a crush on me, Ruthie-Annie," I said. "You know I am irresistible." I felt confident. I gulped four glasses of Manischewitz wine when my parents weren't looking. I was five foot ten and growing. I looked older. Bubba warned me to not eat French fries. She offered to squeeze my blackheads for free. "*No deal*," I said. "Pimples are private property."

Auntie Leah wanted me to be her dance partner. I said no. That week mother asked Estella Mazer to teach me mambo and cha-cha for my bar mitzvah. "You look *Cubano*," Estella said. "You have a nice *Cubano* name, *Rubén, like Rubén Gonzáles*. Let me show you a few steps." I said I was too busy. "But *Rubén*, it would give me *mucho satisfacción*." Mambo terrified me. It was a weird primitive mating dance. Just the idea gave me nightmares of Mrs. Mazer, in a skin-tight black sequin dress dancing with me. In my recurrent wet dream Xavier Cugat played "Mambo Number Five." Mrs. Mazer had her arms around my neck. I wore a black tuxedo jacket and dancing shoes like Arthur Murray. I had no pants, nothing—just a tremendous erection. That year during half the week my voice slipped lower, then for the rest of the week it went higher. In October the Soviets put Sputnik in orbit. I found *Peyton Place* beside my mother's night table. The book was full of lewd steamy sex. Just picking it up made me nervous—I worried Bubba would find me reading the dirty parts. My buddies Mazer and Loeb were masturbating day and night on *Peyton Place*. Their parents read *Peyton Place*. Everybody in the world was reading *Peyton Place*. Finally a book talked openly about everything nobody talked about—sex.

* * *

Herbie said his parents fought. I found Ruthie-Annie's diary. She wrote Sam had sex with her night after night. She wanted

229

a door lock. Was he having sex with the German girls? Ruthie-Annie was making it up, wasn't she? Suppose it was true? In those days who spoke about abuse or sex? It was hushed up. In the Fifties the bad guys were the Commies and before them, the Germans.

* * *

People worried about a Soviet invasion. I worried when I should start having sex. Estella told us Castro was growing in strength in his mountain stronghold in Oriente province. One day he would take over Cuba. Her family was quietly making arrangements to leave Havana. Then there was war at the Suez Canal—the Israelis were fighting the Egyptians. France and England had joined them. My parents worried the Soviets would join in. The Soviets had their hands full with the Hungarian Revolution. In school we heard air raid sirens and recited drills in case of nuclear war:

If there is a nuclear attack while you are in school:

1. *Close all windows. Pull down the blinds.*
2. *Turn off the lights.*
3. *Crouch under a table or desk.*
4. *Bend over in a protective position.*
5. *Kiss your toochas goodbye.*

The world would explode—it might happen anywhere, including my pants.

Dad, maybe we should build a bomb shelter in the basement. "*I really need that*, a d-damn b-b-bomb shelter. I am saving for your bar mitzvah. A b-bomb shelter costs $10,000." Loeb built one in his basement for his family. He stocked up food and water for months, a year. Seriously, Dad, the Russians are going to attack. "Loeb doesn't know what to do with all his money. Seymour, his brother is an undertaker. So the two of them dig a big hole in their b-basement and build a b-b-bomb shelter for their families. Good for him." What happens, Dad, if the Soviets drop the H-bomb? "We drive out to the country somewhere, Gravenhurst, maybe." *But there won't be enough time, Dad.* It can happen in less than twenty-five minutes. "Reuben, stop. Are you B-Bubba?" Father said. "Let *me* worry about it."

That week in shul Rabbi Spiegel told us Nasser's army was crushed—I didn't believe him. I checked with Walter Cronkite. It was actually true. Pinsky, it was all relative, Spiegel preached. Jews would be back in trouble again. Spiegel's motto was never get too happy. In 1957 I had my hands full with Estella Mazer. She taught me mambo, rumba, and cha-cha Tuesdays when Ari was having bar mitzvah lessons at shul and didn't get along with his stepmom. I rode my bike over and brought my bathing suit to her house. I swam in their kidney-shaped pool before my lesson. When I came over Estella was sunning in her bikini speaking Spanish with a dark old woman in a sun hat and flowered dress. "*Rubén—esta es mi abuela*, from Havana, my grandmother," Estella lapsed into Spanish. "She is staying here a few months."

Torture #9. Pinsky, just looking at Estella for a nanosecond gave me an Olympic hard-on. I swam a few lengths in their pool and tried to think of something terrible to get my mind off sex, like polio or nuclear war. After I dried off Estella said it was time for my dance lesson. We did cha-cha and rumba steps in our bathing suits without music. Her *abuela* leaned forward in her chair, nodded and counted, "*Uno, duo, tres. Uno, duo, tres,*" while Estella said to keep still upstairs—downstairs does the work. *Count. Left. Right.* Her *abuela* took my left and right hand and repositioned them, counted in Spanish, watched for moments, then shook her head. A moment later I was dancing with the grandmother. It was easy to be close to the old woman; she was light on her feet. She giggled like a little child as we danced by the pool.

I suspected dancing was sex standing up. I had a permanent erection, day and night. Tuesdays when I rode my bike over to Estella's place, I turned into a giant blow-up penis. One warm afternoon, dancing by the pool with her *abuela* watching I felt I was literally going to explode. Mrs. Mazer must have known because she said I was *growing* coordinated in my movements. She threw her head back. A smile spread over her full lips; she showed her perfect white teeth. I felt the two women were playing me, torturing me, mocking me in Spanish, but then, I tortured myself pretty well without anyone's help. Estella gave me her dance lessons in the air-conditioned master bedroom. Often her *abuela* watched us. Estella put on a dancing dress—to look professional. I saw her body swaying—but why the upstairs master bedroom? Why? Because, Estella explained, the huge hi-fi that Mr. Mazer bought was in the master bedroom and weighed a ton. Four workmen had lugged the beast up the circular staircase to the master bedroom. I figured the Mazers danced rumba nude each night before they went to bed. Then they had sex. Or else they had sex while they were dancing. Or maybe they sipped *mohitos* and had sex on the circular staircase and danced in bed. Or maybe they didn't have sex. I wondered if Estella was trying to seduce me. My mind was going haywire. Estella said I was big for my age. "How come Mr. Mazer is never home when we have our dance lessons?"

"He is busy man, working," Estella said.

"Is he always so busy?"

"He's in Havana two weeks a month with Mr. Karp. I live my life, you know."

"You are a fantastic dancer, Mrs. Mazer. You really are."

"*Rubén*, call me Estella; we are on a first name basis. You are *chulo*."

Sometimes Estella's *abuela* was not around. Then there were only the two of us in the bedroom. "You are a great dancer, Estella. I want to dance as well as you."

"I like your energy *Rubén*. Use that energy, come forward, *vienes, come*."

"I am trying to follow your steps."

"In Cuba the man leads—*the man is boss*—understand? Stand closer. Like this. Hold your left hand out, bring your body closer. Feel me closer to you. Don't press my right hand tight, *lighter*, yes. You are the man, you lead. *You are the one in control*."

"I see."

"Come closer, *Rubén*."

I was the one in control now. I saw the king size bed beside us as we danced. Estella put on a slow dance, *Siboney*. I wanted to dance her into bed.

"Come closer, *Rubén*."

She told me to hold her closer, I edged forward. My penis touched her—two million volts sparked across the room. Incredible. Nobody died on the spot.

"Come closer, *Rubén*."

"I feel your energy, *Rubén*. In Cuba we grow up very fast, you know." She put her cheek to my cheek as we danced. She whispered. "There is the music, the dance, the sea, the air—we dance as children. Feel the music. Dance is life."

Please, Estella—feel the music—dance with me into your big bed. Seduce me now, please. Seduce me. I am ready for you. Estella— even if you are my best friend's mother. Big and red and hard, that's my almost thirteen-year-old shmuck. And I can tell, you absolutely want my steely Jewish stallion. Show me the real dance of life. Yes, and when I get through with you Estella, you will never be the same again. Such *narishkeit* and craziness was going on in my head.

After drawing close I stood a foot away.

"Give more of yourself, *Rubén*. Relax your hips. Release yourself."

You just wait Estella, you just wait until I get through with you; you will never go back to your husband—or any man—not after I get through with you.

233

"I think I need to take a break," I said, sweating, overcome with tension, torn between my lunatic pubescent fantasy and a sober reality that was gradually evolving. I leaned against the bedroom wall. I took a breath.

"Please, no break," Estella said. "You are getting the feel of the dance."

She walked to the hi-fi and put on Tommy Dorsey's *Tea for Two*. "*Si*, start on the left foot, *Uno, dua, cha, cha, cha. Closer—not so far away*." We danced for three straight minutes. Estella patted me on my shoulder. She gave me a twinkling smile. Then we danced another three minutes. My dreams were that Estella was a sex-starved nymphomaniac, ready to unbutton my shirt, unlace my shoes, unzip my pants, and rip my underwear off my body. I sensed she was fed up with Ari's father. I waited for her to make the first move, signalling once and for all that my masculine charms and incredible almost thirteen-year-old good looks would win her over. *Resistance was futile*. Without doubt, Estella was dying for *the big one*—the Reuben sex howitzer. And Pinsky, I swear to God—that is exactly what did not happen. At least not at first—but then it did. We kissed on the lips. Who knows? There was a moment when her eyes gazed back at me unfocused; I could have had her then—*honest*. She waited. But nothing happened. "Learning to dance will be good for your future," Estella said. I did not move. I stood there. I did not want to leave. I held out my arms to her— she was five inches shorter than me. And then she kissed me hard on the lips and it was *craziness, craziness*, I put my arms around her and felt her warm body and then she told me not to worry, *don't worry, don't worry, Rubén, don't worry, Rubén, come here Rubén, come inside me, take your time, Rubén. I can't make babies, don't worry*. And thank God I had already masturbated twice before I cycled to her house for dance lessons, thank God, because I was able to stay inside a whole two minutes, and it wasn't a total fiasco, Pinsky. I swear I had died and gone to heaven and Estella was kissing me and saying *Rubén, don't worry, it is all right. You did fine. That's a nice job, really. And you will get better—yes.*

* * *

When I was young I joked about everything and took nothing seriously. When the clock struck twelve, I took everything seriously. Catastrophe waited for me around the corner. My affair with Estella exploded desire and terror. We had dance lessons when no one was around. I couldn't tell my parents, or Bubba, or any of my friends. Imagine how I felt around Ari. I was doing wrong—although she wasn't his real mother. And then I wasn't sure what to say about Ruthie-Annie's diary. Could something so terrible be true? You'd think, Pinsky, this is a wonderful thing—a teenager's fantasy to have sex with an older gorgeous woman. Estella was sensual, experienced, adoring—hungry—why choose me? I didn't understand whether her husband was impotent or having affairs in Havana or if she was simply curious. All I know is that we made love before my dance lesson, during my lesson, and then afterwards.

Our affair lasted two months, and then, *boom*, my dance lessons were over. And then I was totally besotted with women, obsessed with Estella, Roxanne Greenbaum, and Sabrina Lustig.

* * *

"Moses, you live and hide in the past," Pinsky says. "You avoid conflicts—you retreat from the present. I am concerned about you. Take a good look. You see who I am?"

"What the fuck do you mean?"

"I mean take a look at me, Moses. Don't rely on your *imagination—that is your problem*. Face reality. Face the real world. See me for who I am. Turn around on the couch. Check out

235

this person who has been your analyst and the witness to your *tortures*. What is the date today? Do you understand?" I lift my head off the couch. I turn around and stare at Pinsky.

Pinsky is sitting in his chair taking note, a balding nondescript Jewish doctor in his early seventies. He is wearing grey flannel pants, a shirt, and tie. His left leg crosses over his right. He is waving his pen at me crossly, like a dog he is training that is not performing well. What is the trick? I haven't the foggiest idea. OK, I say. I see you. I know it is October 2008. I know where I am. So what? "Take a good close look. What do you see?" What the fuck are we doing—is this show and tell? "What do you see, Moses? What do I look like?" *What do you look like?* This is not a beauty contest, Pinsky. Your best days are behind you. To tell you the truth you look like a piece of shit. You are old, bald, and out of shape. You might die tomorrow. Does that make you happy?

"Moses. *I AM NOT YOUR BUBBA*. I don't look like your Bubba. I don't speak Yiddish in the sessions. I do not make *gefilte fish*. This is your Bubba-transference. You want me to tell you what to do. You want me to warn you about looming catastrophe and you want to rebel at the same time. See what you do?

"You fixate on the past. Stop repeating it. This is reality. Understand?"

Bubba-lust: men addicted to older women

Montreal Gazette, November 2, 2008

> Professor Reuben Moses created a stir at the McGill Women's Association where he documented the unseen pandemic of men sexually attracted to older women, namely grandmothers. Moses spoke of Mae West, Madonna, Marlene Dietrich, Raquel Welch, Jeanne Moreau, Jane Fonda, Golda Meir and Hillary Clinton, and posited that

the behaviour is related to *The Bubba Complex* …. He cited his survey of men who became fixated on older women … he suggested that the *Bubba* was not an innocent bystander in the complex but desired the desire of the male youth … several women in attendance disrupted his presentation and shouted that Moses halt his vicious male diatribe against the *Bubba* … Dr. Moses explained later that he was not attacking the *Bubba* but stating the obvious … *desire shapes development* regardless of gender. After his presentation an angry chorus of women protested on the street, one of the scores of *Bubba Bunds* that have formed across North America and Europe …

* * *

Outside my office window before M's session an early November snow descends and I see four older women on the street conferring on walkie-talkies. I am puzzled by their militant look. A black van pulls up. Two more women appear, the van rear door opens, and black armbands and placards are passed to women who march in single file holding the placards over their shoulder.

Ban Bubba Bashing, say the signs.

In our session M informs me that his dog walker, Crystal, has quit. Jaffe-Jaffe is high-strung, too shy, and too unsettled. Crystal is terrified to go to the park and let children pet Jaffe-Jaffe. The dog snarls and runs amok on the icy sidewalks. Neighbours are scared stiff of Jaffe-Jaffe; tenants in the apartment stay clear of the dog. They complain of her wailing at night. M has tripled the dog's Prozac. The apartment super warns M several times to train Jaffe-Jaffe to be better behaved. A note has been placed under M's door threatening to assassinate Jaffe-Jaffe. M laughs this away.

CHAPTER TEN

My bar mitzvah suit

L ike my buddies Ari Mazer, Lenny Loeb, Josh Karp, Herbie Faust, Karl Guttnik, and Tzvi Biro, it was *de rigeur* to have a bar mitzvah suit. In the suit, you acted mature and sang from the Torah. You wore the bar mitzvah suit once or twice in your entire miserable lifetime—the truth was you grew out of it in less than six months. It was as useless as a wedding dress but a ritual necessity. Bubba insisted on buying me the suit. *No.* I must buy the bar mitzvah suit, Father said. Torture #10. Bubba wanted me to sing perfectly.

* * *

On call at Mount Zion Hospital, November 2008

Pinsky, on the weekend I am on call. Two overdose patients, a Chinese med student and an Iranian car dealer are medically clear and want to leave ICU. I work with a resident from the United Arab Emirates, *Tahir*, who speaks halting English. I must double-check each case to make sure he gets things right. A depressed Cambodian on the psych ward says she wants a weekend pass. All told I have twelve hospital patients to see Saturday and thirteen on Sunday, not to mention Friday night when I examine eight patients. Who shows up again?—Crystal [who says Zeno will soon be out of the slammer]. On top of that I have to supervise the resident. I try to keep the patients, their diagnoses, the medications, their histories clear in my head. I write down each case because I can't afford mistakes with my stupid ageing memory blocking out names. Pinsky, for good luck I use Bubba's fountain pen for notes, even though the hospital is digital. Suicidal and addicted patients rarely tell the whole truth; the two patients in the ICU say they are fine; they won't try to kill themselves. I don't believe them—you don't take a massive drug dose and end up in ICU for a lark—the med student took two vials of Tylenol—the Iranian car salesman drank a bottle of whisky and polished it off with antifreeze. No social worker is on call for weekends—budget cuts. The resident and I check phone numbers that the Iranian and Chinese patients give us; we contact their GPs and families. It turns out the Iranian patient does have family; he had an argument with his wife, his brother vouches for him, he can stay with the brother, and will be followed up in the crisis clinic. The Chinese med student lied. He has no one; he failed a final exam. He feels humiliated and his Asian family is betrayed. His life is over. We transfer him to the psych ward. If I hadn't checked, this patient would have died. *Tahir* agrees. You recheck everything, diagnoses, drugs, the patients' stories. And you do it over again, to be sure.

"If you check things why be blind to hate notes at your office, vandalism to your car, rose garden, or Blum's car, Sam-Lee's criminal links, or threats on Jaffe-Jaffe. How about the protesters in front of my office before your session? Why not be more careful?"

* * *

November, 12, 2008

Crystal comes to emergency at 2 am. Torture #11.

She hasn't swallowed. She tells me her stepfather was the one who impregnated her.

* * *

My parents drew up a list of guests, spoke to the caterer, Ben Mazer, and inquired about dance bands. Mother discussed dresses for the ladies. Father drove me downtown to his men's store. I stood on a stool. "Stand straight," the tailor ordered. "*Straight. Please.*" I was stooped. Perhaps it was because I had grown three inches taller than my father. Each month I grew more shy and anxious. Was it because I had developed a twenty-four hour erection thinking of Estella? Unlike my past self, I no longer wanted to be noticed. The suit was hauled out in pieces, unstuck and stuck together with pins. In my suit I looked like a banker. Meanwhile, Father talked to himself at night.

I could have folded. Karp bluffed—where do I get 2 G's? I owe Bella ten thousand. Plus the bar mitzvah—Mazer charges a fortune. I have to check waiters and bartenders don't steal my booze.

To relax Father watched horror movies on TV. Business was lousy. Father had huge debt. He gulped Crown Royal when he came home from work. Why not forget my bar mitzvah suit and have a small reception like Tzvi Biro? Father refused. Uncle Max paid us a visit. I sang my entire bar mitzvah portion. Soon I would grow feathers and wake up a Jewish budgie. "*Sing louder,*" Father said. Some days I sang higher than girls in my class. Other days I was bass. We brought the bar mitzvah suit home. Bubba wanted a dress rehearsal. I sang in my suit.

I hung it up afterwards so it would not be creased.

* * *

Two weeks before my bar mitzvah, I amassed two briefcases, six fountain pens, and four travel clocks—none of which

240

I needed. My parents practiced rumba. When we lived on Euclid, life was simple. Now Father paced at night complaining he had lost again at cards, debating if he should be partners with a drug chain or take out a bank loan. All I wanted for my bar mitzvah was a lousy pair of hockey skates. I heard Father mumble about borrowing cash from Karp or red-faced Faust. When I went to bed I heard the Fausts yelling and Ruthie-Annie playing her squeaky violin.

I wondered if Ruthie-Annie's diary was true. Could Sam do that to his daughter?

My mother's grandmother, Reba, died when my mother was thirteen, I was told. One week before the bar mitzvah Bubba and my mother, superstitious, not wanting to tempt the evil eye, said no running, no sports, no over-exertion, and no spicy food. Bubba and Auntie Leah were delegated to keep a watchful eye on me. I was to go to bed each night early. I wasn't permitted to sweat. I was not allowed to ride my bicycle. I stared at my blue bar mitzvah suit, resting on a special wooden hanger in my closet. It was waiting for me. When I stared at the suit it gave me the creeps. People got buried in suits. In bed I heard my heart pound. Three days before my bar mitzvah I was under religious house arrest—I was told to remain home from school. "Why can't I go to school?" I asked. We can't take a chance, Bubba said. You have to stay put. On Thursday, fed up with Bubba's threats, I snuck out of the house with Guttnik. We played ball hockey. I played goal. Karl took a slap-shot that hit me in the nose at about eighty miles an hour. I had a terrible nosebleed. I felt weak. The afternoon air was cool. I developed chills. I figured it was all in my head. I said nothing. The next morning I woke with a pounding headache and a fever of 102 degrees. My glands were swollen. Friday at noon Uncle Max appeared with his black bag. So, again you didn't listen to your Bubba, he said. "I went out for a walk, honest." Uncle Max took his stethoscope to my chest. *Deep breaths.* He looked in my throat. "Will I be all right?"

Stay in bed. Drink juice and take aspirin. We will see.

I had a dreamless sleep. When I awakened it was dark and my sheets were drenched with perspiration. My temperature had dropped. By dawn the fever left. Bubba came into my room. She spoke Yiddish to push the evil eye away. *Poo-poo-poo*. She kissed me.

She spat air away from my body as if she was draining me of a pestilence.

* * *

I dressed in my bar mitzvah suit, put on my shirt, and Father knotted my tie. I stared in the mirror and figured this was how I was meant to look. I sang as I was supposed to sing—as in a dream. In the afternoon I came home from synagogue, slept two hours, and dressed for the evening reception. I ate little. My body was weightless as a shadow. I gave my bar mitzvah speech. People clapped. "Reuben, you look so mature, you were perfect." People I had never seen handed me white envelopes; I passed them to Father. Herbie Faust, without crutches, danced with Ruthie-Annie. His head came up to her tits; he was waiting for his growth spurt. We did the bunny-hop together. I noticed Sammy Faust had not come. Faggie sat glum and alone. Lenny Loeb, Ari Mazer, Karl Guttnik, Sabrina Lustig, Josh Karp, my friends and cousins, were in the bunny-hop line.

Pinsky, the bar mitzvah was not for me—it was for Bubba, my parents, their relatives and friends. I wore my bar mitzvah suit like a zombie. The weight of my family was on my back. I dreaded Father would not pay back the money he borrowed for the bar mitzvah. I screwed up my courage and danced to *Stardust* with Sabrina Lustig. I felt her soft cheek, her warm body.

Three days I had not eaten. The celebration passed before me.

My bar mitzvah suit—R. Moses

A week later Father came to me. He asked for my bar mitzvah money.

I gave him every cent I had. He had to pay Manny Karp back.

November 17, 2008

Frieda Moses, M's ex-wife, leaves a sombre message at my office. She is a respected analyst in the Toronto community, an attractive intelligent woman. Frieda says M's analysis is helping him; M is less depressed and more open—he calls her nightly—he has not shared this with me. Frieda is worried not only about M's snarling dog, but that M has succeeded in alienating hundreds, perhaps thousands of women against him in his work on the *Bubba Complex*. Frieda fears that the *Bubba Complex* will go viral. She suggests that fanatics will harass and possibly attack M.

I recall the small parade of angry women appearing outside my office before M's session.

CHAPTER ELEVEN

Adolescent fixations: O. Pinsky,
November 24, 2008

Mcontinues to attend sessions. He wears a dark suit, dark tie, and a starched white shirt. Is this adherence to the dark suit a carry-over of his link to the past—the bar mitzvah suit? His once sleek black hair is filled with grey. Amidst his constant movements I note more fatigue. By November 24, 2008, M receives another two threatening notes. These notes have little to do with Jaffe-Jaffe but are related to the *Bubba Complex* as Frieda Moses suggested.

Evidently M has more enemies. I get M to focus on the present—I open my laptop to show him an *anti-Bubba Complex* blog. Cavalierly he brushes away my comment. Point blank I tell him about the figure in the trench coat outside my office—is this person prowling his office?

It becomes clearer why M dwells on the past avoiding his present turmoil. To explain this shift away from the present moment, I invoked the concept of trauma fixation—namely that M had, at an earlier phase of his life—*his childhood*, developed a deep attachment to an older woman, suffused with hostile erotic impulses which remained unresolved.

M was not only over stimulated by his Bubba as a child, but at age thirteen he was seduced by his friend's mother, Estella. As romantic as this youthful fantasy appears, in reality it spells disaster for the developing adolescent because of intense sexual excitation flooding the immature ego. M reported that he had read Ruthie-Annie's troubled diary where she wrote of sexual abuse at the hands of her father. He questioned his role as a witness to the atrocities Ruthie-Annie had suffered.

He debated his own wilful blindness.

But here he had to contend with his own unsettled sexual misadventure with Estella.

In the past, in the West, society was critical of premature sexual contact between an older man and a pubescent woman, yet neglected to consider the impact of an older woman wilfully seducing a male youth. My role here is not to take sides in this debate, nor evade analytic scrutiny of the impact of such violations or seductions on the vulnerable female or male ego, but to understand and treat in depth the factors responsible for M's neurosis. Certainly his relationship with his patient Blum re-enacting the role of M's Bubba, proved to be difficult for M.

By all accounts, M was regarded as a superb therapist, knowledgeable and empathic for the most vexing patient. More pressing and critical was the nature of aggression and hostility which M had unconsciously split off and denied. I assumed M had acted out some delinquent acts. When I confronted him about the smearing of feces—he dismissed any responsibility or involvement.

Newspapers, broadcasts, and internet activity on websites and social media pointed to increased public awareness of *The Bubba Complex*; M's work stimulated critical discussion in analytic circles. Media feasted on the term. Several comedians parodied the concept at comedy clubs. When a leading late-night TV talk show host did a satirical skit about Madonna and *The Bubba Complex*, the term became a buzzword. Having a *Bubba Complex* meant infatuation with an older woman. The term, originally intended as a psychoanalytic concept to describe a complex developmental process was appropriated by social media. This subverted M's original intention. The term was shorted to BC and used in texts and twitter as getting *BC'd*.

Just as Frieda Moses predicted, BC went viral. M became a media celebrity.

To burn off tension M compulsively jogged the city streets later at night to avoid being seen.

* * *

Dr. Sandor Gabor had grown up in Budapest. Gabor stated bluntly that M had been overstimulated in childhood—of this there was no doubt. He added two caveats—one: M was prone to vigorously deny and dissociate, and two: there was an unseen factor—an external hostile reality. Gabor, whose office was across the hall from M, had shit placed on his hood and the air let out of his tires. Another puzzling event was the night visitor inspecting my office door; it had happened too many times to be a simple coincidence. Once it had been M's mother paying me a visit. What of the other times? Security had picked up a grainy image, a person with a broad-brimmed hat in a trench coat, then nothing—tape had been placed over the camera. It was impossible to visualize the face. What joined these events? They were linked to M, but how? Had M caused them? Had he succeeded in polarizing groups of therapists and child educators to attack him? Was M, as his analysis illustrated, his own worst enemy?

* * *

Sam-Lee Yan, November 26, 2008

M fills me in on a new unsettling crisis. "Pinsky, Sam-Lee enters my office accompanied by three bodyguards with wireless ear-buds. Under their black suits they sport body armour, flak jackets. The scene is ridiculous. Sam-Lee is sporting a Kevlar vest—the helmet is a ballistic military type. The Serbian-Russian received several death threats. He sent his wife and kids away. The Serbian-Russian is not caving in to criminal types."

M laughs at this crazy charade.

The next week M tells me that the Serbian-Russian, Luka, has been shot dead. M's patient Sam-Lee is unsure whether to attend the funeral of his dead colleague. Police will be watching. So will the Russians, the Chinese, and the Iraqis. If Sam-Lee does not attend the funeral, people will be suspicious. If he does go he will be watched and likely followed. M's laughter is empty. For weeks Sam-Lee has been followed to M's office.

Frieda Moses, November 28, 2008

Frieda Moses phones my office. She leaves a voice message with times when we can talk person to person. She speaks with urgency. While M's depressive symptoms have lessened, he is in peril. We arrange a lunchtime chat the following day. "Normal physician confidentiality is trumped by life-threatening crises," she begins. "I believe that my husband is targeted."

"Targeted for what? Targeted by whom?"

"Targeted for what he has unwittingly done. He has to save patients. He works himself to the bone. He can't stop or hold himself back. He's struggled since childhood—years of analysis—he can't stop work to help others. It infuriates me—I left him, it was his doing. I want him to work on our marriage—we haven't divorced. Did he tell you that?"

"He told me you were divorced."

"No. He turns that around. Whatever he says, I love him. It's true I had an affair with his rival, Karl Guttnik—it was to confront Reuben. You must confront him before it is too late."

"*Me*—confront him? Too late—what do you mean?"

"His dog walker quit," Frieda says. "I go over and walk Jaffe-Jaffe at lunch. It's a short walk, about twenty minutes or so. With me the dog is calm. But when she is alone in the apartment she becomes frantic. She picks up a scent near his apartment—she knows it is not safe."

"She is a nervous dog when she is alone. M tell me that."

"She is nervous for a reason. For months she has sensed intruders."

"What are you talking about?"

"It is a patient, or a patient's partner, or some underworld connection—he has too many cases. When I walked Jaffe-Jaffe two days ago some driver almost ran into us."

"Mmm," I say, thinking. "Intentionally?"

"I think he might have received death threats."

"He never told me that," I say.

"Please—you must try to help him. Try to stop him from working this way."

Like the sky before a storm I see dark shadows spreading over the analysis.

CHAPTER TWELVE

Blum's condition: December 2, 2008

For the last few sessions, Blum appears motivated to work on her issues. It is strange, Pinsky, this *volte-face*, this turn around—I can't explain it. She is no longer late; she is on time. She is eager to start. No longer are there gaping silences, no more classic *kvetch*, or *krechts*, she lies down on the couch with an Obus form [for her back], she associates to her anger and frustration with me. Now she is not reactive, engaged in storms of anger, she is reflective, looking at the shapes of her mood from an elevated safe distance. So it is easier for us to work together. She tells me that she is not withdrawing her complaint—it turns out, she has made several complaints to the college about physicians—she wants to explore her dissatisfaction with me. Ivan has been speaking to her about our work. The fact I saw the two of them together demonstrated that I was genuinely interested in her.

In our relationship I feel—how can I say it—a seedling of trust.

"Dr. Moses, I feel irritation when I come to this office. Sitting in the waiting room, I feel anger. Before I never allowed myself to be early and think about my impatience—but living out these feelings and having the space to think about them, I realize I did not wait for anyone, I began to see that I refused to wait for anyone; I hate depending on people, they always disappoint me."

I feel my eyes burning. "And I disappoint you too, Mrs. Blum."

"*Oh, yes*—like Hermann von Blumenthal and other men in my life, I know that now."

"So what is it then?"

"It was no one; it was everyone—you see *life abandoned me*, Dr. Moses."

"How do you mean, life abandoned you?" Blum turns from me to face the wall.

"When I was a small child I lost my country and my past. Everything dear to me was taken away. My mother was poor and alone. My father had been murdered. His family had been killed."

There is a long silence. She lies motionless.

"I can't bear to lose anything more. I can't bear to want anything. That is why it is so crucial for me to have money, to be self-sufficient, to be independent."

"But you are still alone," I say.

Pinsky, at that moment I was thinking exactly the same thing, we are both alone.

"I have Ivan—you remind me of him—the nose, don't take this as criticism."

"I will try not to take it as a criticism, Mrs. Blum."

"I have my grandchildren, Dr. Moses—I have beautiful twin granddaughters. I see them on weekends. I did not play as a child—but with my twins, yes, it comes back."

I think of my daughters and my three grandsons. I play with them each week.

"Life abandoned me, Dr. Moses, I will not reach out again—you understand?"

"You fear being hopeful—you protect yourself with your work and your anger. It keeps you safe, distant, in control—that is what you are working on in here."

* * *

250

Jaffe-Jaffe's anxiety worsens: December 8, 2008

Jaffe-Jaffe has been acting nervous, Pinsky. Since Crystal quit Frieda walks the dog at lunch. You must discipline a *hund*, Frieda says. Be firm; show you are boss. And then Frieda tells me that she was so worried about me that she spoke to you.

"She loves you and wants to work on the marriage," I say. "She believes you are targeted. Tell me if there have been threats, angry notes, or any unusual events."

* * *

M's superintendent: December 10, 2008

Pinsky, my super calls me during Blum's session. Jaffe-Jaffe won't stop barking. He tries to settle Jaffe-Jaffe, bending down and patting her nose; the dog lunges and snaps at him. Your neighbours are fed up, says the super. You lost your dog walker. I am sick of your hysterical pet. Your dog is a barking nuisance. I don't care if your wife takes the dog for a walk. It's not enough. In the apartment she yelps, she snarls, she whines, she growls, she moans. Send her to a dog psychiatrist. He says twelve words that chill me. *If you don't do something, I will shut her up for good.*

To relieve the build-up of tension I jog at night. You wouldn't believe how lousy Toronto drivers are. These people don't drive cars—they aim them. Someone almost ran me off the road.

My mother's weather report: December 11, 2008

Reuben, your old friend, little Herbie, is very sick. He now lives with his sister who cares for him. He was our neighbour. I heard from the Zaglember Society that the hospital sent him home to die.

Before M's Friday session I see four black cube vans pull up before my office. I count twelve women organized two by two with placards standing on the sidewalk. I see them placing the black armbands on. The *Bubba Bund* march back and forth. The protesters know M comes to see me. He walks to my office from his brownstone. On the far edge of the road I note M in his dark suit scurrying along the snowy sidewalk rushing to see me. He politely waves to the women. He approaches them and carries on a brief discussion which turns into an argument. He shrugs, walks away and turns into my building. I make out their fixed glare tracing him to my office and feel uneasy with M's public persona stirring anger. People have a right to state their views, to argue, to protest, to voice difference. In newspapers, magazines, on television and internet I see images across North America and Europe, groups protesting the denigration of women. M tells me of the growing superiority of women over men and how men resent this. Can this basic truth be what infuriates the protest groups? Could his vandal be a man? What is M so powerfully stirring up in otherwise law-abiding citizens? Is he making himself into an effigy that some irate individuals vilify? Enough, enough, I tell myself. The office door buzzes. I let M into the waiting room.

After the Friday session I decide to follow M.

For the next few hours after our session I proceed by car and on foot to various parts of the city. In our analysis M has told me how he spends his day. I intend to check out his comings and goings, to see what in reality actually happens. Analysis is dependent on the reliability of the patient who is a witness to his own actions, feelings, and thoughts. In certain instances the patient as witness—*his recollection*—is fraught with errors, omissions, and distortions. Put in another way, the patient's memory may be deficient, the patient's powers of perception and understanding may be decreased, the patient may deliberately falsify an account, or the patient may be struggling against his repudiation of a troubling event. The analyst seeks to find a measure of truth and at the same time an explanation for the patient's difficulties.

252

M had discussed his schedule with me.

Upon arising he took Jaffe-Jaffe for a dawn stroll. After breakfast, showering, and changing into his suit, M drove his Volvo to his ground floor office in a brownstone on St. Clair shared with Karl Guttnik and Sandor Gabor. From early morning until midday M saw office patients. Monday to Thursday at lunchtime he came to his analysis with me. In the afternoon he walked to Mount Zion Hospital where he assessed clinic patients, taught residents, and carried out consultations. Here was where he saw the most difficult patients in the afternoon. By late afternoon he walked back to his St. Clair office and then saw analytic patients until evening. On Friday M walked to my office from his brownstone. We had a four o'clock session then M took his mother shopping.

Friday December 12, 2008: following M

I followed him by car that Friday afternoon to his brownstone office. The roads were clogged and slowed by December ice and snow. He drove his Volvo to his mother's apartment a few blocks from his office. He did not see me but I noticed his car had a broken headlight. His shopping took ninety minutes after which he dropped his mother off at a married daughter's. He proceeded to drive to his apartment a half-mile north. I followed him, parked my car a few blocks away, and discreetly waited outside his apartment. A half hour later M changed into yellow jogging shoes and pants, a winter running jacket, a toque and gloves, and emerged with Jaffe-Jaffe. The two were going for a walk. I recognized Jaffe-Jaffe's nervous canter.

I kept a safe distance behind the pair as they walked around a local park. M did not take Jaffe-Jaffe off-leash until they reached an enclosed dog park. He did some stretches while Jaffe-Jaffe ran about with other dogs and then sat down on a park bench. A woman joined him on the bench. I noted she was petting Jaffe-Jaffe and talking to M and the dog. She was too young to be his wife; I assumed she was Crystal, the former dog walker. She was remarkably beautiful and her appearance had an arresting effect on the men in the dog park. She bent forward and touched, or should I say, caressed M on the shoulder. I imagined the onlookers wondered about their relationship—was she a daughter, a friend, a lover? The two became involved in an animated conversation while Jaffe-Jaffe pranced about. Crystal gently brushed M's shoulder twice. I considered Crystal's boyfriend, Zeno, who was to be released from jail, and who, according to M was extremely jealous. No sooner did this enter my mind than a tall bearded dark-haired man in a leather jacket walked before the couple: Zeno, I presumed he had been released from jail early. He was displeased. I was close enough to hear their voices arguing.

I believe M tried to persuade Crystal to return to work as his dog walker.

Zeno appeared angry. Crystal seemed more unsettled.

M and Jaffe-Jaffe left a few minutes later. M turned and walked in another direction. He headed towards the apartment on DuMont Street with Jaffe-Jaffe. It was now early evening and the sky had coloured from dark blue to pitch-black. I drove my car slowly along the Toronto streets and followed M as he entered the foyer and took the elevator. I parked quickly across the street, rushed to the apartment main entrance, pushed the automatic door to the residents' suites; this time it had been repaired and remained locked. A few minutes later a teenager in dark glasses carrying a guitar case departed. I was able to enter and found myself on the second floor outside suite 21 listening to the low growl of a dog and the high-pitched vocalizations of Jaffe-Jaffe. M was at GC's apartment for I heard the baritone voice of a man, then M talking, and a woman's voice in the background. M was seeing GC for PTSD. Why home visits? I saw M pushing a burly bearded man in a wheelchair accompanied by a huge mastiff. One hour later, at about eight-thirty, M appeared on the street without Jaffe-Jaffe. He stretched and began to jog on the sidewalk following a major thoroughfare. I started my car and followed him as he turned southwards; M descended from the sidewalk and ran on the road in the right inner lane. He picked up speed. He sprinted past several parked cars, weaving in and out of winter traffic.

* * *

I had asked M about GC. He told me of a Vietnam medic caught in a roadside ambush who lost both legs. GC lived with his mother and because of his earlier trauma was terrified to leave his apartment without his service dog.

* * *

I returned to my office, made notes in M's files and was about to return home when the night security guard knocked on my door.

"You had another visitor," said the night security guard. "I wanted to let you know. We have an image on our monitor, same trench coat and hat, no distinguishing features."

The night security guard invited me to review his file.

I walked to the security room and checked the building's CCTV bank of monitors. I saw two of my day's patients, M and Blum as they entered and left the building. I saw the mail-woman. I saw the maintenance man clearing snow from the entrance then myself entering and leaving. I saw four cube vans parked in front of the building and twelve angry women march before my office. I reviewed the intruder in trench coat and hat. The images did not reveal any identity.

I thought of Crystal's anxiety, her involvement with M, her boyfriend Zeno, and M's insistence that she get her job back as his dog walker. M strongly believed in the importance of work for others. He followed the path of his tireless Bubba and industrious parents who worked dawn to dusk. Many of his family and friends had fled atrocities in Europe—immigrants, refugees, *DP's* they were called. My own family had escaped the war when I was a child and come to Canada. M was driven by some inner force that neither he nor I could explain. He masked his suffering through self-mocking humour which warded off a sense of ineffable emptiness.

On his Monday session he spoke of his first job, his initiation into the adult world of work.

CHAPTER THIRTEEN

My first job

Bubba said I should get a job. But how do I get a job? Father said to discuss prospects over a deli lunch, man-to-man. A good place for a meal in Toronto was Switzer's deli on Spadina Avenue above Dundas Street. Switzer's had a sign: *Hope to meat you soon*. Inside were cozy wooden booths and a counter where you sat on stools. Father argued Switzer's had the top knishes in Toronto. The beef was spicy, pink, and succulent. The best *kishka* was at Zuchter's deli on Adelaide Street. If you wanted an amazing bowl of soup, you went to United Bakery on Spadina—their split-pea soup had a magic aroma— dill, thyme, pepper, potatoes, served with fresh black bread. *Heaven*! He spooned soup, eyes closed. *Smell it. Taste it*. Dad's favourite was Shopsy's beside the Victory Burlesque. He told me about gangsters like Max Bluestein who nearly got whacked in a nearby tavern and Manny Karp who didn't follow rules. "Jews and Italians love good food—especially criminals. They do their deals in restaurants."

I felt excited to be with my dad. It was great to have him all to myself over lunch. At Shopsy's you ordered cafeteria style: smoked meat, pastrami, corned beef, baby beef, tongue, salami sandwiches, baby dills, kugel, *kishka*, and *gefilte fish*. Shopsy's had pieces of wurst on toothpicks with a sign: "A nickel a *shtikel*." At the back of the deli Shopsy's sold Cuban cigars.

The air was redolent with tobacco and hot pastrami. Father told me about customers at tables, the *schmata* crowd, *ganifs*, shills, and gamblers. Beside the counter, I saw wary meat-slicers, talkative waiters, and the owner Sam Shopsowitz, a flushed corpulent blond man and his young brother Izzie. Yitz was the hawkeye manager. On the walls were black-and-white pictures of Jimmy Durante, Bob Hope, Tony Martin, George Raft, Xavier Cugat, Jerry Lewis, Dean Martin, Red Buttons, Milton Berle, Louis Armstrong—entertainers who ate at the Toronto deli and posed with Sam. I was fifteen and needed a summer job. Dad said maybe we could work something out—a deal. They could use a young guy like you at the CNE, Dad said, confident of my potential. We drove to Spadina Avenue, parking opposite Sammy Taft's store. "I buy my fedoras here," Dad said. "Sammy offers a hat to any Leaf who scores three goals—"

"You mean Sammy started the hat trick?"

"*Sshh*." Dad clapped a finger to his lips as we entered. "You have to be sixteen to work at Shopsy's. I call the manager and deal. I say you are sixteen. Understand?"

"What do I do?"

"Say you are sixteen. When I nod, you stand up."

"But I am fifteen," I said. "What if he asks for my driver's permit?"

"That's what you don't do—see? They will listen to me. First I order food."

I felt shifty and nervous like a criminal. Dad knew everyone. He joked with the headwaiter. They talked a good five minutes. The corned beef was fine, lean and tasty. Dad asked if Yitz was in the store, he'd like to see him. *Get ready*, he whispered. Meanwhile I tried to eat my dill pickle and corned beef without choking. "You'll be fine," Dad said. "Do what I say. Watch me."

Two men entered the deli in pinstripe suits. They sat down opposite us and looked deathly serious. I couldn't tell if they were Jews or Italians, regulars or gangsters, getting ready to kill someone. *Relax*, Dad said. Look, there's Manny Karp with Sammy Faust—he's doing a deal. *Don't worry. Nothing will happen*. Outside, a car honked. I jumped. Yitz came by, a pencil over his ear. He gave me a once over. "What's your name?" I didn't speak. I concentrated on eating my corned beef. I watched my father. I looked at the two men in pinstripe suits. They were slurping matzo-ball soup. I stared at the wall and saw an autographed photo of Jack Benny holding a violin.

Yitz was speaking to me. I didn't hear him. "*I said*, what's your name, boy?"

Dad kicked me under the table. "Reuben, sir," I said. "That's my name."

"Son, you want a job?"

"Yes, sir. Definitely."

"Can you make change?"

"Yes, sir. Definitely."

"He's a good boy, smart," my dad said.

"I'm talking." Yitz bent down and stared at me. "How old are you?"

"Sixteen."

"Son, are you sure about that?" Yitz asked. "You know to make change?" His eyes were black and shiny like polished knife handles. My dad nodded. I stood up. I was four inches taller than my father and six inches taller than Yitz. "You like hard work?" Yitz asked.

"Hard work—yes, sir. I am a hard worker. I am a very, very hard worker."

"Come by the restaurant at the Grandstand, Sunday, the week before the Ex begins. We will fix you up then." To celebrate, my dad bought me an extra sandwich—hot pastrami—and afterwards we finished off the meal with a slice of apple strudel.

Torture #12. They paid me a lousy dollar and twenty-five cents an hour. They gave me a white hat, white pants, an apron, a jacket, and a wooden tray with pockets for bills

and change. There were only a few things on the menu—
corned beef, pastrami, salami sandwiches, dill pickles, hot
dogs, soda pop, coffee, and tea. The restaurant was a circular
building opposite the Grandstand. I worked from eleven in the
morning until eleven at night when the grandstand fireworks
signalled the show finale. Yitz was our boss and I was one of
the slaves.

I was to bring twenty dollars of my own money and that
was my float.

* * *

Pinsky, I didn't know at the time but Karp and Faust were up to
no good. Remember the fire beside our drugstore, well, Faust
made a deal with Karp to set the fire. It came out years later
after Karp had some lackey put a match to two other stores.
Karp was cooking the books for Faust—the tax department
caught them. Sammy red-faced Faust left his wife for some
bimbo. I never quite figured what happened with Ruthie-Annie. My first day at work this guy ordered a corned beef and
gave me a five-dollar bill. I gave him change for ten. I ran the
scene over in my mind twice.

"*Wait*. Excuse me, sir; I think I gave you too much money."

"No, you didn't."

"You gave me five dollars," I said. "I am pretty sure."

"Show me the five-dollar bill," the man said. "I want to
see it."

"I don't have it now."

"Too bad," the man said. "Like you said, you gave me
change for ten dollars."

"You took my money—"

"Better watch what you say, sonny boy," the man said.

I walked to Yitz on cash. The man took his corned beef on a
paper plate with his Coke. He opened the sandwich to put on
mustard and pepper and then started to eat the sandwich and

drink his Coke at the counter. I asked Yitz to call the cops. "No. You keep the bill on the tray right under your thumb—you can show it to the customer. If there's a problem you come to the cash."

"But he only gave me five dollars."

Yitz opened the cash register. "Show me his bill." Yitz pointed to a wad of bills between the two-dollar pile and ten-dollar pile. "Tell me, which five-dollar bill is his?"

"Maybe it is the third one—that one," I pointed, "—there."

"Are you sure?"

"It was folded, like he sort of folded it in his pocket. I can't be sure."

"Listen. You may be right but you have to prove it. Customers don't care if a waiter makes a mistake as long as it doesn't cost them. You make a mistake, you pay for it. That's business."

"You mean there's nothing I can do?"

"Nothing—you just have to be nice to the customers and smart about cash." I looked over to the counter. The man had gone. I figured he cheated me out of five dollars. From then on I kept a close eye on the money the customers gave me. I was furious at the man for not telling me the truth and then I was furious that I was making a lousy dollar and twenty-five cents an hour and had to work day and night to break even. I was furious with Yitz for not getting back my five dollars. I was angry with everyone because I had to order, pay with my float, serve the customer, double check my change—it reminded me of the money I had lost but then I didn't let it get to me because I had to put in more orders, I had to remember customers' faces and the money they gave me, and hold onto the bill and make change. By night end I was down eleven dollars and ten cents. I hadn't made any tips. I couldn't figure out who swindled me out of my money. I wanted to find that first customer and murder him on the spot. Most of all I was angry with myself. This was a big lesson. After the first day

261

it never happened again. I told Bubba what happened. Bubba said keep a smile on my face and be nice to everyone—don't trust a soul.

Pinsky, work was important to me. I told Crystal to get to work; it would be good for her.

On the third day I started making tips. Celebrities came from the Grandstand for a corned beef. In the evening at 10:30 the show was over and there was a massive firework display. The first night, after I lost my entire float, I forgot about fireworks and heard gunfire. It was coming closer. I ducked below the counter, figuring the customer was back with his gangster buddies—they were gunning for a showdown.

Sammy Faust supplied pots and pans for Shopsy's. Faust had *schlepp*—this was before he went to jail. Who should start work but Herbie! He worked as an assistant slicer—preparing corned beef and pastrami. His leg was better but he had a limp. I worried Herbie would lose a finger in the slicer and Ruthie-Annie would blame me. And who was the head slicer?— Guttnik. He was four years older than me and going out with Sabrina Lustig.

I know it's not polite or nice to say but I hoped he would lose all his fingers in the meat slicer.

The next day The Three Stooges came for lunch. My luck, the three of them started to walk to my section of the restaurant. Guttnik and the other two slicers, the assistant slicers, and the cashiers were staring. Everyone at Shopsy's loved The Three Stooges. They were our heroes. Reuben, go get their autographs, Guttnik said. Ask him for tickets to their show. "Lay off," I said. "Get your own tickets, Guttnik." C'mon, Reuben, be a sport. We love their movies. Maybe they will give us tickets. "*Drop dead*," I said. "I have to keep my mind on what they order—so shut up, Guttnik. I'm not losing my float." I checked my bills. I counted change. I stood at attention and waited for The Three Stooges to come closer. I spoke to Moe. I had seen his movies on TV.

"I want three corned beef sandwiches on rye, very lean, no fat on the side," Moe said, "—with sour dill sliced and no mustard inside."

"We never put any mustard inside. It's pure 100 per cent corned beef."

"You'll make it lean. Remember."

"Three up on rye, *lean*," I yelled at Guttnik and Herbie Faust.

"You want *lean to the left* or *lean to the right*?" Guttnik yelled back.

I brought Moe three sandwiches with a sliced dill pickle. There was absolutely no fat on his corned beef anywhere. Guttnik had sliced a masterpiece and Herbie had heaped twice as much corned beef on the bread—the sandwich was a goddamn work of art. Moe took the sandwich. He didn't smile or leave a tip. Sammy Faust came with Ruthie-Annie and Faggie to see Herbie. Ruthie-Annie didn't say a word. Sammy Faust left me a two-dollar bill. The next day Karp showed up with two guys and ordered a pile of sandwiches. He was back in town on business. Karp left me two dollars as well. The one person who left a big tip was Victor Borge—he was a classy guy with a Danish accent who played piano and told jokes. I saw him on TV. I told him he made me laugh. "Laughter is the shortest distance between two people," he said. His real name was Borge Rosenbaum, a piano prodigy, a Jewish refugee who fled the war. He left me a five buck tip.

Frieda calls my office: December 22, 2008

"*Listen*, Moses, I've heard your thousand and one stories of childhood," I say. "Let us talk of the present. Frieda, called this week. She wants to work on your marriage. Frieda says you are not divorced. She never divorced you. She wants you back."

"More bullshit," M says. "*She* left me."

"Frieda worries about your safety. She says she loves you."

"*Love*—she loves me?" M laughs. It is a muffle, a moan, a sigh dressed in a smile.

"Frieda believes someone is out to harm you. Jaffe-Jaffe senses danger. She told me she loves you and is worried. You've been attacked at presentations of the Bubba complex, haven't you?"

"Pinsky, Freud's ideas were also attacked." M's eyes gleam. "My work on the Bubba complex has been accepted for the World Analytic Meeting in Montreal in July 2009. See?"

M disregards my warnings and drifts back to the past.

* * *

"One thing my dad and I did together was watch *Hockey Night in Canada*. Most boys and their dads were nuts about hockey; after all, it was our national sport. Canada had the greatest hockey players in the world. I told everyone at Shopsy's I played hockey; it was a total lie, I played road hockey with a lousy tennis ball and a hockey stick. Bubba refused to let me play ice hockey. She repeated the Mendel story—not only had he lost both eyes now but suffered a head injury and was paralyzed from the waist down. *Dad*, please. I want hockey skates. I am going to be *sixteen*. Every guy has skates. Even Herbie has skates. OK, he said, I will get you skates in the fall."

"Your wife is worried for you," I say. "Why are you talking about the past?"

"Will you stop interrupting? Nobody listened to me as a kid. They were too busy working."

* * *

Everybody loved corned beef especially hockey players. I served Bobby Baun and Carl Brewer—they played defense for the Toronto Maple Leafs. That spring, in 1962, the Leafs won the Stanley Cup. Brewer was shorter than me, but his arms were knotted with muscle. He was one of the most agile skaters I ever saw. Hi, Carl, I said. Have you begun training camp? We started last week, he replied, wiping the side of his mouth deftly with the edge of a napkin. Give me another corned beef, will you? He had short close-cropped hair and iridescent blue-grey eyes. Everything about him was sharp. I hope you go all the way this year, I said. I play hockey too.

Keep your head up, he said.

I wanted to ask questions about how he handled big players, protected his goalie, and passed the puck to his forwards. He made faces at the opposition, got penalties, but didn't fight. I wanted to ask him if he knew he was going to be a professional hockey player.

He took his second sandwich, smiled, and disappeared into the crowd.

Father said Switzer's had the best beef knishes
in the world.—R. Moses

CHAPTER FOURTEEN

Love's torture

Torture #13. Pinsky, before I fell asleep I thought of Sabrina Lustig. I walked past her house each morning on my way to our grade ten English class with Miss Carducci at Vaughan Road Collegiate. For three weeks I composed a love letter: nothing emerged. When I did my homework I drew her face in the margins. When I read books she sat at the top of each page. I dreamt of *Sabrina*. Pinsky, I wore size eleven shoes. My Adam's apple was huge. My testicles expanded. I needed loose underwear to keep them from asphyxiating. Both of them were sweaty making testosterone day and night. I was almost six feet, a half foot taller than Father. I developed a stoop. I tried to put Estella out of mind. Ari said his dad helped Estella's family flee Havana for Miami. Estella had a new boyfriend, her tennis coach—she gave him dance lessons. She never loved me.

* * *

December 23, 2008

M has brought Jaffe-Jaffe to our session. For the moment the dog sits quietly beside her master as he repeats his litany of bygone neurotica. I slap my hand on my knee. I want to jolt M out of his past reveries and shake him into the present. "Look, this is important, sure, *but it went on a half-century ago*. Frieda worries for your safety. You have a serious problem with your patients Crystal and Sam-Lee Yan. We are here in the *present*, Reuben. We can return to the past later. *This is December 23, 2008.*" M ignores me and pats Jaffe-Jaffe.

* * *

Sabrina had curly black hair, twinkling almond eyes, and generous lips that were smiling or pouting—it slayed me to look at her. "Ari, don't tell anyone," I whispered, "I love *Sabrina Lustig*." She sat in the middle row of home class beside her best friend Tina Skolnik, who wore thick spectacles and was basically blind with the naked eye. I sketched Sabrina in school. She wore a white blouse and a grey skirt. She had a perfect body. I worked on my love letter in class; each day I added a phrase or crossed out a word. The love letter had to be perfect. Miss Carducci taught us J. D. Salinger's *Catcher in the Rye* and Shakespeare's *Hamlet*. I tried to steal ideas from Holden Caulfield or Hamlet. Both guys were total losers. In Miss Carducci's English class I passed Ari a new edition of my love letter. What do you think of this version, Ari?

A fatal mistake. Ari passed it to Josh Karp who sat beside us.

"Reuben, what are you and Ari and Josh talking about?" Miss Carducci asked.

"Nothing, Miss Carducci," I said.

"You are talking about *something*," Miss Carducci said as she rubbed her silver neck crucifix. Miss Carducci had straight black hair and thick eyebrows that grew together over her nose. She had a little moustache over her lip too. "You pass notes. I hear you talking. Don't try to fool me."

"There's no note, Miss Carducci," Ari said.

Joshua Karp could not tell a lie. I whispered to him to shut the fuck up.

"I see a note on Reuben's desk. Ari, you bring it up to the front of the class and read it to us."

"Miss Carducci, I can't do that," Ari said.

"Who was the writer of that note?" Miss Carducci asked.

"It was definitely not us," Ari said. "We don't know who did it."

"It was a private note," Joshua Karp, the informer said.

"Is that the honest truth, so help you God?" Miss Carducci said. The class was quiet as a tomb. "I demand to know who the writer of that note is, or else everyone in row four will have a detention," Miss Carducci said. "If Ari and Reuben did not write that note, who did? I will give you ten seconds to tell me the truth or there will be a class detention, all of you. Was it you, Josh?"

"It was *absolutely definitely* not me," Joshua Karp said.

"Whoever wrote the note, stand up?" Miss Carducci began to count. "Ten … nine …" I thought of gulping the note, running from the room, jumping out the window, or diving into a brick wall and smashing my brains to smithereens. There was no escape. "Six … five … four …." Bubba told me I should never lie. I always had to be good. "Three …" Miss Carducci had pulled out the Bible from her desk. The next step was that she would come down our row and ask Ari or me to swear on the Old Testament. She did that when she wanted the truth. The class was Italian, Portuguese, Hungarian, and Jewish— between the Catholics and Jews there was enough guilt to sink a ship. "Two …" At the count of one I raised my hand. Miss Carducci, I am sorry. I wrote the letter. "Reuben. Come to the front of the class. Let us hear you read." Miss Carducci, I said, sitting at my desk, it is *personal*. "Personal notes are not discussed in English. Read the note." I was cornered. The class waited; thirty-two students focused their attention on me. I lifted the paper. I rose from my seat. I walked to the front of the class. Ari stared pitifully at me. Josh Karp looked out the window. I took a breath. I tried not to see the class, least of all Sabrina. I read my letter, slowly, painfully, face down. Each word was a tooth wrenched from my jaw. I declared the most private human feeling—*Desire*. Two people giggled. Tina Skolnick smirked. I felt destroyed.

Dear Sabrina,

You are the most beautiful angel in my universe. When I sleep you are my starlight. When I wake you are the wind that kisses my skin. Sabrina, if the world was going to start all over tomorrow, I would be with you. Sabrina, if the world was going to end tomorrow, I would be with you. Sabrina, would you come out for a Coke with me? You know me from Miss Carducci's English class. I am the curly dark-haired person behind Ari Mazer.

Yours truly,
Reuben Moses Row 4, Seat 5,
Miss Carducci's Home Room 10 B.

I walked to my seat. I didn't look up until I sat in my seat and saw Miss Carducci. Her eyes were dewy. Josh Karp stared out the window. "This is like Dante's poem for Beatrice," Miss Carducci said. I had no idea what she meant. My face blazed with shame.

* * *

December 23, 2008

I can't stomach the colossal grandeur of M's lost loves, his morbid hyperbolic misery. I see where he resides. He spends life lying on a bed of psychic nails.

I urge him to the present. He pats Jaffe-Jaffe and after a moment returns to the past.

* * *

Pinsky, Father unwound at night after long hours at the drugstore, he upped his Crown Royal to a glass and a half, he chainsmoked, he ate pistachios; he watched hockey or TV horror movies. "Dad, you are smoking cigarettes—one after the other. It's a bad habit. You don't get exercise. You cough in the mornings. You're in big debt with these bills, you owe Bubba; you worry all the time. You borrow from Karp. You play cards with him and lose. You borrow from me. You make me anxious, Dad. You are putting on weight. You don't take care of yourself."

Pinsky, each week I told him to stop smoking and gambling. See a psychiatrist, I told him as we watched *The Thing*, a TV horror movie. Dad loved horror movies. The more people that died, or got vaporized, the more excited he appeared. "Now what are they going to do?"

"*The Thing* is there—it is thawing out," I said. "They are all going to die." *The Thing* was indestructible. It was huge, from another planet, and had been buried under the ice and snow for eons. The scientists were total idiots. They were in snowy Antarctica, in the middle of fucking nowhere. We watched as the Thing killed humans. To me, it seemed, Father was rooting for *The Thing*. "Dad … I have a bit of a problem—"

"*Sssh*—this is the best part."

I wanted to talk about sex. Father sold special creams for vaginas and condoms for men. He had penicillin for venereal disease. I figured he was an expert. In health class we learned about syphilis and gonorrhea and pregnancy. I wondered if I had an incurable illness. I wasn't able to stop dreaming about Estella and Sabrina Lustig. I needed to masturbate three times a day just to be sane. "Dad, I have a crush on a girl in class—"

"Relax, Reuben, let's watch *The Thing*. Look, look what's happening now—"

"Dad, I'm going half-crazy about—"

We sat on the edge of our seats watching *The Thing* as it destroyed whatever was alive. *The Thing* was too evil to die. Talking sense to it didn't work. Bullets didn't work. It was too late to freeze it back to ice. "Look at that—will you?" Father said. I closed my eyes. *The Thing* got killed. By the end of the night I was unable to sleep. Sitting with Father in a room filled with thick blue smoke, we watched *Frankenstein*, *The Wolf-Man*, *Dracula*, *The Curse of the Mummy*, *King Kong*, and *The Day the Earth Stood Still*. Father took me to see *War of the Worlds*. I developed insomnia. Extraterrestrials were going to land behind our house. I dreamt of flying saucers. When I woke at night I was paralyzed with fear. I stopped dreaming about Sabrina.

* * *

December 23, 2008

Outside my office as M talks about the past I hear a muffled sound of trucks. Jaffe-Jaffe shifts uneasily on the carpet beside her master. From my chair I make out black cube vans parked on the other side of the street. I crane my neck to see more but only hear voices. Jaffe-Jaffe settles and closes her eyes. I think nothing of it and return to M as he recites life a half-century ago.

Saturday night Father and I sat back and watched TV … at midnight there was the scariest movie I had ever seen. The movie was about a doctor. He was transformed into a horrid evil creature—*Dr. Jekyll and Mr. Hyde*. My throat was in a knot. I had trouble swallowing—Jekyll was losing control and becoming Hyde. I tried to calm my breathing.

"Split personality," Father said. "He switches from nice doctor to his dark side," he said.

"Do people actually have a dark side, a split personality?"

"Definitely."

Pinsky, that movie was my life. Finally I understood. On the outside I was this nice decent Jewish guy—I went to school, did homework, watched my brothers, prayed to God, and tried to tell the truth like Bubba said. The other part of me

271

skipped classes, shot pool, didn't do homework, masturbated, and stopped keeping kosher. I nearly killed my brother with a baseball bat. I broke Herbie Faust's leg in three places—not intentionally. I wanted to rip the clothes off Sabrina Lustig. *I was a raving lunatic.* At night my Hyde took over. Pinsky, I felt like confessing sex crimes to the cops and getting locked up before worse things happened.

I decided to tell Ari the whole story, start to finish.

"Whatever you got," Ari said, "you got it bad."

"Ari, am I normal? Please tell me—you are the only person in the whole world who knows what I think. How do I know what happens when I sleep? Suppose I get out of bed, sleep-walk, and do terrible things—understand? I can't get women out of my mind. They tear me apart."

I tell Ari the truth.

"Ari, I have constant sex dreams—it started with my Bubba."

* * *

At a school sock hop I danced with a grade nine girl, Roxanne Greenbaum. Her parents owned Greenbaum's dairy; she was sort of cute but had a zit on her chin. She reminded me of Ruthie-Annie. On principle I never talked to Ruthie-Annie since her brother's leg got busted. Roxanne wasn't a great student or anything. She didn't keep a secret diary but wore glasses like Ruthie-Annie. Who cared? Roxanne had great lips. Her bum wiggled. She was a hell of a *shmoocher*. We walked to her house—her parents were out—we made out in the basement for four hours.

We basically did everything you could do without taking your clothes off.

We were two wild animals. Pinsky, Roxanne became my sex object. One day, towards the end of November, in Miss Carducci's home room English class, Sabrina Lustig with her dark flashing eyes and beautiful lips spoke to me. "Reuben," she giggled. "When will you take me for a Coke?"

"You're joking, right?"

"No. I loved your letter. It was so sweet. Tina says you are a poet."

"A poet, *get off it*, Sabrina. You *are* joking, right?"

"Reuben, you had courage to do what you did," Sabrina said.

At the end of classes I walked her home. On Thursday afternoon I asked her out for a Coke to the *Bagel-King* restaurant on Eglinton Avenue. We sat in a booth and talked for two whole hours straight. "Sabrina, would you like to go to the December prom with me?"

"Reuben that would be fun, but I have a date."

"A date—who are you going with?"

"Karl Guttnik," Sabrina said. "We are going steady."

"Guttnik? He's in grade thirteen! He's a total egghead."

"I like older men," Sabrina said. "Karl said it's OK if *we* go out for Cokes."

"He said it's OK? How sweet. Is Guttnik the prime minister or something?"

"Karl is already accepted into Pre-Medicine next year at U of T. He will be a surgeon like his big brother," Sabrina said. "What are you going to be, Reuben?"

"Big deal—everybody knows Karl is a complete genius—especially Guttnik. He already does differential calculus and reads Greek for god sakes. He is going to lead a boring life. He will stand first in everything. He will win gold medals, the Nobel Prize. Tell me—what fun is that?"

"I asked you a question, Reuben. What are you going to be?"

* * *

December 24, 2008

Jaffe-Jaffe wakes beside M just as I recall that Guttnik was brilliant, good-looking, and two grades behind me in high school.

273

He married Sabrina, the prom queen and had four children. M's self-mocking exasperates me. He exaggerates misfortune and craves tragedy. I can't get to the bottom of it. He makes me powerless, then I think, it is *transference*. I have become his Bubba.

He needs me to protect him yet he refuses to listen and controls me with his pains.

There is a loud sound coming from the street outside my office—a voice on a megaphone? Jaffe-Jaffe rushes to the window. She barks and lunges. I get up from my chair and follow her.

"Look, you see what is out there? Do you see now?" I point angrily to the street outside my window. M lifts himself off the couch. Jaffe-Jaffe barks uncontrollably, leaping to the window, snarling, baring her teeth. "This is the present, Moses. This is reality. See what you have done!"

Outside protesters stand from the *Bubba Bund*. They have followed M to my office.

They carry large placards and posters. "*Stop Bubba Bashing*."

A series of farting sounds and a thick heavy penetrating unmistakeable aromatic odour permeates my office. I look down.

Jaffe-Jaffe in her rage has lost control of her bowels. Or perhaps she has used her bowels to express what she cannot tell us. Jaffe-Jaffe has deposited two enormous puddles of watery shit on my oriental rug.

CHAPTER FIFTEEN

Back pain: December 24, 2008

I am not sure when I read through all the files Ivan Blum sent me. Blum had trouble lying down on the couch, changing positions was difficult. Back pain—she said she pulled a back muscle in yoga class. She complained her appetite was poor. I assumed it was her low mood. She had been depressed and gone off her antidepressant. I tried to persuade her to restart Celexa. She refused. She was seeing a naturopath, a chiropractor, and a personal trainer. Have you had a medical check-up? No, she said. Mrs. Blum, I am your analyst. It would be a good idea to have a full medical exam. When was the last time you saw your GP? Blum was on hospital boards—she could make an appointment for a check-up at the Mount Zion—she didn't need me. I stopped bugging her. She talked of her lost family— her father, her two older brothers, and a sister.

* * *

Since our separation I walk to my office from my bachelor apartment four blocks from the house where Frieda and I raised our family. Frieda still lives nearby in a new townhouse; I see her in sweat pants *schlepping* our garbage cans to the curb Thursday mornings. During weekends I walk by our old home and gaze at the swings in the backyard where my daughters played. A new family with two boys and a dog has moved in. At night I jog by Frieda's townhouse. Each weekend I visit my daughters and play with my grandkids. "Why are you not with Mom?" my daughters ask. "She is alone and so are you." Frieda dragged out newspapers, boxes, and bottles, the first time I saw her. I was jogging on the other side of the street. I waved at her. She waved back.

Blum comes to our sessions with a heating pad. Ivan has taken her to her GP. Blood tests and X-rays are done. To me, she looks drawn. In the evening, after I see hospital patients I walk back to my apartment. Everything is in boxes. It's been that way for ages. I make dinner and call my daughters. Jaffe-Jaffe has been unsettled, sniffing around the apartment, yelping. I think she misses Crystal, the dog walker. Crystal is considering whether or not to return to her dog walking job. Zeno is not keen on her working for me. Zeno offers to have one of his gang member friends walk Jaffe-Jaffe. No thanks, I say. Amidst the gloom I feel more positive. The Bubba complex has been accepted for the World Analytic Meeting July 2009 in Montreal.

My mother's daily weather report

Reuben, you heard about Herbie Faust, the kalika with polio—I didn't go to the funeral. Josh Karp, Manny's son phoned me—he ended up a police detective. Imagine Manny Karp, in jail, taking cash from Italians and Jews, burning down Faust's stores—an accountant yet. Not one moment were Sammy and Faggie happy. Josh Karp went to the funeral. You know who came? Ruthie-Annie. After you broke little Herbie's leg in three places, she got sick—blaming doctors and you. Her husband died; she never remarried. I gave Josh your number—is that all right?

* * *

276

Sam-Lee Yan asks for an early session. He comes with three bodyguards; his Hummer idles outside my office. He wears a dun-coloured long-sleeved safari suit, with multiple pockets, large enough for body armour. "The safari suit is making a comeback, Dr. Moses. When I worked in southeast Asia and India this was respectable attire. One of my bodyguards carries a vapour analyzer, a Geiger counter, a chemical weapon suit with gas mask—my enemies play tough. I don't want you in any danger." Sam-Lee plans to take an extended holiday. He plops down a special government-issue gas mask for me with a duffel bag containing a chemical weapon suit.

He is leaving right after the session.

"Where you will be staying?"

"I can't tell you."

"Whatever you tell me is confidential."

"Don't put this on my chart."

"Why not?"

"You have no idea who is against me." Sam-Lee Yan writes down where he will be in Miami, shows me the address, and puts the paper into my paper shredder. "Your office is bugged. I can't talk. They will take your files. They will stop at nothing. If I need something I will call."

He leaves me a card.

"Goodbye, Doc. I've paid for two months of cancelled sessions. Maybe I will see you again."

After Sam-Lee departs I open the envelope.

Fifty one-hundred dollar bills are folded inside a goodbye card.

* * *

After Sam-Lee leaves my office I feel uneasy. I check my office for small bugs, wires, any object that could be used to watch me. I disbelieve Sam-Lee, yet he is no fool.

Sam-Lee has seen the dark seamy side of life. He is a survivor and has a sixth sense.

Pinsky, I tell myself that I have done nothing wrong.

PART FOUR

THE LAST PHASE DISRUPTED
ANALYSIS: JANUARY 2009–JULY 2009

CHAPTER ONE

The last phase: O. Pinsky, January 2009

One knows how an analysis begins, but one has little knowledge of how an analysis will end. Our predictions are fallible and like many human projects at the outset we are faced with our limited horizon of skill and knowledge. It is only in retrospect that we can trace the complex skein of external situations and internal mental events that influence life, yet even then, we are faced with approximations. Each time when I replaced my notes at the end of a session in M's file, which had grown to four folders, including diaries, sketches, cartoons, Bubba's recipes, personal reflections, I wondered what direction our analytic journey would take.

The most intractable part of M's analysis—his childhood—which in the past had been hermetically sealed, was now gradually opening itself to exploration. Childhood, as we know, is the most formative stage of human development but adolescence and young adulthood with their turbulent passions and anxieties are the most difficult to face. M's early trauma and seduction by his Bubba [whether directly intended or largely imagined we will never know] paved the way for his hypersensitive and unsettled sexual desire. His premature erotic liaison with Estella, a woman twenty years his senior, ignited a storm of monstrous sexual longing and the impossibility of realizing that goal in later life. Although M portrayed himself as a sex-starved thirteen-year-old virgin, he was not the seducer; Estella violated this young impressionable boy. In a sense this was a form of rape. M's somatic symptoms, his physical and psychological anxieties, were derived from this and his infantile neurosis; I came to understand that he needed to return again to his life over fifty years earlier, to his childhood and adolescence in order to grasp himself in the present. Why did M come for a final analysis in his sixties? And what about the unexplained vandalism—it was not present in his first analysis with Lippman. I had no answers to this question. After January 2009, during the last phase of the analysis, however, I came to see three factors which stimulated his quest—first, he felt "abandoned" by his wife, Frieda, with whom he had been deeply attached despite his compulsive work addiction— her separation had triggered his longing for love and affection. Second, as I have written, M was seeing a patient, Paula Blum, who intensified his intricate feelings of love and hate to older women. Third, at this point M was a grandfather; he was to see from an elder perspective the importance of grandparents to a child and vice versa. He was to experience life's transience. No doubt, the sublimation of these strivings and disappointments was the reason he passionately presented his controversial work across North America in his famous book, *The Bubba Complex* which was criticized more than carefully read.

* * *

Sandor Gabor, who was ninety-four, had lived through two European wars. Gabor had accumulated a deep wisdom of life and psychoanalysis. He informed me of a "sinister element" in M's analytic course—his masochism and hypo-manic denial of external danger.

All else seemed to be moving well ahead. M worked diligently in the analysis, his initial resistance had given way to a growing therapeutic trust, many childhood memories had returned. He shared his romantic adolescent misadventures. He was able to work through his failures with Frieda who now appeared open to reconciliation. Success appeared close at hand.

Regrettably, none of us could identify Gabor's "hostile reality element"—doing so might have prevented the final outcome. M's dog Jaffe-Jaffe for some weeks was aware of an intruder outside his master's apartment. M walked with a limp.

M informed me that he had again almost been run over by an errant car.

I did not inquire further into this, accepting his assertion that Toronto drivers were among the worst and most feared in North America. I failed to see what Jaffe-Jaffe had tried to communicate to her master. I also underestimated Crystal's perceptiveness.

Who would know that the beloved dog had hit upon an enemy?

M's office security had picked up images on the video surveillance cameras of a stranger in a broad-brimmed hat and trench coat. The individual wore gloves, was of average height, but the face was obscured.

That person, I believe, had also come several times to my office.

* * *

A major factor that influenced M's life was his relationship with Herbie Faust. Herbie was a sickly, sensitive child cared for by his sister. After Herbie contacted polio he spent time drawing. A talented young artist, Herbie drew what he saw—flowers, faces, landscapes. His pictures according to M were striking and unique. Ruthie-Annie protected him against any perceived attack. In retrospect she defended an aspect of her vulnerable self, projected to Herbie and others. If she was abused as a child, her actions could be seen as adaptive and necessary.

When I received urgent calls from Mount Zion Hospital, from Bayer's office, and the police contacted me, I considered that some individual or group was definitely stalking M. In consequence, as his analyst, we were both vulnerable. I felt uncertain and insecure. M continued to appear blithely indifferent. I noticed some subtle changes. M had become less restless. He drew closer to Frieda. He planned to work shorter hours. His face was filled with new worry lines. His once sleek black hair had gone grey.

I shall now record what awaited us in the next few months.

CHAPTER TWO

Blum's withering: January 10, 2009

Blum comes to my office holding a cane. I can tell from looking at her that she is in pain. With her inner torments, her constipation and palpitations she gives me an earful, with her back and her gait she is too proud to *kvetch*. Why? Because these problems are related to muscles and limbs on the surface of her body—she can see them, in her conscious mind, she believes they are under her dominion, these ordeals she can work out on her own—without help.

"Where were you?" she asks as I greet her in the waiting-room. "What took you so long?"

I check my watch and note Blum has arrived on time. "Mrs. Blum, this is when we start."

From this point on there is an odd change. Blum comes on time or even a few minutes early. She sees I have a slight limp—from jogging I tell her. I am more worried about your limp than mine, I say. I get her blood-work results and chest X-rays. Something is wrong with her calcium. Her liver functions are out of whack. Her chest X-ray shows infiltration in her lungs. She has lost weight. It doesn't take a rocket scientist to know she is ill. Blum tries to hide this from herself yet it is plain to see. Ivan phones me. He wants her to see the surgeon who first treated her.

Bayer phones in the evening but it is not about Blum. The borderline patient's wife—the addicted dentist who was a gambler—Fine was his name—it was suicide, wasn't it? Fine lost a fortune. His wife kept her maiden name, I believe she is the one harassing me—you recall her? She was the one we called the lawyers about.

Pinsky, I never saw the woman. I only spoke on the phone about her. She had several aliases and was paranoid. I have this problem—name blocking. My mind goes blank.

* * *

January 12, 2009

I call the psychiatry department at Mount Zion. I leave messages for Guttnik and Bayer. I suspect M has blocked out aspects of this patient, Fine.

* * *

Pinsky, at the end of December Bubba complained of arthritis. I shovelled snow from the driveway and helped her down the sidewalk to cross the street. Bubba insisted on taking the bus and streetcar to go to work. I told her to fly to Miami and get away from the cold. In the nights she drank brandy and rubbed Bengay on her body. She snored in the bedroom beside us. Mornings she rose to make breakfast. When I came to the kitchen my parents had left for work. Bubba set down a cup of hot tea and read the *Toronto Star* obits. Her dark hair was silver. Her body gave off a wintergreen aroma. "Reuben. Danny. Come here. Give me a look before you go. A kiss too."

She inspected us before school. She checked my hair, face, nose, coat, gloves, toque, scarf, and boots. She checked Danny too. Benji remained in front of the TV. Soon he would get a lift to school. "Danny is dressed good—but you—Reuben, what are you hiding? Behind your back, what is hanging on those laces? Show me."

I pushed them to the front of my coat. "Skates," I said. "Hockey skates."

"Skates? Those leather boots with knives on the bottom?"

Ari Mazer's skates had no ankle support. Lacing them tight, even on the hall rug was torture. I wobbled and took the skates off. My parents were too busy with work to buy skates. Bubba didn't understand hockey.

"Hockey is not for you to play, Reuben. You must study to be a doctor."

Before and after high school, whenever he let me, I tried on Ari Mazer's skates in our house. One cold day full of courage I walked to the outdoor ice rink. I put on his skates and tied them tight. I held onto the wooden boards. I tiptoed along the ice. My ankles ached. I wasn't able to turn and stopping was impossible. Ari's skates were too big. I slid inside them, not to mention the ice. The worst part was Bubba. The first week of my adventure she hobbled to the rink.

"Reuben? This is what you do—to fall down with Mazer's skates?"

"You want me to fall, I'll fall. Let me show you. Will that make you happy?"

I wanted to die of shame. I let go of the boards. I rushed forward with my left foot, then my right. I dug Mazer's skates into the ice. I gritted my teeth, half-running, half-jumping, sliding. Who knew what possessed me? I shut my eyes. Bubba ranted in Yiddish. I would crash; my lungs would give out. I would get a concussion or become a cripple like Herbie Faust. I lurched forward into an ice-world.

When my eyes opened I was still standing. "*Nu?* So what if you skate?" Bubba said.

* * *

287

The school prom was in February. I invited Roxanne Greenbaum whose parents owned Greenbaum's dairy. I bought her a cheap corsage. We made out most of the night. That year the junior prom queen was Sabrina Lustig and the senior prom king was Karl Guttnik. "Ari, do you have any idea how *revolting* this is," I said. "He stands first, gets early confirmation from university, has the most stunning woman in school, and is crowned senior prom king."

"Guttnik is actually not such a bad guy," Ari Mazer said.

"That's another thing I hate about him."

* * *

January 13, 2009

Guttnik calls me back. Last week there was a minor hospital mishap—patient charts were gone. The secretaries assumed the charts were in my office. After a complete search several files were clearly missing. The missing charts began with the letter *F*.

* * *

During winter holidays, Ari Mazer and his parents went on a Caribbean cruise and stopped in Havana. Castro had seized power. Batista fled the country with three hundred million US. Quietly Italian and Jewish gangsters left Havana and moved to Miami. Beside all the big news, Ari told me (and all his friends) that he got laid on the cruise. *You got fucking laid— that's bullshit*. You're not even sixteen. Reuben, see, here's her picture. Dolores Perón, she's twenty, from Texas. I lied about my age. I said I was twenty-two. I stared at Ari beside Dolores in a bathing suit. Wow, I say—she's stacked. "We had sex six times," Ari boasted. Of course I don't tell Ari that I *shtupped* his mother before and after each dance lesson. Ari Mazer's dad

288

and Manny Karp were living the high life going to Havana every two weeks—they developed a hotel complex on the *Malecon*. Ari told me his family divided time between Miami and Nassau. By this time we heard news about the Fausts. They built a giant hardware chain but were divorcing. That winter the Fausts sold their house. Little Herbie and Ruthie-Annie disappeared from our street.

* * *

Two months before Passover, Bubba's pain worsened. When I came home from school, Bubba was in bed. Danny and Benji were watching TV and fighting. They argued about what channel to watch. "Please, don't yell or scream," Bubba said. "I am feeling sick." I went upstairs to see Bubba. She lay under the covers in her darkened room. On her night table a glass of water held her dentures. They looked like sleeping yellow crabs. "Tell them to turn down the TV set. It is too loud. Tell them not to yell or fight." She shifted in bed. "It is cold everywhere, in all my joints." Uncle Max says to go to Florida, Bubba. "What does he know? I take my pills and still the pain comes." I had never seen her face so pale. Can I get you hot tea? "It's not tea I need. Give me a kiss." I kissed her. You look sick today. "There is ice in my chest. Please, don't tell Yasha."

I phoned Uncle Max. Bubba was too ill to move. Uncle Max arrived with a wooden box, an electrocardiograph. He checked her pulse. He printed out a spool of waves. Bubba was taken to Mount Zion Hospital. Bubba had suffered a heart attack. We said nothing to Yasha.

Yasha's life was a book with two pages. The first page was that he had grown up in Poland, was in the Polish army, and came to Canada. The second page was that he had married Bubba.

Between the first and second page there was an empty white space, a blank, a nothing.

Zaide Yasha, silent as an Easter Island statue.—R. Moses

Thursday I walked to the corner and met Sabrina Lustig at the Bagel-King. We talked about school and drank Cokes. "Have you got a date for Tina's Sweet Sixteen, Reuben?" Sabrina asked.

"Just you—if you want to come with me," I said.

"I told you Karl Guttnik is taking me."

"I was hoping maybe he would get food poisoning or something," I said.

"Karl is very careful about what he eats. He keeps strictly kosher. He washes his hands with special soap just like his older brother, the surgeon."

"Doesn't it bother you that Karl is so perfect?"

Sabrina smiled. "He's smart and handsome. I'm gorgeous and intelligent."

"I bet he doesn't even kiss you on the lips."

Sabrina flushed. "Word has it you see Roxanne. She is only good for one thing."

"She is pretty good for that one thing," I said.

"You should be ashamed. Everyone knows you take out a grade nine Jewish slut."

"Listen, Sabrina, I am not perfect," I said. "I am restless. My mind is all over the place. I get sick with colds and fevers. I don't know how long I have to live. You are beautiful; I want to kiss you. I swear, I will never kiss you—why?—because of Karl. I am a gentleman. Try to understand—I need an outlet for my tension."

"You're seeing that tramp, Roxanne? I hear you make out in her basement."

"Who told you?"

"It's *public knowledge*."

We walked to Sabrina's home. I told her about Bubba having a heart attack and needing to stay in bed. I cried. "It's all right to cry. If you want, Reuben, you can kiss me." Pinsky, we were at her side door on Glencedar Avenue beside Cedarvale Public School. It was dark. Sabrina had her back against the brick wall. I wiped tears from my eyes. For a second I thought about Guttnik, the Nobelprize genius. I pushed him out of my mind. I didn't ask where to kiss her.

I leaned forward, closed my eyes. I tasted her lips. I was in a distant galaxy.

* * *

Bubba's sepia wedding photo showed Yasha in a black tuxedo; Bubba stood in a white dress. A picture was a thousand words but this picture was silent. Yasha's surviving brother Shem had two sons, Meyer, the lawyer, and Yossel, the doctor. Meyer was to be married, Yasha was not invited. Father added, "Yasha does not know." By then I knew more than Yasha. I heard my parents speak Yiddish when they did not want me to know.

"Yasha should not come to the *simcha*," Bubba said. "What would he say?"

I read Ruthie-Annie's diary. It was full of sex like *Peyton Place*. Ruthie-Annie wrote that Sam, her dad, was plunking her. *It was disgusting*.

CHAPTER THREE

Meyer's wedding

Bubba asked me to cut her toenails—twisted and over-grown. I cut them with cuticle scissors. Her heels were covered with yellow calluses, rough as sandpaper—it was all the walking she had done in her life. After her heart attack it was difficult for Bubba to walk. When I drew close to her I saw a blue-white arc around her brown irises. "Your eyes are milky."

"Men used to say I had beautiful brown eyes," she said.

"I am sorry you don't feel better."

Bubba sat up in bed. I saw the veins in her neck. "I loved to dance. I loved telling stories. I was the life of the party." I had never seen Bubba dance. She was the one who watched us, worried, and told stories. Bubba took her purse and extracted a small photo. "Here I am at eighteen." She was striking, with thick hair, bright almond eyes, and circumflex brows.

Life was a riddle. I never saw Bubba as a young woman. Bubba never saw me as an adult. We were destined to look at each other and not see who we were or who we were to become. I stared at the picture for the longest time. Bubba reached into her purse and found another photo. She sat on the grass in a sailor dress beside Yasha. He wore a white shirt, open at the next, dark slacks, and smiled at her. He was young

292

and handsome and they were in love. Bubba wiped a tear. "He was in Pilsudski's army. We grew up in Bendin. Many years after we came to Canada, Yasha wanted to see his family back home. His father had died. His mother was very sick. Your mother was young, Reuben. We had a beautiful older son. I had to work and take care of my mother. It was 1937. Yasha agreed to stay in Poland for the summer. He returned to Bendin with our son to take care of his mother. She needed him to stay. One of his brothers was in Canada. Then the war came. People believed the Germans would be nice to them. We received no mail. We had no idea if Yasha was alive or dead. He fled the city. He lived in the country and hid in a farmer's barn. It was a miracle he lived. He came to Toronto a changed man."

"And your son was Mommy's brother? What happened to him?"

"He was captured. He was killed outside of Bendin." What was his name, I asked. "Reuben," she said. Bubba passed me a faded photo, her lost dead son. Reuben was me. I was Reuben. I was thunderstruck.

February 2, 2009

Blum is too ill to see me. I phone Bayer. He calls the head of medicine and finds a bed on the medical ward. I haven't seen her for weeks. No one knows what is going on. She is acutely ill; she has shortness of breath and back pain. Frieda leaves a message on my cell. "Reuben," Frieda says, "Ivan said she can't keep food down. Did she tell you that?"

"On the phone she tells me she is angry. She is fed up with everybody."

I check my schedule and my hospital duty roster. I tell him I will drop by at seven that night.

* * *

Feter Shem's son, Meyer, the lawyer, was to be married in March. My parents and Bubba were invited. Bubba was weak and short of breath from her heart attack but insisted on coming, Bubba wanted to dance at her nephew's wedding. Sunday afternoon before the wedding I made some excuse to my mother and went to Roxanne Greenbaum's house. Her parents as usual were away working in their dairy. Roxanne had no sisters or brothers. We made out for an hour. I had all her clothes off, her blouse was on the night table, her bras hung on a bedpost; her underwear lay on the floor. I kept my underwear and jeans on in case I lost control—I didn't want to leave telltale shot spots on her walls. If just a single one of my maniacal sperms got loose and landed within twenty feet of her VJ with my luck it would be curtains.

"Roxie, I have to watch my brothers in twenty minutes."

"I can come over to your place," Roxanne said.

"It's better if I go. I have to babysit. My family has a wedding. See you later."

"Listen Reuben, I feel hot all over. I want to do it."

"You want to do it? *You actually want to do it?* But I have no safes."

"C'mon, Reuben, you got me all hot. When you feel yourself getting close to coming, you pull out. It's called the rhythm method. That's what you do."

"Roxanne, I can't take that chance. I don't have a good sense of rhythm."

"You are not going home now, Reuben," she said.

Torture #14. So what did I do, Pinsky? Like an idiot I took off my jeans and my underwear and in no time flat I am inside her. I feel how sweet and warm and juicy she is. Roxie told me she had never had 100 per cent sex with anyone before. Believe me, this was no virgin, Pinsky. She was a fucking gymnast in bed. I didn't bother asking her when she first got laid. All I can say it was hymen-free heaven up there inside her. I was getting higher and higher. It was like Queen Victoria's birthday,

294

I swear, there were sparklers and shooting stars, pinwheels, and whizzing lights. The bed was creaking and the floor was shaking and the two of us were on a roller coaster at Crystal Beach. Then it was too late.

"Look what you did! *Idiot!*" Roxanne said. "Look what you did!"

"What? Oh my God! I'm sorry, Roxanne. I'm sorry. I didn't get out fast enough."

"You should have been faster. Look at all of your sperm. I have never seen so much sperm before. *Holy crap!* What were you thinking?"

"I was distracted."

"If I am pregnant, Reuben, I am not having an abortion—*understand?*"

"Roxie, I am sorry."

"Reuben, you will have to marry me." Roxie ran to the washroom for some soap to wash up. I was thinking of millions and millions of my rioting single-minded sperm rushing frantically headlong inside her vagina looking for fresh eggs. What incredible odds for disaster! Pinsky, it was an absolute nightmare—what the hell was I to do? At the same time my dark side was proud in this moronic way—with Estella and now Roxie my virgin days were behind me. I was proud of my magnificent load of sperm home-delivered inside of her. *A job well done!* What if I went to jail or had to get married or had to join the French Foreign Legion. I felt like fucking her again, why not? When I arrived home my parents were dressed up and angry. Bubba wore her finest clothes.

She looked excited to go to a *simcha*.

Bubba collapsed during the wedding ceremony. It was just after Meyer crushed the crystal glass with his foot, Father said. Bubba closed her eyes. She slipped back in her chair. Father believed she was overcome with joy. *Wake up now, wake up.* Bubba did not move. Uncle Max came over and checked her eyes and pulse. He listened to her chest.

"She's fainted, yes?" Father asked. Two men lifted her out of the shul in her chair. Uncle Max tried to revive her. Rabbi Spiegel ordered the wedding to go on. What more could anyone do? A wedding, our sages said, continues, even when there was tragedy.

It had been a clear, cold winter evening—a beautiful evening for a wedding. My father wore a tuxedo, my mother a silk dress. I saw how elegant and miserable they looked when they came home early at nine. I had put Danny and Benji to bed.

"Bubba is gone," my parents cried.

Pinsky, that night I saw life was an enigma, full of terror. I had a dread of death as a child, but now I realize the feeling had never left me. Bubba was buried the next day. I felt guilt—not just ordinary guilt, or Protestant guilt, or Catholic guilt, no, I felt the loss of my namesake Reuben and the weight of centuries of oppressive *Jewish guilt*. We held *shiva*. Our home was filled with dark-faced mourners. Ruthie-Annie and Herbie came. The mirrors were covered. Mother sobbed until her tears ran dry. Father had to be the strong one. He cried at the cemetery. Bubba had become his mother.

"She wanted to see M-Meyer's wedding," he said between sobs. "It was her wish."

"She was not well enough to go. What if she stayed home?" Mother asked.

"*What if?*—" Father said, "what if she had died at home and not felt joy?"

Pinsky, there is mystery in everything. There is mystery in the ways of the ants, the trees, and animals of the forest. There is mystery in our dark universe. There is a mystery in ourselves we never know. Why did Bubba not tell me of the first Reuben, the real Reuben? *Why?*

* * *

February 5, 2009

Bayer interrupts my Friday afternoon session to tell me hospital security is certain that there was forced entry of the filing system. He convenes a meeting of the psychiatry department—evidence points to a single intruder—surveillance cameras identify a figure in a trench coat and broad-brimmed hat. Bayer assumes the intruder works for Fine—the patient.

The intruder has broken into Guttnik's hospital office and ransacked his desk and files.

* * *

February 6, 2009

Ivan opens the door of his mother's mansion, filled with fine art, and I see the broad marble hallway and main rooms. I note alabaster sculptures in the arches. I walk up the spiral staircase to her room overlooking a French garden.

"She won't leave," Ivan says. "She feels safe here." We stand by her bedroom door.

"How long has she been like this?"

We enter her room. Blum lies propped with three pillows. Her eyes are sunken. Her belly is huge, distended and swollen. Her face is skeletal. "How are you feeling today, Mrs. Blum?"

She points a wobbly finger at me. "Good—already I feel better," she says.

"You don't look well. You've lost weight. You refuse to see our doctors."

"*I see you*. What good do you do? You haven't helped me one bit."

"You must come to hospital." I explain she is an involuntary patient. I explain she is a danger to her health and security. I tap her on her shoulder.

* * *

People from Crystal Beach who knew Bubba came to the *shiva*. The lady from the big cottage with the swimming pool and the little dog came to our *shiva*—here is the strange thing, the woman—Pinsky, I didn't know her name—the young teenager, Polly, who watched the lapdog, Zsa-Zsa, that was Paula Blum. I had seen her when I was a child. All my parents' relatives and friends were at the *shiva* except for Yasha. He had not been invited to the wedding or the funeral.

For Yasha life was a double mystery.

Yasha survived the war but lost his son and his hearing, and no one explained a thing to him. For years I believed him to be a fool. What could Yasha have done? But the truth was that we were the ignorant fools. I sensed he knew more than he let on. He knew that he had done his best to help his sick mother. He knew that he had tried to save his son. He must have known that Bubba had died. The following year he suffered a stroke and lost the power of speech. I never knew his whole story. I was almost sixteen—I had never seen a dead body before— and there, lowered into the earth was Bubba Bella. Bubba, like Yasha, like many tortured souls, had kept her secrets until her last days. I hated and loved her as she loved me; she was the closest person to me in the world. I hated her because she had made me her lost son. There was fresh snow on the ground. It was bitter cold but I was warm in my toque, scarf, jacket, and boots like Bubba wanted. The cantor sang as they shov- elled in smoking earth. *Zaglember Society* mourners came, Leo the butcher, Zlotnik the barber, Karp the *ganif*, my parents, and Faggie Faust. Bubba's room was cleaned, her clothes sent away; the sickroom smell left.

Bubba had spoken Yiddish and told stories of loss. After death her Yiddish stories were gone. The machinka broke. Her *bubba meysehs* vanished. We became modern like everyone.

But the mystery and magic of life left.

* * *

February 6, 2009

Bayer calls me from the hospital. "Moses, this is serious. You have to look through your files. I am being followed. It's that crazy person again—I called the police. They can't do much. They have to wait until something happens, you know." What are you talking about? "My office is ruined. The dentist's wife— she left a death threat. She slashed my tires. Did you write her name down anywhere? What was her maiden name?"

But as hard as I try, the name is gone.

CHAPTER FOUR

The gathering storm: March 2009

Pinsky, I helped my father in the drugstore on weekends. I stocked the shelves, I dumped red Dustbane on the floors; I swept up; I delivered prescriptions; I dropped off flyers door to door. Business was taking a hit from the cut-rate super-pharmacy across the road.

"Reuben, do you think I should sell my drugstore or go in with a chain?"

"Dad—you do what you think is best."

Seven days a week he worked, smoking cigarettes, pacing at night, trying to decide what to do. I worried he was going to collapse or go broke. I told him to see Uncle Max.

He was short of breath walking more than two blocks. He coughed each morning.

"Someone is stealing my safes. I count them each week. Four boxes are missing."

* * *

That was me, Pinsky, stealing safes. Why? Because of Roxanne—after school each afternoon we went to her place and fucked our brains out. I didn't care where she was in her cycle, start, middle, or end. And if she was flush in her period that was better because she was hot and juicy and ready for me. Her parents, slaving at

Greenbaum's dairy, never came home until after seven. By math class at two in the afternoon I couldn't concentrate—I was thinking of *shtupping* Roxie. My marks fell. I worried my dad was going bankrupt. My buddy, Ari, was moving to Miami. His father made a pile of dough—it wasn't from bar mitzvahs and weddings. Ben Mazer made deals with Cubans coming to Miami, he knew the right people. I'm not saying he was with Manny Karp and the Jewish gangs but he had a feel for money and big money was not coming from little folks, right? I missed Ari. I missed Estella. I missed Bubba and so I had sex with Roxie to fill the void.

* * *

March 4, 2009

I meet Bayer in his office at the hospital. A plain-clothes police officer is checking his office for fingerprints. A man from forensics inspects the doors, the filing cabinets. "That person or persons broke into my office last night a second time," Bayer says. "I don't know how the hell *whoever* it was got past security. Guttnik's office was ransacked. I looked through my files."

"What did you find?"

"Nothing—I haven't kept active files on patients longer than ten years. I did find her name, *Anna, Anna Fine*—she was married to that dentist, Fine. Her personal info is nowhere. She used her married name. Guttnik put her husband on medication. He followed him up. Remember?"

"Anna Fine, yes; now I remember. Guttnik saw her for a consultation as well."

"Reuben, I have a question for you," Bayer says, taking a step closer to me. "Why didn't you call back the first time I phoned about this case? Why didn't you call me back the second or third time—look, I know you are a busy guy, but you knew this was important."

"You mean about the patient harassing you?"

301

"You always call back about a crisis. Why did you put it out of your mind?"

"Bernard, honestly, I haven't the slightest idea why I didn't call you back."

"Did you call back the police harassment unit?"

"I didn't call them back either."

"For god's sakes, what is with you? Our lives are in danger. Why put this out of your mind? What the hell is going on? Your name comes up on the news every week about women's groups out to attack you. I know you've had your share of domestic problems with Frieda leaving you for Guttnik. Has that been getting you down?"

"Actually, we are thinking of getting back, Bernard. The future looks good."

"*Well, what the fuck is with you?* Are you on some other planet? What gives? There are protest groups in front of the hospital. They think you hate women. Have you kept your head in the sand, Moses—didn't you hear the news. Guttnik was almost killed this morning."

"Guttnik—you have to be kidding! I didn't hear a thing."

"Guttnik was run over."

"Run over? It's got to be a joke. How you do you mean?"

"Someone driving a car hit him from behind when he was cycling. I am worried myself now."

"No shit." I feel a nervous smirk cross my face. "Is he all right?"

"He's at Mount Zion 12-West but don't see him. He has a broken pelvis, several ruptured tendons, two fractured femurs. The surgeon is not sure if he will walk. What's up, Reuben? It's no joke—why are you smiling? Guttnik is lucky to be alive. Did you have anything to do with this? How come you are not worried like everyone? Reuben, the police want to see you."

* * *

302

Pinsky, I supervised Bayer—Anna Fine was his patient. It's strange—I usually recall old patients, but with this patient it is like London smog in my temporal lobes. I see bare outlines. I remember nothing. Bayer, the smart ass, tries to turn the tables on me like he is the analyst—he is pointing out my problem. Bayer is right—I did put him and the police out of my mind.

* * *

"Reuben," Bayer calls me later that day; "I need your full attention. You have to review your notes—you consulted on her case—there has to be something, some piece of paper, some clue."

"I put my old papers into boxes when Frieda and I separated last year."

"Where are the boxes?" Bayer asks.

"In my apartment—some I threw out."

"Please—open all the boxes and take a look. Do it ASAP."

My mother's daily weather report: March 10, 2009

Pinsky, by now you know my frail ageing mother calls me every morning to warn me about rainstorms, tornados, lightning strikes, hail, vicious rainstorms, blizzards, traffic snarls, fires, West Nile virus, break-ins, plane crashes, car accidents, power blackouts, global warming, not to mention terrorist strikes in the Middle East, Lyme disease, and updates from Homeland Security. She calls after the early Toronto traffic and news. She reads the morning obituary columns and police reports and informs me of hospital deaths, shootings, funerals, *shivas*, and unveilings. She deposits cautionary bulletins on my office phone. Pinsky, my mother, like Bubba, records life's tragic endings. She told me she visited you at the office and said for me to be careful when I jog. You realize this is what I have been up against all my life? Between Bubba and Mother, the outside world is a minefield. To offset ubiquitous misfortune she blesses Sabbath candles for me, Danny, Benji, my late father, Bubba—and all the dearly departed. Morning to night Mother listens to CNN. Like a radio telescope she picks up the dark swirling orbits of adversity cycling our forlorn planet.

Reuben, did you send a condolence to Herbie Faust's sister, Ruthie-Annie? Someone called—I never give out your telephone number to anyone. I am proud of you going to Montreal to talk about Bubba in front of all those important psychiatrists.

* * *

Blum ended up in hospital on the medical ward. It was decided not to transfer her to psychiatry. She was adamant—no chemotherapy. She sensed her deterioration but refused to talk about it. Blum lost her entire family in the war. For better or for worse, she reasoned, her time was up—Ivan and I tried to persuade her to take palliative treatment to improve her quality of life. She told me she wanted a natural death. She worked all her life making shrewd deals, bargaining, dealing with difficult partners. This time there was no deal. If I were to live, I would stay in analysis with you, Dr. Moses. I knew I didn't make it easy; I needed to know you could take my tantrums. I never complained as a child, I had no one to rely on. I am not taking back the letters I sent to the college. It makes me feel better to complain.

The big complaint, I grasped, was not her cancer; it was what she had already lost in life.

* * *

March 12, 2009

At the funeral I saw Blum's buyers, suppliers, retailers, hospital committee members, Hebrew school teachers, UJA executives, her gardener, her homemaker, her life coach, her yoga

304

instructor, her fitness trainer, her menopausal naturopath, her accountant, her lawyer. Her office staff filled the synagogue. I saw Lippman, her first analyst, sitting by himself. Ivan, his wife, and family sat in the front row with Bayer. I noticed Frieda sitting alone. I joined her.

"Reuben, you work with difficult patients," Frieda took my hand.

"Did you hear about Karl Guttnik?" I ask.

"The police want to speak to you. Reuben—I know you didn't have anything to do with poor Karl, did you?" she pauses, uneasy. "A detective asked questions. He asked if you had ever threatened Karl."

"I have nothing against Karl. I wouldn't hurt a fly or a *centipede*. I worked through this with Pinsky. I plan to take a break—a sabbatical. Frieda, can we talk over coffee."

The rabbi starts his eulogy about how charitable Blum was in life. Everyone is dry-eyed except for Ivan and me. Frieda squeezes my hand. "My friends read *The Bubba Complex*. Your concept is clever but divisive and controversial, Reuben."

"So was the Oedipus complex."

"You provoke women. Reuben, people don't read word for word—they text, twitter, and web surf. Who listens carefully? People jump to conclusions. Feminists say you attack the matriarchy."

"I love the matriarchy, Frieda. Will you join me for dinner?"

We went to the cemetery that afternoon. After the graveside service a man came up to me, a face I had not seen for over fifty years. It was the grey informer eyes.

"Joshua Karp? Josh? Is that you?"

"Reuben—yes, it's me. I am a special detective with the Metro Police." He pulled out his ID. "We must talk. I don't want to alarm you. We need to question you about your whereabouts since your colleague Karl Guttnik was almost killed."

"Were you following me?"

"You are a person of interest."

"Josh, OK, I was a shit-disturber in cheder. I am not guilty of any wrongdoing."

"Maybe you are right. So, let's make it easy. Tell me about the last few days. Look, I'm not saying you had anything to do with Guttnik." Karp scribbled notes as we talked. "This file is bigger than Guttnik—it goes back years, to Bayer, to a woman harassing the hospital. She attacked other male doctors. Do me a favour. Phone the police if you get any strange or harassing calls, all right? Now where were you last night?"

* * *

Pinsky, I wasn't sure if Karp believed me. Remember in Miss Carducci's class he turned me in. Karp sent his own father to the clinker—honest. Look, despite my guilt, I have a clear conscience; I swear I didn't run over Guttnik, although the thought crossed my mind several times.

In the evening I took Frieda out for dinner. I felt a certain *tristesse* for Blum's life. Frieda and I talked for hours. We talked about a sabbatical—I planned to take off three months. I never had a holiday longer than two weeks.

We held hands and kissed. She looked radiant that night.

"Reuben, would you like to have a nightcap, your place or mine?"

When we got to Frieda's townhouse I fumbled with her clothes like a teenager—it was my arrested development. *You were absolutely right, Pinsky*. We made love twice that night. Afterwards I lay awake. I thought of my father who dropped dead of a heart attack in his drugstore. I didn't want to die young. I told Frieda we would have a long life. I wanted to move in with Frieda and play with Jonah, Jason, and Jeremy in our new house.

"Life will be different now, Frieda," I said. "I am a changed man. I want to spend the rest of my life with you." I felt unbearably happy. I had my life ahead of me. I had finished a major part of my analysis. I had Frieda back.

Then I remembered I had promised Bayer to look through my files, you know, the files I put in boxes and search for that woman, Anna Fine, the patient I had consulted on years ago.

* * *

I recalled my high school reunion. Graduates from past decades met at our high school. Guttnik, my friend, my nemesis, the genius who had everything I ever wanted showed up. Karl had lost his beautiful wife, Sabrina, to cancer. He was talking to Roxanne. Roxanne Greenbaum—she had remarried twice and ran Greenbaum's dairy. Lenny Loeb arrived sombre-faced in a dark suit; his wife was an accountant and he ran his father's funeral business. Miss Carducci my English teacher showed up—her wool dress smelled of mothballs but she looked the same. Ari Mazer flew in from Miami. He had made and lost and made a fortune in Miami real estate. He heard my name from one of his business partners, Sam-Lee Yan. "The world is a tiny place, Reuben, and I knew you *shtupped* my stepmom— you old goat you."

Pinsky, I felt old and stupid and sad.

* * *

In the morning I went over our plans and kissed Frieda goodbye. We planned to get together after I came back from Montreal. I was to be a keynote speaker on *The Bubba Complex* in July. I was developing a name. TV stations called for interviews. A publisher and two agents wanted to discuss book ideas. Pinsky, I was a media celebrity, more famous than Guttnik or Bayer.

* * *

307

March 13, 2009

At 6 am I returned to my apartment. The door was ajar. I had absolutely forgotten Jaffe-Jaffe's morning stroll. I looked inside. My apartment was trashed, books thrown to the floor; files scattered. My laptop lay smashed on the floor. *Who would do this?*

When Jaffe-Jaffe was alone she preferred to stay my bedroom. I walked into my bedroom. Someone had opened my night table. And then it hit me—whoever it was might be searching my patient list. Why? I looked in front of my bed and to the side.

I saw Jaffe-Jaffe. She was in the corner against the wall, trembling. I stepped closer. My step startled her. She stared at me, quivering. Her back arched in this weird way, her neck hyper-extended. She appeared to lose control. Her eyes were in spasm, she fell to the floor in a heap. She emptied her bladder and bowels. She convulsed.

CHAPTER FIVE

The hostile reality factor—O. Pinsky, March 2009

The analysis appeared to move quickly forward as M resolved his neurotic conflicts. His primary relationship to Frieda was on a firm footing. He smiled as he spoke of a forthcoming sabbatical with her. He appeared relieved to take leave from committee work. He restricted consultations on difficult cases. He reduced his practice to be with his family. He placed great energy on *The Bubba Complex* which elicited attention from medical societies but harsh criticism from feminist groups. He was delighted his paper had been accepted for a plenary session at the World Analytic Meeting in Montreal July 2009. For the first time since I had seen him, M appeared depression-free. He planned to move in shortly with Frieda and resume married life. The fact that Bayer, the chief of psychiatry at M's hospital was the target of a former patient or group concerned me. M was not the least apprehensive and felt pleased with his celebrity. Detective Karp had questioned M who appeared detached and oddly absent. M dismissed the fact that Guttnik had been run over and was critically injured. He put aside that the intruder had broken into the hospital offices of Bayer and Guttnik. Each time I brought this up, M turned away. He did not listen to me. He did not want to think.

March 16, 2009

I was in a towering rage. I rose from my chair, pointed my finger at him and ranted. *Your apartment was ransacked! Your dog was killed! Moses, you put that out of mind?* Are you the one smearing shit and slashing tires, writing threatening letters, and putting dead chickens in parking lots? You were a Goody Two-Shoes at camp, I remember now; you had the bunk beside Sax the shit-disturber, why?—because you admired the way he flung crap at the world. Fury overwhelmed me. I staggered back to my chair and sat down. *It had been M all along.* I was dealing with a criminal mind that masked itself in social decency. Had M killed his own dog? M was sobered by my sudden outburst. As I sat in my chair I wondered if I was dealing with a two-faced scoundrel, a liar, a secret psychopath. How could this be? M confessed he had never hurt a soul. He told me he was still in shock with the loss of his beloved dog, Jaffe-Jaffe.

If that was true, why was he impervious to the reality that someone was out to harm him?

* * *

April 10, 2009

Three weeks later, a clinical-pathological examination of the dog, as well as toxicology taken immediately after Jaffe-Jaffe's terminal convulsion, confirmed that the dog has been poisoned by strychnine, a rodent poison. The dog had apparently eaten some tainted food outside M's apartment.

April 26, 2009

The police request that M change his name and move to a town where he is unknown. There are no further leads. Detective Karp urges M to leave the city. The police offer few suggestions.

M tells Detective Karp he is in analysis with me and cannot be disturbed.

May 15, 2009

Detective Karp phones my office. He asks M to stop his analysis and leave the city. Karp has seen cases like this go badly. M stubbornly resists.

June 15, 2009

I attend M's talk on *The Bubba Complex* at a Mount Zion meeting. Six hundred people are in the audience. The discussant is a feminist; the moderator is an author neutral to psychoanalysis. M presents his views on the male child's first love, reverence for older women, and the centrality of the grandmother. M is articulate but on intimacy he becomes heated as he speaks of love and hate. "The grandmother rivals the mother for a child's love."

His zeal intensified criticism.

June 24, 2009

I have no security system apart from the usual monitoring CCTV devices in office buildings. Has the attacker already traced M to my office? Bayer, as hospital chief, is able to gain protection while in hospital and obtain security for his home. M is often outside the hospital in his private office or seeing me; he does not want his private practice compromised, and security cannot be easily arranged. Reviewing hospital databases, police files, and checking with community organizations leads nowhere. Bayer persuades the reluctant hospital executive board to provide a detective to examine the available evidence, to meet with me, Dr. Sandor Gabor, the office superintendent, and M—in order to review a list of possible assailants.

Detective Karp reads out a list of suspects: Paula Blum—a long shot, the police explain—she has complained to the medical college about M, she expressed hostility towards him, she had unlimited funds—she might have hired someone to intimidate her doctor while she was dying. One of M's current difficult hospital patients—Crystal, for example, had been a violent teenager and had links to biker gangs and drug dealers. Her jealous boyfriend, Zeno, in the past months has been released from prison. Then there is Sam-Lee Yan who suddenly leaves the city and is incommunicado; Sam-Lee is mixed up in shady Chinese-Russian deals and one of his middlemen, Luka, a Serbian-Russian has been assassinated. Karp suggests anyone M had seen, professional or otherwise—for example his mystery patient, the special op, only known as GC; Karp considers Lippman, his former analyst a possible suspect. Yet M is at a loss to name anyone—his natural tendency is to care for others—he cannot imagine anyone as his enemy. Karp cites M's apartment superintendent, filled with rage and hatred for Jaffe-Jaffe. Karp adds on his suspect list M's separated wife, Frieda. The last suspect on Karp's list is Moses himself—a case of multiple personality in which the attacker himself is victim. Unless we have compelling evidence, this option is conjecture. Detective Karp hits upon what I had seen—M's work on *The Bubba Complex*. Were disaffected women so furious that they might attack the man and his theory? I supported this view; protest groups have paraded in front of my office and demonstrated before Mount Zion Hospital. Karp looks up M's name on the internet. He cross-links it with social media sites. In seconds a list of vicious comments on *The Bubba Complex* appears. "Reuben, you are a target," Karp says, having studied FBI profiling. Karp summarizes the essential points.

June 25, 2009: Detective Karp's summary

- These acts of vandalism are connected.
- There is a possibility you know the assailant(s).

- The next act will be more violent.
- Your stalker(s) is more likely female than male.
- Your stalker(s) feels justified in attacking you.
- Your stalker(s) has a personality disorder or is psychotic.
- You cannot reason with stalkers.
- Your life is in grave danger.
- Internet sites indicate multiple threats on your personal security.
- There is a strong possibility that there is not one stalker but several.

Detective Karp convenes a meeting with M, Dr. Gabor, Dr. Bayer, and me at police headquarters. Karp urges M to change his name, obtain new identifying data and credit card information, and close his bank accounts. Karp insists that Moses under no circumstance return to his residence. He orders M to have someone cover his busy practice and move to another city. M refuses. After M leaves Karp says: "There is one situation I have not emphasized—it is rare but must be considered. Dr. Reuben Moses, as decent as he appears, hired an attacker." Karp pauses. "I knew Reuben Moses as a kid," Karp adds. "He was nice. But nice people can do terrible things. Something made this attacker or attackers furious. We don't know what it was. I have a gut feeling—in homicide we often see it. In the majority of cases the victim and killer know each other."

"You mean," Bayer says, "Reuben knows the exact identity of the stalker?"

Karp replies. "He doesn't know the identity—he's had dealings with this person. He may not know that this person has a grudge against him. This person may have enlisted other attackers."

"You forget the unconscious," Gabor says. "There, victim and killer can be the same person."

* * *

June 26, 2009

M's depression has completely disappeared. His face is flushed. His movements are lighter. He feels relief. Yet he is impervious to reality.*

June 26, 2009, 9:45 pm

Friday night, I receive a call from my office superintendent. Someone tried to enter my office. The super tells me the intruder quickly left before any close identification can occur.

---

*In certain cases, the patient, who knows a certain person exceedingly well and is ordinarily in touch with reality, is unable to recall the name or the emotion associated with this individual. Most of these memory problems have their origin in an unpleasant experience separated from conscious awareness by repression or dissociation. This mental process may seem preposterous, but it has been noted too often in clinical situations to be put aside. *S. Gabor.*

CHAPTER SIX

The Bubba Complex goes viral: July 3, 2009

June 23–July 2, 2009

The main conference hall at the Queen Elizabeth Hotel in Montreal holds over 1,000 people. The notion of the Bubba as a central family figure intrigues the July program organizer of the World Psychoanalytic Association. I am assigned a special chairperson for the meeting—a pinched-face young buzz-cut feminist with a bad case of *mittelschmerz*. In the room are analysts, psychiatrists, neuroscientists, teachers, social workers. Before we start I briefly explain to the chairperson, in the same way Oedipus loved his mother, young boys love the Bubba—I am not out to dismiss anyone's theory. I am trying to explain the little *pisher* has sexual and hostile feelings to the grandmother and she to him, right?

The chairperson snarls at me with hooded laser hate in her eyes.

Pinsky, what is psychiatric diagnosis anyway? In the old days there were a handful—depression, mania, paranoia, anxiety, dissociative states, hysteria, obsessions, phobias, perversions, schizophrenia, trauma—not more than fifty. These days, there are hundreds of psychiatric conditions, and every few years new ones are added to our DSM—our

315

psychiatric bible. Does a diagnosis occur in reality or is it something we create? I argue the Bubba complex is real. For the DSM-V, I proposed a syndrome with anxiety in young boys before age thirteen—the Bubba complex. This was not a figment of my imagination. I ran focus groups. I tested controls. The syndrome exists—call it the granny neurosis, if you wish—it exists.

* * *

Most analysts at the Montreal meeting were in their fifties, sixties, seventies, and eighties; several were round-shouldered, stooped like me—grandparents. They would appreciate my work. They wore tweed and corduroy jackets, dark suits, and faded jeans. I saw young people who looked pensive.

My chest tightened; a weight was pressing upon it.

When I spoke about the Bubba complex there was dead silence. Some analysts nodded, others seemed unsettled. Two of my panellists were feminists. They glared at me.

The chairwoman with the buzz-cut spilt her cup of steaming hot coffee over my lap—an accident—sure, more likely a Freudian slip. Before I opened my mouth they said my paper was scandalous. How dare a male analyst place matriarchy in such a dark light?

Isn't this disguised hatred towards the mother?

The feminists savaged me—the Freudians were irate—they said I discounted Oedipus, proposing Bubba supplant the parents. The self-psychologists were vicious. Lesbian, gay, and transsexual therapists were displeased. Lippman and two male analysts spoke up for my paper.

"Moses is not denigrating women," Lippman said. "He is elevating the feminine. We are all ambivalent about the powerful woman. Don't you see?" Lippman was shouted down.

316

Whatever Happened to Bubba in America? NYT, Friday July 3, 2009

> What is the place of the grandmother in modern Western society? This theme was hotly debated recently at a special July psychoanalytic meeting held in Montreal's Queen Elizabeth Hotel. Dr. Reuben Moses, a psychoanalyst, has advanced the idea that a psychiatric syndrome arises from an attachment between the grandmother and child and should be included in the new DSM-V due in 2013. Dr. Moses, citing clinical studies of other analysts, argued that reactive anxiety, hypochondriac obsessions, depression, and other debilitating symptoms are stimulated by traumatic narratives of the Bubba [*Bubba mysehs*] when recited at a critical and vulnerable age to the male child.
>
> The audience's response was largely hostile. Feminists deplored the biased view of matriarchy. Freudians argued that the *Bubba Complex* was a radical repudiation of the *Oedipus Complex*.
>
> Dr. Moses countered that even Oedipus had a Bubba before he had to be escorted from the stage by security personnel …

Needless to say, a wonderful warm, friendly reception awaited me in the hotel lobby—some harridan had organized a hate rally, a pogrom. The crowd was packed with angry women in their sixties and seventies; they waved small signs: *Halt bubba-bashing.*

One woman yelled: "*You*, a *Jewish doctor* should be ashamed of yourself."

A second woman kicked me in the shins. A third punched my arm. I had to laugh at them all. *What a dumb joke!* Two Montreal security officers whisked me to a side entrance.

Pinsky, the one time I say what I really think, the world is out to whack me.

They marched along Boulevard Rene Levesque with placards and signs. *The Bubba Bunds*.

My Montreal hotel phone did not stop ringing.

July 3, 2009, 1 pm: our phone session from Montreal

On Friday afternoon, for relief, I changed and took a
jog through Parc Mont Royal. A dog walker came up to
me: "You're not that analyst who believes in the Bubba
Complex?"

Yes, I said.

She flung a steaming plastic sac of dog turd my way.

I ducked—the bag burst on my shoulder.

I had to laugh at how stupidly she behaved.

It was more hilarious when I arrived back in Toronto.
Bayer called me to say he received a request from the dean
of women's studies to discuss my findings. My story reached
the national news. It was splashed all over TV and in the
papers. But now the tide was turning. Radio and TV stations called me for interviews. Literary agents left me messages. This would be a fantastic book or documentary, they
said. An Afro-American journalist agreed with everything
I wrote—the grandmother was the tree of life for the family.
I got an email from a Hispanic social scientist that said I hit
the nail on the head—the dominant white Anglo-Western
culture had suppressed the grandmother's influence—deep
down—everything went back to the Great Mother. Several
French-Canadian professors congratulated me on my work.
An Italian analyst and two Muslim women phoned—thanking
me, yes, and then an Indian feminist psychiatrist from Mumbai
congratulated me. She asked if I would fly to India to speak
at her university.

Finally the world is waking up. People were listening to me,
Pinsky.

Are you listening, Pinsky? Are you there?

318

* * *

Friday July 3, 2009, 2:30 pm

Our phone connection faded. Twice I re-dialled M. He did not pick up. I left a brief message. I told him that I planned to stop the analysis.

CHAPTER SEVEN

The last sessions: O. Pinsky, Friday
July 3, 2009

"*Y*es, I know you are upset. Let me explain, I am speaking from my Toronto office. Do you hear me? Those voices in the background are the police forensic team and insurance claims adjusters. My office was broken into when you were in Montreal. A lot of damage was done. *I know you're not responsible for the vandalism.*"

"I am listening," Moses says over the phone.

"This intruder rifled through my papers, my books, and my desk. You appreciate the danger of your situation? Someone is after your personal file—that person or persons wanted to know how much I knew. One or more of them traced your where-abouts to my office and has it in for me. Whoever it is knows my work routine, when I come and go. I haven't the foggiest idea who this is. It doesn't matter, I don't want more of the same. In the interest of safety I have made a decision. We stop analysis. For your benefit you must leave town and change your name."

"You are ordering me to change my name?" M says. "You are abandoning me?"

"I am not abandoning you. I am warning you of imminent danger."

"I like my name. I feel safe seeing you. I don't want to stop."

"I know you don't want to stop. I would like to carry on. But it is out of my hands."

"Just because you are anxious … you can't stop seeing me, Pinsky."

"Someone tried to kill Guttnik; someone tried to open my files, someone murdered your dog, Jaffe-Jaffe and threatened others. You know your dog Fidel was murdered as well. Your dog walker, Crystal told me."

"Let me worry about that," M says.

"That's the problem, Reuben, you don't worry about it. You push it away; you deny it. You forget it existed. You make us into two sitting ducks. The police have instructed me to close my office. Detective Karp ordered me to stop practicing. You haven't seen my office—it is virtually destroyed—my paintings, books, art objects, even my couch—ripped to shreds. Please understand I am not rejecting you."

* * *

Friday July 3, 4:30 pm

By the time M returned from Montreal he was greeted at the airport by a scrum of journalists and television reporters. His ordeal in Montreal made news headlines across North America and Europe.

On evening news M appeared bleary-eyed, serene. A reporter pressed for his views on why women were angered. "I am deeply misunderstood," M said.

Initially I experienced shock, fear, and a sense of violation entering my office before my first session at 7 am. I collected myself. I told the patient who entered the waiting room minutes later her session was cancelled. I said I would get back to her later that day to rebook.

321

Minutes later I used my cell phone to call the police and phoned my wife who practices family law and told her that my office was ransacked.

I was shaken but unharmed. She knew about my ordeals with M in the most circumspect way—she said not to touch anything, to wait for the police. She said for me to leave as soon as the police and insurance teams finished their investigation. I glanced through my office ruins. I called each patient that day to inform them that there had been unexpected office damage—all sessions were cancelled.

When my patients asked for the next appointment I was left with a disquieting reality.

I did not know when the next appointment would be.

If my office was no longer safe, my patients would no longer be safe. In minutes the police arrived. The insurance companies were prompt and courteous. They offered to fix the damage by the weekend. I was enraged and helpless. How could I explain this situation to my patients? Would I have a duty to warn them about my attack?

I called my medical insurer and my lawyer. I would see one last patient.

* * *

Friday July 3, 2009, 6 pm

M was visibly distressed, restless, and refused to sit. He stared at my office damage. A locksmith and carpenter from the insurance company changed my lock and repaired my broken door. The police forensic team and two detectives took photos and checked the hallway outside my entrance door.

Karp sat in the waiting room scribbling notes. A squad car idled outside. M said nothing for a minute. His eyes nervously surveyed the panorama of destruction.

322

"I came from my office," M said. "It was broken into—my rose garden was destroyed."

"Did you call the police?" Karp asked M.

"I called Frieda, my wife."

Karp rose from the waiting room. He instructed his detectives to drive to M's office. "You guys can talk for fifteen minutes," Karp said. "Go ahead—it's OK to sit down—just don't move anything. I don't want either of you seeing patients for a while."

My mother's daily weather report

Reuben, I saw you on TV. You know who you made angry? Herbie Faust's sister Ruthie-Annie phoned. She saw you on TV. She says you hate women.

* * *

"I called Lippman from Montreal," M says. "I've seen him off and on for a year."

"At the same time as you see me?"

"I see him when I don't see you—Saturday." M rose and paced about my office.

"I thought you were in analysis with me."

"With you it is analysis." M's pace accelerated. "With Lippman it is coaching."

"Coaching? You get coaching for what?"

"I get advice how to push off with my left foot," M leaned forward and bent his left foot illustrating the motion as he paced. "He gives me power skating lessons. We go to a local rink. We talk and skate, forwards, backwards, sideways, stops and starts, cross-over right, cross-overs to the left, and then I do backward cross-overs. It is therapeutic—body work, right?"

"Let me understand, you see Lippman for hockey skating lessons?"

323

M said, "I called him after I went to my office."

"And you wanted—"

"You are right. I don't need more analysis. Frieda and I are back together. I am not depressed. I have sorted out my past. I sent my mother's last message to Lippman."

"You wanted Lippman to hear your mother's message?"

"It is over between me and you."

"Look, Reuben, our analysis is not over—it is stopped for the time being. This is a temporary pause. Why don't you sit down and relax?"

M sits down and shifts his chair opposite me in the remains of my consulting room. We are alone. Pictures are scattered on the floor in shards of broken glass and shattered frames. My couch has been savagely hacked apart, tufts of stuffing and strips of leather are strewn helter-skelter. Books have been thrown from the shelves. Filing cabinets have been chiselled, hit, and dented with a hammer yet stubbornly refused to open. Papers are strewn across the room.

Karp knocks at the door to the waiting room.

"You have ten minutes left."

M scans my office. "I am sorry. I don't mean to be angry. If it makes you feel better, my office is covered in shit—literally. The surveillance cameras outside my office showed someone in a trench coat and hat—*that person*. As soon as I got off the plane I visited Guttnik in hospital. He looked awful—broken pelvis, two broken legs, a shattered wrist, skull fracture, ruptured kidney, spleen, facial lacerations—he was conscious. He said I had done this. Imagine, Guttnik wrapped in bandages head to foot, doped up on drugs, and as soon as I see him he yells at me to fuck off and go to hell. Everybody is angry at me. I said I was sorry for what had happened. I said it wasn't me. I told him it did not give me any pleasure to see him in hospital. He told me to drop dead. So I waited a minute or two. I collected myself. I told him my life was no picnic either. I told him lots of people hate me and I had a feeling I was next. I had a hunch about who broke into his office and ran him over. I can't be sure."

"It's not one of your patients?"

"It is … and isn't. I think I found the answer when my mother phoned me and left a message."

"You mean the person who was vandalizing?"

"It goes back to childhood. She was Fine when she was married to a dentist—he became a cripple. See, Pinsky? I put her name and face out of my mind—do you believe that? She blamed me because Herbie got polio. She blamed me for breaking his leg in cheder. She hated doctors because they never helped Herbie. She blamed Bayer and Guttnik for her husband dying."

I stare at M, unsure.

"She did this." M picks up a shred of leather couch. "Pinsky, you should have figured this out," M yells at the top of his voice, flinging the leather shred at me. "Where the fuck were you?"

"I am supposed to tell you? You didn't tell me! I should read your mind?"

"You should read my mind because I can't read my mind. It's dark inside."

"Your mind is your mind, Reuben. I am not your Bubba. I won't tell you what to do."

"You should have warned me about her." He lifts a broken picture frame and flings it to the floor in a loud clatter. "What do I do?"

"I tried to warn you," I scream.

Moses runs at me, charging madly. He punches my chest and arms.

We wrestle to the floor in a heap. "You blocked out her name," I say breathless. "Let go of me. How do I recall what you can't remember?"

We struggle for a few moments. Moses clings to me. He has stopped punching. He is clinging to me, limp now. I remember now, at Camp Hello-Goodbye I was his counsellor.

* * *

There is a knock at the door. Karp enters. "Are you two all right? I heard yelling from the waiting room." He looks us both over. "You have three minutes." Like a ref in a boxing match Karp brings our round to a close. He shuts the door and waits outside.

* * *

Friday July 3, 2009, 6:35 pm

"Pinsky, what do I do?" M has gained some composure but paces my office. "Do I tell cops about Ruthie-Annie? Suppose it isn't her." He traverses glass shards, papers, broken frames, a crunching noise as he circles my wrecked office tensely waving his arms. "I need to go for a long run."

"Look, I can't tell you exactly what to do. If you suspect Ruthie-Annie tell Karp, tell the police, and get a restraining order. Hire a security guard to follow you 24/7. Cancel patients. Go where no one knows you. Change your name. Are you going to follow my advice?"

M shakes his head.

"You asked me for advice. I gave you good advice, now you are rebelling against me. I am calling Frieda. I will say that you are not listening to me."

"You are a useless piece of shit, Pinsky."

"Call me useless—go ahead, but you are feeling helpless and angry. Here is a deep interpretation—in your nervous state don't jog tonight."

"Drop dead, Pinsky."

I should have known, it is impossible to talk to a compulsive jogger—they jog through rain, ice, snow, and injuries. I call Frieda and tell her what has transpired. Karp knocks on the door and enters.

"Time is up, *boys*," Karp says.

"There is something more," M says. "It's about Ruthie-Annie."

* * *

M raises his hand like a student in class. Can we stop and talk? M is impatient and irritable. Karp shakes his head. "We need to go. Time is up. We leave all patient charts, including yours in the filing cabinet. I suspect this person has not finished and will be back for your file. We will stake out the office with an undercover officer. You must go."

We walk out of the office. I close and lock my door not knowing when I will return.

On the way out M explains to Karp what he has not yet told us about Ruthie-Annie.

"The truth, now that I think about it, was that I pushed her first, and then she pushed me down the stairs. *I lied*. I read her diary. I understood Yiddish. Her family fled the Nazis; her grandparents were killed during the war. She protected her brother, Herbie. Her diary was a witness. When Sam Faust got angry with life, with everything lost, he beat them. She wrote her father—beaten during the war—entered her room and abused her. I didn't want to believe. I was a child. I was afraid. I did nothing. Did Bubba know? I didn't want to think about it. When her brother got polio and was crippled, when Herbie fell off me when we played piggyback, she hated me. Her husband died. She blamed the doctors, Bayer then Guttnik, who followed her husband. But most of all she blamed me. Her brother died last week."

* * *

327

Friday July 3, 2009, 9:30 pm

The last part of this monograph is based on information presented to me by M's wife, Frieda, Sergeant Detective Karp, police records, hospital charts, and court reports. That evening, while he was out for his night run, at 9:30 pm a car approached my patient M. He heard the car behind him and turned to see it. The driver argued that at that moment M shifted his direction and ran into the car's path. A male bystander who did not identify himself at the outset stated that the driver veered into the jogger's path. M suffered multiple injuries, a broken pelvis, severe internal bleeding, two broken legs, a broken right arm, multiple contusions, facial lacerations, and cranial trauma The unidentified bystander stated M was briefly lucid. The collision occurred in front of his wife`s townhouse. Frieda came out to see what the commotion had been. Her husband lay prostrate on the road.

"You drove into him," the bystander said.

"He ran into my lane," the driver said.

The driver was identified as Ruthie-Annie Faust, aka Anna Fine. The male bystander was Detective Karp. He reported in court testimony that because of my phone call and a hunch he followed M that night. Karp witnessed the accident.

He captured the last scenes on his iPhone.

Friday July 3, 2009, 10:41 pm

By the time M arrived at Mount Zion Hospital, because of extensive bleeding and shock his blood pressure dropped. M lost vital signs. A cardiac code was called. M received cardiopulmonary resuscitation and two defibrillation attempts. Normal cardiopulmonary function was re-established. M had been dead—without vital signs for three minutes.

At one point surgeons considered an amputation of M's right leg because of bone fragmentation and tissue damage.

For the first week doctors witnessed M's life and death struggle. He was in postoperative delirium. Episodically he regained consciousness to say he was sorry. He wanted to clear his name. He called out for me and demanded to narrate his analytic ordeal. M told me of a troubling near-death experience. He rose from his broken body towards a tenebrous region where an opaque visage appeared—a child's face in a cloud. Go home, the child repeated three times. M said the face was Reuben.

I came to visit each day. For the next month it was unclear if M would walk.

He stabilized enough to be discharged from ICU.

He was placed in a semi-private room in the 12-West orthopedic unit with Karl Guttnik who had undergone two further operations to restore his crushed left foot.

CHAPTER EIGHT

Final words

Our analysis had come to an unexpected end. M convalesced slowly from the trauma of the accident. Frieda and their children visited M daily. M's aged mother visited twice weekly. M remained in Mount Zion 12 West beside Guttnik, both recovering from multiple surgeries. M undertook a course of physiotherapy. He ambulated with the assistance of crutches, a cane, and later was able to walk unattended.

Despite his efforts, he was unable to run for months.

This news had a paradoxical calming effect on M.

M had come back from the dead. In those three minutes of death he saw himself suspended above his hospital bed, between the living Reuben and the departed Reuben, viewing his Bubba and her lost son as if they were faces in an approaching cloud.

* * *

Ruthie-Annie Faust was placed in a psychiatric facility for a full assessment, treatment, and later court appearance. She had been suffering from cumulative childhood abuse but had always attended to her frail brother. As a caregiver she had survived her troubled inner world, but when she later lost her husband and then her brother, and then when M's work on the

Bubba went viral and was seen as an attack on women, Ruthie-Annie lost her semblance of normality and re-experienced Reuben as her victimizer. All pain and hatred she had felt in her early years was turned outward. Her father's recurrent physical abuse, his forced entry into her room, his sexual pollutions of her body overwhelmed her. In return she smeared feces over cars, vandalized property, and deflowered M's rose garden—a symbolic way of undoing her sexual debasement and violation. When M left the hospital the first person he visited was Ruthie-Annie.

I had no idea what the two of them said. I asked M what was spoken but on this he kept silent. He said that there was finally peace in their lives.

* * *

I was left with the pervading doubt that I had not seen past M's defensive use of humour. To this day I reconsider how I might have helped M avoid this fate. Apart from Ruthie-Annie everyone loved M, except himself. His destiny was enmeshed in a lost identification with his grandmother and the fate of the other Reuben, a lost Holocaust child, who was never talked about.

If this Reuben was lost in death, Ruthie-Annie's childhood was unspeakably lost in life.

I accepted M's words about Bubba. He loved and hated her—life's elemental forces—the ties that pull us asunder or bind us together.

* * *

An odd coincidence was that at the time M was struck down by Ruthie-Annie, he had addressed his significant life issues. Was it naïve or wishful of me to consider this? For weeks in his hospital bed M debated the Bubba complex with Guttnik who remained somewhat opposed.

331

"You, the *hacham* with two broken legs and busted pelvis—I should feel sorry for you?"

"If I wasn't in a cast, smarty-pants," Guttnik said, "I would break your leg."

If laughter was a form of acceptance and forgiveness, Guttnik and Moses had made up. They shared the same injuries, the same surgeon, and had loved the same women.

They swore in Yiddish to each other.

* * *

Months and years later the Bubba complex is debated in psychiatric and analytic circles. Had M intended his concept to be taken seriously or as a joke? He acted as if his theory spoke a basic truth yet laughed at the unbearable burden of life.

The last time I saw M he gave me a sketch of his first couch and thanked me for completing this monograph.

In this volume I have set out my clinical data, M's notes and drawings, and his Bubba's recipes.

To my knowledge I have not withheld significant events or sessions.

Now the reader may decide.

RECIPES

Bubba Bella and Mother's knaidelach (matzo balls)

2 tablespoons of oil
2 eggs beaten
½ cup of matzo meal
1 teaspoon of salt
2 teaspoons of water or chicken soup
Combine oil and eggs and add matzo meal and salt and blend well.
Stir in water; cover and chill for twenty minutes.
Shape into balls and drop into boiling water.
Simmer.
Cool 30 or 40 minutes.
Makes 8–10 matzo balls.

Bubba's gefilte fish

This recipe requires 3 pounds of ground fish—pike, whitefish, carp, pickerel, a slice of lake trout. Sometimes my Bubba or mother threw in a small piece of salmon too. In the old days this was put in the *machinka*, ground up, and then placed in a wooden bowl, to which was added the following:

2–3 tablespoons of matzo meal
4 large onions
4 teaspoons of salt—more if desired

1 teaspoon pepper
1 quart water
3 eggs
one quarter cup or more iced water
head and bones of the fish

In a pot put 3 sliced onions and carrots, head and bones, and water. Cook until boiling. Add salt.

Chop the mixture until smooth. Moisten hands and shape mixture into balls. Drop balls into boiling stock. Cover and simmer for two hours.

Remove, strain some stock, place on platter, garnish with carrot slices and chill.

Bubba Bella and Mother's chicken belak balls

2 pounds of chicken belak (breasts) ground in the machinka
2 eggs
1½ teaspoons of salt—more to taste
¼ teaspoon pepper
1 onion, chopped
1 can ginger ale
1 juice glass of ketchup
2 tablespoons matzo meal or more
Combine chicken, egg, seasoning, and meal. Mix well. In a pot, add ginger ale and ketchup and boil.
Add balls and bake 1 hour at 350.
Cover and simmer on stove top.

Salami and eggs—my father's favourite Sunday brunch

Slice 5–6 pieces of Chicago kosher salami.
Beat 2 eggs in bowl.
Add a touch of pepper.
Place salami slices on a hot iron skillet.
Allow to fry until salami begins to curl.
Add eggs to skillet.

GLOSSARY

Yiddish [Hebrew] words	English
A bruch	a curse
Aliyah [Heb]	lit., ascent, immigration to Israel
Al-Maleh [Heb]	lit., Oh God, full of mercy, prayer for dead
Areingeshtup	to fill up
Balabusta	a bossy woman
Behamah	an animal, sometimes a cow
besherit	it is meant to be
bissel	a little bit
blintze	a crepe
bobbilach	a type of pastry
borscht	beet soup
boychik	a little boy
bruchas	blessings
bubba, bubbeh, bube	grandmother
bubba myeseh	an old wives tale, a tall tale
bupkes	worth nothing
chalash	faint
chazzar	literally a pig, someone who eats too much

chometz	[Heb] lit., leavened bread, not for Passover
chrain	a pungent mix of grated horseradish and beets
chupped	to grab, to take
daven	praying, usually swaying back and forth
dienst	a maid, housekeeper
dybbuk	a malicious figure that can possess the soul
egilach	a child's eye (diminutive)
epis	something
fageles	lit., little bird[s], delicate, feminine, gay
farshlepter krenk	a chronic ailment, a chronic illness
farshtaste	understand
farshtinkener	rotten
fesilach	a child's foot (diminutive)
feter	an uncle
fingerlach	a child's finger (diminutive)
flumen	prunes
ganif	thief
gans	goose, a fat person
gatkas	underwear, usually long underwear
gay gesundt	Go in health
gay schlaffen	Go to sleep
gehucked liber	chopped liver
gefilte fish	fish balls made from chopped carp, pike, salmon
gay	to go
genug	enough
gevalt! Oy gevalt!	Heavens! Oh, woe is me! Oh goodness!
grebenas	fried chicken skin
gorgel	neck
gornisht mit gornisht	nothing with nothing, useless
Goy	Christian

Goyim	Christians
Goyische	Christian
haggadah	[Heb] lit., telling, a book recited for Passover
Seder	[Heb] lit., order, the Passover dinner
hackmesser	a chopping knife
hacham	wise, a smart one (disparaging), not so smart
hunt	a dog, a hound
Kalika	cripple
Kish mir	Kiss me
kishka	intestines, stuffed derma
knaidelach	matzo balls
knucks	to hit or smack
Koch leffel	a soup spoon, someone who agitates others
kop	head
krechts	a groan, a complaint
kreplach	dumplings
kuchen	cake
kuck	to defecate, to shit
kucker	a defecator, a shitter, a denigrating term
kvetch	to complain, bicker
latkes	pancakes
loch in kop	literally a hole in the head, an idiot
lungeloksch	a long noodle, a tall person
machinka	rotary hand-operated food grinder
madelach	a little girl
maftir	Torah section read by the bar mitzvah boy
mame loshon	mother tongue
mamzer, mamzerim [Heb]	bastard, bastards

mandelbrodt	dessert biscuit like biscotti
mazel	luck, fortune
Megilla	a narrative scroll, a boring tedious account
meschugge	crazy
meschugoyim	crazy people
meyseh	a story
Mohl	a religious person who performs circumcision
Mon	poppy seeds
narishkeit	foolishness
nebach	unfortunately
nem	take
neshumah	a soul, a spirit
nisht	not
noodge, noodging	to push, to pester, to repeatedly bother someone
nu	so
nudnik	a person who pester, irritates, a pain in the neck
paskudnyak	a terrible person
pesadicke	appropriate for Passover
pesadicke shissels	Passover pots
plotzing	to burst, explode, die
polkas	legs, thighs
ponim	face
poo-poo-poo	a benediction to ward off evil eyes
potatonik	potato pudding
pupik	umbilicus, bellybutton, gizzard (chicken)
putz	penis
Rav Natan	Rabbi Nathan
reibeisen	a metal hand-held food grater
rosh	head, beginning

Rosh Hashanah	[Heb] the new year, lit., the head of the year
Schlemazel	luckless, down on one's luck, a loser
schlect	bad, naughty
schlepp	to pull or yank, or to have pull (connections)
schlong	penis
schmaltz	fat, cooking fat usually made from chicken
schmuck	penis
schnoz	nose
schwarzfliegen	blackflies
schwartzekind	a dark child, a tanned child
shandah	a shame, a humiliation
shiksa	a non-Jewish woman
shishels	plates, dishes
shiva	[Heb] seven, lit., first week of mourning
shlepp	to drag, pull, carry
shmata	a scrap, rag, cloth, clothing
schlaffer	sleeper
shoicet	a ritual Jew presiding over animal slaughter
shpilkas	needles, to be on needles, jumpy, restless
shpitzier	to stroll or promenade
shtik drek	a piece of shit
shtikel	a small piece
shtill	quiet, silence
shul	synagogue
shtupp	literally to fill up, to fuck
shveik!	Shut-up! Quiet!
shvitz	to sweat, a steam bath
simcha	happiness, rejoicing, a religious celebration